PRAISE FOR ALYSSA MAXWELL
AND HER GILDED NEWPORT MYSTERIES!

MURDER AT MARBLE HOUSE

"Maxwell again deftly weaves fictional and real-life
characters into her story."

—*Publishers Weekly*

MURDER AT THE BREAKERS

"Intriguing characters and a solid murder mystery."

—*RT Book Reviews*

"Will keep you guessing."

—*Historical Novels Reviews*

Books by Alyssa Maxwell

Gilded Newport Mysteries

MURDER AT THE BREAKERS

MURDER AT MARBLE HOUSE

MURDER AT BEECHWOOD

MURDER AT ROUGH POINT

MURDER AT CHATEAU SUR MER

MURDER AT OCHRE COURT

MURDER AT CROSSWAYS

MURDER AT KINGSCOTE

MURDER AT WAKEHURST

Lady and Lady's Maid Mysteries

MURDER MOST MALICIOUS

A PINCH OF POISON

A DEVIOUS DEATH

A MURDEROUS MARRIAGE

A SILENT STABBING

A SINISTER SERVICE

A DEADLY ENDOWMENT

Published by Kensington Publishing Corp.

A Gilded Newport Mystery

MURDER
AT
BEECHWOOD

ALYSSA MAXWELL

KENSINGTON BOOKS
www.kensingtonbooks.com

eISBN-13: 978-0-7582-9087-8
eISBN-10: 0-7582-9087-X
First Kensington Electronic Edition: June 2015

ISBN-13: 978-0-7582-9086-1
ISBN-10: 0-7582-9086-1
First Kensington Trade Paperback Printing: June 2015

10 9 8 7 6 5 4 3

Printed in the United States of America

*To my beautiful daughters, Sara and Erin,
with all my love. You might not have lived in
Newport, but you are Newporters
all the same. I'm so proud of you both.*

Chapter 1

❦

Newport, Rhode Island, June 29, 1896

I sat up in bed, my heart thumping in my throat, my ears pricked. I'd woken to a high-pitched keening, an eerie, unearthly sound that gathered force in the very pit of my stomach. There had been no warning in last night's starry skies and temperate breezes, but sometime in the ensuing hours a storm must have closed in around tiny Aquidneck Island. I knew I should hurry about the house and secure the storm shutters, yet as I continued to listen, I heard only the patient ease and tug of the ocean against the rocky shoreline, the sighs of the maritime breezes beneath the eaves of my house, and the argumentative squawking of hungry gulls flocking above the waves.

With relief I eased back onto my pillows—but no. The sound came again—like the rising howl of a growing tempest. Throwing back the covers, I slid from bed and went to the window. With both hands I pushed the curtains aside.

And stared out at a brilliant summer dawn. Long, flat waves, tinted bright copper to the east, mellowed to gold, then green, and then a deep, cool sapphire directly beyond my property.

The sky was still a somber, predawn gray, but clear and wide, with a few stars lingering to the west. Like polished silver arrows, the gulls dove into the water with barely a splash and swooped away to enjoy their quarry.

I could only conclude I had been dreaming, even when I'd thought I was awake. Well, I was certainly awake now. I grabbed my robe, slid my feet into my slippers, and quietly made my way downstairs.

I needn't have muffled my footsteps, for as I entered the morning room at the back of the house I found Katie, my maid-of-all-work, as well as Nanny, my housekeeper, already setting out breakfast. The inviting scents of warm banana bread and brewing coffee made my stomach rumble.

"You're both up early," I said.

"Mornin', Miss Emma," Katie replied in her soft brogue.

Nanny's plump cheeks rounded as she bid me good morning, her half-moon spectacles catching the orange flame of the kerosene lantern. "Something woke me. I'm not quite sure what."

"That's so odd—me as well." I picked up the small stack of dishes and cutlery on the sideboard and carried them to the table, noticing the web of small cracks in the porcelain of the topmost plate. Katie looked at me uncertainly, then half shrugged and made her way back to the kitchen.

She had been in my employ for a year now and had yet to grow accustomed to the informal machinations of my household. At Gull Manor we never stood on ceremony; there was no strict order of things, but rather a daily muddling through of tasks and chores and making ends meet. That was my life—by my choice and by the gift of my great-aunt Sadie, who had left me the means to lead an independent life.

Part of that gift included this house, a large, sprawling structure in what architects called the shingle style, with a gabled roofline, weathered stone and clapboard, mullioned windows framed in timber, and enough rooms to house several families comfortably. Set on a low, rocky promontory on the edge of the Atlantic Ocean, Gull Manor was a very New England sort of house, one that seemed almost to rise up from the boulders themselves and have been fashioned by the whim of rain, wind, and sea. Yes, it was drafty, a bit isolated, and required more up-keep than I could afford to maintain it on the proper side of shabby, but it was all mine and I loved it.

Katie returned with a sizzling pan of eggs, and I asked her, "What about you, Katie? What brought you down so early?"

"Oh, I'm always up before the sun, miss. A leftover habit from being in service." She placed the frying pan on a trivet on the sideboard and whirled about. "Oh, not that I'm not still in service, mind you. . . ."

"It doesn't always feel like it, though, does it?" I finished for her.

"No, miss. And for that I'm grateful. Now . . . I'll go and get the fruit. . . ."

Nanny, in a faded housecoat wrapped tight around an equally tired-looking nightgown, heaped eggs and kippers on a plate, placed a slice of banana bread beside them, and went to sit at the table. I did likewise, and when I'd settled in and picked up my fork, I hesitated before taking the first bite. "Have you seen our guest yet this morning?"

Nanny shook her head. "That sort doesn't rise with the sun."

"Nanny! That's unkind. Please don't refer to Stella as 'that sort.' We agreed—"

"We agreed, but I still worry that you're crossing a line, Emma. Out-of-work and disgraced maids are one thing, but . . ." She pursed her lips together.

"Prostitutes are another," said a voice behind me.

Nanny glanced beyond my shoulder and I twisted around to see the figure standing in the doorway. Stella Butler wore my old sateen robe buttoned to her chin. Her ebony hair, tamed in

two neat plaits, hung over each shoulder, making her look anything but a jaded woman. The bruises with which she had arrived
at Gull Manor had faded, thank goodness. High cheekbones and
slanting green eyes marked her a beauty, but today that beauty
struggled past obvious fatigue and the downward curve of her
mouth. She met our gazes with defiance, but the spark quickly
died. She bowed her head and released a sigh.

"I'm sorry. I'm grateful to you, Miss Cross. I promise I
won't stay long and I'll pay you for every scrap of food I eat."

I stood and pulled out the chair beside my own at the round
oak table. I gestured to the well-worn seat cushion. "You'll stay
as long as you need, and as for payment, I'm sure we'll work
something out, something mutually beneficial."

Nanny harrumphed. Without another word Stella scooped
up a small portion of eggs and a slice of banana bread I deemed
too thin, and returned to the table. I was about to admonish her
to take more, that she needed to keep up her strength, but
thought better of it. Stella obviously had her pride, and if she
was going to carve out a better life than the one she'd been living, she would need pride as much as strength.

"I'll be back in a moment," I told them. "I'm going to see if
the newspaper came yet."

"I would think the storm kept the delivery boys from ven-
turing out at their usual time," Stella said without looking up.

"You too? This has been the strangest morning." I glanced
out the window. The sun had fully risen, gilding our kitchen
garden and the yard beyond. A few fair-weather clouds cast
playful shadows over the water. With a shrug I headed for the
front of the house, my slippers scuffing over the floor runner.
Ragged edges and the occasional hole suggested the rug needed
replacing, but it would be some time yet before I could justify
the expense.

It was as I reached the foyer that the wind suddenly picked
up again, sending an unnerving shriek crawling up the exterior

façade to echo beneath the eaves. I hadn't been dreaming. What kind of a strange storm was this?

Bracing for a blustery onslaught, I opened the front door.

"Nanny! Nanny!" I shouted and fell to my knees. Here was no gale battering my property, or any other part of the island on which I lived. The keening and the cries I'd heard, that had yanked me from sleep, were not those of a summer squall.

They were those of a baby, tucked into a basket and left on my doorstep.

Chapter 2

❧

"Land sakes . . . What on earth?"

Nanny bent over me as I gathered blankets and whimpering child into my arms. Gently I lifted it—him? her?—from the basket and stared in mute astonishment at the little face, red and wrinkled and damp from tears.

Watching from the doorway, Katie gasped and Stella let out a whispered oath. The silence that followed declared them as shocked as I.

"Oh, Nanny," I said, staring at this tiny person in disbelief, "how long can it have been here? I heard it crying . . . but I didn't come. I never thought . . . Who would leave a baby on a doorstep?"

Nanny being Nanny, she placed her hands on my shoulders and helped me to stand. "Let's get this child in the house and see if we can't figure out what on earth is going on here."

The first thing I did, after handing the child over to Nanny, was run to the alcove beneath the staircase, where my uncle Cornelius had had a telephone installed for me. First, I telephoned Jesse Whyte, a detective with the Newport police and an old friend. He wasn't at the station, however, and when the man on the other end of the wire asked if I wanted to leave a message, I hesitated, then said I'd call back and quickly hung up.

I stood for a moment with my hand on the ear trumpet where it dangled from its cradle. Why had I been unforthcoming with a member of the police? Didn't I have to report this incident? Yet the very thought of revealing too much too soon, and to the wrong people, raised a prickly warning at my nape. I trusted Jesse Whyte implicitly, and I would wait for him before making my next move, whatever that would be.

However, there was one other person I trusted. I lifted the ear trumpet and turned the crank.

"Operator. How may I place your call?"

"Good morning, Gayla." I knew I would have to trade pleasantries before I could proceed. Gayla and I had known each other all our lives.

"Oh, hello, Emma. How's everyone out your way?"

"We're just fine, Gayla, thanks." I noticed my foot tapping and held it still. "And you?"

"My father's gout is acting up again."

"Sorry to hear it." She started to go on, but my impatience was building. "Gayla," I interrupted, "would you connect me with Dr. Kennison, please?"

"Oh, dear. No one's sick, are they?"

"No, no. It's . . ." I thought a moment, crossed my fingers, and improvised. "Nanny is due for her appointment, is all. But she's fine. So . . . please, Gayla."

"All right. Hold the line. . . ."

The next half hour passed in a blur of activity. Katie had carried the basket into the house and discovered a feeding bottle and containers of Mellin's powdered baby milk that had been tucked in with a small supply of diapers.

"At least someone thought of his immediate needs," she said, though her tone implied that this *someone* hadn't risen much in her estimate. She proceeded to loosen the swaddling and peeked inside. "He's a boy!" Delight twinkled in her eyes.

Meanwhile, Stella had gone upstairs to rummage through the spare bedrooms for light blankets and extra linen we could fashion into swaddling and yet more diapers. Aunt Sadie never had children, so there would be no ready supply of baby necessities stored away in a cedar chest in the attic. As Nanny sagely pointed out, you never could have enough linen on hand where an infant was concerned, and at this point we didn't know how long our visitor would be staying with us.

One thing was certain: This child had been dropped off once, and it wasn't going to happen again, at least not on my watch. I wouldn't be leaving him at the police station or packing him into my buggy for a drive up to St. Nicholas Orphanage in Providence. Gull Manor had already proved itself a haven for strays, and this poor mite was nothing if not that.

In the parlor, I reclaimed him from Katie's arms and sat with him on the sofa. Being no stranger to infants, Nanny had boiled water and mixed a quantity of the Mellin's, so that when he began whimpering again she had the bottle cooled and ready. "By my estimate," she said, twisting to tighten the seal of the rubber nipple, "he's no more than two or three weeks old. A month at the most."

"So young!" Stella entered the parlor and deposited the results of her search on the sofa. "Who would do such a thing?"

"Someone desperate," I replied, looking down as if speaking to the child nestled in my arms. "Someone who had no other choice."

My gaze strayed from the child to Katie, who sat on the floor at my feet, her face turned up to me.

"Someone with nowhere else to turn," she whispered. Tears filled her eyes and my heart broke for her, for I knew she was remembering the unborn child she had lost a year ago last spring—the child who had been forced upon her by an unprincipled youth, and who had resulted in her being fired from her position at The Breakers, the home of my Vanderbilt relatives on nearby Ochre Point.

While Katie blinked her tears away, I carefully tipped the bottle and touched the nipple to a pair of rosebud lips. Those lips immediately opened, drew the nipple in, and latched on with a strength that startled me and made me grin. Sucking noises filled the silence.

"Desperate or not, it's horrible to abandon a baby on someone's doorstep." Stella tossed her head, sending one braid swinging over her shoulder. "Only a selfish, wicked person would do such a thing."

Nanny turned to her with a patience she hadn't previously shown the young woman. "You don't understand. The person who left this child knew about Gull Manor. That's why she came here. It's why *you* knew to come here. Because Emma would never turn away anyone who needed her help. That's what Gull Manor means here in Newport."

"That's right, you're safe here," I said, this time intentionally speaking to the child. He took no heed, too intent on drawing nourishment into his tiny body. All the while, the bottle moved subtly against my palm to the rhythm of each greedy suck. "You may be small, but you're determined, aren't you?"

By the time the milk was nearly gone, those little greenish blue eyes, which had been staring up into mine as if to impart some vital wisdom, began to droop. The others had settled around the room to watch, but now Nanny came to her feet.

"Unless I miss my guess, this little one is in need of a diaper change and a nice long nap." She reached for a folded linen square from the top of the pile we'd made. Stella had also managed to gather an assortment of safety pins, which she'd deposited on the sofa table.

With a twinge of panic it struck me that I had never changed a diaper in my life. In fact, this was the first time I'd fed a baby, and while he had really done all the work, I surmised such would not be the case with diaper changing.

"I'll do it." Katie accurately interpreted my hesitation. She stood and reached for the baby. "I'll take him into the kitchen."

I hesitated in handing him over. "Have you ever done this before?"

She showed me an indulgent smile. "I'm the second oldest of six, Miss Emma."

"I'll help." Stella followed her out of the room, surprising me. I hadn't previously suspected her of harboring maternal instincts. Or was that simply my preconceived prejudice, based on her life previous to arriving at Gull Manor? I loathed to think I'd been judging Stella, that I had in any way blamed her for falling into the oldest profession. As Aunt Sadie had taught me, a woman did what she must to survive, and it behooved the more fortunate among us to help where and when we could.

"What are we going to do?" I asked Nanny once we were alone.

"Do?" She tucked a wiry gray curl into her kerchief. "I believe we're doing it."

"Yes, but, Nanny, we can't keep this baby."

"Can't we? Whoever it belongs to either doesn't want him or can't keep him."

"But even if that's true, there could be relatives who would take the child in if they knew he existed. We can't assume no one wants him."

"Then what do you propose we do?"

Before I could reply, Katie called out my name from down the corridor. A moment later she passed through the doorway with one arm outstretched, a bit of lace dangling from her fingers. "Look, Miss Emma. This was tucked into the baby's blanket. I don't know how we didn't see it sooner."

"Where is he? Did you leave him alone?" Frissons of alarm shot through me.

She frowned slightly. "Of course not. Stella's finishing up with his diaper. Seems she grew up with four younger brothers and sisters."

"Oh, yes, of course. I'm sorry." I wondered at my strong and instant reaction to the idea of Katie having left the baby unattended, that the person in whose charge I had left him had returned without him. It seemed I harbored some surprising maternal instincts as well, and the smile dancing in Nanny's eyes told me she'd noticed, too.

I held out my hand. "Let me see what you've got there."

Katie dropped into my palm an embroidered handkerchief edged with lace—no ordinary lace, mind you, but an intricate pattern shot through with golden silk threads. Puzzled, I searched for an initial worked into the embroidered design, but there were only flowers.

"This was costly," I said.

Katie nodded her agreement. "Do you suspect the mother might be a lady of quality?"

"I don't know. I suppose a maid could have gotten hold of this handkerchief, but the question would be why?" I fingered the tiny yellow and pink flowers and curling pale green vines embroidered on the linen portion of the handkerchief. This was meant to dangle from a manicured hand during a ladies' tea or luncheon, or to ward off a sheen of perspiration during a garden party. "This isn't here by chance. I'm fairly certain of that."

"A clue, then," Nanny said, reading my thoughts as she so often did. "Someone wants us to know where this baby came from."

"A rather obscure clue, though. With no initial or crest of any sort, this could belong to anyone and have come from anywhere, even off island. For all we know, someone brought the child over on the morning ferry."

"Not so, at least not this morning." Nanny reached to take the handkerchief and crossed the room to hold it in the brighter light of the front window. "We all heard what we believed to be a squall before sunup. The morning ferry wouldn't have arrived yet."

Katie's hand flew to her throat. "You don't suppose the poor lad was outside all night?"

"All night?" The very suggestion sent me hurrying out of the room and nearly colliding with Stella, on her way back to the parlor with the baby. We both stopped short, yet the slight jarring the baby received didn't disturb him in the least. His eyes remained closed, his lips working as if still sucking on the bottle.

"Are you all right, Miss Emma? You're as white as a sheet."

I waved away Stella's concerns while my own burgeoned. "I'm fine, but I'm going to call Dr. Kennison again. What in the world can be keeping him so long?"

But I'd no sooner reached the alcove and lifted the ear trumpet when a knock sounded at the front door.

"He's fine, Emma. Lungs are clear, his heart's strong. Has a good grip, too. I'd say this is one healthy little fellow." Dr. Kennison folded his stethoscope and slipped it into the medical bag at his elbow, the black leather worn and cracked from years of steady use.

I sighed with relief as I leaned over the kitchen table and rewrapped the swaddling blankets snug around the baby's pink body, which had only begun to grow plump in the way babies did at several weeks old. Our young man had awakened briefly during his examination, whereupon he surveyed the doctor with a puzzled frown, squeezed the offered finger, blew a bubble between his lips, and drifted back to sleep.

Poor thing. How long had he cried before I finally found him this morning? "You don't see any signs of exposure, then, Doctor?"

"Emma, relax. Even if he had been outside all night, which I very much doubt, don't forget it's summertime. The air wouldn't have done him a lick of harm."

A few minutes later I walked him to the door. "So for now you'll keep mum about this, Doctor? I'd like a chance to discover who he is and why he was left here before too many people learn of his existence."

"If you think that's best. Now, mind you mix his formula exactly according to the directions. I can't tell you how many undernourished infants I see whose mothers added too much water, trying to stretch their supply."

"We'd never do any such a thing." The very notion appalled me and I instinctively hugged the baby closer. "We'll take the very best care of him."

He reached out a finger to stroke the baby's head. "I'm sure you will. If you need me, telephone. Otherwise I'd like to see him again in about a week. Say, Thursday?"

Beyond him through the open door a cloud of dust formed at the end of my driveway, and seconds later a police buggy came into view. "That's Jesse. Someone must have told him I called the station. Well, good-bye, Doctor, and thank you."

The two men exchanged greetings before Jesse made his way to my front door. "Morning, Emma."

"Good morning, Jesse. Did they tell you I telephoned, or can you read my mind now?"

As with Gayla, I'd known Jesse all of my life. We both hailed from the Point, the colonial, harborside section of Newport that had changed little in the past century. Though he was some ten years older than me, we'd forged a friendship based on our common origins and, more recently, through our mutual efforts to solve crimes and see justice done. Jesse hadn't necessarily approved of my involvement in local criminal matters, but neither had he turned down the vital information I'd been able to offer him.

"Read your mind . . ." he said. " 'Fraid I don't know what you mean by that."

It was then I noticed the grim set to his mouth. At the same time, his gaze dropped to the baby in my arms. We spoke at the same time.

"What's happened?" and "Who's that?" jumbled together in a confusion of words. I led him into the parlor.

"Left here?" he said with a shake of his head after I'd explained. "On your doorstep?"

"I know it sounds unbelievable, but it's the truth. I telephoned the station earlier, but you weren't in. If you never got the message, what brings you here?"

Leaning forward with elbows on his knees, he ran a hand through his auburn hair and blew out a breath. "There's been an incident. A murder, Emma. This morning."

"Oh, Jesse. Who?"

"That's just it. We don't know. No one recognized him and he carried no identification. He was a young man, mid-twenties, driving a rented carriage."

"From Stevenson's Livery?"

He nodded. "The death wasn't far from here, where the road curves around Brenton Point. He went off the road into the water—"

I gasped, a hand to my mouth. Nearly the same thing had happened to me last summer. As in my case, I guessed this was no accident. "He was forced off the road?"

"No, Emma, not quite. He went off the road because he'd been shot. Clear through the chest, from dead-on. The best we can figure is someone lay waiting for him, and when he rounded the bend they took a clear shot."

Jesse and I had fallen into a pattern over the past year. After I had proved my investigative skills more than once last summer, he often came to me when a case had him particularly perplexed, as now. We'd mull over evidence and possible motives. Jesse said it helped him see the facts more clearly. I was glad to help, but sometimes I wondered if his frequent visits were prompted by more than protecting Newport from crime.

The baby, awake now, squirmed, and I realized how tightly I

held him. I loosened my arms, shifting him from one shoulder to the other. A shiver traveled my length. "Jesse, this child was left on my doorstep sometime between last night and this morning. Do you suppose there could be a connection?"

"At this point, anything is possible."

My mind raced. I needed to move, needed to pace as I considered these developments. Seeing me struggle to come to my feet, Jesse took the baby from me and settled back in the wing chair, cradling the child as if doing so were second nature. I couldn't help smiling at the picture they made.

Then I turned away, counted off ten steps toward the window, ten back. Mentally I listed the events of this morning, picturing the details as I knew them. I came to a halt. "Jesse, you said he was driving a rented carriage. Was he dressed like a wealthy man?"

"Not at all. If anything, he appeared more like a groom or a groundskeeper. A workman of some kind, certainly."

"Not a man who would have an expensive piece of linen and lace in his possession."

"Certainly not."

"But someone might have given him the handkerchief we found in the swaddling, perhaps at the same time she entrusted him to deliver her child here." I fell silent and began pacing again. Jesse watched me, gently jiggling the baby against his chest. I came to another halt. "But then who would murder him?"

"Someone who didn't want the child traced here. Someone who didn't wish to hurt the child, but who wanted to make certain the one person who delivered him here could never tell anyone."

A possible scenario formed in my mind. "Either the mother is desperate to prevent her family from learning of her pregnancy, or the family . . . or perhaps even the child's father . . . wants the boy hidden away and the mother to never learn where."

"Either is entirely possible, *if* there's a connection between the two," Jesse conceded. "That's still a big *if* at this point."

"Yes, but I think the latter is more plausible. I can't picture a mother—someone who has just brought life into the world—being capable of taking a life so cold-bloodedly. I believe I know where to start searching—for the mother, that is. And something tells me if we find the mother, we'll find your murderer."

"Be careful of stretching again, Emma."

"How many times have I been correct in the past?"

That silenced any further protests he might have made. The baby kicked his little legs and Jesse changed his position to a more upright one, which seemed to satisfy the little fellow.

My heart squeezed. They presented so homey a scene Jesse could almost have been the boy's father, except for the complete difference in their coloring. Where Jesse was fair and auburn haired and possessed keen blue eyes, the baby's eyes were a deep blue-green that suggested they would turn dark—as dark as the nut-brown hair dusting the crown of his head.

"You know, you're a natural at that," I said to him. Just then shuffling into the room, Nanny twittered lightly in agreement.

"I don't see how you'll ever find the mother unless she wants to be found," Jesse said, apparently choosing to ignore my observation.

I chewed my lip to hide the smile that refused to go away, and went to sit beside Nanny on the sofa. "Tomorrow night is June thirtieth and Mrs. Astor will be holding her annual ball to kick off the summer Season. I'm on the guest list—well, not strictly as a guest, mind you. I'll be working, taking notes for my Fancies and Fashions page. Every member of the Four Hundred who's in Newport will be there. It's as good a place as any to begin asking questions."

I glanced over at Nanny, who agreed with one of her sage nods.

"And what makes you think a woman who gave birth so recently will be at that ball?"

"She'll have to be," I replied to Jesse. "If my suspicions are correct and the mother is a society lady, she'll make every effort to attend the ball to quell any rumors that might have sprung up during her confinement. A woman can't simply stop making her usual appearances without her peers noticing, not to mention wondering and whispering. She might get away with the excuse of having been ill, or visiting relatives in the country or some such, but she'd be desperate to reenter society as soon as possible and have everyone see her carefree and happy and, more to the point, laced tightly into her corset."

Jesse winced. "Sounds painful. Not to mention unhealthy."

"It is, on both counts." I smoothed a hand down the front of the sprigged muslin I'd hastily donned earlier. I wore stays, but not nearly as tightly as fashion dictated. In the past it had been a source of disagreement between my aunt Alice and me. "Loose stays suggest loose morals," she would often admonish. Only to add in a rush, "Not that you are of loose morals, Emmaline. Heaven knows you are not. But one does not wish to give a wrong impression, does one?"

Jesse again shifted the baby from one shoulder to the other, his large hands fumbling when the blanket began to unwind and a tiny foot dangled freely. I bit back yet another grin and came around the sofa table to help tuck those miniscule toes safely back in. I pretended not to notice the blush suffusing Jesse's face or how he avoided my gaze.

He said, "I'm still not sure why you're so convinced the mother is a society lady. She could be a lady's maid or even a laundry maid. And if the murdered coachman was involved, he could have been the father, all too eager to hide the evidence of his indiscretion."

"Then why murder him?" I shook my head. "It makes more sense that he was murdered to preserve a secret. And who more than anyone else would wish to hide the evidence of an illegitimate birth?"

When neither Jesse nor Nanny answered, I threw up my hands. "A member of society! Someone with heirs or who stands to gain an inheritance, or who wishes to preserve his reputation, along with that of the woman who birthed the child."

"Emma," Jesse said, "rage knows no class distinctions. Rich or poor, an angry brother or father might have shot that man, not to mention we haven't yet found a definite connection between the two occurrences. Anyone could have gotten hold of that handkerchief. Have you considered that the mother might want you to believe the child hails from a wealthy background in the hopes you'll do better by it?"

"As if that would make any difference to us," Nanny replied with a huff.

"No, it wouldn't." I resumed my place beside her on the sofa. "But it might to a lot of people. Jesse does have a point, one I hadn't considered. A desperately poor mother might have thought she was influencing us by leaving a false clue. Perhaps she thought that rather than delivering him to an orphanage, we'd find a good family willing to take him in, or we'd raise him ourselves."

If Nanny thought I wouldn't notice the sudden change in her posture, or how she clutched her hands in her lap, she was greatly mistaken. "Nanny! Do not even think it. We cannot keep this child."

She turned to me with a wounded expression. "Why not?"

"Lots of reasons! For one, a child needs parents—two of them. The state isn't likely to let me adopt him, or even foster him for any extended length of time. Isn't that right, Jesse?"

"I'm afraid so," he said.

A sudden and wholly unexpected rush of disappointment temporarily knocked the breath out of me. I struggled not to show it. Good heavens, did I, despite my protests, hope this little boy would find a permanent place in our household?

"What about me?" Nanny puffed up with self-importance. "I was married for nearly thirty years."

"I realize that, Mrs. O'Neal, but . . ." Jesse suddenly looked uncomfortable. His cheeks colored again, the curse of his pale complexion. "It's your age, Mrs. O'Neal. The courts might deem you, to be blunt, too old to take on an infant."

Nanny pursed her lips, and Jesse turned his attention back to me. "They might allow you to keep him while a search was made for his next of kin, but that's about all, Emma. Since you're unmarried, it's unlikely they'd allow you to adopt him. For now, though," he added with a wink, "what the courts don't know won't hurt them. See what you can find out, but only about where this fellow belongs. Leave the murder to me."

I nodded, only half listening. My reaction to the prospect of the child's leaving continued to shock me. If I felt this way within mere hours of his arrival, how would I feel days from now? Or weeks—or however long it took to find his rightful home? Would I be able to simply hand him over to a stranger?

Now when I chewed my lip, it wasn't to hide a smile, but to bite back wholly unexpected, stinging tears.

Chapter 3

Jesse settled the baby back in my arms. "This certainly wouldn't be the first time a family abandoned an inconvenient child," he said. "Thank the stars whoever it was had sense enough to bring him here, where he's safe." He spoke those last words roughly and quickly dropped his gaze again. "You know, Emma—"

"If his family is wealthy," I interrupted, "there could be an inheritance at stake. He could be in danger if his existence sets that inheritance in dispute. Until we know more . . ." I trailed off and he nodded. Whatever he'd been about to say before I interrupted hung in the air between us. A year ago I'd glimpsed a portion of Jesse's heart—a portion he'd apparently set aside specifically for me.

I had yet to decide what to do about that. He was a good man and despite the ten years' difference in our ages, he and I had so very much in common, not the least of which involved being born and raised in Newport, and having rarely gone anywhere else—or wishing to. We were of a kind, he and I, and yet . . .

I simply didn't know. Other girls were wives and mothers by

my age, but I felt no rush to enter that arena. Perhaps it was because I'd been independent for too short a time, and relished my individuality far too much to give it up—for anyone.

"In the meantime," Jesse said, "I'll send officers out here to check on you several times a day. The chief won't like it, but . . ."

"No, Jesse. We'll be fine. Until we know more, it would be better not to speak of this, not to anyone."

"All right, but I'm still sending the men." He smiled sadly, and I felt the double impact of my last statement. I'd been referring to the baby, but to Jesse, perhaps my words meant we would not speak of our hearts or where the future might lead us.

Yet, who was I trying to fool? Myself? Perhaps. Jesse? Probably not. Whenever I saw that gleam in his eye, it was the arms of another man, Derrick Andrews, that I imagined around me, and I believe Jesse knew it.

He said good-bye and with my shoulder I nudged the door closed behind him, then leaned against it and snuggled the baby's head beneath my chin. Another summer had barely begun and already I found myself embroiled yet again in deception and murder, not to mention once again lost in the confusion of my own longings with no answers at hand. I let out a breath, and from deep inside me a tear squeezed its way to my eye and rolled down my cheek.

At the sound of footsteps coming down the hall I wiped the tear away on my shoulder and pasted on a cheerful smile.

Katie stopped before me and reached out her arms. "Can it be my turn to hold 'im now, miss?"

This household was becoming perilously attached to our little visitor.

The next morning, Nanny and the girls, as I'd come to think of Katie and Stella, were out beyond the kitchen garden, each taking turns walking with the baby. *The child needs fresh air,* Nanny had declared, and out they went. I'd remained behind, thankful for the solitude as I planned my strategy for the evening to come.

I'd be attending *the* event of the season, already dubbed so by all the newspapers and the majority of the Four Hundred—that magical number of society's most elite men and women who fit comfortably in Mrs. Astor's New York ballroom. As merely a poor relation of the Vanderbilts, I held no place among that hallowed number, but what good was it to hold the most extravagant ball of the summer unless representatives from every newspaper in town, not to mention those from New York, Boston, and Providence, were there to capture all the sumptuous details?

I would be reporting for the Newport *Observer*, but the details I sought involved more than place settings and silver, or which debutant outshined the rest with the latest fashion from House of Worth. I counted on my Vanderbilt relatives being there, especially the younger ones. With Gertrude I'd have access to the upper rooms, where ladies' maids would wait to freshen frocks and redress ill-behaved curls. Such feminine gatherings were always reliable sources of the latest gossip. With Neily I could approach gentlemen and the older society matrons—who viewed him as excellent marriage material for their daughters—without appearing impertinent.

My questions must be subtle and typical for someone in my position. Who had attended the spring balls? Who had traveled abroad? Which house parties offered the most interesting activities? Such probing, among enough individuals, would gradually assemble a picture of the past several months, including who had been where and when, and who had been absent. Four hundred might sound like a large number, but in reality comprised a close-knit community where everyone intimately knew everyone else—and their business. By ruling out enough individuals, I hoped to whittle down the possibilities and from there discover the identity of the baby's mother.

Unless, of course, my hunch about her hailing from society proved completely wrong.

A knock at the front door interrupted me, and I was both surprised and pleased to discover Marianne Reid on my doorstep. Marianne, a woman only a few years older than I, originally hailed from England, and dire circumstances upon her arrival in this country had brought her to Gull Manor briefly last summer. Like Katie and Stella, Marianne had needed a place to stay and a fresh start in life, the first of which I'd been only too happy to provide. The second came from an unexpected source. Through the influence of my half brother, Brady, and the intervention of my Vanderbilt cousin Neily, Marianne had been hired as a lady's maid to one of society's most glamorous debutants.

"Marianne, what a lovely surprise." Upon seeing her looking fresh cheeked and so much healthier than when we'd first met, I reached out to draw her inside. "What brings you to Gull Manor?" I stopped, suddenly fearful. "I hope there's nothing amiss at the Wilson household?"

"Not at all, Miss Cross," she replied in her lovely accent. "Miss Wilson sent me. I have something for you." She stepped back outside and bent to retrieve a large box of heavy white cardboard from the stoop. I was dumbfounded when she held it out to me. "Miss Wilson sends this with her compliments."

"What in the world?"

"Open it, Miss Cross!"

Marianne's enthusiasm worked its influence on me. Taking the package into my front parlor, I practically clawed the twine off the box and flung open the top. Next I tore aside layers of gold-foil tissue paper and could not contain a gasp of amazement.

"Oh, Marianne . . ."

"It's for tonight, Miss Cross. Miss Wilson hopes you're not offended by her gesture, but she thought perhaps you might want something special for the Season-opening ball. She apologizes for it being last year's design. . . ."

Marianne's explanation went on, but I didn't hear it. Beneath my slightly shaking fingertips lay folds of the most beautiful silk I'd ever beheld. Ever so gently, one might say reverently, I grasped the fabric and lifted the evening gown from its shiny nest. In a lustrous cerulean blue that outshone the clearest summer sky, the gown unfurled to pool its hems at my feet, revealing patterns of large and small roses framed by borders of leaves, all embroidered in a deeper shade of the same blue. Gossamer ivory lace dripped from the plunging neckline and shoulders, and from a cinched waistline the gown flowed in straight, hip-hugging lines in front and flared to a generous, graceful train in back. Simple, yet . . .

"I've never seen anything so beautiful," I whispered. Good heavens, in the past couple of days my front stoop had certainly yielded astonishing deliveries, so unlike the usual newspapers and bottles of milk. I looked up at the Englishwoman. "Is it . . . ?"

"It's a Worth gown, yes."

"Oh, my." Even my cousin Gertrude had never given me one of her Worth gowns.

"Miss Wilson wants you to have it because of how nice you were to Mr. Neily when the rest of the Vanderbilt family . . ." Marianne nipped at her bottom lip. "I won't say another word, Miss Cross, but both Mr. Neily and Miss Wilson wished to show their appreciation."

After spending the autumn and winter abroad—to be near Grace Wilson—Cornelius Vanderbilt the younger had returned to his New York home only to have his father banish him to Newport for his defiance. Uncle Cornelius and Aunt Alice didn't approve of Grace and probably never would. Though Neily had had the family's Newport "cottage" all to himself, he instead stayed with me for much of the spring, and I couldn't blame him. The Breakers, however luxurious, was a cold and lonely place for a young man on his own.

"Mr. Neily is more than my cousin, he is my friend," I said, "and I'll do whatever I can to help him. I only want to see him happy."

Marianne nodded but looked distinctly uncomfortable, no doubt at this very personal turn in the conversation. Sometimes I forgot about the invisible barriers between servants and their supposed superiors. I didn't think of myself as superior, but it was obvious Marianne saw my familiarity as a line she must not cross.

I wouldn't press her. Instead, I held the gown up to my shoulders. "Do you think it will fit?"

The question immediately reestablished our respective stations, as it was meant to do, and with restored confidence she regarded me with the critical eye of an experienced lady's maid. "I believe it will do quite nicely, but Miss Wilson instructed me to make any alterations needed. We can get started now, if you like."

"I wouldn't dream of keeping you, especially when Miss Wilson needs your services for tonight. Nanny can do some quick nipping and tucking later." Her eyes lit up at the mention of Nanny. I hesitated, uncertain, then decided this woman had more than earned my trust last summer. "Marianne, would you like to squeeze in a visit with Nanny and Katie before you go? Can Miss Wilson spare you a little longer?"

"Oh, I would, indeed, and yes, I'll make sure I'm home in plenty of time to attend to Miss Wilson."

"Good. There's someone else I'd like you to meet. And then there's a matter I'd like to discuss with you."

"Oh?"

"I believe there is something you can help me with, Marianne, if you're willing."

"Good gracious, Miss Cross, after all you've done for me? Whatever it is, rest assured I'm more than willing."

"I assume you'll be accompanying Miss Wilson to Beechwood tonight?"

"Of course. I'll be upstairs with all the other maids, waiting in case Miss Wilson should need me."

I smiled at my good fortune. With Marianne's help at Mrs. Astor's ball tonight, I'd be able to be in two places at once.

"Oh, Nanny," I said hours later as I stood before the swivel mirror in my bedroom, "you've worked your magic yet again. This gown might have been made for me."

Half disbelieving, I stared at the unfamiliar image reflected back at me. Grace Wilson's cerulean gown flowed like tropical waves down my torso, caressing every curve with a perfection never before achieved, before plunging from my hips to the floor in a gleaming silk torrent every bit as dramatic as a waterfall.

"The dress *was* made for you, sweetie." Nanny slipped one last pin into my hair, piled at the crown of my head and held in place by a wreath of silk flowers that matched the ivory lace at my neckline. "Mr. Worth just didn't know it at the time."

My hand flew to my mouth to stifle an uncharacteristic giggle. "I hardly recognize myself. Oh, but, Nanny, I can't possibly keep it after tonight."

"Why ever not?" She stood back to admire her handiwork, her arms folded across her bosom, her chin tilted in satisfaction. "From what Marianne said, Miss Wilson meant this gown as a gift. Besides, I've done too much altering. It won't fit Grace anymore, and being the youngest daughter she doesn't have a younger sister to give it to. Surely you can't imagine her bestowing a hand-me-down on one of her *married* sisters."

"Heaven forbid." I pulled on my evening gloves, and couldn't resist turning and gazing over my shoulder at my reflection. "I believe this train is the most elegant thing I've ever seen."

Nanny grasped my shoulders. "*You* are the most elegant thing I've ever seen, Emma. It's not only the dress. You're a natural beauty, and I don't care who wears what tonight—no other young lady holds a candle to you. Don't you ever forget it."

"Oh, Nanny." My eyes misted and I hugged her. She held me tight for all of three seconds . . . enough time to remind me that while my mother might be far away in Paris and unlikely to return any time soon, there was no shortage of parental love in my life.

She gently nudged me away. "You'll wrinkle. Now, where's your purse?"

I picked up the drawstring bag from my dressing table. A homemade item of simple design with a braided cord and a tassel added by Nanny, the sapphire blue purse wasn't a perfect match but somehow complemented the gown nicely. "Have Katie and Stella hitched Barney to the gig?"

Before Nanny could answer a call came from below. "Miss Emma! A carriage has arrived for you!"

"A carriage?" Gathering up my skirts, I hurried downstairs, with Nanny close at my heels, or as fast as her bulk would allow. In the doorway I gazed out at a pretty little two-seater brougham with a driver sitting high in his box, and pulled by a pair of matching grays. But there was no crest on the side panel to identify the owner. "Who in the world?"

My heart hammered in my throat as a possibility leaped to mind. I hadn't seen Derrick Andrews all spring, had believed him to be gone from Newport, perhaps indefinitely. Had he returned and—

A footman jumped down from the rear bumper and came to the door. "Miss Cross? Miss Wilson requests the pleasure of your company on the way to the Astors' ball."

"Oh! Thank you . . . and please tell her I'll be out presently."

I said a quick farewell to Nanny and Katie, but then I hesitated. "Where's . . . ?" I glimpsed Stella through the parlor doorway, pacing back and forth with the baby. I quickly detoured inside. "I'm sorry, I just couldn't leave without . . ." I leaned to press a kiss to his brow, and whispered, "I'll be doing everything I can for you tonight, little one. Here, let me hold him for just a moment . . ." I reached out.

"Emma Cross, what are you thinking?" I dropped my arms and straightened like a child caught sneaking a taste of a cooling pie. Nanny's scowl only increased my chagrin. "One burp could bring up that child's last meal and set that dress to ruin."

She tossed my wrap around me and shooed me to the door, but once again I dallied. "Now, mind you lock the door behind me and do not open it to anyone except Jesse or one of his men."

"Go!" she ordered with a nudge. Even as the footman helped me into the carriage, I noticed Nanny didn't shut the front door, but stood watching, the pride I'd seen earlier in my bedroom evident again on her kindly features.

"Good evening, Miss Cross. I'm so glad you didn't leave on your own before I got here. I should have called ahead, but this was a bit of a last-minute decision on my part." Grace Wilson smiled at me from her corner of the velvet seat. She extended her hand, her arm gloved to above the elbow in glossy satin, a wide diamond cuff encircling her wrist. More diamonds glittered in the tiara that framed an elaborate arrangement of golden red curls. I saw nothing of her gown, hidden beneath a black velvet cape. She looked like a princess, and for a moment I felt a surreal sensation of moving in a dream.

"Thank you so much, Miss Wilson," I finally managed to say. I shook her offered hand and she gave mine a squeeze. "Such a lovely surprise. I didn't realize at first that it was you."

She laughed lightly. "No, my parents aren't ones for crests or coats of arms."

Yes, I'd known that, actually. Despite being vastly wealthy, the Wilsons weren't keen on displaying it the way many of the Four Hundred were, my own Vanderbilt relatives included. While so many of Newport's summer elite resided in European-inspired villas and palazzos, the Wilsons seemed content with a shingle-style mansion not much bigger than Gull Manor.

"And this gown, it's . . ." Searching for words, I smoothed the folds in my lap.

"Perfect on you, and you need say no more. Besides, I owed you a debt. Marianne has proven to be a most proficient lady's maid."

"Now that, Miss Wilson, is a lie," I said with a chuckle. "You could have found any number of much more qualified lady's maids. Marianne was new at it, and I know you only took her on as a favor to me."

"Yes, because you're Neily's cousin . . . and his friend." She hesitated, glancing out the window as the driver made the turn onto Ocean Avenue. "I wanted to talk with you, Emma—may I call you Emma?"

"Of course. I'd like that."

"Good. And you may call me Grace." She looked out the window again, and I sensed her gathering her thoughts before she turned back to me. "I wanted to talk to you about Neily. I know he stayed with you after his father sent him out of New York a few months ago."

"Banished him," I corrected her.

"Yes, because of me."

Because Cornelius and Alice Vanderbilt vehemently disapproved of Neily's association with Grace, though why, I couldn't understand. They called her a gold digger, yet her father was vastly wealthy; they called the Wilsons nouveau riche, yet much of society considered the Vanderbilts new money as well; they said she was too old for Neily, yet Grace's twenty-five years set her at a mere three years older. Hardly scandalous.

Grace and I barely knew each other, yet I suddenly found myself the recipient of her intimate confidence. Unable to look her in the eye, I studied my hands in my lap as I replied, "It was very hard on him. Neily isn't the sort who thrives on contention."

"Do you blame me for his troubles?" The question came in a

small voice very unlike that of a debutant, as if my opinion meant something to her, as if she dreaded my disapproval.

I shifted on the seat to face her more fully. "Not at all. It distresses me to see Neily and his parents so at odds, but I certainly don't blame you. Neily knows what he wants. And, like his father, once his mind is made up there is no changing it."

That seemed to satisfy her and she relaxed with a sigh. "You know, his parents aren't coming tonight."

"No, I didn't know that." But I might have guessed. The dispute between Neily and his parents had begun nearly a year ago, ever since he and Grace had danced at his sister's coming-out ball last summer. I remembered how Aunt Alice had charged me with keeping an eye on the pair, making sure they didn't steal off somewhere together and reporting back if they did. I'd reluctantly agreed to the task, only to shirk my responsibilities in the wake of a murder I witnessed shortly after.

But that is a story best left for another time.

"They're staying home specifically on my account." Grace's assertion shook me from my memories. "The family is fast closing ranks against me, Emma. Cornelius and Alice, William, Frederick—all of the older generation, with the exception perhaps of your aunt Alva."

I grinned. "No, she'll support you just to enrage the others. But what I fail to understand is why Alice and Cornelius object so strongly. After all, Carrie Astor married your brother, Orme. No one has a more narrow sense of proper society than Mrs. Astor. If *she* didn't object to *that* match, then—"

"Oh, but she did, Emma. My goodness, she considers us upstarts every bit as much as your relatives do. But Carrie was determined and Mrs. Astor had no choice but to accept the match or lose her daughter. I'm afraid Neily's parents are going to prove much more stubborn."

"The Vanderbilts are nothing if not stubborn," I murmured with a shake of my head.

"Even Gertrude feels we should end it rather than continue to defy their parents."

"Gertrude!" It surprised me that Neily's sister would take sides against him. It hadn't been very long ago that Gertrude exhibited her own rebellious streak, though in truth she never stepped far beyond the boundaries of her parents' expectations. Yet I'd noticed changes in her in these past weeks since she'd returned to Newport. She seemed older, a good deal more mature than last summer, and ready to take her place as an adult in society. There were even stirrings of a coming engagement.

"I'm sorry to hear that, Grace. What will you and Neily do?"

"We'll do what we've been planning all along." She shook her head as if I'd asked an absurd question. "We're going to marry, and soon."

"Oh, dear." If storm clouds had been gathering this past year on the Vanderbilt horizon, I felt fairly certain the storm was about to break. And it was going to be a fierce one. The time for delicacy had ended. I said, quite bluntly, "You do understand that Uncle Cornelius has threatened to disinherit Neily if he marries you."

"I do and I don't care. I'll have enough for both of us."

That sent my hand shooting out to grasp hers, the fabric of our gloves hissing out a warning. "Oh, Grace. Do you really think Neily could be happy living off his wife's money?"

"I . . ." She frowned, looking uncertain and even fearful. "What else can we do?"

"Grace, Neily is working toward a master's degree in engineering with every intention of obtaining employment in the field. He is intelligent and dedicated. But we both know he'll never make the kind of salary that will keep the two of you in the kind of luxury you're accustomed to."

"I'm willing to make sacrifices."

"Are you? Do you even know what that will mean?" I almost suggested she spend a few days with me at Gull Manor but held my tongue.

Her gaze locked with mine and tears glittered behind her lashes. "Then . . . you're against us, too."

"No." I released her hand and gave it a gentle pat. "No, I'm not against you. If you and Neily are quite certain you have the fortitude to stand up to the entire Vanderbilt family—"

"We are."

"Then this is one *almost* Vanderbilt"—I pressed a hand to my breastbone and the string of tiny pearls that had been my aunt Sadie's—"who will support you. But you must fully understand what you'll be facing. No illusions, Grace. It shan't be easy."

She blinked her tears away. "Knowing Neily has your friendship will make it easier."

"You both have my friendship."

"Then any time I can do anything for you, Emma, you have only to ask."

"Actually, there is something . . ."

Chapter 4

It seemed the stars themselves lit the way from Bellevue Avenue to Beechwood, Mrs. Caroline Astor's Italianate villa overlooking the sea. Gas lanterns swung gently from lines strung from tree to tree, while luminaries formed glowing snakes along both sides of the driveway that circled the fountain and its surrounding flowerbeds. Our progress from street to house took almost as long as the entire trip from Gull Manor, as countless carriages ahead of us deposited family after elegant family beneath the archways of the porte cochere.

Our conversation had turned to lighter topics—Grace's winter in Italy, her spring in Paris, and the excursions, parties, and shopping she had enjoyed. Neily had been present throughout most of those months, which she termed a happy, carefree time. In spite of the Wilsons' lack of open ostentation, they lived nonetheless luxuriously, and I schooled the incredulity from my features as Grace spoke of their extravagances as casually as I spoke of the weather.

Yet I paid careful attention to the details, and her chatter provided me with ample information to rule out a number of young ladies as having potentially birthed a child in recent weeks. The delay in reaching the house also provided me with an opportunity to broach the subject foremost on my mind, yet without revealing too much about the baby in my care. It's not that I had cause to distrust Grace, but this sudden friendship of ours, if that was what it was to be called, had yet to be fully tested. I thought it best to err on the side of caution and not mention my newest visitor at Gull Manor.

"There have been rumors among members of the press," I said to her, not liking to lie but seeing little alternative, "of an indelicate nature . . ."

With just those words, she understood my meaning. "Do tell? Who, may I ask . . ."

I happily fell back on the truth as I explained that I hadn't yet discovered the identity of the woman in question, but that not only could an inheritance be at stake, but the child's welfare as well, and for that reason I wished to ascertain his origins.

"But how did you hear of this?"

Here I utilized a reporter's first line of defense. "It would be unethical of me to reveal my sources. But may I count on your assistance?"

"You'd like me to . . ." Her eyes narrowed as she sought to comprehend.

"Merely talk to your acquaintances, ones you haven't seen in recent months, as you normally would. Nothing more sinister than that, I assure you."

"And you say the child's welfare could suffer?"

"Indeed."

"And you know the whereabouts of this child?"

"I do," I said, and left it at that. Would she probe further? Her eyes narrowed again speculatively; then she nodded.

"Then, yes, of course, I'll do as you ask, and I'll let you know if I uncover anything significant."

The way she warmed to my subterfuge made me smile. Finally, it was our turn to disembark. Liveried footmen handed us down from the brougham. Immediately we became absorbed into the controlled crush of newly arrived guests, were escorted into a foyer glittering from the light of a tremendous crystal chandelier, and swept in a current of chatting, laughing ladies up a flight of stairs. Music and voices poured from the ballroom and followed us along an upper corridor, until a woman in the tailored black of a lady's maid opened another door for us and we stepped into a bedroom suite.

The trappings of femininity instantly surrounded us. Ribbons, lace, taffeta—it seemed these items flew through the perfumed air with lives all their own, until my senses processed the scene and I recognized that lady's maids were removing capes from their mistresses' shoulders and smoothing frocks, adding petticoats, jewels, and headdresses left off for the carriage rides, adjusting bodices, and changing serviceable leather shoes for delicate silk dancing slippers.

Marianne, who had apparently arrived sometime earlier, hurried over to us. She and I traded pointed glances; then she walked us into an adjoining dressing room. Obviously set aside for singularly important guests, it was quieter here. There were only two other ladies being attended to by their maids, and I immediately recognized the regal figure of the woman just then inspecting her maid's handiwork in a full-length, gilded mirror. The maid herself stood anxiously by, awaiting her mistress's assessment.

Mrs. Mary Goelet, Grace's older sister, turned away from the mirror with an appreciative nod, and I felt rather than heard her maid's sigh of relief. I curtsied when Mrs. Goelet's gaze fell upon me, and endured the weight of her curiosity as she tried to place me. We'd met previously, though I'd not spoken with her in nearly a year, when I'd gone to nearby Ochre Court, her Newport cottage, searching for my cousin Consuelo. She slowly took in my gown, an act that rather reduced me to an insect beneath a magnifying glass. She no doubt recalled the garment from whichever ball she had attended with Grace last summer. I received an "Ah," as she apparently remembered me, followed by the swift abandonment of her regard as she came forward to embrace her sister.

"High time you arrived, Grace. What kept you?"

"Oh, May," Grace said lightly, her lips dancing over the single syllable of her sister's nickname. "What was the rush? Miss Cross and I had a lovely ride over together. You do remember Emmaline Cross, don't you?"

May acknowledged me with something between a hello and a grunt, admonished her sister not to take too long, and swept imperiously out of the room. With a little roll of her eyes Grace took her sister's place before the mirror and Marianne went to work. First she removed the velvet cape, and for the second time that day I gasped in awe at the image of beauty before me.

I had believed the gifted cerulean gown to be uniquely exquisite, but Grace's gown far outdid my own and left me gaping. Silk moiré of neither cream nor blush, but a shimmering, translucent combination that exists only inside seashells, formed the basis of the gown, with an overlay of black velvet swirls reminiscent of wrought-iron scrollwork. The bodice molded to Grace's lovely figure, spilled over a gentle bustle, and flowed with breathtaking simplicity to a four-foot train. Little shirred sleeves combining the two fabrics added balance to the skirt and emphasized Grace's shapely arms.

Marianne added a petticoat, made some minor adjustments to the gown, attached ribbons to the tiara and entwined them in Grace's curls. Then she turned her attention to me. I let her fuss for a few minutes, but as soon as I convinced both her and Grace that the achieved results were the best that could be hoped for, I hurried back into the main bedroom. This had been Carrie Astor's suite when she was a girl, before she married Grace's older brother.

Cousin Gertrude's face was the first to greet me, and in seconds her expression transformed from mild pleasure at seeing me to out-and-out astonishment.

"Emmaline . . . my goodness . . . you look . . ."

"Oh, this?" I was very tempted to toss my head as many of the other young ladies would have done and declare the gown nothing special. I couldn't do it, not even in jest. "I'm a bit overwhelmed by it, truthfully. It was a gift from Grace Wilson."

My cousin's nearly black brows converged, her scowl making me wince even before she spoke. "Since when do you accept gifts of that sort—of any sort—from the likes of Grace Wilson?"

It was then I remembered what Grace had said, that Gertrude believed Neily and Grace should go their separate ways.

She didn't allow me time to explain, but went on. "You don't understand what you're playing with, Emmaline. Letting Neily stay with you during the spring upset my parents enough—"

"It did? Why? He didn't wish to be alone in that giant house."

"It involves more than that and you know it, Emmaline. Mother and Father feel you're taking Neily's side, and heavens, if they saw you in that dress, why, they'd . . ."

"It's only a dress, Gertrude, and I am not taking sides. If Neily needs me, I'm only too happy to assist. The same goes for all of you, including your parents."

"Yes, well . . ." She broke off, compressing her lips as her gaze shifted over my shoulder. Judging from the direction, I guessed Grace had entered the bedroom and probably stood watching us. I used Gertrude's sudden muteness, however ill-tempered, to change the subject.

"You spent most of the spring in New York, in the city and Long Island, yes?" When she nodded absently, I rushed on. "I'd love to hear all about it. Why don't we walk downstairs together and you can tell me whom you saw and where you went—all the exciting news."

That seemed to rouse her from her resentments. With a murmured instruction to her hovering maid, she slipped her arm through mine and we made our way through the crowded room. Before we stepped into the corridor, however, I glanced back and caught Marianne's eye.

She nodded once, and I knew she would move about the room discreetly listening to the gossip, and once all the ladies descended to the ballroom she would strike up conversations with the other maids, probing, as I had asked her to, for hints that any of their young mistresses had been "indisposed" in recent months, and whether any male servants had gone missing lately. As to her divulging my secret to her mistress, I had no worries. Marianne had sworn secrecy with a vehemence that raised no doubts.

"Uncle William and the boys were with us for most of the spring," Gertrude was saying as we reached the staircase, "and we were often with the Delafields and the Havemeyers and their cousins from Ohio. Oh, and the Newbolds and the Camerons turned up everywhere we went. The Camerons were supposed to have gone abroad, but there was some problem with the yacht . . ."

"Oh? And were Miss Catherine and Miss Ann Cameron in attendance as well?" I pictured the sisters in my mind. Ann in particular was a dark-haired girl with brown eyes that turned green in certain light . . . rather like my small guest's. But in the next breath Gertrude silenced my speculation by confirming that yes, both the Cameron girls were at hand during the spring season.

In a bright salon off the ballroom we lined up behind other guests, were announced by the butler, and were received briefly by Mrs. Astor amid a lush display of potted palms and American Beauty roses—her favorite flower. She spared a few polite words for Gertrude, fewer still for me, but then I was neither friend nor guest, but there to capture the night's glorious moments for my newspaper column.

Before we passed through to the ballroom, Mrs. Astor called me back. She drew herself up so she could gaze down her nose at me. "You will be discreet, of course, Miss Cross. I cannot have you badgering my guests as they endeavor to enjoy themselves. Unless you are first spoken to, you may use your eyes and ears only to report on the ball."

"Yes, ma'am. Discretion is part of my job."

"That's a lovely dress," she observed as I again started to move away. I couldn't help smiling at her disapproving tone, or how she glanced sideways at her social advisor and companion for the evening, a short, round-faced man with a snub nose and a great, grizzled mustache. Ward McCallister often filled in at such events for William Astor, who preferred a quieter life at his upper New York estate. I myself had seen Mr. Astor in Newport only once, and that had been years ago as he boarded his steamer to leave the island.

Mr. McCallister gave a snort and raised his shaggy eyebrows, and he and Mrs. Astor nodded in silent agreement—no doubt that a girl of my social station should know better than to overstep her bounds; Worth gown or not, I was still nothing more than a wealthy family's poor relation.

Gertrude and I parted soon after entering the ballroom. She drifted into a group of friends while I moved along the wall and found a discreet doorway from where I could observe without interruption. As I usually did, I took a writing tablet and pencil from my purse and began jotting down the details I'd need for my Fancies and Fashions page, all the while on the alert for any clues that might lead me to the baby's mother.

The orchestra played a cotillion, the current favorite, and an array of bright silks and severe black eveningwear filled the dance floor. In pairs men and women formed two long lines and performed the frolicking steps that harkened back to the once-popular quadrilles of decades ago. Hems flounced and coattails fluttered, a dazzling display captured in the numerous French doors that were paneled with mirrors.

Poised in bas-relief above each doorway, images of Poseidon and Aphrodite presided over the proceedings, while the herringbone pattern of the parquet floor mimicked ocean waves. Along with the brilliant chandeliers overhead, brass wall sconces lit the scene, each one fashioned to look like ribbons of flowing seaweed. The overall effect was one of a charmed, underwater backdrop meant to enhance rather than overshadow the main spectacle, that of the very cream of the Four Hundred dancing, smiling, and yes, strategizing in their finest attire and priceless jewels.

I had always admired Beechwood, more than I cared for either The Breakers or my aunt Alva's Marble House. Though magnificent, those houses were also hard and frigid and somehow vacuous. Not of *things,* for both houses were chock-full of treasures and luxuries of every sort, but of warmth and life, of that cozy spirit that made a house a home.

Designed in the Italianate villa style, Beechwood was certainly grander than the shingle-style houses like my own, yet possessed a lighter, airier, and more genial atmosphere than either of the houses owned by my relatives. A person could more easily live here, move about, breathe ... without fearing to damage one's surroundings. Beechwood had been designed to delight those who lived within its walls, while The Breakers and Marble House were intended to strike awe into the hearts of those who did not.

Even as I took in these surroundings, I kept a sharp eye out for anything unusual. Eventually I abandoned my doorway and began a circuit of the room's perimeter, stopping to greet guests and, when invited to converse, ask questions and jot down notes. Where I met with reticence from those less familiar with me, I admit to defying Mrs. Astor's edict and using my carefully collected facts to inquire after their newest yachts, the renovations to their New York mansions, the plans for their daughters' weddings, et cetera. A few well-chosen words of flattery usually went a long way in loosening tongues.

Much to my frustration, all seemed as it should. I'd begun to despair of learning anything useful that night, when my gaze fell upon a singularly unhappy face, one I recognized. With renewed vigor I set off at once in her direction.

"Miss Gordon," I said when I reached her, injecting the correct mix of cordiality and polite deference into my voice. "How lovely to find you here. Do you remember me?"

Daphne Gordon was a girl some three years my junior with wispy golden curls, pale eyes, and a sturdy frame that hinted at future plumpness. For now her youth leant a healthy and pleasing roundness to a figure clad in pale rose satin. She returned my greeting with a puzzled expression that gradually cleared to one of recognition. "Miss Cross, is it?"

"Yes, Emma Cross. We met here at Beechwood a year ago, when Mrs. Astor dedicated her new rose garden. I'm covering the ball for one of our town newspapers. Your family are good friends of the Astors, as I recall?"

"Indeed. We're staying here at Beechwood as Mrs. Astor's guests." Her reply held no enthusiasm, nor did her expression convey pleasure. Quite the contrary.

I pasted on my most professional, yet still amiable, demeanor. "Are you enjoying yourself tonight? I couldn't help but notice, as I entered the ballroom, that you appeared rather disconcerted."

"Disconcerted." She spoke the word as if testing out a new flavor of wine. "No, Miss Cross, not disconcerted. Bored. Horribly, dreadfully bored."

"How can that be?" I swept an admiring glance over the ballroom. Had she become immune to the splendors of her set?

"Because I'm tired of"—she waved a hand in the air—"all of this. If you must know, I was dragged here—quite against my will." She flicked her gaze to the group ranged behind me, and I glanced over my shoulder to recognize several members of the Monroe family. Daphne Gordon had been orphaned several years ago, after both of her parents died in a house fire. Daphne, about thirteen at the time, had been placed with the Monroes, who were relatives—distant ones, which had puzzled closer family members at the time. I remembered my parents discussing the matter. An aunt had sued for custody, but the will had been clear. The courts upheld her parents' wishes and Daphne Gordon, along with the lumber fortune she inherited, was placed under the protection of Virgil and Eudora Monroe, presently standing directly behind me.

I was about to make some mollifying reply when my gaze landed on an object that stopped me cold. Instinctively I reached out a hand, almost but not quite touching the beaded purse that hung from a gold chain looped around Daphne's wrist. "Good heavens!" slipped out before I could stop it.

Her own gaze followed mine. "Oh, this. Do you like it?" Unexpectedly, the corners of her mouth tilted in a small smile. She lifted the purse so I could admire it closer. The fabric matched the rose silk of her gown, but it was the lace trim that most intrigued me—and startled me. Unless the lights were playing tricks, I recognized the pattern. I gaped, but she didn't seem to notice. "Mr. Monroe and his elder son, Lawrence, recently returned from a trip to Belgium. They brought back many bolts of handmade textiles, including this lace. Lawrence suggested the pattern for this purse."

"It's extraordinary," I said breathlessly.

"There is more lying about, if you'd care for some."

Except for the emphasis she had placed on Lawrence's name, she showed no sign that the intricate-patterned lace shot through with gold thread meant anything special. Artifice? I couldn't rule it out. I'd learned in the past year not to base assumptions on appearances alone. I had been fooled before.

"Did you also spend time abroad this spring?" I asked in hopes of learning more about Daphne's immediate past. Was tonight yet another affair in a long and tiring series of social events beginning in early spring? Or was this a first and unwelcome foray back into society after a lengthy absence? I scanned her waistline, cinched tight within her corset, and the press of her ample bosom pushing against the Queen Anne neckline of her bodice.

She shook her head and sighed. "I've been nowhere interesting of late, Miss Cross, and tonight is no exception."

I maintained a calm exterior while speculating that perhaps her discontent indeed stemmed from having recently borne an illegitimate child. I had been accused often enough in the past of stretching my facts to fit my suspicions, but then again my instincts had just as often served me well. "You could always plead a headache if you long to be away. I'd be happy to accompany you upstairs." And ask more questions along the way, I added silently.

"Thank you, but I'm afraid I cannot. I was told unequivocally I must remain until after the midnight supper. Only then may I slip upstairs to my guest room. Oh, Miss Cross, how weary I've grown of such traditions."

"What do you mean?"

"Ball, suppers, being put on display in order to find a husband. . . ." She paused, her eyes suddenly misting.

Mention of husbands fueled my speculation that the Monroes might have a reason to marry off Daphne at the first opportunity, perhaps because they feared recent events could destroy her reputation—and their own.

"All across the country—the world—times are changing, Miss Cross. There is progress and innovation, and new notions of achievement and personal endeavor. But not for us. Not in families like those here tonight. We are trapped in the past, in notions of old money and propriety and—oh! Things that shouldn't matter anymore."

"Yes, I wholly agree," I said truthfully. Her passion raised my earnest sympathies, for she reminded me of my cousin, Consuelo, who only months ago had been manipulated into an unwanted marriage. I reached out my hand to Daphne. "My dear Miss Gordon . . ."

I got no further. An arm fell between us, a silk-gloved hand latching on to Daphne's upper arm. Eudora Monroe was what many would call a handsome woman—tall and big-boned, with steel gray hair piled high and dressed with jewels, her jaw square and stubborn, her eyes dark, direct, and entirely without sentiment. I instinctively stepped aside for her, and she spared me the briefest nod. With a low murmur, she ushered Daphne away so insistently I easily imagined her dragging the girl if she had shown any resistance.

A humorless chuckle caught my attention and I looked up to see the Monroes' elder son, Lawrence—the one Daphne had mentioned—leaning against the wall. How long he had been there I didn't know, but I had the sensation he'd been watching us, that he had witnessed Daphne's brief outburst and Eudora's hasty effort to stifle her.

"Is she all right?" I asked him with no attempt to hide my concern.

Tall and trim and broad through the shoulders, he had his mother's obdurate jaw, her wide mouth, but not her eyes. For where hers revealed little, Lawrence's eyes revealed his thoughts to all who would look. I looked now, and stepped back, and almost wished I hadn't spoken to him. His expression had blackened, became somehow twisted, and he followed my backward progress with an arrow-sharp hiss of a whisper.

"Try asking my father if Daphne is all right."

Chapter 5

Lawrence Monroe pushed away from the wall and shouldered his way through the crush. What had his caustic reply meant? I couldn't very well walk up to Virgil Monroe and ask him about his family's troubles. I didn't dare approach him at all without a proper introduction. Quickly I scanned the room until I found the face I sought.

Before I made my way to my cousin Neily, another familiar face stopped me in my tracks and left my mouth hanging unfashionably open. Our gazes connected, and for the briefest moment the sentiment I witnessed sent my stomach sinking to my feet, for I glimpsed awkward reluctance, a wish to avoid, followed by resignation as he started toward me.

"Emma. How nice to see you. You look lovely tonight."

"Derrick. I hadn't thought you would be here. It's been such a long time—"

"Mother," he interrupted, and I only then noticed a woman held his arm. She stood rigidly at his side, sweeping me up and down with a judgment that gave no quarter. I wanted to shrink away but held my ground. "May I present Miss Emmaline

Cross." No smile softened the stiff line of his lips. No reassuring light entered his eyes. "Miss Cross, my mother, Mrs. Lionel Andrews."

"How do you do?" Her chin inched upward as she spoke, and she did not extend her hand to shake mine. Lavinia Andrews was a beautiful woman who hardly showed her fifty-odd years. Dark-eyed like her son and raven-haired with only the faintest traces of silver, she possessed the slender figure and porcelain skin of a much younger woman. Yet there was nothing youthful or inexperienced about her bearing.

I lowered my outstretched hand when she made no move to grasp it. "I'm very well, thank you, and pleased to make your acquaintance."

"I've heard so much about you. From my son," she added unnecessarily. Her mouth, too, became a flat, harsh line.

"All good, I hope."

Her eyebrow went up. I smiled, a forced effort, for I detected no warmth in this woman's opinion of me, or in the way Derrick's attention seemed focused everywhere but on me. We might have been the barest of acquaintances, and in truth I hadn't seen him since last winter, when he had suddenly disappeared without so much as a good-bye. "It's been many months since you've been in Newport," I said to him. "I can't help but wonder why you bothered purchasing a home here."

He had the grace to blush, but only slightly. I referred to my own childhood home on the Point, which Derrick had bought from my parents last summer before I'd even known the property had gone up for sale. The loss had come as a devastating shock to me, yet beneath the layers of perceived betrayal—by both Derrick and my absentee parents—I'd experienced a disconcerting thrill. Derrick would now be tied to Newport indefinitely . . . and that would give us more opportunities to get to know each other properly. . . .

Except that he hadn't been here, at least not for long. And I didn't know why, for he hadn't seen fit to offer any explanation. He had simply left, and now here he was, his manner inscrutable and perplexing, and his mother staring daggers at me.

"Yes, business kept me away." He touched a hand to his pomaded hair while his eyes darted again about the room. "I . . ." Suddenly he frowned. "If you'll excuse me—us. Mother, I see . . ."

I didn't learn whom he saw. Before he finished the sentence the two of them simply walked off, leaving me summarily dismissed. Not to mention angry and confused.

And hurting. Derrick had proposed to me last summer, and I had turned him down. Even now I believed I had made the only right decision. Circumstances had thrown us together amid a whirlwind of chaos and danger, and with emotions running high, I couldn't trust that whatever feelings we had developed were real and lasting.

But in saying no, had I lost his regard entirely?

"Good evening, Emmaline."

"Neily! I was just looking for you." I wanted to fall into my cousin's arms—yes, I needed one of those hugs he used to give me when we were children and I'd fallen and scraped a knee, or simply felt lonely and sad. Derrick had left me wanting to weep against Neily's shoulder, but instead I embraced him quickly and remembered I had a task to carry out.

He pulled back with a broad grin. "Sorry Brady's still stuck in New York. Father's got him researching some land options on Long Island. He should be able to get away in a week or two."

"As long as he keeps out of trouble." We shared a laugh, both of us knowing that trouble always seemed to find my incorrigible half brother.

Neily held my hands and swept my arms out wide. "You look stunning tonight, cousin!"

"I had help."

"I know. Grace thinks the world of you. I hope you won't be cross, but she told me what you confided in her earlier."

"I thought she might, and I hope you don't mind my asking for her assistance."

"I don't." He grasped my hand and held it up between us. "But only if you confess the whole truth. Who is this child whose mother you're trying to find? And don't tell me it's some vague rumor you heard down at the newspaper office."

I hesitated for as long as it took to inhale a breath and release it. I drew him into a doorway where no one would overhear. "All right, but this is in the strictest confidence. No one can know, other than those I've already told."

He only looked at me steadily, waiting.

"Yesterday, I found a baby outside my front door."

"The devil you say!"

I explained briefly, and when he began to ask questions, I cut him off. "There's something I need you to do. Can you introduce me to Virgil Monroe?" I spotted him again across the way, a man whose looks, like Lavinia Andrews's, belied his age. He stood as tall and straight as his son and filled his tailored evening clothes to perfection, and though his hair had silvered completely, it was full and thick and made a stylish frame for his distinguished features. "There's a question or two I'd like to ask him. I know his ward, Daphne, but I certainly can't approach the man on my own."

"Surely you don't think this child originated with the Monroes?" His eyebrows went up. "With Daphne?"

"I don't think anything—yet. But Daphne is apparently unhappy, and it has something to do with Mr. Monroe." I told him what Lawrence Monroe had said to me.

Neily tugged at the new growth of beard on his chin. "That may be. Monroe is a tough old bird to be sure, but I just can't fathom—"

"As I said, I'm not accusing anyone of anything at this point. I have very little to go on. Ruling out possibilities is as helpful as finding clear leads."

"All right." He held out his arm to me. "I'd be honored to escort you, Miss Cross."

For an instant his gallantry transported me across the years to when we were children and used to play at being grown-ups. Yet at the same time I realized Neily probably wanted nothing so much as to perform this favor for me and return to what interested him most—Grace Wilson. I grasped his arm and we set off.

Unfortunately, my quarry had slipped the net. He'd migrated out to the dance floor, partnering a striking brunette I judged to be several years older than myself, and a good deal more sophisticated judging by the grace with which she executed the dance steps. She seemed to be leading Virgil Monroe, rather than the other way around.

That Mr. Monroe would dance with this woman was nothing strange. On the contrary, etiquette deemed it only polite for even married men to dance with a wide variety of partners so that no woman suffered the ignominy of being a wallflower. I recognized something familiar about this particular woman, though I couldn't yet define what.

Neily turned me about and then we were dancing only steps away from the couple in question, where we might easily fall into conversation once the music paused. For now they seemed locked in a conversation of their own, oblivious to those around them. I strained my ears to listen, but the surrounding voices and music proved too much.

Suddenly their voices hit a crescendo. They came to an abrupt halt and released each other. Fury burned in the woman's dark eyes. "If you wish to bully me," she hissed, "I'm afraid you must stand in line behind my brother."

At that, Virgil Monroe chuckled—meanly, I thought. The brunette raised the hems of her gold silk gown and swept imperiously away without a backward glance. My original intentions forgotten, I turned to Neily.

"Who was that?"

"Don't you know?" When I shook my head, he said, "My dear, that's the widowed and wildly wealthy Mrs. Judith Kingsley."

I continued to look at him blankly.

"Derrick Andrews's sister."

I went about my business during the remainder of the ball, but Neily's revelation continued to gnaw at me. Derrick giving me the cold shoulder . . . bullying his sister . . . Was this the man I thought I knew?

And just what was the connection between his sister and Virgil Monroe?

Concentrating became a challenge, but it mattered little since I uncovered nothing else of interest as I continued to interview the guests, though I did rule out several more possibilities for the baby's mother. I'd decided against approaching Mr. Monroe after what I'd witnessed. It seemed the man had a way of bringing out the worst in women. But with the Monroes staying on at Beechwood for the next week—that much I'd found out from Virgil's wife, Eudora—I'd surely find another opportunity to question the man, or perhaps I'd have Neily and Grace do it for me.

Soon after the midnight supper I asked Grace if she'd mind if her driver brought me home. Before slipping out to the carriage, I climbed the stairs to see if Marianne had anything significant to report from her time spent with the other maids. As I reached Carrie Astor's former bedroom, male voices drifted from around the corner of the corridor. I hesitated, immediately on the alert. There shouldn't have been men in this part of the second floor. It had been reserved exclusively for the use of the female guests.

Then again, with the ball still in full swing downstairs, they wouldn't have expected anyone to be within hearing range. They spoke in low, tight murmurs that raised the hair at my nape.

"You can lie all you want, but I know your little secret," one said. "I promise you, you won't win this time."

With my hand on the doorknob, I froze. Who knew what secret? I willed them to say more, but silence followed, then footsteps. Quickly I turned the knob and stepped inside, but before I closed the door behind me I peeked over my shoulder. Without glancing my way, Virgil Monroe passed under the light of the electric wall sconces. His eyes were blazing, his face aflame.

Good heavens, he seemed to raise discord with everyone he encountered. Had he been the one who spoke? Or had he been the silent one? Another set of footsteps approached, and this time I opened the door wide as if innocently stepping out.

A second man stopped as if startled and glared at me. He was younger than Virgil, and while his features were smoother and stronger, the family resemblance was obvious. I smiled politely.

"Good evening, sir."

His mouth twitched; then he simply looked forward and kept walking, his long legs making short work of the corridor. I turned back into the room and gestured to a maid sitting in view of the doorway.

"Did you see that man who just passed? Is he by any chance related to the Monroes?"

"He certainly is, miss. That's Wyatt Monroe, Mr. Virgil's younger brother. He'll be piloting his sailboat in tomorrow's races." Her lips tilted in a dreamy smile. "He's a handsome one, and ever so sporting. His team is sure to win."

When I arrived home I changed from Grace's beautiful gown into an infinitely more comfortable cotton nightdress. Even as I breathed a sigh of relief to be out of binding stays and that impossibly delicate fabric, I allowed myself the luxury of running my fingertips over the embroidery and imagining myself wearing the gown to yet another function. I would not, of course. Grace's gift had warmed my heart, but it was her friendship I valued. That, and the fact that this dress would fetch a price that could help support numerous orphans for a good long while. I couldn't possibly keep it knowing that. Tomorrow Katie and Stella could take it into town, to Molly's Dress Shop. Molly would fetch a good price for it, and I would send the proceeds to St. Nicholas Orphanage.

Then I tiptoed across the hall and into Nanny's bedroom, careful not to wake her. I found the child on the upholstered bench at the foot of her bed, asleep in the dresser drawer Nanny had emptied and lined with blankets. As I bent over him I made a mental note to have Katie and Stella find him a proper cradle in town tomorrow.

I reached in to gather him up, and his little eyes popped open. He barely uttered a sound, just some soft gurgles as I settled into the easy chair opposite the bed. I held him to me and rested my cheek on his little head, and released the tension of the past hours.

I couldn't help feeling I'd failed him, that I'd go on failing him. Marianne had added no insights from the other maids. I had learned nothing tonight but that strife existed in the Monroe family, just as it did in countless other families. True, there had been the lace trimming Daphne Gordon's purse, but hadn't she told me Mr. Monroe brought back bolts of the stuff? Which meant any lady of means might have obtained some by now.

That wasn't all that troubled me. How different Derrick had been—a stranger. And his mother couldn't have made her sentiments any clearer. I was not for her son . . . and it would appear that, last summer notwithstanding, he agreed. Those reflections depressed me further, and rather than wallow I pushed my personal concerns aside and returned to contemplating the link between the Monroe and the Andrews families.

Instinct urged me to explore that link further, as well as discover what was making Daphne Gordon so unhappy. Two unhappy women—Daphne and Judith Kingsley—both connected to Virgil Monroe. What did it mean? And how did Derrick fit into the mix? That last question again reminded me how little I knew of Derrick outside of his life in Newport—a life that hadn't spanned much more than a couple of months in total.

I rocked the baby gently, seeking comfort in those tiny, flawless cheeks, his softly rounded brow, his silky, wispy hair. As I inhaled that uniquely baby scent deep into my lungs, a near certainty—the night's *only* certainty—burned a little hole through my heart. If I couldn't find his family, he might live out his childhood in an orphanage.

"No," I whispered. "We will not let that happen."

"Emma . . . ?" Nanny stirred on the bed a few feet away. I might have known the slightest sound would wake her. "Is Robbie all right?"

"Robbie?" The name sent a stab of warning through me.

She sat up and reached for the spectacles on her bedside table. "Katie's idea. Says it's for her brother back in Ireland."

"Oh, Nanny, we shouldn't be naming him. He's not ours."

"We need to call him something. We can't very well keep calling him *the baby*." She flipped the covers back and swung around to sit on the edge of the bed. "Did you learn anything useful at the ball?"

I shook my head. "This isn't going to be easy."

"When is anything ever easy?"

That made me laugh, a single breathy note in the darkness. Robbie's hand found my braid hanging over my shoulder and tugged. Yes, despite my protest, he was already Robbie to me. Nanny was right—he needed a proper name. He wasn't some inanimate object, however carelessly he had been left on my doorstep. He was a person, an individual, and deserved to be acknowledged as such. His name would likely change once he left us, but for now . . . Robbie he was.

"How did he do while I was gone?"

The moonlight outlined Nanny's rounded cheek as she

smiled. "Just fine. He's such a good little fellow. Almost as if he knows he's a guest and mustn't make much fuss."

"That's right," I said, gently trying to untangle Robbie's fingers from my plaited hair, "a guest. We all need to remember that."

She adeptly changed the subject. "Tell me what you observed tonight."

Once I had, she moved across the room to me and gathered Robbie from my arms. "Ask questions if you must, Emma, but stay away from Virgil Monroe. I remember him from years ago, before he married. A young hellion, he was. The type who takes what he wants and never pays the piper. There were even rumors about a young woman . . ."

"He ruined her?"

Nanny shrugged. "Nothing was ever proved. Whoever she was, she disappeared along with any family members who might have raised a complaint."

"Disappeared?"

"He obviously paid them to go away."

"Oh, Nanny, what if Virgil Monroe hired that poor carriage driver to bring Robbie here and then murdered him to prevent him from telling anyone. What if Robbie is Daphne Gordon's child?"

She looked down at the baby. "Anything is possible. That's why you need to be careful. Have you considered that Robbie—and all of us—might be better off if we never discover where he came from?"

Chapter 6

Early Wednesday morning I hastily scribbled an article for my society column. The details of America's most illustrious names—Vanderbilt, Belmont, Fish, Forbes, Oelrichs, et cetera— along with the styling of gowns and jewels, the china and silver gracing Mrs. Astor's table, and the many dishes served to her guests at the midnight supper, flowed from my hand almost by rote, from habit and experience much more than any effort of my mind. No, my thoughts remained tangled in the mystery of little Robbie, along with a strong premonition that kept leading me back to the Monroes. When the delivery boy came with our newspaper, I sent my article off with him and didn't give it another thought.

That afternoon I returned to Beechwood with my tablet and pencil, but this time dressed casually in a linen day dress meant for tennis, a hand-me-down from my cousin Gertrude.

The rear lawns bustled with activity—badminton, tennis, bowls, and croquet. White and pink flowers on flowing green vines decorated the round tables lining the arched loggia that wrapped around the rear and south sides of the house, while down on the lawn, long rectangular buffet tables, shaded by bright-colored pavilions, held platters overflowing with glazed duck, roasted partridge, stewed pheasant, and seared fillets of beef; there were lobster tails and crab croquets, pickled oysters, buttery clams, and a multitude of refreshing summer salads. Some of the guests sat on the shaded loggia while others strolled as they nibbled from small plates. Footmen circulated with trays of champagne and colorful hors d'oeuvres.

Nanny had warned me to steer clear of Virgil Monroe, and for now I wouldn't have to worry about that. He, along with twenty of the other male guests, were down at the harbor, at the New York Yacht Club stationhouse. In about half an hour's time they were to sail their vessels along the coast and hold a race some several hundred yards out from the cliffs behind the Beechwood property. It seemed Mrs. Astor had planned every entertainment possible for her guests.

A weary-looking Daphne Monroe, her face shadowed by a wide straw hat pulled low over her brow, stepped into my view. She seemed listless, uninterested in the goings-on. Had she slept badly? Did worries keep her awake? "Miss Gordon, hello. How are you today? Feeling better than last night, I hope?"

"Should I be?" She tersely excused herself and walked off.

A shadow fell across the place where she had stood. "It seems my ward could benefit from a lesson in manners."

"Mrs. Monroe . . . I . . . good afternoon," I stammered. Frankly, that the woman addressed me at all left me flustered. Despite my Vanderbilt relatives, most of the older guard—especially those allied socially with Mrs. Astor—considered me only slightly above the status of a servant.

"Forgive her behavior, Miss Cross," she said, surprising me further. "We've spoiled her. Not hard to do considering her history, but perhaps we didn't do her any favors with our lenience."

"There is nothing to apologize for, Mrs. Monroe. I'm sure

Miss Gordon doesn't mean to give offense, and be assured there was none taken. How are you enjoying the festivities?" Becoming all business, I pulled my tablet from my purse and set my pencil to paper. I sent an admiring glance at her sapphire blue frock with its silver satin inset, scalloped hem, and Medici-style collar. The colors and cut flattered her build, making her appear more queenly than simply large. "Is that an Augustine Martin you're wearing?"

She looked impressed. "Yes, it is."

"Stunning . . ." I went on to ask her the usual questions about the weeks leading up to her arrival in Newport. She seemed only too gratified to supply me with details, though they did little to answer the real questions lurking in my mind.

"Goodness, it's hot out here." She pulled a fan from her purse and snapped it open. With a start I recognized the lace pattern.

"That's a lovely item." I tried to sound impressed yet casual. "It reminds me of the purse Daphne carried last night. The lace is from Brussels, I believe?"

"Correct again, Miss Cross." Her lips flattened to a thin line.

"A gift from your husband?"

Suddenly she snapped the fan closed and thrust it in my direction. "Here. You may have it. I believe it would suit you well, Miss Cross."

"Oh, Mrs. Monroe, I couldn't . . . I didn't mean . . ."

"Nonsense, I insist. I could always have another made." She pressed the fan into my hand and strode away in the direction Daphne had gone.

I stared down at the ivory lace shot through with golden thread. Surely this could not have been a valued gift or Mrs. Monroe would not have parted with it so indifferently.

Yet another woman with a reason to scorn Virgil Monroe?

I found Grace some minutes later. She wasn't engaged in any of the lawn sports or chatting at one of the tables, but stood alone beneath her parasol near the base of the lawn, looking out past the Cliff Walk at the ocean. The skies overhead were clear, but steely clouds banked low on the horizon.

"Shouldn't they have been here already?" she murmured as I moved beside her.

"Do you mean the sailboats?" Four buoys had been placed in the water, marking the turns the boats would take on a course that kept them always visible to those watching from the cliffs.

"Yes, Neily's in his uncle William's ketch. Oh, Emma, I wish he wasn't. Racing can be dangerous."

"Don't worry. Neily's quite a good sailor. All the Vanderbilt men are good sailors." I touched her shoulder, prompting her to cease her probing of the empty waves. "Grace, what can you tell me about the Monroes?"

"The Monroes? If you mean Virgil and Eudora..." She compressed her lips and glanced over her shoulder at the party behind us. "My sister, May, tells me all is not happy there."

"I thought not. Do you know why?"

"Indeed, I do." She inched closer and lowered her voice, not that there was anyone close enough to overhear. "There are whispers that he wants to leave her."

"You mean a divorce?"

"Shh!" Grace cast another backward look across the lawns. "But yes. Up until two or three years ago it would have been unheard of, but ever since last year when your aunt Alva and uncle William divorced... well... it's not such an outlandish idea anymore, is it? Not the scandal it once was."

It took me a moment to come to grips with the fact that my own relatives had wrought such a drastic change in society. But given my aunt Alva's stormy disposition and her insistence on having her way, I shouldn't have been surprised.

This development concerning the Monroes shouldn't have surprised me either. Daphne, Lawrence, Eudora... even Virgil's younger brother, Wyatt, exhibited sure signs that all was not well within the family.

"Do you know which is officially seeking the divorce?" In Aunt Alva's and Uncle William's case, the sentiments had been mutual, but Uncle William had allowed Aunt Alva to initiate the proceedings. It had been the gentlemanly thing to do.

Grace shook her head. "I only know as much as I do because May's housekeeper is the sister of the Monroes' housekeeper in New York." Her face suddenly became animated and she raised a hand to point. "There they are!"

To the south, four sets of tiny, gleaming triangles bobbed over the waves. The party behind us saw them, too, and shouts went up. People pushed closer to the Cliff Walk, and numbers—in dollars and cents—were called back and forth as wagers were made.

As two small sloops, a yawl, and a ketch made their way toward us, so, too, did the clouds. The waves kicked up, prompting fresh speculation and additional money to exchange hands. A favorite was declared as the boats entered the course—one of the sloops pulled out ahead, followed by Uncle William's ketch, *Defender*. Besides Uncle William and Neily, *Defender* was manned by William's two sons and his youngest brother, Frederick. Behind them came Mrs. Astor's son, John, in his yawl. Grace's older brother, Orme, who was married to Carrie Astor, and several other men formed that crew. Behind them came the smaller of the two sloops, owned by Mr. Stuyvesant Fish.

My gaze swerved back to the lead craft. "Who is in the Monroes' sloop?"

"Virgil and his brother, of course," Grace said. "And his two sons, Lawrence and Nate. The boat is called *Vigilant*."

"I don't believe I've met Nate Monroe."

"No, he's younger than Lawrence. Sixteen or seventeen, I believe. He wasn't at the ball last night."

I squinted to make out the figures on the boat. "That's only four. Isn't there a team of five on each boat?"

"Yes, you're right. I believe the fifth is Derrick Andrews."

"Derrick?"

Grace turned to me with a surprised look. "Do you know him?"

"We're . . . acquainted. I didn't know he was such a good friend of Virgil Monroe." Once again, it struck me how much I didn't know about Derrick Andrews.

"Virgil and Derrick's father, Lionel Andrews, go back many years. They're heavily invested in each other's business concerns. Virgil is invested in several major newspapers, including the Providence *Sun,* and Lionel is just as heavily invested in Virgil's textile interests and his transatlantic shipping company. In fact, the families often travel abroad together. We've often seen them in Paris or Italy together."

The Monroes' vessel cut through the water, widening the lead over the others as they approached the first turn. I searched for Derrick on board, wishing I'd thought to borrow a pair of binoculars. "Did you see them all in Europe this spring?"

"Oddly no. Oh, we saw Virgil and Lawrence, but Eudora, Daphne, and Nate stayed home this time. None of the Andrewses was there at all."

I held my hat against the wind. "Are you certain? Perhaps they merely weren't in the same places at the same time as you."

Grace laughed at that. "Emma, trust me. If the Andrewses had been in Europe this spring, I'd have known about it." She studied me a moment. "Is this idle curiosity, or does it have to do with that little matter you're investigating?"

Something in her tone prompted me to ask, "Did Neily tell you what I told him?"

"Well . . ." She looked slightly embarrassed. "Yes, he did. I know the child is at Gull Manor. I'm sorry . . ."

"No, it's all right." I smiled a reassurance. "It's nice to see that you confide in each other. As for your question . . . the truth is, I'm not sure." Before I could elaborate, a fat raindrop splattered the grass at my feet. More followed in rapid succession. Grace let out a little squeal and grabbed my hand.

"Come, let's make a run for it!"

Across the lawn others were scurrying for the shelter of the house. We reached the loggia and Grace kept going through a set of open doors into the ballroom. I stopped along with a small crowd of heartier individuals who huddled beneath the roof, watching the boaters who were suddenly battling the unexpected squall.

The ocean had turned iron gray, the waves as sharp-edged as kitchen knives. Those boats were manned by seasoned sport sailors, yet I held my breath as I watched each vessel pitch and heave. The two in the rear, John Astor's and Stuyvesant Fish's, were already heading south after taking the first turn in the course. Now they kept going, hugging the coast as they made their way around the island and toward the safety of Narragansett Bay.

"Well, that's certainly a relief," a woman said. Despite much of her face being hidden by a flowered, beribboned hat that resembled an overdecorated cake, I recognized the tall brunette as Stuyvesant Fish's wife, Mamie. She made her way to the ballroom doors and stepped inside.

That left Uncle William's ketch and Virgil Monroe's sloop. My stomach clenched as I considered how many people I cared about were on those boats. Uncles William and Frederick, Neily, William's two young sons . . . and Derrick.

"They're having a devil of a time," announced a man who stood near me. He held a pair of binoculars to his eyes.

"Why don't they turn and follow the others?" someone asked.

"They can't," another replied, pointing. "Looks like they're caught in the currents."

"And they're too close to one another. . . ."

The man with the binoculars lowered them to his side, and

with a look of apology I snatched them from his hand. The sloop and the ketch were indeed close—too close—and the wind barreling over the waves threatened to send them crashing into each other. Through the rain and at this distance I couldn't make out individuals, but I could see them all scrambling to tighten the sails and secure the lines.

I gasped as the *Vigilant*'s boom swung wildly around from starboard to port. Behind me, a woman shrieked. On board the men ducked, narrowly missing being hit, but as the boom swung out over the water again the boat tipped onto its side. My heart reached up into my throat even as cries of dismay erupted around me. A hand squeezed my arm. I lowered the binoculars to discover Grace once more beside me, her eyes large with fear.

"Oh, Emma . . ."

"That wasn't Neily's boat," I said quickly. No, but Derrick was on that sloop. I craned my neck, wishing away the rain and the distance so I could more clearly see what was happening. Grace let go a breath, but the worry didn't release its hold on her features—worry that pulled my own features taut with an almost painful tension. Another woman elbowed her way through the crowd, her flawless skin blanched of color, making a sharp contrast with her ebony hair.

"Good heavens. Derrick . . ." Mrs. Andrews pressed her fingers to her mouth and stared out at the rain-blurred view.

"They'll all drown," another female voice said, and I turned around to find Daphne Gordon and Eudora Monroe standing side by side and clutching each other's hands. It was Daphne who had spoken, and now she cried out, "We must do something!"

"There is nothing we *can* do," Eudora Monroe told her with anxious shakes of her head.

"I'm sure they'll be all right," I said with little conviction. I turned back around to face the water. The sloop tipped again, this time towed by the current toward Uncle William's *Defender*, also banked sharply on its side. My own stomach seemed to drop out from under me as the mast from the former seemed about to crash into the hull of the latter. Grace gripped my arm like a vise. I drew her closer and wrapped an arm about her trembling body.

Cresting waves obscured the vessels, sending up a collective gasp among the spectators around me. When the waves broke, the *Defender* straightened and skipped over the water away from the sloop, putting a safe distance between them. But the *Vigilant* tilted sharply again, the boom once more swinging out of control. Mrs. Andrews cried out. Daphne's sobs filled the air while Mrs. Monroe murmured a steady stream of words to calm her.

My heart clogged my throat and my pulse hammered in my wrists so that I could hardly position the binoculars I raised in my free hand. The sloop was once more upright, but the mast had splintered, the shattered section and broken boom pitching riotously in the waves. I caught my breath and held it as two men leaned out over the port side. They reached out and latched on to something in the water, and to my horror I realized that something was an individual. They gripped handfuls of clothing and heaved until they dragged what appeared to be a lifeless body up, over, and onto the deck. There he lay sprawled on his back, unmoving.

"Who is it?" I asked aloud. Even with the binoculars I couldn't make out the features, not of the prone man or the others. It was all a watery blur, the images muted and gray upon the darker gray background of sea and sky.

"What's happening?" Grace demanded. "Can you see Neily?"

"What about Lawrence?" Daphne shouted.

Before I could answer either of them, Mrs. Andrews made her own hoarse demand. "Do you see Derrick? Where is Derrick?"

"I don't know. . . ." Fear made me queasy. No matter how

coldly he had treated me the night before, or how much this woman apparently disdained me, I could not wish either ill. I clamped my teeth around a wordless prayer that he would be all right.

"Thank God," a man in the crowd shouted. "The Life-Saving Service is on the way!"

This time I released Grace to raise the binoculars in both my trembling hands. Sure enough, two official cutters sliced through the rain and churning waves. Within minutes one had rendezvoused with Uncle William's ketch. The other continued until it reached Virgil Monroe's sloop.

With a gasp of relief I said, "Thank goodness, they'll be safe now."

Yet when I swerved my sights back to the foundering vessel, it was to realize there were only four men on board. The binoculars slipped from my grasp to clatter to the marble-tiled floor.

Someone else had gone over. Someone had been lost.

Chapter 7

❦

Mrs. Astor's guests crowded into the ballroom, a somber gathering waiting for news. The buffet tables had been carried inside at the first drops of rain, but not many people ventured toward them. I certainly had no appetite. How could this have happened? How could the elements have dared defy Mrs. Astor and wreak such havoc on her festivities?

One by one Mrs. Astor assembled those most affected by the day's events and ushered them upstairs to her private parlor. Grace and Gertrude, Mrs. Monroe and Daphne Gordon, Mrs. Andrews and her daughter, Judith Kingsley, all followed Caroline Astor up the Grand Staircase in heavy silence. She had not sought me out, but I brought up the rear nonetheless. Five of my relatives had been directly involved, not to mention Derrick. As we arrived on her parlor threshold she eyed me as if contemplating sending me away, but both Gertrude and Grace reached out their hands to draw me into the room.

"Shouldn't we telephone someone in town?" Mrs. Andrews plucked nervously at the lace on her sleeve. "The hospital, or the Life-Saving Service station?"

"Don't you think someone would telephone here if there were any news, Mother?"

Something in Judith Kingsley's tone caught my attention. I glanced over at her in time to catch the petulance on her features before she schooled them into a more suitably apprehensive expression. I studied her a moment longer, remembering her anger of the night before, aimed at both Derrick and Virgil Monroe. Could her resentments be so powerful as to overshadow any concerns for their welfare? Had she not realized someone on that sloop had most likely drowned?

Daphne Gordon, on the other hand, appeared almost inconsolable. She had collapsed into a side chair near Mrs. Astor's escritoire. Her face in her hands, she sobbed quietly while Mrs. Monroe stood over her rubbing her shoulders and patting her hair. Unlike Judith Kingsley, whatever hostilities Daphne had harbored the night before seemed forgotten in her anxiousness over the fate of family members. Mrs. Monroe at times dashed away tears of her own with the backs of her knuckles, but otherwise maintained a brave face for her ward. I wondered how she managed it. Her husband, two sons, and brother-in-law were all on that boat.

For the moment, Grace and Cousin Gertrude seemed to have forgotten their differences. I saw no disparaging looks pass between them. Unable to keep still, I went to the window that looked out at the ocean. The rain had tapered to a light drizzle. Earlier, the remaining men on Virgil Monroe's sloop had been rescued by one of the Life-Saving cutters. Then, using pulleys and winch, the cutter had towed the damaged sloop away. The other cutter remained in the vicinity and several other vessels joined it, a mix of pleasure craft and fishing vessels. Apparently word had spread through Newport. The boats fanned out over the water in what looked to be about a mile in each direction and were methodically sailing in an almost gridlike formation.

"Some of those boats look like volunteers from the Yacht Club," Grace murmured. I jumped at her voice; I hadn't heard her approach. "How splendid of Neily's sailing comrades to join the search. I do hope—" She broke off, swallowing.

"You mustn't worry," I said firmly. "It's certain Neily is safe in town by now. Whoever they're searching for fell from the Monroes' sloop, not my uncle William's ketch."

"Emma is right, Miss Wilson." Gertrude had come to stand at my other side. The dark slash of her brows pulled inward. "You needn't worry about Neily. My brother is my concern, and my family's."

Had I believed them to have reached a temporary truce? How wrong I was. My cousin's rudeness sent me whirling to face her. "Gertrude . . ."

"It's all right, Emma," Grace whispered.

"I've already telephoned over to The Breakers and told them what little I know." Gertrude went on as if she hadn't committed an unpardonable slight against Grace and, by association, me. "The very moment there is any further news I'll rush home to tell them. They're worried, of course, but I reassured them the ketch appeared sound as it sailed off with all crew members aboard."

Grace ignored her and stared out at the activity on the water. "Whom do you suppose they're searching for?"

I shook my head, my teeth clamping the insides of my cheeks. Though I wished ill fate on none of the men aboard the sloop, I refused to consider that it could be Derrick lost to the waves. He and I had last parted on such uncertain terms, and I couldn't help but blame myself for that. For the better part of last year I had sent him mixed messages, offering my regard one moment only to withdraw it the next. Why? Because I feared where that regard might lead me. Because I wasn't yet ready to commit to him or any man. Because . . .

Because in truth I doubted that he or any man could form an attachment as swiftly as he had . . . to me.

Me—plain, ordinary, unexciting Emma Cross. Surely what had aroused Derrick's interest had been the danger we had shared in facing death on more than one occasion. Oh, I'd cited my desire to remain independent, to achieve success in my life and my career on my own terms and in ways that would be considered unseemly for a society wife. I'd pointed out the differences in our backgrounds and how I'd never fit in with his upper-class family.

But I'd had plenty of time in the interim to examine my motives and admit the truth, at least to myself. I had feared that once the excitement had worn off, so, too, would our infatuation with each other. It seemed sometime last winter he had realized something to this effect, or perhaps he had simply grown tired—or bored—with my insistence that we not become too deeply involved too quickly.

And now . . . I gulped in a breath. Now we might never have the opportunity to discover if we could have developed something more lasting. My throat tightened at the thought—at the possible loss. At my own stubborn stupidity.

"Ladies, come and have some tea," Mrs. Astor beckoned from behind us. "You'll feel better."

I doubted it, but after blinking away the mist that had gathered in my eyes, I dutifully took a seat on one of the two Louis Quinze sofas that faced each other. A pair of footmen poured tea, which Mrs. Astor herself graciously passed around, even offering me a kindly smile as she placed an exquisite, floral-patterned Meissen cup and saucer in my hand. Either in all the commotion she had temporarily forgotten that I was not one of her honored guests, or seeing me flanked by Gertrude Vanderbilt and Grace Wilson had elevated me in her esteem, at least temporarily.

An hour dragged by, seeming more like several. We spoke in

whispers and drank endless cups of tea while continuing to gaze out the windows as if the men for whom we waited would suddenly appear in the sky. Finally, at the sound of raised voices below, we thrust cups aside and, in a flurry of skirts, sprang to our feet.

We entered the ballroom to discover Neily had arrived with the Monroe brothers and their uncle Wyatt. Their clothing hung about them in sodden wrinkles, their hair encrusted with salt and plastered to their foreheads. They were speaking with John Astor and Stuyvesant Fish, who also must have returned while the ladies and I had been upstairs. I saw no sign yet of Virgil.

Or of Derrick. Was he somewhere in the room, speaking to one of numerous knots of people? I tried to discern his voice among the murmurs filling the room. My heart thumped more forcefully with each moment I didn't find him.

Gertrude spotted Neily and started to go to him, but Grace was too quick. She hurried by and cast herself into his out-stretched arms. I remembered the feeling, after more than one harrowing experience, of running into Derrick's arms and not caring who saw. Gertrude set her hands on her hips. She tensed as if about to hurry toward them, but I came up behind her and grasped her elbow. She turned to me with a scowl and opened her mouth to protest.

"Give them a minute or two," I whispered in a rush, and in-dicated with a sweep of my gaze the numerous stares pinned on us. "You don't want to make a scene."

"They are already making a scene and it isn't right," she whispered, but lowered her arms and assumed a more ladylike stance.

"Perhaps that's not for us to judge," I whispered back.

She ignored me, and called out, "Neily, what about Uncle William and the boys, and Uncle Frederick?"

"They're all fine," he said, lifting his cheek from Grace's hair and putting several proper inches between them. "They've gone back to Rough Point."

Rough Point, situated at the southern end of Bellevue Avenue, was Uncle Frederick's estate, and where Uncle William and his sons often stayed when they weren't on his steamer yacht, *The Valiant.* The news of their safety sent a surge of relief through me.

Though she still appeared anything but happy, Gertrude voiced my own thoughts. "Thank goodness they're safe."

At the same time Grace had rushed to Neily, Eudora Monroe and Daphne Gordon did likewise to Lawrence and Nate Monroe. As Grace had done, Daphne seemed oblivious of surrounding stares and threw herself into Lawrence's embrace. From over her shoulder the young man tossed his mother an unapologetic, almost defiant look . . . as if this show of affection was something forbidden . . . something heretofore concealed.

I hadn't long to contemplate that before Nate Monroe staggered to a table and collapsed into a chair. He was as pale as the surrounding walls and seemed light-headed, about to faint. Someone produced a snifter and pressed it into his palm and, when he barely responded, helped raise the glass to his lips. Nate sipped and then sputtered. His coughing brought silence to the surrounding voices.

Eudora went to him, sank to her knees, and took hold of his free hand. "What happened out there? Where is your father?"

"Where is my son?" Lavinia Andrews demanded, the panic in her voice echoing my own rising anxiety. "Where is Derrick?"

When the boy said nothing, his uncle, Wyatt Monroe, raked his fingers through his hair, making it stand up in dark spikes. His eyes were bloodshot; his skin loosely hugged the bones of his face. Virgil's younger brother, the handsomer, sporting brother, seemed to have aged decades at the hands of the storm.

"He's safe, Mrs. Andrews," he said. The breath whooshed out of me. Relief weakened my knees, until his next words hit me with physical force. "He took in some water, but the doctors say he should recover."

"Water?" Mrs. Andrews's startled gaze met my own before darting back to his. "You mean he nearly drowned?"

"We fished him out before that happened," Wyatt assured her.

"And my husband?" Eudora Monroe was still kneeling at Nate's feet, holding his hand in both of hers.

Nate tried to reply, but it came out choked and garbled. With an arm still around Daphne, Lawrence said, "It was awful, Mother. As soon as the waves kicked up, Father lost control of the rudder. It was almost as if—" He stopped, biting down on his lower lip. He angled a gaze at his uncle.

"Tell me," Eudora demanded in a tone that made both her sons flinch.

Lawrence released Daphne and approached his uncle. "Uncle Wyatt, you realized it, too, didn't you? Am I imagining things? You're the most experienced sailor among us. What was your sense of it?"

"If one of you doesn't explain this instant..." Eudora gripped the arms of Nate's chair and pushed to her feet. "What should Wyatt have sensed? What did you all see out there?"

Once again she glared at each family member, and only then did I realize her eyes were dry—quite dry, unlike Daphne's and her younger son's. Nate's tears fell openly and his shoulders visibly shook, so that I longed to go to him and offer what comfort I could. I stood rooted to the spot, however, waiting, as everyone else in that room waited, for some explanation.

Lawrence spun on his heel to face his mother, but it was Neily who spoke. "It seemed to be more than the storm that sent the sloop out of control. Each of the four boats was hit with the same wind, and the same currents dragged at our rudders and strained the sails. We had trouble navigating the ketch, true, but it wasn't until the Monroes' sloop came at us that we were in any serious danger."

He paused, and Grace asked quietly, "What are you saying?"

"Something wasn't right about how the sloop was handling. As if the problem stemmed from the vessel itself and not the weather."

"That's right." Lawrence fisted his hands. "I *felt* the sloop shimmying in the water before the storm hit. There was an odd vibration in the lines I'd never felt before. I called over to Father to tell him as much, but he didn't seem to hear me. He—" He broke off, swore under his breath, and made his way to a seat beside his brother at the table. "Oh, God . . ."

His head fell into his hands. Eudora stood looking down at him, at both her sons. Foreboding settled heavily in the pit of my stomach.

"Where is your father now?" Eudora asked, her voice a mere rumble of its normal pitch.

In answer, Lawrence lifted his face and stared out the French doors facing the sea.

A half an hour later I arrived at Newport Hospital on Friendship Street just off Broadway. Grace had lent me use of her carriage. She had offered to accompany me, but I had insisted she stay behind with Neily. I thanked the driver and sent him back to Beechwood to collect his mistress. I'd worry about getting home later.

The air inside reeked of dampness from the rain mingled with antiseptic and lye soap. Lavinia Andrews and Judith Kingsley had entered only minutes before me. I waited at a respectful distance as they were greeted by a doctor who explained Derrick's condition. I pricked my ears, and terms such as *fluid on the lungs* and *possible pneumonia* sent ice through my veins. I held my tongue and saved my questions for later.

Finally, the doctor offered to escort them to Derrick's room.

I started forward, but Lavinia noticed me then and held up the flat of her palm. I stopped short as if she'd pushed me. "My son's health is a private matter, Miss Cross."

"I'm concerned about him, too, Mrs. Andrews."

Her eyebrow rose in a show of disdain. "I suggest you return to your home. I'll have someone deliver a message to you once we are more certain of Derrick's condition. Unless you have a telephone?" Her expression said she didn't think someone like me would possess such a luxury.

I didn't bother to correct her. She had placed pointed emphasis on *my son*, in effect staking her claim and negating any hold I might have believed I had on Derrick. Her attitude toward me stung, but in a way I could hardly blame her. Her only son lay in a hospital bed in serious condition. Why should she worry about the feelings of a young woman she scarcely knew? Yet Derrick and I had a history of facing danger together, and I wasn't about to go anywhere until I knew he would be all right. Resolutely I chose a chair in the lobby and settled in. Mrs. Andrews and her daughter regarded me with no small degree of exasperation before apparently dismissing me and following the doctor up the stairs.

Time passed, and I began to wonder if I should call for a hansom to take me home. At the sound of heels clicking on the steps I jumped up from my seat. Judith Kingsley approached, her expression grim.

My heart sank even as I clung to hope. "Will he be all right?"

"The doctor said we won't know for another day or two. He swallowed quite a lot of water and is heavily sedated. They'll need to observe him for the next forty-eight hours, perhaps longer. I suggest you go home, Miss Cross, and leave Derrick to Mother and me."

That was all. She offered no further reassurances, no thanks for my concerns, not even a softening of her haughty expression.

"Mrs. Kingsley, your brother and I are friends—"

"Only friends?" she interrupted. She raised her eyebrow at me, and if I hadn't known she was Lavinia Andrews's daughter previously, there would have been no doubt now.

"Truthfully, yes. And as his friend, I feel I have a right to—"

"Miss Cross . . ." She moved closer and dropped her voice to a murmur. "My mother would like you to know this: You gave up any right to be my brother's acquaintance, much less friend, when you took a prostitute into your home. Oh, yes," she added at my look of surprise, "we know all about that. Did you think you could keep such a secret in a town like this?"

"I took in a young woman in need of shelter and a fresh start," I said stiffly.

"Call it what you will. You are not the kind of person our family wishes to see fraternizing with my brother. Now, if you'll excuse me . . ." With that she turned on her heel and began the ascent to the second floor.

Outside, I stared unseeing into the road in front of the hospital. My temples throbbed and like an insidious fever my anger ran alternately hot and cold inside me. The sound of my name snapped me from my daze.

"Emma, over here!" Neily waved me over to his curricle. Grace squeezed over to make room for me on the leather seat. I climbed up and settled in with a sigh.

Grace reached for my hand. "Is Mr. Andrews going to be all right?"

"I don't know. They're going to observe him for the next few days."

Neily leaned around Grace. "Your friend, Detective Whyte, wants to see you, Emma. He called over to Beechwood after you left. That's why we're here. We'll take you over to the station."

"Why me?" I had no desire to discuss theories with Jesse, not just then. I wanted only to go home, receive a hug and a cup of tea from Nanny, and hold little Robbie. I sighed again. Robbie. I shouldn't have allowed Katie to name him. We had no claim on the child, no lasting ties.

Just as I had no true ties to Derrick . . .

"The detective has been interviewing everyone who was involved in the accident," Grace explained.

I shook away a sudden urge to cry and focused on the matter at hand. "Yes, but I wasn't . . ."

"You *were* watching through binoculars," Grace reminded me. "Several people remembered that. Someone must have mentioned it to him."

We arrived at the police station to find a dozen or so of Mrs. Astor's guests milling in the lobby and the large open office beyond. How strange, the sight of so many fashionably dressed people in that harsh, utilitarian place, with its electric lights, bare walls, and dull wood floor. I saw no sign of Mrs. Astor herself. I did see Eudora Monroe and her brother-in-law, Wyatt, sitting near Jesse's desk. Jesse, however, was nowhere in sight.

Leaving Grace and Neily talking to a group in the lobby, I made my way into the main room and over to Jesse's desk. "Mrs. Monroe, are you all right?"

Her pale face supplied the answer, but she drew herself up and met my gaze. "My sons are being questioned, Miss Cross. Both of them. They wouldn't let me be there."

Judging by his absence, I guessed Jesse was one of the officers questioning the boys. "Don't worry, Mrs. Monroe. They're in good hands, I can promise you. Where is Daphne?"

"She stayed behind at Beechwood. There was no reason for her to come. I put her to bed with a cool compress before we left. Her nerves are all a jumble. Mrs. Astor will look in on her."

I touched her shoulder. "I'm sure she'll be fine. But how are you holding up, ma'am? Is there any word?"

"My husband has not been found, if that is what you're asking."

I searched her face for signs of grief, for the threat of tears. As earlier, her eyes were dry. I remembered the lace-edged fan she had given me so blithely earlier in the day. I still had it. I opened my purse and drew it out.

"I should return this to you, Mrs. Monroe, especially now."

She held up a hand, not to take the item but to shield herself from it. "No, Miss Cross, you keep it. Really."

I was confused and flabbergasted. I flicked a glance at Wyatt Monroe, who had been watching our exchange in silence. He stared back at me, his nostrils flaring and his upper lip slightly curling. "How is Derrick?" he asked.

"He's been admitted to the hospital," I said, unnerved by the bluntness of the question, and by his use of Derrick's given name with me. Did he know about our friendship? Had Derrick spoken of me to this man? "They need to observe him for signs of pneumonia."

"Humph." He crossed his arms over his chest.

"I'm sorry? Is that supposed to mean something?"

"Two men fell in, Miss Cross. Only one came out."

"What are you implying?"

Before he could answer, the door to the police chief's private office opened, and the Monroe brothers walked out. Lawrence was scowling. His younger brother, Nate, had obviously been reduced to tears yet again. Their mother sprang out of her chair and rushed over to them.

Jesse stepped out of the office, saw me, and waved me over.

Wyatt came to his feet and brushed my arm to catch my attention. He was a tall man, athletic in build, the type who obviously spent more time in pursuit of outdoor activities than sitting in an office. If Virgil was the family's financial expert, Wyatt was the seasoned sportsman. "I am implying that Derrick Andrews is either one lucky bastard or a guilty one. He dove in after my brother. By the time I reached the side of the boat to pull them back in, only Derrick was there. My brother was nowhere to be seen. Now, why do you think that could be?" He tipped his head to me in dismissal. "Miss Cross."

He walked away, leaving me shaking where I stood.

Chapter 8

✦

A policeman in blue stood in the private office, but at a word from Jesse he nodded a greeting to me and left. Police Chief Rogers, a barrel-chested man with sharp features yet kindly eyes, rose from his seat behind the desk. "I'll leave you two alone."

Jesse closed the door behind him. "The Life-Saving Service will continue the search, but at this point Virgil Monroe is presumed dead. And it's quite possible the storm isn't solely to blame."

"Have you questioned his brother yet?"

It wasn't so much my question as my deadpan tone that seemed to take Jesse aback. "I've questioned all of the Monroes. Why?"

I didn't want to voice what Wyatt Monroe had just insinuated—that Derrick was responsible for Virgil falling overboard. I couldn't believe that. But what reason would Wyatt have to implicate Derrick? According to Grace, their two families were longtime friends. Derrick wouldn't have been part of the race crew otherwise.

Of course, that didn't mean Derrick and Wyatt hadn't argued recently, or that they hadn't harbored some secret resentment toward each other, giving Wyatt reason to accuse him.

"Emma, I called you in here because I've been told you were watching the race through binoculars."

I blinked away my speculations. "Yes, that's true."

"Did you see anything unusual occur between the men?"

I thought back. I'd been so focused on the effects of the wind and rain that, in truth, I'd hardly noticed the individual actions of those on board. "I remember the boom swinging wildly back and forth, and the men ducking out of the way. I was sure someone would be knocked over the side, but they all avoided being struck."

Jesse grasped my arm and led me to a chair facing the desk. He perched himself on the edge of the desktop. "Did you notice who manned which position?"

"No, they were all scrambling, reaching to secure lines and tighten the sails. With the rain, I couldn't make out who was who."

"So you couldn't say, for instance, if Derrick Andrews left his starboard position before he jumped in to allegedly save Mr. Monroe."

I pinned Jesse with my gaze. "Wyatt told you he believes Derrick is responsible for Virgil being lost, didn't he?"

"He expressed that sentiment, yes."

Spots of fury danced before my eyes. "Have you considered that he might be trying to shift attention away from himself? After all, who among those men knows more about sailing, and about that boat in particular? Wyatt Monroe is the sportsman of the family. I was told it was *his* sailboat they raced."

"Paid for by Virgil," he corrected. Jesse leaned back on his hands and regarded me for a long moment. "Lawrence Monroe told us the boat was handling oddly before the storm kicked up."

"He said the same thing earlier at Beechwood. It raises important questions about Wyatt's actions before the race."

"Explain."

"Don't forget, Wyatt should have inspected the vessel before the race." I grasped for any fact that would remove suspicion from Derrick. "If anything had been tampered with, he should have noticed, shouldn't he? Unless he sabotaged the *Vigilant* himself."

"And his motive for doing so?" Jesse posed the question with a lift of his chin.

In other circumstances I might have grinned as I rose to the challenge of his question. But not now, with so much at stake. "I heard Virgil and Wyatt arguing last night at the ball. One of them said, 'You can lie all you want, but I know your secret. I promise you, you won't win this time.'"

Jesse gave me a deferential nod. "I admire your recall abilities, but what were they arguing about? The race? Or something more serious? And who spoke?"

"They were hidden from me at the time and I don't know their voices well enough to distinguish one from the other, but I saw them immediately afterward and they both appeared furious. As to what 'it' may be, I don't yet know. But Wyatt having a motive to murder his brother makes much more sense than assigning Derrick the blame."

Where I expected concurrence, Jesse's expression turned so grave my stomach tightened in warning. "Actually, Wyatt supplied us with a possible motive. Did you know the two families' fortunes are somewhat linked?"

I hesitated, not at all liking this sudden turn. "Grace Wilson mentioned something to that effect, yes."

"Wyatt claims Virgil had been doctoring his financial reports, misrepresenting the profit margins. His investors have taken a loss as a result, including the Andrews family."

My twisting stomach now dropped to my feet. I didn't wish to hear another word, yet I knew I had no choice. "That's a serious charge. Can he prove it?"

"It has yet to be verified, but that's not all. Wyatt says Virgil was quietly buying out New England and upstate New York newspapers. Most of the transactions were conducted through one of his smaller subsidiary companies, essentially hiding his identity. These were mostly small publications, but he was in the process of buying controlling shares of the Providence *Sun*. A process halted by his untimely death, I might add."

"Oh, Jesse . . ." My throat closed and I gasped for air. Jesse was on his feet and patting my back in an instant, though that only made me sputter more.

He went to the door and swung it open. "I need some water in here, *now.*"

I'd all but recovered before he pressed the cool glass to my lips, but I drank dutifully nonetheless. I wrapped my hands around the glass and Jesse backed away to resume his perch on the desk.

As soon as I could trust my voice, I said, "I don't care what motives he might have had. Derrick Andrews did not cause Virgil Monroe to fall overboard."

"Can you be as certain he didn't seize the opportunity to jump in and hold the man under the water until he drowned?"

"Yes, I'm certain, dammit!"

My vehemence took even me aback. Jesse went quiet, his pensiveness weighting the air between us. My spine gone rigid, I stared back defiantly. Was Jesse *hoping* to prove Derrick guilty? He made no secret of his affections for me, and I didn't doubt he had guessed part of my hesitation in returning them stemmed from my own conflicted feelings for Derrick. Did he see this as a way to be rid of a rival?

"Jesse . . . surely you can't believe—"

"Right now," he interrupted in the brisk tone of a policeman, "every man on the *Vigilant* is a potential suspect. The vessel is being examined for intentional damage, and the Yacht Club records will be checked to see when the boat was last inspected, by whom, and who had been aboard last before the race. We'll also verify each man's whereabouts the day before, as well as look into each one's relations with Virgil Monroe. That's where you come in, Emma, if you're willing to help."

I relaxed in my seat. I should have known better than to believe a good man like Jesse would jump to conclusions no matter how personally convenient they might be. I smiled weakly. "What can I do?"

"Exactly what you're already doing in your search for the baby's mother. How is he, by the way?"

"He's doing just fine." My smile grew. "Getting lots of attention."

"Good. Keep asking questions. Mrs. Astor not only refused to speak with us today, she's put her foot down when it comes to allowing us access to Beechwood. She says the accident didn't occur on her property, so there's no reason for us to intrude on her or her guests' privacy. That's why we had everyone transported here for questioning."

"The incident involved *her* guests." I shook my head at the obstinacy of Mrs. Astor's set, their insistence that they should live by different rules than the rest of us. "I believe with Grace's help, I can return to Beechwood." The weight of my purse in my lap reminded me of something that could prove important. I opened the clasp and drew out Eudora's fan. "I had already turned my focus to the Monroe family. Look at this." I handed him the elegant piece. "See the lace? It matches the handkerchief Katie found with the baby. I believe it's possible Daphne Gordon is the mother."

He frowned. "The Monroes' ward?"

"Merely a theory at this point, but one that needs investigating. Something is making Daphne terribly unhappy, and Eudora doesn't seem to want to let her speak of it. She pulled

Daphne away from me at the ball last night. And that's not all."
I shifted forward on my seat. "When I asked Lawrence if
Daphne was all right, he said I should ask his father that ques-
tion."

"Are you saying . . . ?"

"Like you, I don't wish to jump to conclusions. But yes, I'm
saying it's possible Virgil Monroe fathered a child on Daphne
Gordon. Which opens up new motives for someone wanting
the man dead, doesn't it?"

Jesse raised a hand to his chin. "It most certainly does. But
remember this, Emma. If Virgil Monroe and that child are connected, his may not be the only death involved. There was also
the carriage driver."

"Have you identified him?"

"No, and we haven't received any reports of missing per-
sons. It's as if he appeared out of thin air and disappeared back
into it."

"An abandoned baby and two dead men," I mused. "It
couldn't be coincidence."

"Not just *dead* men, Emma, but possibly two *murdered* men,"
he corrected me. "Remember that. This is dangerous business and
I don't want you doing more than asking general questions and
reporting back to me. No overstepping your bounds like you did
last summer. Understood?"

"Of course, Jesse." I held his gaze without blinking. "I experienced enough excitement last summer to last a lifetime."

"I need to use the typewriter, Ed. Now, please."

"Why?" My fellow reporter at the Newport *Observer*
glanced up at me from his seat behind the only desk in the office
we shared, not that I used it very often. His eyebrows waggled
dramatically. "Got a big tip on the latest fashions coming out of
Paris?"

I didn't consider myself a violent person, but it was all I could do not to smack the stupid grin off Ed Billings's very average face. There was nothing remarkable about this man. He was of average height and build, with nondescript brown hair and eyes—eyes that looked upon the world with a startling lack of compassion or sense of fairness. Eyes that rarely displayed any emotion except a perverse kind of humor, typically derived at the expense of someone else.

Today that someone was me, but that was nothing new.

"You're not using the typewriter, Ed," I pointed out. "If you would simply move your chair so I could get by . . ."

The typewriter sat on a small table behind the desk. Without waiting for Ed to decide whether he would be accommodating or not, I made my way past him, and if I pushed his chair, assisted by its castors, so close to the edge of the desk he was forced to suck in his overhanging belly, well, it couldn't be helped. Besides, I was exhausted, emotionally and physically, but I had no intention of returning home until I'd placed my article about today's distressing events into the hands of my employer, Mr. Millford.

I sat, removed the canvas cover from the machine, wriggled my fingers a few times to loosen them, and began tapping away. Soon enough I sensed Ed craning his neck to see over my shoulder.

"What's got you all fired up?"

"Someone died today, Ed. At Beechwood."

He sprang up from his chair. "Why didn't someone tell me? Why didn't you telephone here, Emma?"

I didn't look up from my typing. "Why should I? I was there. I witnessed the events firsthand."

"That's beside the point. This should be my story. I'm the *Observer*'s hard news reporter."

"No, you're not, at least not exclusively. Mr. Millford ran my story about the murder at Marble House last summer." I glanced over my shoulder briefly. "Remember?"

I returned to my article, pressing the keys with a renewed vigor that almost drowned out Ed's next words.

"That little carrot he tossed you? That was nothing. That was to stop your whining. You shouldn't have read more into it, Emma. I thought you were smarter than that."

My hands flew off the keyboard, throwing the room into sudden silence. I turned. Started to speak. Breathed in sharply. Burning waves engulfed my face—could he see it? His infuriating grin persisted, no longer merely mean-spirited but downright malevolent. Spiteful. He stood over me, leering, his very posture demeaning in a way that felt calculated. For the briefest moment the walls closed in and I almost feared him.

And then I remembered that Ed Billings was all bluster and no substance—just like his articles, where the sensational always took precedence over the facts.

I inhaled, much more calmly this time, and turned back around to face the typewriter. "If you'll excuse me, Ed, I have a story to finish before the presses stop for the night."

"We'll see about this, Emma."

"Mmm. Yes, all right."

"I'm going to speak to Mr. Millford."

He plodded loudly out of the office, but I'm sure he still heard my reply of, "You do that, Ed."

When I could no longer hear his footsteps, my fingers stilled. The truth was, except for a few stories about minor thefts on the island, I hadn't delivered any hard news to Mr. Millford since the Marble House article last summer. Would he allow me to cover this story now? It was vital he did—vital to me, at least. I refused to let Ed Billings publicly accuse, try, and condemn people I cared about. Nor could I let him follow a trail that might lead to Robbie. Under no circumstances must that happen.

I read over what I had typed so far, a fair account of an incident the police officially still considered an accident. No need to mention Wyatt Monroe's accusations, or Jesse's disclosure that the *Vigilant* might have been tampered with. None of those things had been proved yet. A prudent reporter would wait.

I would be prudent.

"I don't know, Emma . . ." Mr. Millford's voice faded and I fidgeted with the telephone wire as I waited for him to continue. What didn't he know about? My article was straightforward, wasn't it? Then why hadn't he run it yet? Why was he calling me that next morning, Thursday, to express his hesitation?

"It feels as if . . ." He paused again, then said, "As if you're holding back. Being too careful. Maybe we should let Ed take over this one."

"No!" My shout prompted a cry from Robbie, just then being carried down the stairs in Katie's arms. In my mind's eye I could picture Mr. Millford flinching, then frowning. I hurried to control the damage I had just inflicted on my cause. "Mr. Millford, just as with the Marble House murder, I was there at Beechwood. I'm a firsthand witness. If I'm being careful—and I'm not saying I agree with that assessment, not entirely—but if I am, it's because I'm waiting for the facts to unfold before rushing to judgment. Which is what Ed would do. You know he would, Mr. Millford."

A murmuring sound came over the wire as he apparently mulled this over. Again, I pictured him frowning, perhaps this time running a hand over his hair. "Ed might do that on occasion, but he also sells newspapers."

"Yes, but—" I cut my own argument short, suddenly unable to defend myself. I *had* held back, and it wasn't the first time. Last summer I reported on the Marble House murder, but I had swept a good many facts under the rug. I'd done so for my cousin Consuelo's sake, but all my good intentions didn't prevent a certain guilt from nudging at my reporter's soul. Once again, I found myself facing the same conundrum. But what choice? Either water down the truth, or allow people I cared about to go down in a froth of scandal whipped up by Ed Billings. Was my journalist's integrity worth more than their futures?

"Mr. Millford," I began anew, "I—"

"All right, you can continue with this one, Emma. But if Ed turns up any interesting developments, I'll run his articles, too."

"Then you'll run mine? The one I handed you yesterday? On the front page, in my name?"

"E. Cross, like last time, and page two, I think."

"Mr. Millford . . ."

"That's all for now, Emma. Good-bye."

He ended the call before I could manage to push an appropriate response past my lips.

Later that day I visited Rough Point to see how Uncle Frederick, Uncle William, and his two sons fared after their brush with the ocean storm. Like Neily, they were all well, though shaken, and could only tell me that they had also noticed the Monroes' sloop dragging awkwardly through the water right before the wind picked up. Uncle William remembered thinking the other vessel wouldn't maintain its lead for long unless they regained control.

I found that odd. The sloop had appeared to those of us on Beechwood's loggia as having been in the lead since rounding the southern tip of the island. If the boat had been tampered with prior to the race, how could it have sailed out ahead of the others so easily? And what could have developed during the race that caused the boat to falter before the storm hit?

I arrived home to hear my telephone jingling once again.

"Emma, it's Jesse."

My pulse jumped. "You've learned something?"

"We're not certain it didn't happen during the storm, but the rigging on the sloop's main mast appears frayed, which caused the line to fail, possibly even before the mast broke." He sounded rushed, and I could imagine him at his desk amid the bustle of the busy police station.

"What does that mean exactly?" I tried to picture how the sloop had struggled against the waves and wind. Fraying resulted from friction, from being rubbed against—or by—a rough object. Surely the lines had been strained to breaking against the wind, but would that have resulted in the rope wearing out? "What would the result of such fraying be?"

"Once the line snapped, the boom would have swung out of control or fallen. Specifically, to the port side given the prevailing winds during the storm."

"But even before the line failed, the boom would have been difficult to control, no?"

"That's correct."

"And you believe that resulted in Virgil Monroe falling overboard?"

"There's nothing conclusive. With the boom out of control any number of the men could have been swept overboard. However, Wyatt Monroe's position of port trimmer put him most in the line of danger."

"That makes no sense." I thought a moment. "What positions did the others hold?"

"Lawrence Monroe was the main trimmer, and your friend, Derrick, manned the starboard trimmer position."

I ignored his subtle emphasis on the word *friend*. "What did Nate do?"

"Tactician. He basically had to keep track of the wind shifts and relay the information to the others, while they trimmed the sails and shifted course accordingly."

I considered these facts in silence until Jesse said, "Emma, I just wanted to let you know. I really must go. . . ."

"Wait. Something isn't adding up here. The fraying on the rigging should have been noticed during the inspections before the race, and that suggests it was done intentionally afterward. Yet the damage would have been most detrimental to Wyatt, not Virgil. Whoever did the tampering couldn't have known a storm was brewing, but . . ." I fell silent again, thinking.

"Emma, I can ring you later tonight—"

"Don't hang up," I practically shouted. I moved closer to the call box and spoke directly into the mouthpiece. "What if whoever frayed the rigging did it to stage what appeared to be an accident? Maybe the plan was simply to push Virgil from the boat while the others were distracted, and put the blame on the faulty lines. But then the unexpected storm struck, making the pretense of frayed rigging unnecessary." A scenario took full shape in my mind and I gasped.

"What? Are you all right?" It was Jesse's turn to raise his voice.

"Jesse, what if Wyatt frayed the rigging because he planned to stage the accident and make it look as though he himself were about to go overboard? Who would most likely hurry to his rescue?"

"I assume you mean his brother?"

"I do. Not to mention that Virgil's position put him closest to Wyatt, so it would make sense that he would have been the first to reach for him. But even if the others tried to intervene as well, Wyatt could have managed to fall overboard and take Virgil with him, drowning him in the waves before the others could fish them out."

"Stop right there." Jesse's policeman's voice startled me. I jerked the ear trumpet away and suddenly understood how a criminal felt when told to halt or his pursuers would shoot. His next words floated across the several inches I'd put between myself and the device. "You're stretching again, Emma. That scenario is too convoluted to hold water. I telephoned because I promised I'd keep you apprised of developments, not to feed your wild imagination. I've got to go. If you think of any sensible possibilities, let me know."

He hung up, leaving me holding the ear trumpet in the air and staring at the call box with my mouth half open. I didn't know whether to be insulted or despondent that my old friend would speak to me that way. For a moment I considered calling back and giving him a dressing down.

My own words played back in my mind . . . and I realized Jesse was probably right. Crimes were usually simple—it was the aftermath and the attempts to cover up that became convoluted, to use Jesse's word.

Still, in my mind the frayed rigging spelled tampering, a clumsy attempt to make an intentional drowning appear accidental, the result of a swinging boom. And the fact that the boom would have struck either the starboard or port trimmer implied even more an attempt to make Virgil's death appear accidental. He would hasten to assist the struck man, and in turn be tossed overboard and left to the mercy of the waves.

Gently I replaced the ear trumpet to its cradle. My theory seemed ludicrous, not to mention impossible to prove.

But somehow, I *would* prove it. Or so I hoped.

On Friday I returned to Beechwood, this time not only with Grace, but also her sister-in-law, Mrs. Orme Wilson, formerly Carrie Astor. Which meant, of course, that on the way over in Grace's carriage I could not speak openly about little Robbie or my suspicions concerning Virgil Monroe. Carrie's mother had asked both women to come and help her entertain her unhappy guests. When we arrived, Mrs. Astor looked less than pleased to see me again, but she could hardly voice her disapproval when her own daughter treated me as a friend.

Carrie Astor Wilson was a slender beauty, with dark, lustrous hair, large eyes, and a delicate nose and mouth. Despite her mother's rigid social standards, I had always felt at ease with Carrie, and she had been a favorite of my cousin Consuelo's. In fact, she reminded me of Consuelo now, in both looks and manner, and a sudden sadness came over me. I'd seen my cousin every summer for as long as I could remember, and she had always been like a younger sister to me, so much more so because neither of us had sisters of our own.

It suddenly struck me that this summer, for the first time, I would receive no invitations to Marble House, or desperate telephone calls begging me to come and comfort her after one of her mother's infamous tirades. Last November Consuelo married the ninth Duke of Marlborough and moved away to England. It might be years before I saw her again.

"Do you play bridge, Miss Cross?" Mrs. Astor asked as she herded us out to the loggia, whose graceful arches mirrored those of the porte cochere at the front of the house.

"I'm afraid I don't, ma'am."

"Good," she said rather too heartily, so that I took it as a slight. But then she gestured beyond the two garden tables obviously set up for card games to where Daphne Gordon stood staring out at the ocean. "Neither does Daphne. Perhaps you might keep her company while the rest of us play a few rounds."

"I'd be only too happy to," I said quite truthfully. I had come to ask questions, and I couldn't think of a better person to begin with, or under better circumstances. With Eudora Monroe's attention on her cards, she was less likely to steal Daphne away from me again.

Voices drifted from inside the house, and a moment later several ladies stepped outside. I recognized among them Grace's sister, May, and their mother, Melissa. Eudora walked between them, wearing dark blue moiré with thin black stripes—somber colors for summer, to be sure, but not quite what one would consider mourning attire.

Mrs. Astor bid them take their seats. Before Grace moved to take hers, I shielded my mouth with my hand, and whispered, "Isn't this a bit odd, setting up for bridge when one of the players' husbands has just died?" I glanced over at Eudora again. "And she's wearing half mourning at best."

"I thought you knew," Grace whispered back. "Mrs. Monroe is refusing to declare her husband deceased until the search has been exhausted."

I gazed out at the heaving waves. The weather had cleared, but whitecaps dotted the vista. "The rescue ships are gone."

"Yes, but she hasn't given up hope that he might wash up alive somewhere on the island."

"After two days?"

Grace shrugged.

"Come, ladies," Mrs. Astor called. "Let us begin."

Grace went to the table where her mother and sister already sat with Eudora Monroe. I stood watching a few moments more while footmen carried out trays of lemonade, tiny sandwiches, and colorful petits fours. Eudora plucked up a sandwich and nibbled at the corner.

I didn't understand her at all. She had practically tossed her fan, a gift from her husband, at me as if it meant nothing to her, yet she refused to accept his apparent death. At the same time, however, she was enjoying an afternoon of cards—albeit a quiet occupation—when most wives would be lying in their beds, incoherent with grief.

Was she a bereaved woman who kept her feelings close, or had her husband's obvious demise left her wholly unaffected? I would have to talk to her to find out, and to do that I would need to find a way to be alone with her.

For now I crossed the loggia to join Daphne near one of the fluted columns supporting the loggia's beautiful arches.

"Good afternoon, Miss Gordon," I said as I reached her. "How are you holding up today?"

She turned to me with a serene, one would even say contented, countenance that took me aback. "I'm well, Miss Cross. And you?"

I hardly knew how to answer. Three nights ago she had been on the verge of tears, with nothing but complaints about having to attend one of the most important balls of the summer. And now, after the death of her only father figure . . .

She went back to staring out at the ocean, tilting her cheeks up to the breeze and closing her eyes in apparent enjoyment. "Such a beautiful day, isn't it? I don't know how the others can concentrate on cards with such a glorious view available to them."

"I'm glad to see Mrs. Monroe up and about," I ventured, but received only a nod and a murmured "yes." It seemed Daphne was not of a mind to offer up any insights. An odd sense settled over me that Wednesday's events hadn't occurred, that I'd only imagined the boat race and storm and Virgil Monroe falling overboard. How else to explain this utter lack of effect upon either Eudora or Daphne? Yet the fallen coachman had not been imagined, nor Robbie, whom I'd held and fed and walked up and down my kitchen garden that morning.

I tried another tack. "And how are your brothers doing? Nate in particular seemed quite distraught."

She turned to regard me so quickly that I flinched. "Nate and Lawrence are *not* my brothers, Miss Cross. Let us be quite clear about that."

"I beg your pardon. I only meant—"

Her brow smoothed. "Yes, I understand. But remember, I have only been with the Monroes a few years. It's not as if the boys and I grew up all our lives together. We aren't as familiar as all that."

"I see."

"But as for your question, you are correct. Nate is despondent over his father, although, like his mother, he has not given up hope."

"And Lawrence?"

She fought another smile and fingered the collar of her ivory tea gown, and a little shock went through me as I again recognized the lace that had first sent me on my quest to Beechwood. It edged the sailor-style collar and the cuffs of her dress. Though we stood beneath the shade of the pavilion roof, the gold threads woven into the pattern shimmered with light.

Her attention had wandered, and I roused her by gently repeating my inquiry.

"Lawrence is rather more stoic than his brother." Her smile peeked out yet again, though only a quick appearance before she compressed her lips. "Don't misunderstand. He is horrified by what happened. He simply isn't one to express his feelings openly, and he understands that it does no one any good to wallow in misfortune."

"I'm sure Lawrence must be doing all he can to help Nate through this difficult time."

"He is trying to. He and Nate aren't always the closest of brothers."

Much like Virgil and Wyatt, I thought. "Perhaps sibling closeness isn't fostered in the Monroe household. I believe Mr. Monroe and his brother sometimes had their differences. Some families seem to thrive on competition, especially among the male members. Would you say that's the case with the Monroes?"

"Now that you mention it, yes, Mr. Monroe did encourage a certain competition among the boys, though he targeted Nate most of all. 'Be like your brother,' he would say. Or, 'Why aren't you as good at everything as Lawrence?'"

I made note of the word she had used: *targeted.* "So he favored Lawrence over Nate?"

"I wouldn't exactly say that either. He favored Lawrence when it suited his purpose to do so."

"And when it didn't?" I pressed, though gently, so as not to let her realize I was doing so.

Here the resentment she had revealed to me at the ball returned to score her forehead and pinch her lips. "Then he would simply dismiss Lawrence, or belittle his requests. And mine, and his wife's—" She broke off suddenly, her eyes widening with an emotion I couldn't read. Fear? Not quite that, but anxiety of some kind, to be sure. She glanced over her shoulder at the card tables. "Listen to me," she said with a soft, nervous laugh, "speaking ill of the deceased. Forgive me, Miss Cross. I suppose I'm not as composed as I might appear."

"That's quite all right, Miss Gordon. In times like these, it helps to unburden oneself."

"Thank you, Miss Cross. I—" She broke off once again, then pointed toward the cliffs. "Here they come now!"

"Who?" But I needn't have asked. Two figures in masculine clothing stepped through the gate in the hedge that separated the property from the Cliff Walk. Daphne raised her hand to wave, and one of the figures waved back and quickened his step.

"Come say hello, Miss Cross," she said, before circling me and hastening down the veranda steps to the lawn. She began to run and then apparently remembered herself, for she lurched to a more sedate pace. Nonetheless, she continued as if on tightly wound coils that could bounce out of control at any moment.

Not about to miss an opportunity, I followed her more slowly so as not to attract undo attention from Eudora or the other ladies. Their voices droned on, indicating their focus was still on their card game.

Daphne reached Lawrence and for an instant I thought she

was going to throw herself into his arms. They both stopped short with several feet between them, but even so I had the unshakable impression of their being wrapped in an invisible embrace. I saw it in the tilt of Lawrence's smile, in the rise and fall of Daphne's shoulders. Nate had fallen behind his brother and only now caught up, but when he should have stopped to greet Daphne he continued on. I bid him good afternoon as he passed me. He scowled and grunted in return.

"Nate seems upset," I said when I joined the other two. I searched Lawrence's face for signs he and his brother had argued. Where his mother's eyes were midnight dark, his were a lighter brown with golden flecks that presently flared. Anger? I couldn't be sure.

"I had agreed to walk the cliffs with him, searching for any evidence of my father. Nate is hoping . . ." He swallowed. "We didn't find anything."

"I told Miss Cross Nate is having trouble accepting what has happened," Daphne said, her voice a soft caress that had an immediate effect on Lawrence. His eyes cleared of their turbulent emotion, leaving him as serene as I'd first found Daphne.

"This must all seem rather bizarre to you, Miss Cross," he said. "Bridge games, being out walking—our family never did do things in the usual way. I hope you won't judge us too harshly, but as long as the police insist we remain in Newport— until Father's death is resolved—we must get on as best we can. For a Monroe, that means staying occupied."

"I explained that to Miss Cross as well," Daphne said. "She's been wonderfully accommodating."

I waved away her praise, and asked Lawrence, "How is your uncle? Is he here?"

Lawrence shook his head. "Since the sloop is no longer habitable, he has been staying here, but I haven't seen him yet today. It's not like him to sleep in."

"He must have gone into town," Daphne said. "Probably to

supervise the inspection of the sloop. You know how he is about that boat. Heaven forbid someone touches something in the wrong way . . ." She rolled her eyes.

Lawrence voiced his agreement. To me it sounded as if Wyatt Monroe was more concerned about his boat than his brother. But then, so far the entire family seemed less than disturbed by Virgil Monroe's drowning.

Had anyone cared about the man while he lived?

I knew I'd earned my keep about an hour later when Mrs. Astor caught my gaze and gave me a nod. Acknowledging me with even that small gesture meant she apparently approved of how I had engaged Daphne and Lawrence in strolling about the gardens and, later, enjoying an impromptu picnic on the lawn in the growing shadow of the house. One of the worst fates in the eyes of a woman like Caroline Astor was to have any of her guests at loose ends.

The bridge game ended. Mrs. Monroe came to her feet and with the back of her hand pressed to her forehead declared herself worn out. Instinct sent me to my feet as well. I could follow her into the house, offer to escort her up to her room to see to her comfort, and attempt to strike up a conversation. Yet as I climbed the loggia steps I saw very real smudges of weariness beneath her eyes. If I had any doubts, they ended when she swayed and Grace's mother moved swiftly beside her and slipped an arm about Eudora's waist. Even if I had offered my assistance, I could not in good conscience have probed the woman with questions about her husband, not then. I would have to return to Beechwood another time.

Carrie decided to stay on, but Grace and I left soon after. If I had lost an opportunity with Eudora Monroe, I gained one now in being alone with Grace.

"This afternoon was not what I expected," I said as the carriage swung out onto Bellevue Avenue.

I didn't need to explain. Grace nodded. "The Monroes are a complex family. Had my father been lost, you would have found all of us in blackest black and weeping on each other's shoulders. But then, my father and Virgil Monroe are two very different men."

I reached under my chin to untie my hat ribbon, removed the simple straw and silk-lined boater, and leaned my slightly aching head back against the velvet squabs. I thought about my own parents and my sense of their having both abandoned and betrayed me by moving to Paris and selling the house I grew up in. Yet in my heart I knew if anything happened to them, I would react with anything but indifference. "It's sad to think his family might not have held him in the highest regard. Perhaps they simply register their grief differently than most people."

"He was a difficult man to like," she replied candidly. She pulled her lace gloves from her fingers, and I caught myself examining the pattern, half expecting to see the gold-threaded design brought back from Brussels by Virgil Monroe. It was not the same, of course, and I shook my head at my fancies.

"Daphne told me he often belittled the family's requests," I said. "If that's true, it seems rather cruel of him."

"Daphne has good reason to say that. It's not commonly known, but she and Lawrence wish to marry."

"I hadn't known that, but it doesn't surprise me after seeing them together. I take it Mr. Monroe disapproved?"

"'Disapproved' is an understatement. From what I understand he downright refused to allow it and ordered them to never speak of it again."

"But why? Was it because she spent the last several years in their household, almost like a sibling?" Before Grace answered I remembered what Daphne had said. "I mistakenly referred to Lawrence and Nate as her brothers, and she nearly bit my head off."

"Yes, I imagine such a reference would be a sore point for her. But from what I've heard—and mind you this came from my mother's personal maid, who had it from Mrs. Monroe's maid—Virgil didn't deem Daphne's inheritance significant enough for his son."

"Won't she inherit her father's fortune?"

"She will, indeed. But after her parents died without male heirs, their lumber companies were sold off. I believe your uncle Cornelius bought one of them, to supply his railroads with ties."

"Did he?" I hadn't known that, but it made sense since Uncle Cornelius never let an opportunity pass him by.

"Daphne's inheritance is a fixed amount," Grace went on, "without company stocks or prospects of increasing in any substantial way. Apparently Virgil wished to expand his own interests with his sons' marriages in order to create a family dynasty. Much like your own relatives established through the generations."

True, I was no stranger to the ambitions of parents. Consuelo hadn't wanted to marry the Duke of Marlborough, but she hadn't been able to withstand the pressure from her mother, who was intent on elevating her branch of the family to European nobility. There was another example much closer to home these days—sitting right beside me, in fact. Neily's parents didn't deem Grace, or her family, good enough for their son. They wanted someone with an older pedigree, without the slight taint of scandal fueled by rumors that Grace's father had profiteered during the Civil War.

"This explains the grievances Daphne expressed at the ball," I said. "I know how she felt about Virgil's interference, but what about Lawrence?"

"I'm afraid we've exhausted the extent of my knowledge." Grace gazed out the window into the lengthening shadows. We had just passed the gated entrance to Rough Point and were turning onto Ocean Avenue. Light traffic passed us in the opposite direction; a carriage ahead of us turned into Bailey's Beach, where late-day swimmers splashed about in the shallows or sipped cool drinks beneath the awnings near the pavilion. "I'm afraid I'm not a confidant of either Daphne or Lawrence." She sat back and turned to me again, her eyes narrowing. "You don't think Lawrence . . . ?"

I shook my head quickly. "No, please understand that I tend to think aloud. It's my way of organizing the nonsense floating around in my brain. I certainly don't mean to accuse anyone of anything, especially a young man who just lost his father."

"A possibly angry young man," Grace whispered. I could practically see the churning of her thoughts, because the look on her face was an all-too-familiar one. Surely it was the same look of concentration I assumed when I was piecing together evidence.

It was one thing for me to play investigator. It was quite another for the daughter of a member of the Four Hundred. Grace had been sheltered and pampered her entire life, and to someone like her, Virgil Monroe's death might seem a great, mysterious adventure. I knew better. I had learned all too well how quickly an ordinary situation could turn lethal. I had experience in fighting back—in fighting for my life. Grace did not.

"A lot of young men become angry with their fathers at one time or another. Take Neily, for example." I didn't finish, but let the obvious hang in the air between us. Grace's next words surprised me.

"Speaking of Neily . . . I telephoned him from Beechwood before we left. I . . . ah . . . " She looked away, nipped at her bottom lip, and played with the tasseled cords of her purse. "Would you mind terribly if he were to meet us at Gull Manor when we arrived?"

I placed a hand over hers. "Not at all."

"It's become difficult finding time together, you see. His parents have been keeping a close eye on him, and when he *has* come to see me they've had terrible rows about it. It could place you in an arduous position, so I really shouldn't ask—"

"Grace, truly, it's all right. While I have no desire to argue with my relatives, neither will I stand down from something I believe to be right. Besides, with a brother like mine, I've had to stand up to Uncle Cornelius and Aunt Alice more times than I can count. I'm happy to report that so far there have been no permanent rifts."

Neily was in fact sitting in the parlor with Nanny when Grace and I arrived home. My heart squeezed at finding him holding Robbie and looking down at him with something approaching awe. He came to his feet immediately upon seeing us, offered me a look of mixed guilt and apology, and then showed Grace a broad grin.

"Oh, Neily," she said before he could speak. She crossed the room to him and cupped her hand over Robbie's head. "He's darling. And how darling to see him in your arms. Why . . ." She raised the same hand to dab at the corner of her eye. Was she imagining a similar family scene, but in a home shared by Neily and herself?

She surely looked out of place in my home, like a flower among a garden of weeds. Shame crept hot along my neck as I regarded my lumpy settee with its faded pillows, my scuffed area rugs, and the faint paths of soot that traveled up the walls from my oil lamps and the old gas sconces.

Then I glanced at Grace again and realized she hadn't noticed any of this, or if she had, she didn't care. All that mattered to her in that moment was Neily and the promise of their future. If any doubt lingered in my mind, Grace banished it by turning to me, her eyes filled with gratitude, and mouthing a silent thank you.

We gave them a few minutes to fawn over the baby, after which Nanny smoothly reclaimed him. She and I slipped out and went to the kitchen, leaving Grace and Neily alone. We fed and changed Robbie, but my thoughts kept me distracted. An idea had formed, and I was waiting for the right moment to put it into action.

Chapter 9

A̶t the sounds of Neily and Grace preparing to go their separate ways, I hurried back into the main part of the house. "Neily, I'm wondering if you might do me a favor."

"Of course, Emma. Anything at all." It was Grace who had spoken. She addressed her next comment to my cousin. "After how good she has been to us, can there be any other answer?"

With a fond expression that tugged at my heart, Neily raised her hand to his lips. Then he turned to me. "What may I do for you, Emmaline?"

"I wish to take a look at the Monroes' sloop. Can you escort me into the Yacht Club? Tonight?" Like all the Vanderbilts, indeed virtually the entire Four Hundred, Neily was a member of the New York Yacht Club, and its station here in Newport. I was not, and neither were my parents. Even if they had been in the country and were able to afford the exorbitant membership dues, they would not have joined. Mother's first husband, my half brother Brady's father, had gone down with a yacht and she swore she would never have anything more do with sporting boats—or men who sailed.

"We're going sleuthing, are we?"

Grace's question came all too eagerly and I realized my mistake. "No, Grace. I want to go after dark, and I think it would be better if Neily and I went alone—"

"Don't be silly." She tossed her head, rustling the ribbons and silk flowers adorning her hat. "Dark or daylight, Neily and I are both members. What better diversion than three friends wishing to view the yachts moored along the pier. Even if we're seen inspecting the sloop, other members will simply assume we're curious." She wrinkled her nose and tilted her head. "But why do you need to bother? Weren't the police going to check for tampering?"

"They already have, but it's not exactly signs of tampering I'm looking for," I clarified. "I'm more curious about who was positioned where on the boat, and what their role was as part of the crew."

"That doesn't sound very dangerous."

"Grace, please, I just think—"

"If you believe it could be dangerous," Neily broke in, "then I don't think I should bring you, either, Emmaline."

Somehow I managed to convince him, just as Grace convinced me to let her accompany us. A few minutes later Neily climbed into his curricle while Grace and I boarded her carriage. Her driver brought us to Shady Lawn Manor, her parents' mansion just off of Bellevue. Neily followed, though he took a roundabout way there. Last summer his father's financial secretary, Alvin Goddard, put tails on Neily at Cornelius's request. Mr. Goddard no longer occupied this earth, but that wouldn't have thwarted Uncle Cornelius's plan to spy on Neily and keep him under his thumb.

We dined informally on the veranda at Shady Lawn and waited until dark, whereupon we squeezed into the curricle and drove into town. We had no trouble entering the Yacht Club.

As Grace's and Neily's guest, no one questioned my presence there.

The New York Yacht Club station Number Six comprised a two-story, boxy building with upper and lower porches in front and a cupola used for spotting incoming yachts. In back, a pier extended into the harbor.

"Where to first?" Neily asked as he held the door open for Grace and me.

"Are there any records kept on informal races?"

"Of course. Everything is recorded," he replied with a note of exasperation, as if my question were a ridiculous one. "This way."

The large main room consisted of tables and chairs, a fireplace, and a service bar where incoming yachters could find coffee and light refreshments. There was also a telephone for arranging transportation to the various summer cottages and accommodations in town, or for summoning the Life-Saving Service in the event of an emergency.

A few people milled about or sat at tables, the women in summer-weight fabrics emboldened with vibrant stripes and military tailoring, the men in sporty linen suits. A man with thinning white hair and a mustache fashionably turned up at the corners moved through the assemblage asking questions and jotting down replies. I assumed he was a Yacht Club official recording these newest arrivals. Activity bustled beyond the rear-facing windows as steamer trunks were unloaded onto the pier and yacht captains prepared to cast off and anchor their vessels farther out in the harbor.

Neily led us through the main room and into a smaller corner office. Mahogany shelves lined two of the walls, stuffed with books, ledgers, and periodicals. A formidable oak desk sat beneath the main window, its surface gouged and pitted from years of use.

"This is the administration room and records library," he said. A counter ran along a third wall, where another telephone was mounted. Neily lifted a ledger book from the counter and flipped through, holding the page he sought with a finger and waving me over. "This is what you're looking for, I should think."

I took the volume from him and set it back on the counter. Neily moved a kerosene lamp closer. Columns that spanned the two open pages before me recorded the details of each vessel registered for the race the day of Mrs. Astor's lawn party. Each column bore a heading: *Displacement, Length, Beam, Draft,* and *Sail Area.*

"What do these designations mean, and remember you're speaking to a landlubber."

Neily obliged, but other than the correlations between the size and power of each ship, the technicalities meant little to me. A notation stated that Wyatt and a Yacht Club official had inspected the vessel the day before the race; no issues were recorded.

A faint discoloration on the page caught my eye, one I easily could have missed. Ordinarily I would have disregarded it, but I had come here searching for any clue, however miniscule. "Neily, pull the lamp closer."

He did and I leaned lower. On the lines indicating the helmsman and port trimmer, I ran my fingertip over the names, *Virgil Monroe* and *Wyatt Monroe,* respectively. The paper felt raised and hardened beneath the ink.

"Do you have a pocketknife on you? Or anything with an edge?"

Neily reached into a coat pocket and handed me his money clip. "Will this do?"

"Let's try it."

After handing him the bills, I placed the edge of the silver clip on the paper and carefully scraped back and forth. A few moments later, I'd collected a small pile of shavings in the crease of the book and uncovered two different names on the ledger lines.

"They were reversed," I said with a grim smile. "Whoever did it used paint the color of the paper to hide the fact."

"Clever," Grace said with a hint of admiration.

Neily looked over my shoulder at the page. "So Wyatt had originally registered as helmsman, and Virgil as port trimmer. I wonder why the change."

"More importantly," I said, "whatever the reason for the switch, why hide it with paint?"

"You'd be surprised." Grace hovered at my other side. "Some of these older members are sticklers when it comes to the records. The very idea of scribbles and corrections makes their administrative skin crawl. It could simply have been an attempt to keep the ledger neat and tidy."

"I suppose . . ." I stared down at the names, my face tightening with concentration as I tried to make sense of this new information. "Who usually captained the *Vigilant*?"

"Wyatt," Neily said. "He's considered an expert helmsman, has won loads of races. He might even have taken the America's Cup last year if the winds hadn't shifted and allowed Uncle Willie's team to outmaneuver him on the last leg."

I gripped the book and lifted it off the counter. "Who initiated the switch—Wyatt or Virgil?" I didn't expect an answer. As was my habit, I was merely voicing my thoughts out loud.

Could Wyatt have convinced his brother to take the helm in order to stage the accident? It almost made sense . . . almost . . .

I slapped the book back down. "I need to see the boat."

Neily gestured toward the main room and the door that led to the pier.

Gaslit globes illuminated the area, each reflected in the black water like a shivering full moon. The men I'd seen earlier were gone, and the newly arrived yachts had been moved back out into the harbor for mooring. Only a dozen or so boats filled the slips along the pier and a few others were anchored close by— so close one might have leaped from deck to deck like stepping-stones. A low hum of voices could be heard from inside, and farther out the buoys tolled and light waves slapped along hulls and pilings.

The night watchman strolled around the corner of the building, whistling a tune. He saw us and touched his cap brim in greeting. "Good evening, Mr. Vanderbilt. Miss Wilson." He offered me a polite smile before continuing his patrol.

Grace had been right. The three of us together, specifically two ladies escorted by a gentleman, attracted less notice than if Neily and I had come alone. That might have raised questions in the watchman's mind, but as we were, we formed a socially acceptable group of young people simply looking at the boats and enjoying the evening air.

He disappeared around the far corner of the clubhouse. I set off at once down the pier with Neily and Grace following. The damaged sloop bobbed gently in its slip. The vessel sat low in the water, its broken mast a jagged shadow against the sky. The shattered boom lay lengthwise across the deck like a drunken sailor. I held my skirts and hopped down from the pier. Neily stepped down beside me. Grace stayed on the pier.

"If you'd like to wait back at the clubhouse, it's fine," I whispered up to her. Why I whispered I couldn't say, since we hadn't tried to hide our presence from anyone. I suppose my clandestine reasons for being there made me feel suddenly shy of using my full voice.

"No, that's all right. I'll wait here." However, it wasn't long before she crossed the pier to view the sleek ketch across the way. That was fine with me. Better Grace stayed occupied while I poked about.

First, I went to examine the rigging on the main mast. With only one lantern mounted several pilings away, I struggled to make out the details clearly. I picked up the severed lines and slid them between my fingers, distinctly feeling where the hemp thinned and the fibers had snapped. I pointed this out to Neily.

"Could one of the crew have weakened the line, planning to sever it completely at the right moment during the race?"

He squinted a bit as he fingered the rope as I had done. "It's possible. He'd have to wait until everyone else was occupied, though, or someone would have noticed."

"Perhaps while maneuvering through one of the turns in the course," I suggested.

"Possibly."

"Who in the crew would be in the most likely position to accomplish this while the others were busy?"

He considered, then said, "The main trimmer, actually."

"Lawrence?" My pulse gave a little leap. Virgil refused to allow him to marry Daphne. Did Lawrence love the girl enough to commit patricide?

I didn't want to believe it, nor did it fit with the conclusions I had thus far drawn about the young man. True, on the night of the ball he had revealed an angrier, darker side, but only momentarily. The hours I had spent this afternoon with him and Daphne had been pleasant ones. Despite the obvious pall hanging over the day, Lawrence—and Daphne, too, now that her doldrums seemed to have passed—had been cordial, accommodating, and intelligent, and had even shown a quiet sense of humor.

Or had I simply resolved to pin my suspicions on Wyatt and ignore other potential suspects? His anger toward his brother had been clear and palpable, even from down a hallway and around a corner the night of the ball. Wyatt had also been too quick to implicate Derrick, as if to cast suspicion away from himself.

"Can you show me exactly where each man would have been positioned, and what his duties were?"

To demonstrate, Neily moved around the deck, from port to starboard, stem to stern, carrying out a pantomime as he explained the various functions of the crew.

"And so when the boom swung around to port side," he said as he concluded his tutelage, "Wyatt could easily have been slammed in the chest or back or even the head. In that event, he wouldn't likely have been able to overpower his brother."

I sighed. "So my theory would make a lot more sense if Wyatt had captained the sloop, instead of Virgil."

"There's another possibility. Wyatt might have been the intended victim."

"Then how is it his brother is dead?"

"That would be the whim of storm and sea. Nothing is ever certain out there, Emmaline. But do you really wish to know what I think?"

I regarded my cousin in the darkness. The beard he had grown in recent months, shaped to a dapper point beneath his chin, wasn't all that made him seem years older than a summer ago. Neily had matured, grown wiser and more seasoned, no longer merely the pampered son of a millionaire, but a man in his own right who did as he saw fit, who deserved respect.

"I'd very much like to hear what you think," I said fondly.

"I think Virgil's death was an accident. I think the frayed ropes are merely a coincidence, somehow overlooked during the inspection. Yes, I know—" He spoke over me when I began to protest. "To miss something as important as frayed ropes is unconscionable, and yes, Wyatt is an expert sailor. But that doesn't mean he never makes a mistake. Or that he didn't rush the inspection. As it is, the boom did fall during the storm—a combination of failed rigging and heavy wind and seas. But again, an accident."

"I don't believe that." I glanced around at the damaged vessel. "Even Wyatt and Virgil's sons don't believe it was an accident. And I will not stop probing until I find the truth."

Turning away, I moved to the helm and placed both hands on the wheel. One question I hadn't asked yet was if Virgil had been holding on with two hands, how much force it would have taken to dislodge his grip and send him overboard. My back still to Neily, I started to do just that when I heard a grunt and a thud.

"Neily?" Before I could turn around, hands encircled my neck. Fingers wrapped around my throat, followed by something rougher, harsher.

Rope. Tightening, squeezing. I flailed my arms, trying to reach behind me. My throat closed and the night turned blacker. Screams ripped through the air, not my own but from somewhere far off, strange and echoing. . . .

Consciousness exploded into a thousand watery shards. Bitter salt flowed into my mouth, my throat; I bobbed and coughed and thrashed. The salty sting blinded me as a shattered blur of dim light and inky blackness shot terror through me. My ears filled and the brine enveloped me whole. I kicked and struggled, my body weighted, legs tangling, arms grasping at nothing. The world slipped around me as I sank. . . .

I fought back, and a burst of air knifed my lungs. I tried to scream, but only a rusty groan emerged through the sandpaper coating my throat. I went under again, knowing I must make myself heard; knowing I'd die otherwise.

Something solid struck my shoulder. Immediately I twisted and found it with my hands. A piling. I wrapped both arms around it and tipped my head back as far as it would go, until my lips and nose inched above the waterline. The air stung going in, but I sucked greedily, desperately, and clung to a single thought, only one: Stay alive.

Those screams I had heard reached my ears again. Now they formed my name and I recognized Grace's voice. Footsteps shook the pier. Two pairs, one clattering and light, the other heavy, clunking over the boards and making the piling tremble against my ribs. I tried to call out but again my voice emerged like an unused hinge.

A pair of hands thrust beneath my shoulders and tugged, hurting me, threatening to rip my arms from their sockets. I didn't resist but kicked against the water to propel myself upward. The harbor and my soaked skirts warred with our efforts, but those determined hands won out, hauling me up and over the side of the pier. The rough edges of the boards scraped cruelly against my hip bones, thighs, and knees, but again I didn't resist, almost welcomed the pain as a sign I lived, that my end would not come at the bottom of the bay.

My body convulsed, sending me onto my side in a fit of coughing and retching that purged the water from my body. The force of it all but turned me inside out, rent me in two, and seemed to go on forever.

And then I lay on my back with the night sky arcing above me and the water pouring from my clothes to soak the boards beneath me. My lungs heaved and clawed with every breath. My mouth and throat burned. Beyond that, numbness claimed me, and even my brain swam in a sea so devoid of thought even my terror flowed gently away. That was, until Grace sank to her knees beside me and seized my hand. Her cheek fell against my shoulder, and she sobbed and shook and for some reason repeated over and over again how sorry she was. Her own horror filled me, reminding me how close I had come to never gazing up at the stars again.

It was the night watchman who finally lifted Grace from me. His concerned face blocked the sky from my vision, and he asked me if I knew my name.

As good a question as any, I supposed, in the process of reclaiming one's life.

"I'm Emmaline Cross," I rasped out. "Emma."

"Oh, thank God above." Still kneeling on the pier, Grace lifted her hands to her face and cried into her palms. Neily crouched beside her and reached for my hand.

"Emmaline . . . Are you all right? Can you sit up?" His words slurred slightly, and suddenly I remembered the thud I had heard right before the rope—or whatever it had been—tightened around my throat.

I freed my hand from his and pushed against the pier in an effort to sit up. Water poured off me in rivulets. "I believe so. . . ."

Neily gently grasped both my hands. In a moment I was upright. Boats, sky, and water tipped dizzily, then righted themselves. My hand went to my throat as I tried to swallow away the lingering pain. "What happened?"

"As near as I can tell, someone crept out of the hold and knocked me on the head from behind." As he spoke Neily shrugged out of his suit coat and wrapped it around my shoulders. I shivered violently, though not so much from cold as from shock and fright.

"Neily was coming to as the watchman and I came running back down the pier," Grace blurted. "Oh, Emma, I'm so sorry!"

I shook my head, as much to clear it of its remaining fog as to show my puzzlement. "Why do you keep saying that?"

"Because I walked away." Her eyes glittered with tears. "I grew bored while you and Neily examined the *Vigilant.* I was looking at the other boats closer to the clubhouse. If not for that . . ."

"If not for that, you might not have brought the watchman . . . Mr. . . . ?"

"Dawson," the man supplied.

"You wouldn't have brought Mr. Dawson as quickly as you did, Grace. And then I might be—"

"Don't say it." She clenched her fists. "Do not!"

"Let's get Emmaline inside," Neily suggested, and helped me to stand. My legs shook and threatened to give way. Neily held me about the waist while Grace moved to my other side and did likewise. With the two of them supporting me and Mr.

Dawson taking up the rear, we made our way down the pier and into the clubhouse.

"Good heavens!" a man bellowed at our entrance. Other voices chimed in. There were gasps and soft cries from the women. "Did the lady fall in?"

Grace waved away the questions as she pulled out a chair for me at the nearest table. Neily carefully lowered me into it and sat beside me, scraping his chair closer as if to catch me should I begin to fall over. Grace sat at my other side, the two of them like flanking sentinels. Someone—I didn't see who—draped a blanket across my sodden shoulders.

"Did you see what happened?" Neily asked Grace. "Did you see who it was?"

"No." Grace's face went taut. "I heard a strange sound and looked over to see you fall. Someone stood behind you, and he was holding . . . I don't know . . . a pipe or club or something. But it was dark and he had his collar turned up. Then he lunged for Emma and I . . . I just ran to find Mr. . . . ."

"Dawson," the man said again.

"It was horrible," Grace went on, and part of me thought she had no idea just how horrible. "I heard the splash, but I had rounded the corner of the building by then. I didn't know which of you had fallen into the water until we came running back and I—I couldn't see you anywhere, Emma. Then I knew. Oh, how awful. You poor, poor dear—"

"Grace," I interrupted with a rasp, then stopped to swallow and clear my throat again. "Did you see the person leave? Which way he went? How could he have gotten away without passing you on the pier?"

A woman brought a steaming cup of tea and placed it in front of me. I thanked her, but my hands trembled so hard I feared spilling the hot liquid down my front.

"Maybe he dove into the water and swam," Mr. Dawson said.

"Or he leaped from boat to boat." Neily winced, and Grace reached across the table to press a hand to his cheek. "Are you all right? Does your head hurt terribly?"

"Like the dickens," he said, "but that doesn't matter at the moment. Mr. Dawson, please use the telephone to summon the police and the hospital. My cousin needs an ambulance—"

"No, I don't! No ambulance. Please just call the police station and specifically ask for Jesse Whyte. If he's not there, tell them it's imperative he be notified." The watchman nodded and set off into the records office to use the telephone there. I turned back to my cousin. "Neily, what do you mean he could have leaped from boat to boat? Is that how he got to us?"

"It's possible, but I believe he was on the *Vigilant* when we arrived. He must have heard us coming and hid below. After he heard Grace shouting for Mr. Dawson, he tossed you overboard and leaped from deck to deck." He stood up. Through the windows he surveyed the moored vessels. He pointed toward the dock that ran parallel to the seawall. "The boats are close enough to each other that, if he were athletic enough to jump the distance between each one, he might have made his way right to the seawall without needing to use the pier. While getting you out of the water kept us busy, he could have climbed the fence and kept going, with no one inside the clubhouse any the wiser."

"Someone athletic, and with a keen knowledge of boats and this yacht club." In my mind, the clues all led in one direction. "Wyatt Monroe. Oh, he's frightfully clever, isn't he?"

But perhaps not clever enough.

"I wish you'd stop looking at me that way," I said to Jesse some thirty minutes later. Despite my objections, he'd brought me to Newport Hospital to be sure my attacker did no lasting damage. I had swallowed a bit of water, to be sure, but not enough to warrant admitting me for observations. I had gone into the water unconscious, but the shock of hitting the waves had revived me immediately. My swimming instincts, weak though they were, had kept me from submerging for long and the doctor declared my lungs clear.

"I regret ever involving you in this investigation." Jesse showed me his fiercest policeman's scowl, but I refused to cringe.

Sitting on the examining table brought me on a level with his height, and I met his gaze steadily. "I became involved the moment someone dropped off an infant on my doorstep. It would have been ill-advised not to tell me of the carriage driver killed out by Brenton Point. If little Robbie or any member of my household is in danger, I need to know about it."

"Well and good, but I asked you to investigate the mother, not the murderer."

His voice rose in exasperation on that last word, and in the same moment Neily and Grace entered the examining room from the hallway. Grace stepped between Jesse and me like an avenging warrior.

"Inspector Whyte, do you not comprehend what our Miss Cross has been through tonight? You are not to harass her, or I'll have my father speak to your chief."

Jesse colored, and I bit my lip to hide a grin.

"Miss Cross understands me, Miss Wilson," he said after taking a moment to regain his composure. "I only want to see her safe and not running headlong into dangerous situations." His gaze narrowed and shifted to me. "As she is so intent on doing."

"Now see here, Whyte." Neily placed a placating hand on Jesse's shoulder. "A stroll along the pier is nothing out of the ordinary, and we could hardly have guessed someone was lurking in the *Vigilant*'s hold."

"I understand that, Mr. Vanderbilt. But trouble seems to follow our friend here."

"And so do results," I said in my own defense. But I softened my voice and offered him a conciliatory smile. "Jesse, I'm fine. My neck is a bit sore, but it will heal. It's Neily we should be worried about. Did the doctor look at that lump?"

Neily touched the back of his head, and for a nightmarish moment I was transported back to last summer, when my brother had awakened from a knock on the head to learn he was the prime suspect in a murder investigation. And then there was Derrick, also struck on the head during yet another investigation that same summer.

My goodness, Jesse was right, though perhaps not in the way he thought. It was the people around me—those I cared about most—who seemed to encounter the greatest danger as a result of my activities. That was a notion deserving some serious thought.

I promised myself I would do so at the first opportunity.

"The doctor doesn't think I suffered a concussion," Neily was saying. "But he's given me instructions for tonight just in case." He touched his coat pocket, where I assumed he had a written list of the doctor's advice.

"I'm relieved to hear it." Then, to Jesse I said, "Are you going to bring Wyatt Monroe in for questioning?"

Jesse raised his eyebrows. "None of you can identify the attacker. I have no evidence it was Mr. Monroe."

"You can still question him," I persisted, buttoning my damp carriage jacket back up over my equally soggy shirtwaist. Without a word Grace slipped to the other side of the examining table and reached to gather up my hair and twist it into something resembling a bun at my nape.

"True, but only if he's willing to cooperate," Jesse replied.

"He had a motive and he has the expertise to have pulled off his brother's death. Except . . ." I paused as a thought occurred to me—my last memory before the attacker struck. "In the end, it was the storm that swept Virgil overboard. Yet from what I observed on the boat, and what I saw the day of the race, it should have been Wyatt knocked overboard by the boom. And they had switched crew positions at the last minute—did you know that?"

"No, I didn't." Jesse frowned. "How did you discover that?"

Neily replied, "It's in the records book at the club. Emmaline discovered the original entries had been painted over to look like no change had been made."

Jesse flashed me a gleam of admiration, albeit a reluctant one. "As if someone didn't want the change to be a clue for us to find."

"Exactly," I said. "And right before Neily was knocked out and the rope went around my neck, he said it almost seemed as if Wyatt had been the intended victim and Virgil the murderer . . ." I shook my head with a laugh. "Which is ridiculous, of course, since Virgil is the one who died."

"There was the other thing I said, too," Neily reminded me. "That Virgil Monroe's death might merely have been an accident and all the rest nothing but coincidence."

"No." I shook my head again. "There have been too many coincidences, and too many deaths. Jesse, consider the possibility that Virgil might have fathered Robbie and Wyatt found out."

Grace gasped at this, but I went on.

"This might be what the two were arguing about the night of Mrs. Astor's ball. Perhaps Virgil killed the coachman after he delivered Robbie to Gull Manor, to forever prevent him from telling anyone the whereabouts of the child. Then perhaps he planned to kill Wyatt to silence him as well . . . or"—I hopped down from the examining table—"perhaps Wyatt planned to kill Virgil to avenge Robbie's mother, who had been wronged, and Virgil, suspecting as much, changed the crew positions. . . ."

Jesse crossed his arms, yet he didn't mock my theories when I expected him to. "I'll admit circumstantial evidence points in the brother's direction."

"And clears Derrick Andrews of suspicion. He could not

have attacked Neily and me tonight. He's still here, in a room upstairs."

"All possibilities need looking into," was all he conceded.

"Thank goodness," Grace said brightly, an obvious tactic to end the subject. "Now that that's settled, Emma, are you ready to go home?"

"Not quite. I'd like to check on Mr. Andrews first."

My legs still weak, I held the banister tightly as I made my way up to the second floor. Along the corridor, there were two wards that each held six beds. I bypassed these. The door I sought stood ajar and I poked my head inside.

To my disappointment, Judith Kingsley sat at the bedside. She saw me and launched herself out of the chair like a charging bull. Her momentum sent me backward to the middle of the hallway. She stopped a few feet away.

"What on earth happened to you? You look as if you crawled out of the bay."

I had forgotten about my appearance. Though I no longer trailed water with each step, my clothes were still sodden and hung limply around my frame. Despite Grace's efforts to secure my hair into a twist at my nape, I could already feel tendrils slipping loose. "I had a bit of a mishap," I began, but Mrs. Kingsley cut me off.

"My brother is sleeping and cannot be disturbed, Miss Cross. Why did the staff let you up here?"

I regarded her dark green walking suit, her meticulously coiffed hair, and the enmity simmering in her dark eyes. What had I done to incur such animosity, other than hail from the unfashionable side of the island? "I'm here on another matter," I said, "and wished to check on your brother. How is he?"

"He is not well, Miss Cross, as one might expect of someone who went through what he did."

"Has he spoken at all about the race? The accident?"

"Accident?" She pursed her lips. "No. What can one expect

him to say? He has not yet been told he's a suspect. Until his doctor releases him and our attorney can be present, the police must wait."

"Don't worry, Mrs. Kingsley. Plenty of people know Derrick would never do such a thing."

"I suppose that is for the police to determine."

The statement shocked me and I winced. "What do you mean? Your brother is innocent."

"I mean . . ." She moved closer, bearing down on me with an almost threatening air. "My brother had as much reason as anyone to see Virgil Monroe dead."

"You can't believe—"

She shrugged, her head tilting to an imperious angle. "As I said, I believe the police should handle it, Miss Cross. It is none of my business who killed Virgil Monroe. And if my brother is responsible—well, the law is the law, is it not?"

My mouth opened, but no words came out. A buzzing filled my ears and the corridor spun slowly in my vision.

"Judith, what on earth are you doing? Have you left your brother unattended?" Mrs. Andrews appeared on the upper landing, huffing slightly from the effort of the climb. She held her skirts and proceeded down the hallway at a brisk stride.

"Sorry, Mama. I was preventing Miss Cross from disturbing him."

"I was only checking on him," I was quick to say.

"Yes, well." The older woman looked me up and down. "Judith, wait for me inside."

Mrs. Kingsley turned on her heel and swept back into Derrick's room.

"Miss Cross—"

Breathing deeply to regain my equilibrium, I held up a hand. "I had no intentions of interfering. I merely wished to see if Derrick was recovering."

"I understand." Her words were civil, but her expression remained shrouded. "I also understand you've been asking a good deal of questions. Oh, yes, Mrs. Astor mentioned it to me when she visited here this evening. Did you think she wouldn't notice the actions of someone in her home?"

My chin went up. "I have good reasons for asking questions, Mrs. Andrews, none of which I care to explain now."

"Is one of your reasons the desire to see my son exonerated of all suspicion in the matter of Virgil Monroe's death?" Here her voice wavered and her aristocratic beauty slipped to allow a glimpse of a haggard, anxious mother. In that moment, my heart went out to her.

"Yes, Mrs. Andrews. I don't for an instant believe Derrick would cause another person harm." *Unless it was to protect someone he cared about,* a voice inside me whispered.

"Then look to Lawrence Monroe," she said.

"Lawrence?" I had thought she was about to implicate Wyatt. "You mean because his father wouldn't allow him to marry Daphne?"

The woman nodded. Apparently, Lawrence and Daphne's relationship was fairly common knowledge.

"I understand Lawrence would be disappointed, but surely not enough to commit patricide."

"A broken heart is as much a reason to commit murder as greed or revenge or the need to silence a dangerous secret, Miss Cross. But I wasn't referring to the situation with Miss Gordon, although that might be relevant as well. I happen to know Virgil Monroe was planning to divorce his wife."

If she expected to shock me with this information, I disappointed her. "This doesn't come as a surprise to me, Mrs. Andrews. I understand divorce is a scandalous notion in most families, but I still can't picture Lawrence Monroe murdering his father for it."

Her jaw tightened and her delicate nostrils flared. "No? Even when Virgil Monroe planned to leave her with next to nothing—less than she brought into the marriage? Now that he's dead, of course, she keeps her dower's share and her sons will no doubt allow her to continue in the style to which she has become accustomed. Everyone wins. Especially Lawrence, who loves his mother, and who is now head of the family and controls the better part of the fortune."

She didn't wait for a response from me, but turned and entered her son's room, shutting the door behind her. I wanted to call after her, to demand to know how she came by this information. Somehow, though, I didn't doubt the validity of her claims. There were few secrets among their set, and Lavinia Andrews didn't strike me as a woman who would resort to lies.

Or would she, to save her son?

Chapter 10

I received a telephone call from Grace early the next morning.

"Emma, my mother just heard from Lavinia Andrews. Her son is doing much better, and she and her daughter will be spending most of today on their steamer out in the harbor for some much-needed rest." She paused, then continued in a sheepish tone. "I thought you might be interested to know."

"Thank you, Grace." Could she hear my vast relief across the distance? "What about his father? I'd been told Lionel Andrews was on his way to Newport, but I didn't see him at the hospital last night."

"Mama said he's already come and gone." She released a mirthless chuckle. "He stayed long enough to assure himself his son would recover nicely and caught the next train back to Providence."

"How cold." Lavinia Andrews might not be the warmest individual, at least not to me, but no one could accuse her of indifference toward her son.

"Don't linger on the phone with me, Emma," Grace said eagerly. "Go. Despite what my mother said, you never know when Mrs. Andrews or Mrs. Kingsley might return to the hospital. Do not squander your opportunity."

"You're right. Thank you, Grace."

"I'll see you soon?"

"Yes, I'd like that. Very much." As I exited the alcove, I heard Nanny's heavy footfalls descending to the hall, along with Stella's lighter ones. Stella carried Robbie down the stairs, for which I was grateful. I often worried about Nanny overburdening herself.

When they reached the hall Stella placed the baby in Nanny's waiting arms. "I'll go help Katie with the laundry," she said. "Oh, good morning, Miss Cross."

"Good morning, Stella, Nanny." I reached out to touch Robbie's round chin. A little hand came up to grip my finger. "How is our young man this morning?"

"He drank his bottle in record time," Nanny said. "I'm going to walk him in the yard, where I can keep an eye on the girls in the laundry yard." She winked.

I had a sudden qualm. "Nanny, I've been so busy, and that's meant Robbie's care has fallen mainly to you. I'm sorry about that. I was going out today to see Derrick Andrews at the hospital. But now I think I'll stay home—"

"Don't be ridiculous." Nanny all but whisked Robbie out of my reach. "My darling boy and I are getting on just fine. There is no reason for you to worry about me, or to stay home when we both know a certain hospital room is where you wish to be. Now, go get ready."

"You're quite certain . . . ?"

"Emma Cross, do I have to tell you more than once?"

"No, Nanny, you don't. As long as you understand that he isn't *your* darling boy. We can't keep this child, not permanently."

"What if you never find his mother or any other relatives?

Are you telling me you'd drop him off at St. Nicholas's? Really, Emma?"

She moved closer, holding Robbie practically against me, bringing his soft, baby scent to waft beneath my nose. He stared up at me with that wise, wistful gaze of his, one that gently penetrated straight to one's heart. My arms came up and Nanny transferred him to me, so that his legs dangled in their blanket from the crook of my elbow and his cheek, noticeably chubbier than mere days ago, nestled against my bosom.

My heart turned over and my throat tightened.

"Well?" Nanny arced an eyebrow over the rim of her spectacles.

"You're an evil one, you know that, don't you?"

She smiled all-too-sweetly.

"I don't know what I'll do if I can't find where he belongs. I . . ." I raised him up and kissed his forehead. "I just don't know."

Nanny moved to take him back. "There now. You go and get ready, and give Mr. Andrews my best when you see him."

I didn't know what to expect from Derrick. The last time we had seen each other had been at Mrs. Astor's ball, when he couldn't have made it plainer that he no longer had time for me. Since then the Derrick Andrews revealed to me assumed a form I no longer recognized. A man who bullied his sister, and who resented his father's business associate—enough to want revenge?

My feet dragged as I reached the upper landing. The sharp, antiseptic smells worked their way to the pit of my stomach and increased my anxiety. What if his mother and sister had returned? What if he didn't wish to see me? What if he treated me with the same cool indifference as at the ball?

His door was closed. I knocked softly.

"Come in."

The rumble of his voice sent a shivery sensation through me. With a fortifying breath that stung of bleach and lye soap, I turned the knob and stepped inside.

"Emma!" Despite the surprise with which he spoke my name, his voice sounded raspy and breathless, as if he'd been running. The effect, I realized, of his having swallowed so much seawater.

"I'm sorry," I said rather stiffly. Here, face-to-face with him, I felt my resolve drain away, leaving me uncertain and ill at ease. "Am I disturbing you?"

"Of course not. Come in. Sit." He gestured to the chair beside the bed. I pulled it away from the wall and positioned it where he could see me easily without shifting his position.

I settled and dropped my purse in my lap. "How are you?" Even to myself, I sounded unnaturally formal, almost cold. It wasn't how I wished to sound, but I found I couldn't shake the hurt of our previous encounter. My gaze fell on the blanket covering him to mid-chest, the flowers on the table across the room, the treetops visible through the window.

"I'm better. Especially now."

Something in his voice drew my eyes to his, and I saw . . .

I saw what I'd been missing these many months, since long before Mrs. Astor's ball, when he disappeared from Newport without a word. Yet the emotion simmering in his dark eyes only confused me further. Was this some sort of game to him, bestowing and withdrawing his regard, only to bestow it again at his convenience?

A sudden pang reminded me I had treated him in similar fashion. But my uncertainty stemmed from very real misgivings concerning our differing backgrounds, misgivings he claimed not to share. Was he giving me a taste of my own medicine, then?

Had coming here been a mistake?

"And you, Emma? Are you well? It's been a long while—"

"Yes, it has."

"Emma . . ."

I shook my head, gathering my purse into my hands. "I just wanted to be sure you were well. I really must go. . . ."

"Emma, don't leave." He lifted a hand from the mattress. "I'm sorry. I was a cad at the ball. I know that. I wanted to speak with you, but—"

"You don't owe me any explanations, Derrick. I am glad to see that you're recovering. I've worried about you, of course."

The corners of his mouth lifted, though not quite in what one would call a smile. "As you'd worry about any poor soul. You're always looking after people, aren't you? Tell me, have you rescued anyone lately?"

"As a matter of fact, yes. Her name is Stella." For some reason his question had made me defensive. "Do you think it's a game?"

"No, no, I don't. I think it's magnificent. I think you're the most generous person I've ever known." He struggled upright until he was sitting propped against his pillows. He reached out again. "Are you generous enough to forgive me for my unpardonable behavior?"

Whatever hurt and anger I'd harbored simply melted away. I grasped the hand he extended, and suddenly I was sitting on the edge of the mattress, drawn there by a single tug. Derrick's arms went around me. I dropped my cheek to his shoulder. We stayed like that some moments before he pulled back, smiled into my eyes, and brushed his lips across mine.

However sweet that last act, it reminded me where we were: in a public hospital, where any nurse, doctor, or visitor might walk in or pass the open door and see us defying all decorum.

Quickly I scooted back to my chair.

"Don't go," he said, reaching out to stop me.

I swatted his hand away, then stooped to retrieve my purse, which had fallen to the floor. "All we need is for your mother to walk in. She already detests me."

That clearly took him aback. "What went on while I lay here oblivious to the world?"

"Suffice it to say she doesn't approve of your association with me. But surely you already knew that." I glanced over my shoulder, relieved to see an empty corridor. "Derrick, since you asked, there is news to tell you. It's about Virgil Monroe. You do know he—"

"Drowned? Yes, my mother told me."

"Did she tell you the rest, about what Wyatt is saying?"

"What is Wyatt saying?"

Then no one had told him. "Perhaps it isn't my place to enlighten you. . . ."

"Emma, if there is something I should know, simply tell me. My mother has been as evasive as all get out, and Judith says little about anything when she's here. So, please, what is Wyatt saying?"

I drew a deep breath and let it out. "That when you jumped in after Virgil, it wasn't to save him, but to hold him under. He's claiming you murdered his brother for financial reasons."

"Oh." His mouth closed, and he stared back at me a long moment. Then, "I see. And did he explain what those financial reasons are?"

"Yes, he said Virgil had been buying up New York and New England newspapers and was quietly in the process of buying your father out. In addition, he had been cheating investors in his companies, your family included."

Derrick's eyes grew more and more shadowed as I spoke. "And this is my motive for murder?"

"In Wyatt's opinion, yes."

"And yours?"

"No." I leaned forward and, decorum be damned, grasped his hand in both of mine. "Never. You needn't even ask." I nearly blurted the details of the night before. Surely the person who attacked Neily and me on the *Vigilant* was the same person responsible for Virgil's death, and clearly it could not have been Derrick who attacked us.

But I held my tongue. I didn't want Derrick to think that was the only reason I believed in him. Instead, I said, "That's why I've been asking questions, trying to discover what really happened. You're not the only person with a possible motive. It seems everyone aboard the *Vigilant* that day had a reason to resent Virgil Monroe."

"And couldn't it simply have been an accident?"

"Neily thinks so, but I believe there are too many coincidences, including the rigging having been tampered with."

"The rigging?"

"It was frayed."

"That's not possible. The inspections—"

"Yes, I know. The inspections should have revealed any defects in the lines. Has Jesse been to see you yet?"

"No. What does he believe? Does he think I'm guilty?"

"Don't worry about Jesse." My gaze drifted back to the swaying treetops, heavy and dark with summer growth. "He's dedicated to finding the truth and seeing the right person charged for the crime."

"Is he? Then why can't you meet my eye?"

I looked back at him and compressed my lips.

"Oh, Emma, just ask me what happened when I jumped in after Virgil."

I removed my hands from his and clasped them tightly over my purse. "I don't need to ask."

"I think you do."

I swore under my breath. He was right. I hadn't wanted to admit it, but I *was* curious about what occurred in those moments when both he and Virgil went overboard. "Fine. What happened in the water? Did Virgil struggle against you in his panic and disorientation? Did the waves tug him from your grip?"

"Neither," he said levelly. "I never found him. The waves were fierce and the water had all but turned black. I could neither see him, hear him, nor reach out to grab him. There was nothing I could do. I could hear the others shouting my name, but I dove under a few more times—I don't know how many— kicking and reaching but never coming in contact with anything but water. The waves tossed me about and turned me every which way. The next thing I knew, I was on the deck on my back. Then I passed out and woke up here."

He went silent, but his unspoken question shivered in the air between us. I answered it without hesitation. "I believe you."

He released a breath and sank deeper into the pillows behind him.

"Derrick," I said, eagerly moving on from what had obviously been a painful recollection for him, "tell me about Nate Monroe. How was his relationship with his father?"

"Like that of many second sons. Virgil was a demanding father and not the most lenient or tolerant. From what I observed, Nate constantly sought his father's attention and approval but rarely received it. But that's common of most second sons. I don't think it's a reason the boy would want his father dead—if that's what you were thinking."

"I don't know. . . . What about Nate and Lawrence? Do they get along?"

Derrick waggled a hand back and forth. "With several years between them they don't have much in common."

I thought back to the previous afternoon, when Nate and Lawrence had returned from combing the cliffs for any signs of their father. Their expressions had appeared neutral, until Daphne went running to Lawrence. It was then a sneer had darkened Nate's young features.

"Nate doesn't approve of Lawrence and Daphne, does he?"
"Come again?"

"Lawrence and Daphne. They wish to marry, but Virgil wouldn't allow it."

"Is that so?"

"Didn't you know?" I realized the answer for myself. "Of course you didn't. You're too old to be Lawrence's confidant, and Virgil certainly wouldn't have discussed such an intimate family matter openly, especially one he had already dismissed from his own mind. But I can tell you this. Nate doesn't approve of the match any more than his father did. I wonder why?"

"Who knows? He's young, still a boy. Perhaps any sign of affection between men and women annoys him." Derrick yawned and I realized I'd kept him talking too long. But I had one more question.

"Speaking of siblings, why don't you and your sister get on well?"

He stiffened as if a warning bell had sounded. "Who says we don't?"

"She did," I said frankly. "At the ball, she told Virgil if he wished to bully her, he'd have to stand in line behind you. Do you know what she meant? And was there a problem between her and Virgil?"

"I'm sorry, I don't know. Virgil was probably trying to give her some fatherly advice, which he sometimes did. As for me, I admit to looking out for my sister and attempting to oversee her financial affairs since her husband's death two years ago, but there are no ill intentions on my part. If Judith doesn't appreciate my efforts, she'll simply have to put up with them. I'm her older brother." His voice had turned stern, distant. I felt him avoiding—something. But I decided not to push. The chasm that had existed between us seemed in danger of reopening, and I felt desperate to prevent that from happening.

"I should go. You need your rest." I gathered my purse and stood. This time he didn't protest, but nodded faintly. "Have they told you when you might go home?"

"Another day or two." I could see his thoughts were drifting; the fatigue had caught up with him. I started to take my leave when he said, "Where are they staying, my mother and Judith? Are they at Beechwood?"

"No, according to Grace Wilson they're staying on your family's steamer. Why?"

His eyes narrowed. "Now that I'm recovering, I don't trust her not to leave."

"Who?"

He shook his head as if awakening from a daze. "Emma, would you do something for me? Would you deliver a message?"

I readily agreed.

"When you see my sister, would you tell her I said please not to leave Newport until I'm out of the hospital and able to speak with her privately. Will you tell her that, Emma?"

"Certainly. Is there a reason I can convey as well?"

"A . . . family matter. She'll understand." He smiled, suppressing another yawn. "Thank you. And thank you for coming to see me."

There it was, that distance again. Not like it had been, not tipped with ice, but still ringing of dismissal. *A family matter*, he had claimed. Something private he would not share with me because I was not family, or a close enough friend to be trusted. Yet hadn't I avowed my trust in him only minutes ago? Apparently, the sentiment went one way only. I leaned to press my hand to his, wished him well, and left.

Our encounter continued to trouble me as I walked down the street to where I'd left my horse and carriage. Barney, my aging roan hack, stared balefully up at me as I removed the feedbag that kept him contentedly occupied during my visit with Derrick. He nosed my shoulder affectionately, reminding me of little Robbie at home, what a good little fellow he was and how he liked to cuddle and be cuddled.

It was then I realized I hadn't told Derrick about the child, and I wondered why. Last summer I would never have kept such information from him. Had I been too focused on discussing all the possible motives that led to Virgil Monroe's death? Or had our closeness been irreparably severed, never to exist again?

I decided not to wait until I happened to run into Judith Kingsley to deliver Derrick's message. Something was amiss in the Andrews family, and a niggling sensation convinced me it tied in, if not directly to Virgil's death, at least to similar tensions festering among the Monroes.

I hired an old friend, Angus MacPhearson, to row me out into Newport Harbor. Though not much older than Brady, Angus looked twice that at least. Years of transporting passengers back and forth on the windswept waters of Narragansett Bay had weathered his fair complexion and scored twin maps of intersecting lines at the corners of his eyes. Only his red hair, held back with a leather boot lace, still flamed with a youthful brightness.

"Are you getting into trouble again, Emma?" he asked mildly as he cast off and steered away from his boat slip on Long Wharf.

"Trouble, me?"

"Last time I rowed you out into the harbor, you ended up running away from godless brigands on Rose Island in the dead of night. If anything had happened to you, Brady would've wrung my neck."

"You heard about that, did you? Either Brady needs to mind his business, or I need to stop confiding in him."

"Oh, now, Emma, what concerns Brady's little sister concerns him."

"When you see him you can tell him I merely rowed out to visit a friend. I assure you there will be no brigands aboard

Lavinia's Sun." I held the brim of my straw boater to keep it from flying off in the breeze. We passed a tugboat hauling a barge piled high with lumber. New construction and renovations never ceased in Newport, not even for a day.

"So no more half-baked schemes?"

I chose to ignore the question. "*Lavinia's Sun* is coming into view. Can you row a little faster, please?"

"Funny how those hoity-toity men name their boats after their wives. Seems like bad luck to me, considering how most of those marriages turn sour about a month after the honeymoon." He raised and dipped the oars at no greater pace than before I'd made my request. "I suppose it keeps the old crows happy."

"Lavinia Andrews is hardly an old crow," I said, not that it mattered to Angus. He only grinned, his cracked lips parting to reveal a missing tooth.

A few minutes later we reached the side of the three-mast steamer. Angus carefully brought us alongside the ladder and then held my hand as I swung my foot onto the first step. Once I'd gotten a good grip on the railing he let me go, and I continued up to the main deck. A porter met me at the top, and I announced my errand.

I was in luck. Mrs. Andrews was not on board, but Judith Kingsley was presently lunching in the aft saloon. He asked if I was expected. I hinted that I'd promised to call at my earliest possible convenience, and that no, I would not be staying long enough to join Mrs. Kingsley for lunch. I didn't bother to explain that she would never extend me that courtesy.

When I stepped down into the richly paneled saloon Judith didn't immediately look up, perhaps assuming a servant had entered the room. She wore a high-waisted tea gown of peach taffeta with wide lace sleeves and a matching collar, and my gaze was drawn to the pattern. But no, this lace matched the gown's color and bore no resemblance to that found with Robbie, or used on Mrs. Monroe's fan and Daphne's purse.

The porter announced me, and when she glanced up the color fled her cheeks. Her eyes sparked with something approaching outrage, but to her credit, she said, quite calmly with only the barest hint of indignation in her voice, "Thank you, Henderson."

The man bowed and left us, and I walked farther into the room until her voice stopped me.

"What are you doing here?" She came to her feet, her thighs knocking the little folding table in front of her and threatening to send it and its contents crashing to the floor.

"I'm sorry to disturb you, Mrs. Kingsley. I saw your brother this morning—"

"How dare you? Mother forbade it."

"Yes, but Derrick is fully awake now and has a say in who may visit him."

"Perhaps he's too polite to send you packing."

It was my turn to blanch. Derrick had essentially done just that—sent me packing with his sudden bout of indifference. I schooled my expression. I wouldn't let her see how much that had hurt. "Perhaps. But he gave me a message for you."

"I have no interest in hearing it." She sat back down and plucked a dainty, triangular sandwich from her gilt-edged plate.

"I'm afraid you have no choice, unless you cover your ears. But the message is a simple one. Derrick asks that you please do not leave Newport until he is out of the hospital and can speak with you privately. That's the whole of it."

"Is it? It is truly, Miss Cross?" Her sudden vehemence took me aback and I retreated an involuntary step. "I suppose you consider it no great inconvenience, this order my brother sends me."

"I don't believe it was an order, Mrs. Kingsley. He did say please."

"Oh, he did, did he?" She sprang to her feet once more, this time seizing the edge of the table and thrusting it off its legs. Tea and soda water and tiny sandwiches went flying, the table crashed several feet away from her, and Judith Kingsley stood shaking, her skin flaming, her eyes scalpel sharp.

I'd lurched backward another several steps, out of harm's way. Although I didn't want to leave her in this state, having been the cause of it cast doubts on my being at all helpful to her. A bellpull dangled behind her, where I couldn't reach it without risking bodily harm. I held up my hands.

"I'm sorry to have upset you—"

"You can tell my brother this is what I think of his *please* and his cursed request. Tell him I'll leave Newport whenever I wish. And he may very well stay away from me."

"He only seems concerned about you."

"He should be concerned about himself, and with what the police might discover about Virgil Monroe's death."

"Surely you don't think your brother had anything to do with that, Mrs. Kingsley. What reason could he have had to murder a family friend? And don't tell me money was involved. I know about Virgil Monroe's financial double-dealing. Derrick might have been angry, but we both know it would take more—much more—to spur your brother to such a fury." Unlike Judith, I thought, who seemed able to fly into a rage at the slightest provocation.

She clenched her teeth so fiercely the corners of her jaw pulsed. "Accept a bit of advice, Miss Cross. Mind your business and stay out of mine. Or you *will* regret it. Now leave, and do not make the mistake of returning here or ever speaking to me again."

With that she turned her back on me.

Chapter 11

That evening I sat with Robbie beside the kitchen garden and searched the night sky for answers that were not to be found. My visit with Judith had left me shaken. What happened between her and Derrick to cause such animosity? True, he had expressed a brother's concern for her financial affairs and perhaps her personal ones as well, and Lord knew I'd resent Brady's interference in my private matters, but beneath my annoyance I would understand his good intentions.

Such thinking always brought me round to the same conclusion—that I perhaps simply didn't know enough about Derrick Andrews to be forming judgments about his character. He had always seemed to be a good man—the best of men—but the truth was that I'd seen only the surface, what he had allowed me to see.

His sister, on the other hand, had showed me her worst, and had done so unapologetically. She seemed ready to toss her brother to the wolves, as it were, by practically accusing him of Virgil Monroe's death. Yet she'd been less eager to give a rational reason why, which suggested her claim stemmed more from hostility than any real belief in Derrick's guilt.

At the same time, I had learned enough about the Monroe family to begin questioning my own beliefs about who killed Virgil. I had been so certain of Wyatt Monroe's guilt, but now I considered whether one or perhaps both of Virgil's sons might have had a hand in his demise.

The sons . . . and perhaps their mother as well. It made a sinister kind of sense. Virgil had been about to divorce Eudora and leave her next to penniless. The prospect of such a fate would arouse the deepest panic in a society matron used to her luxuries. Unlike me, such a woman would not know how to go out into the world and earn her own living. Now, however, she could depend on Lawrence to see to her comforts.

Then there was Nate, who had vied for his father's approval and rarely received it. Eudora might have appealed to him as well. Perhaps she doted on the boy—I hadn't thought to question Derrick about their relationship. If that were the case, persuading him to do her bidding might not have been a difficult task. Had the brothers worked together under their mother's guidance?

Robbie's little arm came up and he indulged in his favorite game—that of tangling his fingers in my hair. It didn't matter how I wore it, he always managed to get a grip. The tug he gave jolted me, even as my last thought brought me up short. I was all but accusing Eudora Monroe, if not of murdering her husband, then planning his death and setting the events in motion.

Robbie clung with a determination that foiled my attempts to free myself. I lifted him higher on my shoulder to lessen the tension of his tugs. My thoughts drifted to Daphne. Had it truly been her lack of fortune that prompted Virgil to disregard her as a potential daughter-in-law? A chill slithered up my spine and I could hardly bear to follow the train of my thoughts. A notion hovered, a cold, creeping abomination I could not dismiss.

I gazed down at Robbie and sighed. "If only you could tell me who your mother is," I whispered, trying to picture Daphne's features in my mind as I traced those soft baby ones with my gaze. "Is it Daphne Gordon? And was Virgil Monroe your father?"

With another determined yank, a sharp pain seared my scalp. I reached again for Robbie's hand. He tugged and tugged and I yelped and jumped to my feet. His eyes popped wide with surprise, and then alarm. He let out a whimper, and then another.

"Oh, I'm sorry! Please don't cry. Don't cry!" I swayed and bounced in a gentle dance to soothe him. He didn't cry, but instead loosened his grip. I rocked him a few more times and then resumed my seat on the wooden bench. His bottle sat balanced on one of the slats. I raised it to his lips and he latched on.

"You're such a good little boy," I said in a singsong voice. "You hardly ever cry and you're no trouble at all to anyone. Yet the moment I mentioned Daphne's name, you pulled my hair, just as if you were trying to tell me something." I dipped my forehead and pressed it to his. "But were you telling me I'm right? Or that I'm wrong?"

I simply couldn't see Daphne Gordon plotting murder, no matter the circumstances. Yes, I'd been wrong before. I knew women were as capable of murder as men. But Daphne wore her heart on her sleeve; she seemed so guileless.

But what if I was right about Robbie's origins and Eudora had discovered the truth? How could she not, with Daphne living under her roof? Motives for wanting her husband out of her life seemed to be piling up.

"Thank you for staying behind to watch Robbie," I said to Stella on Sunday morning. Nanny stood before the hall mirror pinning her very best hat into place, a flattish, black felt number with an upward curve to the back, blue and green plumes, and a smart satin bow. Katie, in her sky blue frock that matched her eyes, waited outside on the drive with the carriage.

"It's my pleasure, Miss Emma," Stella said. "Besides, the congregation of your church doesn't want me there."

My heart went out to her, and I gave her hand a squeeze. Part of me wished to contradict her, for I knew the congregation of St. Paul's to be a tolerant and forgiving one. But no assurances would convince Stella until she had forgiven herself first.

Until she came to me one day a few weeks ago, she had made her living, shall we say, *entertaining* Newport's wealthy men while their wives directed their ongoing social activities. In wintertime, when the elite abandoned our island, she had turned to a less illustrious clientele, mostly sailors and other brief sojourners. She never shared the details of her experiences with me, except to say that in many instances, her poorer customers were kinder than the rich. The fresh bruises on her arms and beneath her eye the day she arrived at Gull Manor attested to the fact.

Today I saw no sign of that desperate woman, but for the ghosts of regret and shame that continually haunted her eyes. She had piled her ebony curls loosely and allowed tendrils to fall charmingly around her face, and wore one of my cousin Gertrude's castoff morning gowns. I had to admit the rose-striped muslin complemented her coloring to better advantage than it did mine, and she might have been any respectable young woman enjoying a Sunday morning by the sea.

But if Stella were ever to live a normal life, she must leave Newport and make a fresh start where no one would recognize her, and where the judgment of others, whether real or perceived, would cease to trample her spirit.

Nanny declared herself ready to go. In the parlor, Robbie stirred and let go a few soft cries from the cradle Katie had found for him in town the other day. Stella hurried in to him, and Nanny and I, along with Katie, squeezed into the carriage for the trip to town.

Just the sight of St. Paul's white steeple grazing the sky calmed nerves I hadn't realized were jittering inside me. The simplicity of the sanctuary with its soothing, whitewashed walls and unassuming oak woodwork brought me a further sense of peace. I settled into the pew beside Nanny, her shoulder warm against mine, and closed my eyes as the first notes of the organ, soon joined by the choir, rose to fill the room and reverberate inside my heart. I let out a long breath and with it released the tensions and uncertainties that had plagued each day of the preceding week.

Would the new week, dawning here amid music and prayer, bring answers and resolution?

Two young acolytes, dressed in the cassocks Nanny had sewed for the church, stepped out from behind the altar screen to set the candles aflame. The sight of their youthful faces sent my thoughts drifting back to Robbie, and I suddenly wished we had brought him. There were other infants present, along with children who would soon be tramping downstairs for Sunday school. How sweet to be holding his bundled little body in my arms, taking turns with Nanny and Katie, of course, and introducing him to the serenity to be found in our forthright Methodist service. But we could not have brought him without being inundated with a barrage of questions we would be unable to answer.

Still, I wondered . . . had he been christened yet? My instincts told me no. Had either of his parents attended church? This church? If I was at all correct about his origins, Trinity Church would be the more likely choice for wealthy summer residents.

Had Virgil Monroe been a believer? Or any of the Monroes, for that matter? And what of Judith Kingsley. Could that troubled woman find solace, as I did, in hymns and liturgy and simple, straightforward sermons?

During the prayer requests, I found myself raising silent hopes for her, for her brother, for all of the Monroes, and for our sweet Robbie.

Grace and I returned to Beechwood the following afternoon. This time I received no disapproving looks from Mrs. Astor when we were announced. If anything she appeared relieved to see us.

She received us in the morning room, but quickly led us upstairs. She knocked on a door, which was promptly opened by a lady's maid in a sensible black ensemble.

"Yes, ma'am?"

"Is she feeling any better?" Mrs. Astor asked.

"Uh . . . no, ma'am. The same."

"Have you gotten her to stop . . . ?"

The woman in black pursed her lips and shook her head.

"Then take it away from her, you fool."

The maid looked about to retort in kind, but then turned about and went back into the room. Grace and I exchanged puzzled glances, which we cut short when Mrs. Astor turned around to speak to us.

"I don't know what to do," she said in a hissing whisper. "She seemed fine until yesterday. You both saw her the other day. But now—this!"

"What's wrong with her?" Grace craned her neck to see into the room. "Is she ill? Have you telephoned for a doctor?"

"A doctor won't be of use in this instance." Mrs. Astor took on a pained expression. "Grace, I don't mean to upset you with this. But I thought . . ." Her gaze shifted to me. "Miss Cross, I thought you might be able to talk to her. Reason with her."

"Me?" I traded another glance with Grace. "But I hardly know Mrs. Monroe. What about Daphne, or her sons? And what exactly ails her?"

Mrs. Astor looked scandalized. "Daphne? I couldn't very well send a young girl like Daphne in there, could I? The very idea. Besides, Mrs. Monroe has asked for you specifically."

"Me?" I repeated. Not my most eloquent return, but I could think of no reason why Eudora Monroe would wish to see me. "I . . ."

"Please, Miss Cross." It was more a demand than a plea. I once again sought Grace's support.

She took my hand. "We'll see her, if you really think it will help, Mrs. Astor."

The older woman's brows converged. "Oh, not you, Grace. Only Miss Cross." She drew Grace from me and led her back down the corridor. Over her shoulder she said to me, "I'll have coffee sent up presently."

"Coffee?"

Thoroughly puzzled, I entered the room. Mrs. Monroe sat— or slumped, I should say—in a floral chintz overstuffed chair beneath a tall window. Bright sunlight haloed her hair, accenting tufts that had come loose from their pins. Unlike when I'd seen her wearing half mourning the other day, today she wore black bombazine buttoned up to her chin, as if she had only just accepted that she had reason to grieve.

She didn't see me at first. On a low oval table beside her a coffeepot sat, a cup and saucer beside it. Strong-looking black liquid filled the cup, but no steam rose, as if the coffee had been poured some time ago but had not been touched. The maid stood in front of Mrs. Monroe's chair looking down at her with what appeared to be resigned disapproval, her back straight, her hands clasped at her waist. Quiet but strained tones signaled some sort of disagreement.

A lady's maid who dared disagree with her employer?

"I said give it here, Prewitt. You've no right to take it away."

Those were the words I deciphered. However, to my ears they sounded more like, " 'V'no right t' 'ake it 'way."

Mrs. Monroe started to struggle to her feet but fell back into the chair, her head hitting the fortunately upholstered frame.

"Now, ma'am, I'm only doing what's best for you, and on Mrs. Astor's orders. You'll thank me later, I promise you that."

"You impertinent girl!" Again, the words were slurry and half formed. "You've no right!"

Miss Prewitt gave no response. Her back remained as straight as ever, her hands still clasped in a show of patience.

"I'll send you packing. You'll never work again."

"Mrs. Monroe, good morning," I said, pasting on a cheerful smile. "That will be all, Miss Prewitt. I'll take over from here."

"Good luck," she murmured as she crossed to the other side of the room.

Just what I would do, I had yet to figure out. I'd taken care of my brother under such circumstances more times than I could count, but an inebriated man was easy. You removed his shoes, tie, and coat; stretched him out on the nearest flat surface where he would least likely injure himself; and chastised him in the morning over cups of strong coffee.

Well, the coffee Mrs. Astor promised hadn't yet arrived, and the old pot had obviously gone cold. And I couldn't very well chastise a woman I hardly knew.

But I could listen.

"Prewitt, bring Miss Cross a chair!"

The maid hastened to comply, and after mouthing to me, *I'll be nearby,* she slipped out of the room.

I stood behind the chair and leaned, placing my hands on the gold leaf frame. "Mrs. Monroe, I see you're feeling a bit—"

"Where did she put it?"

I didn't have to ask what she meant. "I'm afraid I don't know. I didn't see. But I agree with Miss Prewitt. It's for the best."

She scowled, or tried to. Mostly her lips fell open and one

eye closed, leaving the other glaring vaguely somewhere over my shoulder. I braced for her demand that I find her more alcohol from somewhere in the house.

"Oh, Miss Cross, it's my fault. All of it."

Startled, I circled the chair and sat. "What's your fault, Mrs. Monroe?"

She waved a hand in the air and then let it flop to her lap. "Virgil. He's dead because of me."

I stifled a gasp and struggled to appear calm. "What makes you say that, ma'am?"

She clutched the chair's arms and leaned forward. I leaned, too, until our faces were mere inches apart. The sweet, fiery scent of brandy threatened to make me sneeze, but I wrinkled my nose and stifled that as well.

"I wished it on him," she said, and fell back against her chair like a tossed rag doll.

I blew out a breath. Very gently, as if speaking to Robbie, I said, "Mrs. Monroe, one cannot cause someone's death by wishing."

"Oh, yes, one can." To me it sounded like "Oooh, 'essun can." She tapped her bosom twice. "I did."

"No, Mrs. Monroe. I'm happy to say you are innocent of blame." Was she? I was less than confident of that assertion, and now that I had her talking I intended to take advantage of the fact. Coaxing information out of a tipsy widow might not have been my most honorable act, but when it came to investigating murder, no methods were off-limits. Besides, for some reason she *had* asked to speak to me. "Surely you never truly meant to wish your husband ill."

"Oh, but I did. Trust me. Scoundrel. Thought he was clever, but I knew what he was up to. Knew all along."

"And that was?" I believed I already knew the answer: the divorce and her resulting poverty if he had gotten his way.

"Unfaithful lout. Been cheating—for years. 'Course, they *all* cheat. But this time . . . ah, this time . . ." She lifted her hand, pointing a shaky forefinger in the air. "That's why he was leaving me, for this one. With all the rest, I never worried. I knew he'd come back to me. But *this* one . . ." Her face reddened and she trembled, not in fear or from cold, but pure rage, as Judith Kingsley had trembled yesterday.

I reached over to pat her hand and said some calming words to soothe her. Then I asked, "Who was she?"

Instead of answering, she said, "He'd been meeting with her right here on the island. Thought I didn't know. Why else had he arrived before me? Weeks before. He didn't stay here, oh, no. He stayed . . . I don't know where. Somewhere secluded, I'd wager. Somewhere even his closest friends didn't know about. Carrying on like the junkyard mongrel he is. Was."

"Are you certain he arrived on the island weeks ago?"

"What?" She seemed to have drifted off, and my question startled her awake. "Oh. Where else would he have been?"

So she wasn't certain. She was merely guessing. Still, it sounded like an educated guess to me. "Think, Mrs. Monroe. Who could this woman have been?"

"How should I know? I searched through his things . . . couldn't find anything. Oh, so clever, that one. Always so discreet." She spat that last word like a blasphemy.

I needed to pose my next question carefully. "What about your children? Were they with you while your husband was away?"

"Nate was at school. Where else would a boy of sixteen be? Lawrence . . . where was Lawrence?" She snapped her fingers. "Oh, yes. Europe. With *him.*"

She was losing focus, confusing one period of time with another. "Yes, but after that, when you believed your husband was in Newport."

She dismissed the question with a shrug, and I began to wonder if her present condition was not so much a result of recent events but . . . well . . . habitual. Especially considering how unhappy her marriage had been.

"What about Daphne, then? Was she in New York with you all spring?"

"Daphne . . ." She frowned as though struggling to remember her own ward. "Oh, yes, she is the reason I wished to see you, Miss Cross. She needs a friend, someone her own age. . . ."

"Yes, I'd be happy to be Daphne's friend, Mrs. Monroe. But returning to the events of last spring. Was Daphne in New York with you the entire time prior to your trip to Newport?"

"No, she left to visit other relatives." Her features became pinched and she slumped deeper into her chair. "Virgil insisted she go, but I didn't approve. They all fought over her when her parents died. Wasn't about the child, though. No, indeed. It was about her father's money—all that lumber money—and who got to control it. Greedy vipers. That's why the court gave her to us. . . ."

Her slurring words continued, but my mind had seized on one thought: Daphne had gone away last spring, and Lawrence had traveled to Europe. A new scenario formed in my mind, and I marveled that I hadn't considered it before. Perhaps Virgil hadn't violated his ward. Perhaps Daphne and Lawrence had succumbed to the temptation to which so many of their age secretly fell prey, especially when forces were at work to keep them apart. Oh, it happened more often than anyone would admit, and families "took care" of the matter just as discreetly as it occurred.

Daphne had been miserable at the ball, and bitterly resentful of the control the Monroes held over her life. She indicated they were eager to marry her off—thus forever preventing a liaison between her and Lawrence. Could it be their child even now cuddled in Nanny's protective embrace at Gull Manor?

I had one more question for Mrs. Monroe. "When did Daphne arrive in Newport?"

Her gaze narrowed and she wriggled to a more upright position. "You're asking an awful lot of questions, Miss Cross."

"Am I? I'm sorry. I thought it might help to talk and, well, I suppose it's in my nature to be curious." I gave a weak chuckle, at the same time lamenting my poor luck that Mrs. Monroe would choose that moment, when I was so close to finding out pertinent information about Daphne, to become lucid enough to recognize my snooping for what it was.

"You're a reporter, aren't you?" She said *reporter* as she might scullery maid or laundress.

A knock at the door forestalled my reply. Miss Prewitt entered with the promised coffee, with a covered platter beside it. Only one cup and saucer occupied the tray. Since I doubted I'd glean any further details from Eudora Monroe, I stood.

"I'll leave you now, ma'am. I hope you'll soon be feeling better. If there is anything I can do for you or your family, please call on me at Gull Manor. It's on Ocean Avenue."

The woman waved away my offer as though fanning at an unwelcomely hot breeze. I didn't mind; I couldn't leave the room fast enough. I wanted to find Daphne before my courage failed me. Whether Robbie's father was Virgil or Lawrence, I was almost certain now that Daphne was his mother.

After the bright bedroom, the dimness of the corridor half blinded me and I nearly walked face-first into a wall.

A wall of a chest, that is.

I pulled back just before the moment of impact and looked up—and up—to discover the owner of the beige linen suit coat and checked waistcoat with which I'd nearly collided.

"Here again, Miss Cross?" Wyatt Monroe gazed down the length of his nose at me, his steely-eyed scrutiny raising the hairs at my nape.

I schooled my features to as neutral an expression as I could muster. "I was just visiting with Mrs. Monroe." Should I mention her compromised condition, suggest she might need her brother-in-law's support? Nothing in his cold eyes encouraged me to do so. I backed up another step. "If you'll excuse me. I'm hoping to visit with Daphne before I leave."

He made a sound somewhere between a *hmm* and a *humph*. My gaze fell to his hands, curled lightly into fists at his sides. Even in the wide corridor, he seemed too big, too powerful for my comfort. I could easily imagine those hands wrapped around a ship's rigging. . . .

And the rigging wrapped around my neck. Goose bumps showered my shoulders. I darted around him too quickly to appear casual. "Good day, sir."

"Miss Cross," he called before I'd gone far.

I turned.

"Incessant questions very quickly become tiresome. And you have been asking incessant questions, haven't you?" He turned his back to me and continued down the corridor in the opposite direction.

The words *what do you mean by that* leaped to my tongue but went no farther. I hadn't asked Wyatt Monroe any questions since seeing him at the police station the day of the murder. Someone must have told him I'd been making inquiries.

Who? And why?

Saving that for later, I hurried down to the drawing room hoping to find Daphne there, or to come upon Mrs. Astor, who could direct me to the girl's whereabouts. I ran into Nate Monroe instead.

"Back again, Miss Cross?" Nate's question echoed the one his uncle had just asked me, and with as accusatory a tone. The boy sat with a book near the empty fireplace, away from the sunlit windows. I walked closer, trying to make out his features. Why would someone sit in the shadows if one wanted to read? Was he hiding there in the drawing room?

"I'm looking for Miss Gordon, actually. Have you seen her?"

His gaze remained on his book. "I believe she's with your Miss Wilson. Outside." He jerked his chin toward the windows that overlooked the rear lawns.

I should have left then to go find them, yet something in Nate's bearing raised my curiosity. I moved closer still, stopping at the end of the sofa that faced Nate's chair. "You don't like her much, do you?"

"Is it obvious?" he asked, without looking up from his book. He shrugged. "The truth is, I find her behavior appalling."

A sixteen-year-old disapproving of another young person's behavior? I studied him, trying to read the lines of unease around his eyes and mouth. On the surface he was a slighter, more youthful version of his brother, Lawrence, yet with a significant difference. Though Lawrence exhibited few outward signs of aggression or assertiveness, he held himself with the quiet confidence of an elder son, with that innate sense of knowing one's place in the world and being comfortable with it. Nate, on the other hand, exuded a tension that suggested he was unsure of the space he occupied, as if he hadn't yet discovered where he fit while at the same time trying his utmost not to show his uncertainties.

"What has Daphne done to earn your disfavor?"

His book landed on the table beside him with a startling thwack. Nate came to his feet. "She has dishonored my father's memory. She and my brother, Miss Cross. They're secretly engaged—did you know that?"

I shook my head, too disconcerted to speak.

"My father isn't even in his grave yet. He might never lie in a grave because his body may never be found. Yet Daphne and my brother couldn't wait to defy his wishes in this disgustingly blatant way."

"That's a harsh assessment. If they care about each other—"

"I couldn't give a dog's bone what they care about, Miss Cross. It isn't right. My father had his reasons for refusing to let them marry."

"Such as?"

Would he have answered? A footman entered the room, first apologizing to Nate for the interruption and then addressing me. "Miss Cross, I have an urgent message for you from The Breakers. . . ."

Chapter 12

My anxiety must have shown on my face, for the moment Grace saw me she offered to leave Beechwood with me. She quietly withdrew the suggestion when I told her where I was going. One of Uncle Cornelius's own carriages awaited me on Beechwood's drive to whisk me the few streets over to The Breakers on Ochre Point. Aunt Alice herself ran out to the drive and opened the carriage door when I arrived.

"Hurry. Cornelius isn't home at the moment, but we mightn't have much time."

Once the footman helped me down she took my hand and hurried me inside. Together we scurried across the Great Hall with its ceiling that soared three stories high to painted clouds above our heads as if on a perpetual summer's day. I detected nothing sunny about Aunt Alice's disposition today. She brought me into the music room, which I knew to be her favorite in the house.

I understood why the beautiful room brought her both pride and pleasure. Gilded pilasters traveled up soft gray walls to a dramatically coffered ceiling dominated by a tremendous oval medallion and two enormous crystal chandeliers. Softening the effect of all that gilt and carving were rich wooden floors, intimate groupings of crimson velvet furnishings, and sweeping golden draperies. Red roses burst in a tumble of color from the marble fireplace at one side of the room, while the grand piano stood framed by a rotunda of arched windows.

I didn't understand, however, why she had chosen this room in particular, until she spoke next. "If Cornelius happens to come home, we'll simply say I asked your opinion about setting up for next week's concert and dance. He knows I value your eye for detail."

"Aunt Alice, what is this all about? Is Uncle Cornelius ill?"

"No, nothing like that. Sit down." She gestured to the chairs and sofa that graced an Oriental rug before the fireplace.

I sat, but Aunt Alice remained standing, her arms folded across her bosom. "I lunched with some of the ladies while Gertrude played tennis at the Casino today. Mamie Fish was among them, and she told me . . ." She brought her stout, sturdy frame up taller, which admittedly wasn't very tall. "She told me Neily and that Wilson woman have been carrying on in the most disgraceful way for months in Europe and now here, under our very noses."

"Mamie Fish said they're carrying on disgracefully?"

"Not in so many words, not exactly that. In fact, she didn't realize she was telling me anything I didn't already know." She began to pace, her afternoon gown swishing over the diamond-patterned parquet floor. "She was merely commenting on what a lovely couple she thought they made. Lovely—bah!"

"Aunt Alice—"

"I won't have it, Emmaline. I won't! And I won't have you helping them."

Oh, dear. I felt myself shrinking into the cushions behind me and made an effort to sit up straighter. "I haven't been helping them," I lied, and rather smoothly I must say. "I am Neily's friend as well as his cousin. I've merely lent him a sympathetic ear when he needed it." I decided not to mention my growing friendship with Grace.

"Well, don't!" Her barked command made me jump.

"Aunt Alice, be reasonable. Neily and Grace have a lot in common, and they truly care for one another."

"Don't be ridiculous. Neily has things in common with every debutant among the Four Hundred. He can just as easily bestow his affections on one of them. But this Wilson woman . . . that Wilson *family*." She had paced until her back was to me, and now she whirled about, her hands clenched at her sides and her figure a dark silhouette against the brightness of the windows behind her. "Do you know that during the Civil War her father ran blankets past the stockades to supply them to the Rebel armies?"

"I suppose even the Rebels had a right to keep warm," I murmured. Thankfully, she didn't hear or I'd surely have been admonished for my impertinence.

"That was the beginning of his fortune, and the rest came from speculating once the war was done. He puts on airs of being a New York banker, but those Wilsons are a common sort, lower than low."

I refrained from pointing out that the first Cornelius, the Commodore, came from a modest Staten Island family and had built his fortune by ferrying dry goods along the Hudson and East rivers in New York. Hardly illustrious beginnings.

Aunt Alice wasn't finished. "He's been lying to us, Emmaline. Keeping us in the dark while he dallied with that woman, only to return to New York a few months ago with talk of marrying her. He upset his father terribly."

"I'm sorry to hear that, Aunt Alice." This was no lie. It grieved me to see such discord in the family.

"I need your help, Emmaline."

"But what can I do?"

"You can talk sense into Neily. Help convince him of the very real consequences he'll face if he marries that Wilson woman—"

"Mother!"

Aunt Alice and I both jumped. Neily stood in the doorway, shaking with anger.

For a moment Aunt Alice wavered. She emitted a little "oh" at the sight of her son and seemed tongue-tied and uncertain what to do next.

Neily strode toward her, stopping a yard or so away. "I won't have you speaking of Grace that way. She is Miss Wilson, or Grace to those who feel any affection for her. Otherwise you are not to speak of her at all."

"Oh," Aunt Alice repeated, this time with the full force of her indignation. "How dare you speak to me that way?"

Neily plowed a hand through his hair. "Mother, I have tried being civil. I've tried waiting, hoping you and Father would eventually see reason. It's clear to me now that will never happen." He glanced over at me, where I sat half cowering behind the satin pillow I held like a shield in my lap. "I'm sorry you have to hear this, Emmaline. Sorry Mother saw fit to put you in the middle of a family feud."

While I struggled for something appropriate to say, he turned back to Aunt Alice. "But know this. Grace and I plan to marry before the summer is out. With or without Father's and your blessing. We certainly aren't going to wait for your permission."

"Good God."

All three of us turned as if yanked by puppet strings toward the figure in the doorway.

Aunt Alice gasped. "Cornelius!"

He shook a fist in the air. "You *will not* marry her! I will not allow it, Neily!"

"You have no choice, Father."

"Don't I? We'll see who has choices when you are cut off." He pressed a fist to his breastbone. "And we'll see if that woman will still have you when you're penniless."

"I'll never be penniless, Father. I have an education. I'm perfectly willing to earn my way in the world."

"Is that so? Then we'll see who will be willing to cross me by hiring you."

In a burst of motion Neily bore down on his father. I sprang up from the sofa, alarmed, not knowing what to expect or how I might intervene. The tension between the two men stretched to breaking.

"This is not about Grace," Neily said in a dangerous murmur. "This is about control. About you finally understanding that you can no longer command me as you'd like."

"Be careful what you say to me, Neily." Cornelius's voice rose in warning.

His son took no heed. "This not only enrages you, Father, I believe it terrifies you. The great Cornelius Vanderbilt finally coming up against someone who has decided to push back, who cannot be persuaded or bullied or bought. How's that, Father, something all your millions cannot buy—my obedience. My life. *Me.* Oh, how that must truly stick in your craw."

"Neily!" Aunt Alice swept to his side and attempted to grasp his arm. He pulled away, half turning, and I saw his profile, taut like a bull goaded to charging. His arm came up—I thought only to hold it out of his mother's reach—but she flinched and drew back as if he'd been about to strike her. Cornelius lunged.

"Uncle Cornelius, no!" I screamed, or perhaps I merely whispered, for no one seemed to hear. With both hands Cornelius shoved at Neily's chest, sending him stumbling backward with a clack of his teeth as his head snapped forward. Neily caught his balance and then his whole body coiled. For a terrible moment I thought he'd rush headlong into the attack.

But he only stood there, glaring at his father, his breath heaving in and out. Aunt Alice's features contorted with horror and helplessness. She held herself utterly still, as though afraid if she budged, she'd unleash some terrible reaction.

Uncle Cornelius was the first to move. He stepped toward Neily, paused, then took another step that wobbled. In the next seconds I realized how old he suddenly appeared, how the pouches of fatigue beneath his eyes robbed them of their hawk-like clarity, how his skin had lost its luster and stretched thinly across his cheeks and nose, making him seem frail, infirm.

All that passed through my mind in the time it took Uncle Cornelius to take a third step, for his knees to buckle, for him to topple over backward, and for the leader of the railroad industry—one of the richest and most powerful men in America—to collapse in a heap on the floor.

"Cornelius!" Aunt Alice fell to her knees beside him. She seized his hand, held it to her lips. She slapped his cheek lightly, pressed her ear to his chest. "I can't hear his heart. Oh, good Lord, I can't hear his heartbeat!"

I hurried over and sank to the floor at his other side. "Unbutton his coat." As I gave the order I held my fingers in front of his nose and detected a faint stirring of breath. "He's breathing." Once Aunt Alice fumbled his coat and waistcoat open I pressed my ear to his shirtfront. What I perceived alarmed me so much I sat immediately upright. "Mason!" I cried out. As I did, a sobbing Aunt Alice let her head fall to her husband's shoulder.

My voice echoed across the house, reverberating in the vacuous space of the Great Hall. Seconds later, the butler who had been fired a year ago, but who in the interim had been persuaded by Uncle Cornelius to resume his post, ran into the room with two footmen in his wake. "Good heavens!" he said as he lurched to a halt and balanced on the balls of his feet.

"Call the hospital," I ordered. "Tell them we're coming, and have a carriage readied. We'll use the brougham, so we can lay him across the seat." I looked down at my uncle. His face had drained of color. His mouth was open and slack, his eyes closed, his breathing frighteningly shallow. "We need something to carry him on. A thick blanket, perhaps, anything that can be used as a stretcher." When no one moved, I came up onto my knees and reared my head. "Go!"

I retrieved a pillow from the sofa and placed it beneath Uncle Cornelius's head. Aunt Alice's weeping filled the room. Neily stood off to one side, looking dazed and nearly as pale as his father. Now, without a sound, he came closer and knelt beside his mother. Gently he reached out to place his hand over hers.

"Mother, I'm sorry."

She snapped upright, her face tearstained and her eyes blazing. "Get out!"

"Mother?"

"Get out. Go." She shoved at him as her husband had done. "Leave this house and never come back."

"Aunt Alice," I cried out, "you don't mean that."

"Indeed, I do! If you don't leave this instant, Neily, so help me I'll send for the police." She reached for my arm and struggled to her feet. "I'll—"

I moved between them, facing Aunt Alice and essentially blocking Neily from her view. "There's no need for that." I glanced over my shoulder. "Neily, you'd better go. Please. There'll be time later to sort this out."

"But . . ." He rose but hovered, his uncertainty written in the pain of his expression.

"For now, Neily," I said firmly. From the Great Hall came voices and the bustle of the butler and footmen returning. "I'll keep you informed, I promise."

He hesitated for a moment more, then with his head down walked from the room. My heart broke for him.

Some two hours passed while I waited with the family at Newport Hospital. A Mr. Bryant, the hospital's chief administrator, had met us at the street door and led us to a downstairs room used for meetings.

A rectangular table dominated the center of the space, while a well-worn, camel-colored sofa and four serviceable wooden chairs stood crowded together at the end farthest from the door. What the room lacked in comfort it made up for in privacy, being out of the way of the main lobby and common waiting room.

Our arrival had stirred up a frenzy of activity as doctors and nurses scrambled to prepare everything needed to examine and care for Cornelius Vanderbilt. Though muted by the walls, their voices remained a constant presence none of us could ignore. Orders, directions, questions, and occasionally the urgent ring of the main telephone disturbed our own somber vigil as we waited for what felt like an eternity. It was as if we had mobilized an army and in a way we had. I entertained no doubts that these people would fight to save my uncle's life.

Aunt Alice sat in the middle of the sofa, flanked on either side by Gertrude and her young sister, Gladys. In their bright summer frocks the three of them looked hopelessly, almost comically, out of place in the utilitarian room. Reggie, seventeen and all arms and legs now, sprawled in one of the stiff-looking chairs beside Alfred, his studious, eighteen-year-old brother. Uncle Cornelius's two brothers, William and Frederick, sat at the table leaning close together and speaking in hushed tones.

I spared a moment to study my youngest male cousin. Haggard shadows dragged at Reggie's eyes, suggesting a sleepless night, but I suspected another culprit. Puffy cheeks and the bloated skin across his nose spoke of the bourbon for which Reggie had developed a taste at far too young an age. Did his family not see what was so obvious to me? Did they choose not to see?

I looked away. There were problems enough to face. Reggie's, serious though they were, would have to wait.

I spent most of my time pacing and staring out into the hall-way for any signs of approaching doctors, only to report back to my aunt each time with disappointing news.

"What can be taking so long?" She held both Gladys's and Gertrude's hands in her lap. Gladys laid her cheek against her mother's shoulder and stared silently up at me with large, solemn eyes. "Why won't they let me see him?" Aunt Alice lamented. "It's a bad sign, isn't it?"

"No, Aunt Alice." I clasped my hands at my waist in an attempt to appear calm. "I'm sure it's merely a sign that they're taking the very best care of him."

"Perhaps we should have conveyed him onto the steamer and brought him back to New York. He might need a specialist." Her chin quivered. "Who knows where the doctors here received their education?"

Footsteps halted any further debate. The doctor who had spoken to Aunt Alice upon our arrival entered the room. Uncles William and Frederick, and Cornelius's two sons, all came to their feet at once. Aunt Alice and the girls sat nervously waiting, their backs rigid and their chins raised in expectation. Tears filled Aunt Alice's eyes but didn't fall.

The doctor silently walked the length of the room, making little eye contact until he stood in front of her. "Mrs. Vanderbilt," he said in a kindly voice, and she visibly shuddered. The room suddenly seemed smaller to me, as if the walls had closed in; the voices and commotion of the staff became a dull echo in my ears. "Your husband has suffered what we call a stroke of apoplexy. It's when—"

"I know what it is," she replied. She released Gertrude's hand to dash away the single tear that spilled over. I couldn't remember the last time, if ever, I had seen Alice Vanderbilt so vulnerable, and the sight of her faltering courage seemed akin to the earth trembling beneath my feet. "Will he live?" she whispered.

"Yes, we believe he will, so long as he doesn't suffer another attack." The man spoke softly, as though he feared disturbing a sleeping patient, though there was none housed nearby. "But he'll have challenges ahead. We don't yet know the extent of the paralysis, but there is almost sure to be some."

"Oh, my Cornelius!" Aunt Alice dabbed at another tear. Her daughters pulled closer in a show of support. Gladys sniffled and tears pooled in her eyes. Gertrude had clamped her bottom lip between her teeth, something she did, I knew from experience, when she struggled to keep her emotions under control.

"Will the paralysis be lasting, Doctor?" Uncle William asked.

"We can't yet tell. He may need a variety of therapies. Thermal waters are often helpful. He'll certainly need a long convalescence with as much rest and as little disturbance as possible. That means he must not return to work any time soon."

"He won't, Doctor. I'll see to that." The stubborn determination returned to Aunt Alice's voice. "I'll see to it that nothing and no *one* disturbs him."

My stomach sank; I knew to whom she referred. Neily wasn't here. I didn't know where he was presently, and I could only guess at the despair and guilt he must be feeling.

With a silent signal to Gladys and Gertrude to help her up, Aunt Alice stood. "May I see him now?"

The doctor hesitated before nodding. "He's sedated and sleeping, but I don't see the harm in it. No more than two at a time, mind you. Come, I'll show you to his room."

The family filed to the stairway, the doctors and nurses parting for them like whitecaps around a yacht. I followed them only as far as the upper landing. As fond of Uncle Cornelius as I was, I didn't feel it was my right to intrude on their time with him—not just now. Instead, I headed in the opposite direction.

I wanted to check in on Derrick, tell him what happened, and let him know I had talked to his sister aboard *Lavinia's*

Sun. As reticent as he had been concerning Judith and his troubling relationship with her, I wondered how he would react to the news of her bizarre behavior toward me. Would he feel moved to confide in me?

His door was closed, so I knocked, softly at first and then, receiving no answer, I gave a few sharper raps with my knuckles. Still nothing. Was he sleeping? Or had he been released? I felt a stab of sadness at the thought of his having returned home without letting me know. I turned the knob and pushed the door inward.

An empty bed greeted me, the covers tossed into a bundle against the footboard. Puzzled, I opened the door wider and stepped inside.

The smell hit me first, a stench that filled my nose and triggered a primal, unspeakable horror. My stomach heaved at the sight confronting me. Blood smeared the back wall, and beneath it sprawled a body—a man in a summer suit, its ivory weave dripping scarlet. A scream tore from my throat.

I must have passed out, because the next thing I knew I was half-crouched, half-slumped against the wall beside the door. A woman stood over me, her hand on my shoulder. I didn't immediately recognize my surroundings. Bright sunlight streamed through a window opposite me, but my vision and my thoughts remained a blur.

I narrowed my eyes to bring the woman into focus. Her face was smooth, youthful, her cheeks pink and pleasantly rounded. Her hair was pulled back beneath a white kerchief, and she wore a simple pale blue dress covered by a starched white apron. Her expression registered concern . . . no, anxiety . . . and fear. Why?

"Miss, are you all right? Miss . . . Oh, my goodness—Emma?"

"I . . . Who are you?" Recognition struck. "Hannah Hanson?"

"Yes, Emma, it's me. It's been a long while. No, don't try to stand, not just yet," she added when I attempted to pull my feet beneath me. "I found you like this and . . ." She cast a furtive glance over her shoulder, and I saw that we weren't alone. A small commotion occupied the space near the back wall, several men in shirtsleeves I took to be doctors.

And the blood, smeared and dripping down the wall behind them.

My limbs went cold and a wave of dizziness sent the room spinning. I groaned, but at the same time I fought Hannah's restraining hands and pushed to my feet.

"Derrick." The name was little more than a gurgle in my throat. "Oh, Derrick . . ."

Tears scalded my eyes and throat. My chest ached as if encircled by a tightening iron band, and my legs felt as if liquid had replaced the bones. Hannah thrust an arm about my waist and I leaned heavily into her side. But I reached out, my hand open, fingers stretched and shaking . . . tears streaming. The men standing over the . . . the body . . . didn't turn around, didn't acknowledge me in any way. They moved in their orderly fashion, murmuring in their calm manner. Damn them. How could they be so blasted calm? "Derrick. No. Oh, please no . . ."

"Emma, if you mean Derrick Andrews, the patient who occupied this room, that is not him." Hannah spoke slowly and clearly. "He was discharged and left the hospital earlier today."

Still I fought her, trying to conjure the strength in my watery limbs to pull away. Her words fell like gibberish against my ears until she tugged me none-too-gently around to face her, framed my cheeks in a pair of firm hands, and repeated what she had said.

"That is not Mr. Andrews. I don't know who it is, no one has told me, but . . . Come. The police are on their way, and we can wait for them somewhere else."

"Not—not Derrick?"

She shook her head adamantly. "No."

I fell against her ample side, and I could only credit her nursing skills and her experience dealing with light-headed patients for my not falling to the floor on my face. She aimed us toward the door, but before we reached it a man in a dark blue uniform rushed in. I recognized Scotty Binsford, who had attended school with my brother years ago. He stared first at the body on the floor, then blinked at me. "Emma, what are you doing here?"

I answered his question with another. "Who is he?"

"I don't know, I've only just arrived." He moved past us to the group congregating around the body. There he placed his hands on the shoulders of two of the doctors, parting them as he would reeds at the beach. He bent at the waist, drew in a deep breath, then straightened and returned to me. "Emma, it's Wyatt Monroe."

My eyes went wide, and my gasp stopped the doctors in their tracks. I ventured toward them. Hannah tried to catch my arm, but I sidestepped her and kept going, at the same time declaring, "I have to see."

I stopped short a few feet away, appalled and nauseated by what I saw. Wyatt Monroe lay on his back, staring blankly up at the ceiling, a several-inch gash nearly dividing his throat in two. Judging by the amount of blood beneath and all around him, there couldn't have been a drop left in his body.

"Oh, dear God . . ."

Scotty gripped my elbow; Hannah slipped her trustworthy arm once more around my waist and pressed me to her side. "Come, Emma. You've seen enough for now. Let me take you away from here."

I let her guide me, but stopped yet again when we reached the doorway. "Scotty, how did you get here so quickly?"

"I was already here. The station sent me over when we learned Mr. Vanderbilt had been brought in. Just a precaution, seeing as who he is." He glanced over his shoulder at the victim, shook his head, and made a sound beneath his breath—probably an oath, and who could blame him? "I guess I'll call the station now and send for more men and the coroner."

Hannah brought me up to the third floor, where a small dormitory had been improvised for the nurses to catch a few hours' sleep in between their shifts. A cramped kitchen area provided a few cupboards and a stove. Hannah made tea, and she and I sat at a round table beneath the slanted eaves and narrow dormer windows.

"I'm sorry we had to meet again under these circumstances, Emma. But it *is* good to see you."

I blew at the steam rising from my cup. "How long has it been since you went off island?"

"Four years. We were just girls when I left. I went to live with my aunt in Providence and studied nursing at Roger Williams Hospital."

"Do you like it? Nursing?"

She smiled. Hannah had always been a pretty girl, with golden brown hair and blue eyes, and a smile that always made one feel she meant it. "Very much," she said. "But I missed Newport. When I heard of an opening here, I jumped at it. I've only just come back. It's been about two weeks, I think."

"Your parents must be very happy." The Hansons lived on Chestnut Street, not far from my house on the Point, and her grandparents had owned a butcher shop in town until they retired to a cottage near Sachuest Beach in Middletown. "Nanny will be pleased to hear you're back. She and your grandmother still keep up."

"Do they? I'm glad."

We sipped our tea, falling into a thick silence. There was so much to catch up on, so much to say after four years. We had been friends as girls—real friends, with shared secrets and favorite games and special rhymes we made up about the places and people we knew. How long ago it seemed. How lovely and carefree. But how does one happily reminisce when a man lay but a floor below in a pool of his own blood?

Yet I couldn't turn my thoughts to Wyatt Monroe's death either. The shock had been too great, and the implications too weighty to contemplate. I had seen him but a few hours ago at Beechwood. He had been my main suspect, both in his brother's death and my near drowning at the Yacht Club. The question nagged at the edge of my mind: What did his murder mean?

"I heard about Adelaide," Hannah said.

My gaze snapped to her face. "What? Oh . . . yes." Adelaide, who had also played with us as children, but hadn't always wanted to include Hannah, especially when an invitation came to play with my cousins at The Breakers. Oh, at those times Adelaide wanted me all to herself. Little had she known Hannah had accompanied me on those summer afternoons far more frequently than Adelaide.

"Such a shock, and so very sad at the same time." Hannah tilted her head and set down her teacup. She reached across the table to cover my hand with her own. "Emma, are you all right? Shall we have one of the doctors take a look at you?"

I smiled, a weak effort, and shook my head. "No, I'm all right. I just want answers. I want to talk with Jesse—you remember Jesse Whyte, don't you?"

"Indeed, I do."

"Emma." As if I'd summoned him with my thoughts, Jesse stood in the doorway. The look on his face made me shrink against my chair and drop my gaze. It wasn't hard to guess his sentiments. *Another murder, and here's Emma in the thick of it, as always.*

"Jesse, I was only in that room to see how Derrick Andrews was doing," I found myself explaining. I got no farther.

"Yes, I'd like to talk to you about that," he said. "Come with me, please."

I frowned, finding his blunt request rude and wondering

why he simply didn't sit down with us at the table. Hadn't he recognized Hannah? But then I remembered we sat in the nurses' dormitory, where men were never allowed, not under any circumstances.

I excused myself to Hannah and promised we would catch up soon.

My feet dragged as Jesse led me back to Derrick's hospital room. "Must I . . . ?"

"We needn't go in. Besides, the body has been removed." He stopped outside the door. "Tell me exactly what happened, exactly what you saw."

I went over it, trying to remember every detail as it had happened. There wasn't much to tell. "I learned from Hannah that Derrick was released earlier in the day."

"About an hour earlier, I'm told. Have you heard from him?"

"No, why?"

He didn't answer and I didn't like the look on his face.

"Jesse, what are you thinking? Surely not that Derrick—"

"The coroner estimated the time of death to be within one to two hours before he examined the body. Derrick Andrews was the last person in the room."

"That's ridiculous! What about the nurses and doctors? Hadn't someone come to clean the room and change the linens?"

Jesse gave a grim shake of his head, took me by the hand, and led me downstairs. He brought me into the lobby, now empty, where we took seats close together in the corner. "As you could see when you entered the room, the bedclothes had been left at the foot of the bed, as if someone had hastily vacated. Derrick's things were gone, but with the distraction of your uncle being here, no one remembers exactly what time he left the premises, or if he left alone or accompanied."

"And that means what?" When he again didn't answer, I held out my hands. "Anyone could have followed Wyatt Monroe here and into that room."

"Then where is your friend?" His question held a note of accusation, so much so I almost blurted that Derrick was not my friend.

In truth, I didn't know anymore whether he was or wasn't.

"He could be anywhere," I said. "At home."

"He isn't. We checked."

"On his family's steamer, then."

"We checked there, too. No."

"To whom did your men speak, his sister?" My tone dripped sarcasm.

"I believe they spoke to the steward. Would he lie?"

I ignored the question. "Then tell me, Jesse, what is your theory?"

He sat back in his chair. "This isn't a theory, mind you, but a possibility. We both know Wyatt Monroe implicated Derrick in Virgil's death. Now that Derrick has recovered and was allowed visitors, Wyatt might have come to confront him with some sort of proof, and was murdered for his efforts. As I said, not a theory, but a possibility that needs to be investigated."

I leaned forward, crowding him where he sat. "Impossible."

"How so?"

"If Derrick is a murderer, who tried to strangle me and pushed me off the *Vigilant*? It couldn't have been Derrick. He was here that night, not yet well enough to go anywhere."

I raised my brows; he pulled his low. "I don't know. Perhaps what's throwing off this investigation is that there are two guilty parties."

"Do you *want* Derrick Andrews to be guilty?" I scowled.

"You know I would never allow personal feelings to interfere with a case, Emma. At least I hope you do." He searched my features. "Good grief, I hope so."

"Where have you been, Emma, and what on earth has been going on in this hospital? We heard a scream, and men tramping about like soldiers on the march. Mama is ready to lodge a complaint."

After Jesse left to continue his investigation, I made my way back upstairs to where I should have stayed earlier, with my relatives outside Uncle Cornelius's room. How I wished I hadn't been the one to find Wyatt Monroe. How I wished his death had nothing to do with me.

Wearily I grasped Cousin Gertrude's hand. "You don't want to know, not now. How is your father?"

"He's resting comfortably, the doctors say, but how can one know for certain? Oh, Emma . . ." Her features crumpled. In the next instant I was holding up a distraught Gertrude, our arms around each other, her chin on my shoulder.

"He's strong, Gertrude. The strongest of men."

"He isn't really, though. He's not young anymore."

"I mean in spirit. No one has a tougher spirit than your father." I pulled back to look at her. "If he wishes to be well, then he *will* be well."

That brought a ghost of a smile to Gertrude's face, but a fleeting one. "That was once true, not so very long ago. But the situation with Neily is taxing him terribly. Mother told me what happened. How dreadful! Gladys doesn't know," she added quickly with a glance over her shoulder, but her sister wasn't in the corridor. "Oh, Emma, this is all Neily's fault."

"Do not do that, Gertrude. Don't lay blame. Neily is your brother and he needs you just as much as your father does. They're both stubborn, but they're both good men."

This time her smile lingered, sad though it was. "Dear Emma, you're always on everyone's side. Don't you find it exhausting?"

"No, I'm grateful for all of you."

She examined me up and down. "Yet I think you *are* exhausted. You're looking thin. Come home with us later. We'll see that a good meal goes into you."

I shook my head. Someone waited for me at Gull Manor, and

I very badly craved the sensation of a warm, soft cheek against my own. "I need to go home. But I'll check in tomorrow to see how your father is faring. If there is any change in the meantime, please let me know."

I bid the rest of the family good-bye, kissed Aunt Alice, and made my way outside. Uncle William escorted me, and a lucky thing, too. The gathering dusk did little to conceal the line of reporters stretched along the street, and a barrage of questions hit us the moment we were recognized. Was Cornelius Vanderbilt dead, most wanted to know. Others shouted for confirmation about the rumor of a murder at the hospital. There must have been men from as far away as Tiverton, New Bedford, and by now even Providence. I also spotted my nemesis from the Newport *Observer,* Ed Billings, among them. In fact, Ed was the first to call out our names, alerting the others. I stared at the ground and refused to meet any of their gazes. Uncle William wrapped a protective arm around me, put his head down, and charged us clear of the line to his waiting phaeton. He instructed his driver to bring me home.

I arrived at Gull Manor to a sound that sent my anxiety spiking yet again and propelled me down the corridor into the kitchen. It was a sound we'd rarely heard around here in the past week, which frightened me all the more.

Baby Robbie's face was a shocking crimson, and his lips shook around piercing howls that proved he possessed a formidable set of lungs. He kicked and flailed in Nanny's arms. She had been pacing and bouncing him, but stopped when she saw me in the doorway. She accurately read the alarm on my features, for she immediately smiled, and said, "He's fine. Just a bit of colic."

"He sounds like someone is poking him with a hot iron."

"Yes, well, babies always want to make sure we know when they're uncomfortable. That's their job. Ours is to fix whatever ails them."

"Where are Katie and Stella?"

"They weeded the garden today *and* cleaned the big rug in the front parlor. It needed it, after Robbie's afternoon bottle came back up. I gave them an early supper and sent them to bed."

I walked to the kitchen counter and leaned for support. "Should we call Dr. Kennison?"

"For a bout of colic?" Nanny flashed me a condescending look. "You won't remember, but you were quite a colicky baby yourself."

Robbie's howls had subsided slightly when I'd entered the room, but now they continued with renewed vigor. My instinct was to run away to somewhere quiet, but I held out my arms instead.

"I'm glad I don't remember that. Here, I'll take him for a bit." She passed him to me so that his little torso faced mine, his head and trumpeting mouth beside my ear.

"How is your uncle?" she asked as she settled into a chair at the kitchen table.

The day's events tumbled back like loose boulders, and I marveled that those few minutes of worrying over the baby had provided a brief respite. "Out of danger, but not well. The doctors predict a long recovery, and he might never regain his full health again. Oh, but, Nanny, that's not even the worst of what happened today." I lowered my voice as if to keep the truth from reaching Robbie's ears. "Wyatt Monroe is dead. And it happened right there in the hospital."

"Dear Lord, Emma, what happened?" She hopped up from her chair and filled the tea kettle. A sense of relief flowed through me. I truly needed one of Nanny's strong cups of tea.

"I found him in Derrick Andrews's room. He'd been murdered, apparently with some sort of dagger."

"Someone stabbed him? A vigorous man like that?"

"Someone obviously overpowered him. Perhaps snuck up on him. I don't know."

"Tell me what you *do* know, sweetie."

Robbie's cries increased. I rocked him more vigorously and raised my voice to be heard. "Believe me, Nanny, you don't want the image of it in your mind. I wish to heavens it wasn't burned into mine."

She lit the stove. "You needn't coddle me, you know. And while you might think you don't wish to discuss it, I always say it's better to talk than to bottle everything up until the cork pops."

"His throat was slit."

The kettle landed on the burner with a clang. She returned to the table. "Someone was angry with that man."

The irony of that statement forced a laugh from me. "Aren't murderers always angry with the person they kill?"

"No, they aren't always. People murder for lots of reasons. To hide a crime or a secret. Out of revenge for a wrongdoing. But this—this is *rage*, Emma. Pure, crazed, blind rage."

"I hadn't thought of it that way, but I believe you're right. Which only convinces me further that—" I broke off, realizing I hadn't yet told her everything. Robbie's little fingers found one of my own and curled tightly around it. He yanked, as if to prompt me to go on. "What makes this even worse is that the police are suspicious of Derrick. He'd been released from the hospital, but the last I heard he was nowhere to be found. That, combined with Wyatt's accusations that Derrick jumped in after Virgil to drown him rather than save him, has put him at the top of the police's list of people with motives."

"Derrick would never—"

"Of course he wouldn't. He doesn't have that sort of rage in him. I'd know if he did."

Would I? Hadn't I realized in recent days how little I knew Derrick Andrews? But I had more substantial evidence in support of his innocence. "If Derrick Andrews is a killer, then who attacked me at the Yacht Club while he lay in his hospital bed?" I shook my head. "I was so certain it was Wyatt who attacked me, and Wyatt who sent Virgil into the sea."

Nanny remained silent for a long moment. Too long. "What are you thinking?" Robbie was finally quietening, and I spoke in a murmur.

She did likewise, yet her low tone didn't rob her words of their impact. "Emma, what if the police agree with you that Wyatt killed Virgil and attacked you? And what if they suspect Derrick knew this and murdered Wyatt to protect you?"

"Jesse didn't say that. He never implied . . ." But then he hadn't implied much, only that Derrick had been the last person in the room before Wyatt arrived, and that his subsequent disappearance warranted asking him questions. And he had speculated there might be two killers. . . . "Oh, Nanny."

"I don't believe it for a minute, of course." The kettle began to steam and she got up to put the strainer and tea leaves in the porcelain teapot. She took two mugs down from the cupboard above the counter.

"No," I said. "I'd never believe it either."

Nanny brought mugs, spoons, and the sugar bowl to the table. "He does think the world of you, Derrick does. He risked his life for you more than once last summer."

"What are you saying?" I shifted Robbie to the other shoulder. I could sense him tiring. His body lay limp against mine, his whimpers halfhearted at best. "Risking his life for me is one thing. Killing for me is quite another. Besides . . ." I stared down at the table. "His affections for me have somewhat diminished over the past year."

"I doubt that very much, Emma." She seemed about to go on, but a knock on the garden door startled us both. Through the window, my cousin Neily stared in at us, his face a study in shadows. Nanny blew out a breath and went to the door. "Goodness, Mr. Neily! You scared us half to death."

"I'm so sorry, Mrs. O'Neal. The front of the house was dark, so I walked around. I was hoping for news of my father. I'll go if—"

"Don't be silly," I called softly to him. "Come in. Nanny's just brewing tea."

He shuffled in, his hat in his hands, his head bowed. "Emmaline, I also wanted to apologize for today. You shouldn't have had to witness that."

"Neily, for better or worse, you are all my family. I want you to know I'd never take sides."

He reached out to press his palm to Robbie's head. "Is it possible not to take sides?"

Nanny took another cup from the cupboard. I said, "I believe it is. I believe you and Grace truly care for one another and that your parents are wrong to want to keep you apart. I won't turn my back on you, Neily, but I'd never turn my back on them either."

"And if they asked you—no, *demanded* that you take sides—then what?"

I grinned and gestured for him to sit as Nanny returned to the table with the teapot. "Haven't you learned by now that the surest way to ensure I *not* do something is to demand I do it?" I sobered. "Now, about your father, and other things that happened today . . ."

Chapter 13

I stayed up late that night writing an article that brought me no satisfaction. It wasn't a very long piece, only a couple of paragraphs, but contained facts I certainly wouldn't allow Ed Billings to distort. Sometime around one o'clock in the morning I tossed down my pen and quickly reviewed the details of Uncle Cornelius's apoplexy, having made no mention of the distressing events that led to the attack. My heart weighed heavily for him, for Neily, for the entire family. Tears stained my pillow when I finally crawled into bed.

I found little respite in dreams, but woke frequently, each time certain I had heard the telephone jangling with terrible news. I feared for Uncle Cornelius's life, for the future, and yes, for my own sense of security, for these Vanderbilt relatives of mine helped fill the large gap left when my parents moved away to Paris.

After only a few hours' sleep I drove into town and delivered my account to Mr. Millford.

"Ed also wrote something up last night," he told me, pointing to a typed article on his desk. While my blood pressure surged, he placed my handwritten page beside Ed's, scanned both, and regarded me with a sad expression. "I'll run yours, Emma. It seems only right."

"Thank you," I murmured. I felt no triumph in having won out over my rival.

From the *Observer* office I went to the hospital, parking my carriage a couple of streets away and running along the sidewalk to dodge the reporters who continued to mill outside the entrance. Those who recognized me shouted questions, but I kept my head down and pushed on past. I didn't see Ed among them. Perhaps after turning in his article last night he had moved on to another story.

"Aunt Alice, have you been here all night?" I exclaimed upon finding her sitting at Uncle Cornelius's bedside, holding his hand. Her haggard appearance certainly suggested she hadn't slept much, if at all.

She waved away my concern. "I'm fine. One of the nurses brought me a bit of breakfast a little while ago."

"Where are the others?"

"I sent the children home. Willie and Frederick were here most of the night, but I sent them home at dawn. They didn't want to go, but I insisted."

I went to the bedside and gazed down at Uncle Cornelius. One eye drooped lower than the other, and the corner of his mouth sagged. My throat constricted and I gripped the back of Aunt Alice's chair for support.

"He's going to be all right, Emmaline." Her bluntness sounded more like a command that I believe her, rather than a simple reassurance. I felt compelled to obey.

"Yes, Aunt Alice, I'm sure he'll be just fine. But you need to keep up your strength, too, and not overtax yourself."

This, too, she dismissed with a wave. "Bah. I'm strong enough for the two of us." She leaned farther forward. "Do you hear me, Cornelius? I'll pull us both through this. You follow my lead, you stubborn old goat, and all will be well."

Without relinquishing his hand, she sat back and looked up at me. "I'm sure you have better things to do than stand here watching him sleep. I'll make certain you're notified if there's any change."

"I don't want to leave you alone. . . ."

"I'm not alone, dear. I'm with Cornelius." She smiled. That brave gesture, and the softening of her voice when she called me *dear*, as if it were me needing to be comforted, brought on a stinging threat of tears. I bent down and kissed her, and promised to return that evening.

I repeated my duck-and-run tactic outside and soon the voices faded into the background as I trekked the short distance back to Barney and my carriage. I cannot say what made me stop before turning onto the side street and look around me. A noise? A sense of being watched?

I saw only the reporters, their figures grown smaller in the distance. A few carriages rumbled by. The wind stirred. I started walking again, but a distinct rustle in the shrubbery beside the corner house made me stop again.

"Derrick?"

I immediately felt foolish. Why would Derrick be skulking around in the bushes? He had no reason to hide from me. Then it struck me that I didn't yet know if he had been found and questioned about Wyatt's death.

Not death. Murder.

Another rustle carried on the breeze, but instead of craning my neck to discover the source, instinct sent me hurrying to my rig. Whoever did kill Wyatt was still at large, perhaps watching, waiting. My final steps were running ones and I practically leaped onto the seat and then fumbled to release the brake. "Come on, Barney. Please go faster," I added when he assumed his typical leisurely pace.

He didn't, but then neither did anyone jump out at us from the side of the road. Had those noises been my imagination? My lack of a decent night's sleep? Perhaps, but that didn't negate the danger of a murderer on the loose. One who might be well aware that I had been asking questions.

Wyatt had known—he had said as much to me—but now he was dead. Of my list of suspects, that left Virgil Monroe's two sons. I refused to entertain the notion that Derrick could have transformed into a crazed murderer. What if Lawrence and Nate had alibis? Then who?

I craned my neck to glance behind me several times. There were carriages following me, but why wouldn't there have been? The reins trembled in my hands as I thought over every detail I could remember about the day Virgil Monroe had fallen overboard, and everything I had learned in the aftermath. Several people might have wanted him out of the way, and I had no doubt the feeling might have been mutual—

I pulled on the reins so hard Barney stopped with a lurch and whinnied in protest.

"I'm so sorry, Barney! Forgive me."

Carriages swerved around us, a couple of them sending unkind words in my direction, admonishments about women making poor drivers. I barely heard them. Was barely aware of anything but the thought that had brought me up sharp.

What if Virgil Monroe hadn't died that day at Beechwood?

That could be why Derrick never found him—because Virgil swam away beneath the waves. It could be why his body still hadn't been found. It could be why evidence pointed to sabotage of the *Vigilant*, but with Wyatt, not Virgil, as the intended victim.

A possible scenario took shape in my mind. Virgil planned to "accidentally" knock his brother overboard, but the unexpected storm posed new dangers. Perhaps Virgil's going over the side *was* accidental, but instead of dying he saved himself, and murdered his brother yesterday.

Could he have slipped into the hospital unseen? The answer came instantly: Of course he could have. In the distraction of Uncle Cornelius being brought in, all he would have needed was a coat with an upturned collar, perhaps a hat pulled low—techniques I myself had used in the past to disguise my identity.

And now . . . Virgil might even now be planning to "wash up ashore," miraculously alive.

Much more gently than I had stopped him, I set Barney in motion. Our next stop would be the police station. Jesse might pooh-pooh my newest theory, but he would at least hear me out. I wouldn't leave until he had.

By the time I turned onto Marlborough Street, I'd begun to feel foolish again. Virgil Monroe having faked his own death? Then sneaking into the hospital to murder his brother in cold blood? I shook my head. Still, I drove my buggy into the lot behind St. Paul's Church, handed Barney over to Mr. Weatherby, the sexton, and crossed the street to the police station. What would I say to Jesse?

It wasn't Jesse's face that drew my immediate attention inside, it was Derrick's. He stood in the main room with his derby in his hands. A moment later a uniformed policeman addressed him and the two started in my direction.

I identified the moment he spotted me by the resigned reluctance that entered his eyes, as though he would rather have turned around and gone in the opposite direction. That look almost made me want to do the same. I almost didn't want to know what had occurred before my arrival, or why he was being escorted by an officer. I futilely wished the rain had started much earlier that day at Beechwood, and that vile race that had so altered our lives had never occurred.

"Derrick," was all I could think to say when he reached me. Voicing any other thought running through my mind would have been prying, and he had already made it clear that he had no intentions of confiding in me anymore.

"How is your uncle?" he asked in a quiet voice.

"Holding his own, I think." I fought against it, but I couldn't prevent casting a questioning glance at the officer.

"It seems I am under house arrest." Derrick smiled apologetically. "This gentleman is to ensure I arrive home, and then he and others will stand watch to make sure I stay put."

"Oh, Derrick. I know you didn't do anything wrong. Soon the police will know it as well."

"Time to go." The policeman nudged Derrick's arm.

"Please excuse me, Emma." Derrick tipped a bow; then he and the officer moved past me.

Deciding to be more angry than upset, I continued into the main room. I walked right up to Jesse's desk and leaned with both hands braced on the edge.

"Just what do you think you're doing?"

"Good morning, Emma." His smile said he was glad to see me. The look in his eyes said he would rather have avoided this confrontation. "What can I do for you?"

"House arrest? With what evidence?"

Jesse gestured for me to sit in the chair facing his desk. I hesitated, not feeling particularly cooperative. However, realizing I'd soon attract attention, I complied. But not without a good huff.

Jesse leaned forward. "Look, Emma. This wasn't my idea. Don't look at me that way, I'm telling you the truth. Mr. Andrews was found at home late last night. Very late."

"He must have been with his family on their steamer."

"He wasn't. We posted someone there. But that's not all. He came down here voluntarily this morning, but refused to produce any real alibi for his whereabouts at the time of Wyatt Monroe's murder. He claimed he was merely 'out walking.'"

"Walking? Where?"

"He won't be specific. Around town, places he'd never been before. Tell me, Emma, why would a man recently released from the hospital go for a lengthy walk around town, rather than go home to bed?"

"Because he was sick and tired of being cooped up?"

He released a breath and shook his head. "Doubtful."

"He didn't murder Wyatt Monroe."

Jesse took a long time in replying, his scrutiny hot on my face. "I hope not, Emma, for your sake."

"For Derrick's sake," I corrected him. "I care about justice and he is an innocent man."

Jesse nodded without looking as though he agreed with me.

"Oh, but I came down here for a reason," I said, suddenly remembering my original errand. "I came from the hospital, and before I got back in my carriage, I could have sworn someone was following me, hiding behind the bushes near a house."

"Did you see anyone?" He leaned forward again and spoke with a new urgency. "Emma, until this is resolved, I'd feel much better if you didn't go out alone. At least bring Katie with you—"

"Yes, yes, I'll be careful. No, I didn't see who it was, but I was certain someone was there." Had I been, or was I convincing myself after the fact to suit my purposes? My next words lent credence to that notion. "We both know it couldn't have been Derrick, since he was here."

Jesse picked up a pencil and began rolling it between his thumb and forefinger. "Who do you think it might have been, then?"

"You'll say I'm crazy."

"Probably." He dropped the pencil and gestured for me to continue.

"Jesse, what if Virgil Monroe didn't die when he fell overboard?"

"That's crazy." His expression turned sheepish. "I'm sorry, but the man went over the side and—"

"And maybe swam to shore."

"In those high seas?"

"It isn't impossible. Do we know how good a swimmer he was? Or is?"

"No, I suppose we don't."

"It bears looking into, doesn't it?"

Jesse didn't answer. He just sat there with a corner of his mouth quirked. I stood, preparing to bid him good day. Before I did, he said, "You may visit him, you know. I could give my consent for it."

"Visit . . . Derrick?"

He nodded.

"Thank you, Jesse." I suddenly wanted to run around the desk and hug him, but I didn't. Just as well, considering what he said next.

"See if you can find out where he went after leaving the hospital. He might be willing to confide in you." I could see by the tight knotting of his brows that he took no pleasure in the thought of Derrick trusting me.

I decided to relieve his discomfiture by telling him the simple truth. "I doubt it. Derrick Andrews doesn't consider me a confidant. Not anymore."

When I left Jesse I had no intention of visiting Derrick. None. With my chin set to a determined angle, I climbed into my carriage and coaxed Barney to a walk, but when I should have headed south toward home, at the last minute I turned northwest instead. Minutes later I entered the Point.

A uniformed patrolman stood outside my erstwhile childhood home, which my parents had eventually divided into three

flats, one on each level, and—most notable of all—sold a year
ago to the man I had come to visit.

The policeman straightened to attention as I stopped Barney
in front of the house, then relaxed and waved when he recognized me. "Good morning, Emma."

"Good morning, Scotty. They assigned you to stand guard?"

"Until later this afternoon, yes. Are you here to visit our
prisoner, or are you checking on one of your tenants?"

I winced at the word *prisoner,* and again at *tenant.* "My family doesn't own this house any longer, Scotty. Your *prisoner*
does, but please don't call him that. He's innocent."

"I hope so, Emma. For your sake."

I tried to hide my surprise at his parroting of Jesse's sentiments. Did everyone know of my association with Derrick Andrews? Did I wear my heart so plainly on my sleeve?

But then Scotty added, "You're a trusting soul, Emma. You
believed in Brady when he was in trouble last summer. I
wouldn't want to see your faith in people shaken."

I touched his forearm briefly. "Thank you, Scotty. Is it all
right if I go inside? Actually, I'm here at Jesse's request," I
added in a lower tone.

He nodded knowingly. "He sent you to see what you can
find out?"

I wasn't at all sure yet what I intended, but I didn't dissuade
Scotty of his assumption.

He glanced up at the façade of the house, to the second-story
apartment that Derrick had taken as his own when the old tenant moved out. "The windows are open. See that he keeps them
open, and if you need me, just shout."

"I don't think it will come to that, but again, thank you."

With that I climbed the four steps to the front door, where
the tiny vestibule had been sectioned off from the first-floor
flat. A staircase led up to the two apartments on the upper lev-
els, and as I ascended, memories of climbing those stairs to bed

each night brought a tightness to my throat. A sense of unreality settled over me. This house had once been my home . . . and today I came as a guest.

I had tried, over the past year, to be stoic. Realistic. My father earned his living as a painter, mostly landscapes but with the occasional portrait as well. An artist's life is far from a lucrative one and my parents had needed the funds from the sale of the house. But they hadn't told me—hadn't warned me. Neither had Derrick when he entered into negotiations with them through his lawyer. I had been the last to know, and then only when the transfer of ownership had been finalized, when it was too late for me to do anything about it.

What could I have done? Admittedly very little. I didn't possess that kind of money, and my pride would have prevented me from asking Uncle Cornelius for it.

Pride and memories and a sense of loss—those seemed to be the only lasting legacy of my childhood. Knocking on Derrick's door drove that fact deeper still.

"Who is it?" He sounded puzzled and didn't wait for my answer before opening the door. He obviously hadn't been expecting company, for he wore no tie or waistcoat and was buttoning up his coat, which he must have donned hastily. Softly he exclaimed, "Emma!"

"I hope I'm not disturbing you."

"I'm surprised they let you in."

"Scotty—the policeman outside—is an old friend."

"Newport is full of old friends of yours, isn't it?" I wasn't sure if a sardonic edge accompanied those words or not. He stepped back and opened the door wider. "Won't you please come in?"

I hesitated. "I wish you would stop that."

"Stop what?"

"Being so blasted polite." I walked past him into a parlor that had once been my parents' bedroom—so familiar, yet made so entirely foreign by new furnishings and Derrick's personal effects.

"I apologize. I hadn't realized politeness was offensive to you," he said, following me into the room. We stood facing each other, both of us stiff, ill at ease.

"It is offensive when accompanied by an obvious attempt to set me at a distance." Oh, good Lord, had I really said that? I hadn't meant to. I had intended to keep my pride wrapped as tightly as a cloak against a winter wind.

So much for that.

"Is it acceptable for me to offer you a seat and bid you to make yourself comfortable?" A corner of his mouth tilted.

With my own lips pursed I scanned the room and chose the hard-backed chair at the writing desk, turning it to face into the room. The chair had already been pulled out. Had I interrupted him in the middle of writing a letter? Or perhaps an article for the Providence *Sun,* his family's newspaper. I didn't glance at the desk, deeming that too much of an intrusion of privacy, but I had chosen the chair solely for its distance from the easy chair and brass-tacked leather sofa. For some reason I needed that space between us. The open, front-facing windows flanked me, the semi-sheer, unbound curtains blowing inward with the breezes. I thought of Scotty down below, ready to run up to save me if I needed him.

Directly across from me hung a telephone that had never been there before, the oak stained dark, the brass shining, and the ebony gleaming. I noticed, too, wires where previously there had been none, running up the walls to electric sconces.

"You've made improvements to the house, I see."

"I hope you approve."

"It's your house now to do with as you please." I heard the resentment in my voice and tried, not altogether successfully, to school my features to conceal my displeasure.

An awkward silence fell, broken by Derrick clearing his throat. "May I offer you some refreshment?" He pointed toward the one-time dressing room that had been renovated into a small kitchen. Beyond that would have been my bedroom, and then Brady's. Briefly I wondered what use he had made of those rooms.

"Derrick, why won't you tell the police where you went after leaving the hospital yesterday?"

"Ah, I see. Did your friend Jesse send you over to question me? Did he think a softer touch might persuade me to reveal the dark and deadly truth?" He sat opposite me on the Chesterfield sofa, yet the distance between us proved not nearly as safe as I'd hoped. I felt him all too keenly, felt the force of whatever electromagnetic forces continually drew us toward each other.

"Don't make a joke of this," I retorted, perhaps too harshly. But he *had* touched upon the truth of the matter. "You wouldn't be under house arrest if you had been forthcoming. Are you . . . ?"

"Am I what? If you have a question, by all means, ask it."

"Are you protecting someone?"

"Such as whom?" He held up a hand when I opened my mouth to express my exasperation. He gestured to the cushion beside him. "Come here, Emma. Please," he added when I didn't move.

I hesitated another moment before rising and crossing the room to sit beside him. "All right. What couldn't you tell me with a few feet between us?"

"I can only tell you if you swear to me this will never reach Jesse's ears, or anyone else's."

A sudden, cold fear spread through me. "You're frightening me. Derrick, what did you do?"

"Your word, Emma."

I didn't hesitate. "Yes, yes, I swear."

He studied me another second or two, and seemed to reach a

decision. "I didn't murder Wyatt Monroe. Or Virgil, for that matter. I went off island yesterday."

"That's it? I never believed you murdered anyone, but why couldn't you have admitted to going off island to Jesse? You weren't under house arrest yesterday and could come and go as you pleased. Now by refusing to cooperate—"

"I left Newport at my mother's request." He fell silent and showed me his profile as he watched the curtains stirring. I wanted to prompt him but realized the value in holding my tongue while he gathered the wherewithal to confide in me.

As he once did so easily, without a second thought.

"My sister left early yesterday morning without a word to my mother," he said at length. He spoke to the curtains, rather than to me. "Mother was concerned about her and asked me to go after her and find out why she left."

"And did you find her?"

"I did. She was in North Kingstown, waiting for a train to take her back to Providence, or so she said. I had a brief glimpse of her ticket, though, before she tucked it away in her purse. I'm certain the destination was New York. Otherwise why wouldn't she have boarded the northbound train right here in Newport? My father did."

Newport only ran northbound trains between here and Boston. Boats and mainland railways provided the only routes south. As his question seemed rhetorical, I asked one of my own. "What happened once you found her?"

"She returned to Newport with me. Reluctantly, but she returned. She's back on the *Lavinia's Sun* with my mother."

"I don't understand. Why the secrecy, and why can't your sister be allowed to travel if she wishes? She's not a child."

Derrick sprang up from the sofa, startling me. He went to the chair I'd vacated and leaned to grip its back. His shoulders knotted, straining his coat, and his head went down. His effort to compose himself filled the room with waves of tension that had me holding my breath. Finally, he turned back around. He met my gaze, but his head was still down, his eyes hooded.

"In the two years since Judith's husband passed away, she has been . . . different. Not simply grieving, but angry, resentful, at times volatile, especially in the past year. She has spent her money wildly, consorted with heaven only knows whom, and has disappeared for months on end. Not once but several times."

I took this in, working it over in my mind. My nerve endings began to buzz. "Is that where you were in the spring? Looking for her?"

"I searched for her last winter. By spring I'd hired a private detective, but again to no avail. Then she suddenly just showed up at home one day."

"How long ago did she reappear?" I could barely keep a trill of excitement from my voice.

"Two months ago."

"Oh." My growing eagerness suddenly deflated. With Judith disappearing for long stretches at a time, I'd suddenly entertained the notion that perhaps Robbie might be *her* baby. But that couldn't be, not if Derrick had seen her two months ago. She would have been six or seven months gone and surely showing the evidence of it. No, whatever had kept Judith away from home must have been another matter. With a sigh I said, "This is why she accused you of bullying her at Mrs. Astor's ball."

He nodded. "She didn't appreciate my interference."

"Derrick, all this secrecy, your avoiding me—why couldn't you have confided in me?" The hurt I'd been feeling all along made my voice tight, plaintive. I could do nothing to prevent it.

"I'm sorry, Emma. Perhaps I should have, but it was a difficult situation. I—"

"No, don't apologize," I said quietly, trying to tamp down my pain, my bitter disappointment. It wasn't his fault that I had assumed too much, that I had believed myself entitled to more than he felt able to give me. "Your sister's life is none of my business and I respect that. But why not be honest with the police?"

"And make Judith's situation a matter of public record, the topic of gossip and scandal? Destroy her chances of ever remarrying and finding happiness? Thank you, no."

"You could lie and merely say—"

"Lie to the police? They'd almost surely discover the truth and I would look all the more guilty."

"But you have a legitimate alibi and—" I bit down, not sure I should continue.

"Go on. And what?"

"Well, I have a theory about who might have murdered Wyatt, but the police won't take it seriously unless we can exonerate you first." I hurried to explain. "I posed the same possibility to Jesse this morning and he all but dismissed it, but . . . Derrick, what if Virgil Monroe didn't die in the water? What if he's still alive?"

His eyes widened. Several seconds passed before he spoke. "You mean he faked his death?"

"Precisely. But before you ridicule the idea—"

"I wasn't going to." He raked his hair back off his brow and returned to sit beside me on the sofa. He stared down at his hands, fisted and braced on his knees. "Are you thinking he was able to swim to shore during the storm?"

"Was he a good enough swimmer, do you know?"

"He wasn't a young man . . . but he wasn't infirm either." His brow creased in a show of concentration. "Last summer, during the Relay for Charity at Bailey's Beach, Virgil swam a hundred yards in the race."

"Did he do well?"

He made an open-palmed gesture in the air. "His team didn't win, but I believe they finished respectably."

"Then he *was* a good swimmer. Or *is.*"

"I don't know that anyone could have swam in those seas, Emma."

"He might have clung to one of the buoys used to mark the race course until the waves subsided."

Derrick paused, seeming to weigh that likelihood. "Then where is he?"

"Hiding. Watching. You see, I didn't simply snatch this theory out of the air. I had a look at the *Vigilant*, as well as the registration records. Did you know Wyatt was supposed to captain the boat during the race, but the position assignments were altered at the last minute?"

"There isn't much unusual about that."

"Perhaps not, but it does seem unusual to have attempted to cover the change with a thin coating of paint in the records book. And then," I added quickly before Derrick could comment, "I realized with the new positioning of the crew, it made far more sense if Wyatt had been the intended victim. Don't you see? Someone—perhaps Virgil—attempted to stage what appeared to be an accidental swinging of the boom to knock the port trimmer overboard. In this case, that would have been Wyatt. Except the storm kicked up and caused a true accident, that of Virgil going over instead."

"I don't know . . ." His gaze clouded with uncertainty. "There are a lot of *ifs* to consider. My guess is, if Officer Whyte didn't immediately reject this notion, it was out of friendship."

Frustration sent me to my feet. "I was all but convinced of Wyatt's guilt, and now he's dead. That surely rules out the possibility of any of this being accidental. So who do you think is to blame?"

"I don't know." He tilted his head to look up at me. "If I did, I'd tell you. But while powerful men like Virgil accumulate no shortage of enemies during their lifetime, I can see no reason why anyone would want to murder Wyatt. This may sound harsh, but he was of little consequence to anyone."

"Except perhaps to Virgil himself."

With a long exhalation Derrick stood. "You should go, Emma. You've already stretched the limits of propriety by staying so long."

"You're going to be stubborn about this, aren't you?"

"And you're going to respect my confidence and not go to the police with what I've told you, correct?" When I didn't answer, he reached out and lifted my chin in his palm. "Don't you see, Emma, my going off island doesn't prove I didn't kill Wyatt. I might have done so right before I left the hospital. The information would do little to exonerate me, and could damage Judith's reputation irrevocably."

I let my chin rest in the warm strength of his hand another moment. "With what you're facing, how can you be so calm?"

He gently drew me closer, until his lips touched my forehead. "Dearest Emma, I am far from calm." He suddenly set me to arm's length. "Write an article. About my being under suspicion, essentially under arrest, which I am."

"Why on earth? You haven't been formally charged. There is no reason—"

He was nodding, a shrewd grin dawning. "Yes, there is. Running an article in the *Observer* about my alleged guilt might entice the guilty party to grow careless. And then perhaps he'll show his hand. But, Emma . . ." He lifted my chin again. "Write the article and then step away. No further involvement, understand?"

"What if this doesn't work?" I whispered. My stomach twisted into knots. "What if you remain the chief suspect?"

"I'm innocent."

"Innocent men go to prison. Brady almost did."

"I won't."

The adamancy of that avowal made me wonder. Did he have a plan to elude the authorities if it came to that? I found myself hoping he did, yet at the same time not wanting to know. I just hoped if he did have a plan, it was a good one.

Chapter 14

I returned to the *Observer* office after leaving Derrick. Had I found the article about Uncle Cornelius difficult to write? This one drew pain from every part of me. I handed it to Mr. Millford, ignored Ed's questions as well as his protests that he was the hard news reporter and this wasn't fair, and made my way, numb and unseeing, back outside.

"Barney," I said wearily as I took up the reins, "bring me home."

An overwhelming sense of having condemned a friend, of having betrayed him—no matter that this was his idea—hardened like cement around my heart. I wanted Nanny. Needed the familiar embrace of Aunt Sadie's creaking old house. Longed to hold Robbie and press my cheek to his little head.

After settling Barney in his stall, I entered the house through the kitchen. Voices from the front parlor traveled down the corridor to me. As if in mockery of my mood, laughter rang out—laughter that could not have come from Nanny, Stella, or Katie, and certainly not from Robbie. I tossed my hat to the kitchen table and hurried to the parlor.

"Brady!" I cried. "You're here!"

"A bit obvious, little sister, but if there is any confusion, yes, here I am." Sitting in the wing chair, he lifted Robbie from his shoulder and handed him off to Katie. Then he rose and crossed to where I still hovered in the doorway, not quite able to believe my eyes. "You're looking well," he said, and drew me into a tight embrace. "A bit harried, if you don't mind my saying so, but well."

"Oh, Brady." I got no further. Anything I wished to say became lost in my tears. With exhaustion and disheartenment nearly crushing me, I clung to my half brother. He exclaimed something I couldn't make out, I had become that insensible. I believe Nanny might have patted me on the back, and Katie murmured gentle words as she carried Robbie from the room. This I saw through my watery vision, while poor Brady's coat turned sodden beneath my cheek.

Though I hadn't yet found my composure, Brady loosened his hold on me, pried my arms from around his neck, and led me by the hand, as he used to do when I was little, to the sofa.

"Nanny filled me in on a lot of what's been happening. Robbie, Virgil Monroe, his brother . . ."

"Do you know about Derrick?" At his quizzical frown, I said, "Oh, Brady, he's a suspect. Wyatt accused him of drowning Virgil, and now Wyatt is dead, too. I found the body in Derrick's hospital room. Now Derrick is under house arrest, but he didn't do it. He has an alibi . . . generally speaking. He says it won't suffice, but I believe with some critical analysis of the timing and how long it would have taken him to reach North Kingstown—"

Brady placed his fingertips over my mouth. "Shh, Em. You need to slow down, because you've lost me. If I know Nanny, she'll be bringing in tea in a few minutes. We'll drink it, and then you'll start over and tell me everything."

True enough, Nanny brought tea, of a good strong Irish variety that fortified me and steadied my nerves. I started at the beginning and told Brady everything that had happened while he'd been in New York. Relating the distressing tale didn't solve anything, but having the whole of my immediate family around me—at least the ones who would never abandon me—served as a balm that somehow made me believe the truth would eventually prevail. For the first night in many, I slept soundly.

The next morning, the paper boy delivered the morning edition of the *Observer*. Mr. Millford ran my article about Derrick on page two. Had this been any other article about any other subject on the face of the earth, seeing it on page two would have been a personal triumph after finding my other news pieces buried farther in. Not today. Although the article citing Derrick's apparent guilt had been his idea, I still couldn't shake a dismal sense of having wronged him. And of having compromised myself in writing an article I didn't believe in.

The morning melted into afternoon with further discussions between Brady and me about the various possibilities and scenarios that might explain the murders. With Brady playing devil's advocate at every turn, it seemed we could reach no agreement.

"Virgil alive, Em? I can't fathom it. Not with the kind of squall you're describing."

"A competent swimmer might have managed it."

"A *superior* swimmer might have managed it. Someone more athletic than Virgil. Wyatt, for instance. He was the sportsman of the family."

"Yes, but Wyatt didn't go overboard."

A knock at the front door cut short our debate. We had been sitting in the kitchen with Nanny while she prepared the dough for the evening bread. We all froze and my gaze darted to her.

"Where is Robbie?"

"Katie and Stella brought him upstairs for his nap."

Yes, I had known that, but we didn't often have visitors at Gull Manor and the knock had rattled my nerves.

"It's probably Mr. Neily," she said, her arms floured to the elbows.

"I'll go see." I rose from my seat, but then I heard Katie's voice in the downstairs hall.

"May I help you?"

This time I traded a glance with Brady. "A stranger. Katie wouldn't question Neily or any of our other friends that way."

"I'm here to see Miss Cross," a familiar and youthful voice said.

"I know who that is." Knowing, however, didn't make me any less bewildered. Why would Lawrence Monroe visit me, unless something had happened to Daphne? I hurried into the front hall to discover it wasn't Lawrence after all. It was his younger brother, Nate.

"Oh," I said without hiding my surprise. "Nate. What are you doing here?" Perhaps not the most hospitable greeting, but I simply couldn't imagine what brought him.

"Miss Cross, forgive me for disturbing you. I hoped I might have a word with you."

The last time I'd encountered Nate Monroe had been in the library at Beechwood. He had been scowling, complaining about his brother and Daphne carrying on in spite of his father's wishes. The memory made me wary of his motives for coming to Gull Manor, but I remembered my manners. "Please come in, Nate. My brother and I were just having tea. Would you care to join us?"

A throat clearing behind me alerted me that Brady had followed me into the hall. I gestured into the parlor. "We can have it brought in here."

Nate removed his straw boater but didn't move to follow me. "I need to speak to you alone, Miss Cross. Please."

I studied his face, noting how the petulance of a sixteen-year-old boy warred with the dignity of someone much older. He was an oddity, this younger son of the Monroe family, and now my curiosity burgeoned. After brief introductions, I asked Brady to excuse us. I didn't have to see his lopsided grin to know he'd be eavesdropping from the discreet grate in the wall that connected this room to the formal dining room, allowing for the flow of air in the summer and heat in the winter. I led Nate into the parlor.

"Please have a seat." I gestured to the wing chair. I settled onto the sofa. "Now, what seems to be the matter?"

"It's Lawrence and Daphne. I need you to talk sense into them, Miss Cross."

"Me? What makes you think I should become involved, or that I hold any influence over either of them?"

"Oh, you do. Daphne thinks the world of you."

My stomach tightened. Cousin Consuelo had thought the world of me, too, and last summer my aunt, Alva Vanderbilt, had sought to use my influence over her daughter to persuade her to willingly marry the Duke of Marlborough. The results of my interference had been all but disastrous.

"And perhaps you'll tell me why they need someone to talk sense into them, Nate."

"They're planning to elope." His eyes briefly flared with that Monroe temper I had become so familiar with over the last week.

"Does your mother object?"

"Mother doesn't know. She's beside herself with grief over my father."

That didn't sound right. From what I had learned of Eudora Monroe, she had abhorred her husband, and if she felt anything at all about her husband's death, it was merely the guilt of having wished ill on another human being.

But I certainly couldn't point that out to her son.

"Nate, I'm not a member of your family. It would be inappropriate for me to intrude."

"Please, Miss Cross." He tapped his hat against his knee repeatedly, a show of nervous energy. "Our family has suffered so much. We don't need any more upheaval. If Daphne and my brother won't see reason, the very least they can do is wait to carry out this plan of theirs. You speak of what is inappropriate. Surely marriage during this time of mourning would be most inappropriate."

"All right." I stood. "I'll come to Beechwood and speak to Daphne, but I cannot make any promises."

"Thank you, Miss Cross. Thank you!" He practically leaped out of the chair. His rueful grin grazed my heart and reminded me of just how young he was, and how lost and truly frightened he must feel at the loss of his father and his uncle. How could he help but believe this elopement might deprive him of his elder brother as well? "I'll bring you over. I came in Mrs. Astor's cabriolet, and we'll both fit."

"But we've waited so long already," Daphne said with a wounded expression some twenty minutes later. "And besides, it is none of Nate's business."

She and I strolled among Mrs. Astor's prize roses, a soft sea breeze stirring the blossoms and raising their heavenly scent. I inhaled the fragrance as I considered whether I should have stayed home and refused Nate's plea that I become involved. I had learned the dangers of advising people on the subject of marriage. What if my counsel went horribly awry again?

I reached out my fingertips to touch a velvety crimson petal. "Nate is very young, Daphne. And I believe he's feeling vulnerable. What youth wouldn't, with all he has been through? I under-

stand Lawrence's and your wish to be together, but perhaps waiting until things have settled would be the wiser decision."

"But one never knows what might happen in the interim.
What if some calamity were to keep us apart again?"

A door on the loggia opened, and Lawrence Monroe came
through one of the arches and down the steps. He approached
like a charging cougar, his gait long and coiled, his face set and
determined.

"Miss Cross," he called out before he'd reached us, "am I to
understand you are attempting to talk my fiancée out of marrying me?"

"Mr. Monroe, I am doing no such thing. I'm merely pointing
out the wisdom of waiting until a more appropriate time when
you wouldn't have to elope. When . . ." I thought quickly.
"When Daphne might have a church wedding with your friends
and family in attendance, a stunning gown from Mr. Worth, and
a wedding feast to dazzle your guests and keep them talking
about the event for months afterward."

That stopped Lawrence in his tracks. His chest rose and fell
sharply, and he pinned a burning gaze on Daphne. At a slower
pace he continued to us. When he reached us he raised a hand
to stroke Daphne's cheek. She blushed and ducked her head,
smiling prettily.

"Yes." Lawrence drew the word out, then repeated it in a low,
almost sensual murmur. "What were we thinking, Daphne? You
deserve all that, and more. Miss Cross is correct. To marry in
haste would be to deprive you of the pleasure of planning a
beautiful wedding, one we'll remember for the rest of our
lives."

"I only wish to be your wife," she replied. I slowly backed
away from them and turned to gaze out over the water and the
cloud-specked sky.

"You *will* be my wife, but first you must be my bride. The
loveliest bride in the world. It's worth waiting for, Daphne."

"But—"

"No, I was foolish to suggest we rush. There is no reason for haste." Lawrence's next words plunged to a murmur, yet reached my ears nonetheless. "Father is dead."

Was he? Dared I tell them of my theory?

Lawrence spoke again. "He can no longer forbid us, or prevent us from doing as we please. We are free, my darling. Free."

When he might have sounded happy, his voice had instead sharpened with resentment and no small amount of disdain. I waited, braced, for Daphne's reply.

"You're right. He can no longer hurt us. Thank you, Lawrence."

At those last words I peeked over my shoulder at them, keeping my chin low and my face shaded by my hat brim. Lawrence grasped the stem of a rose, and with a snap he broke it off from the bush. Daphne smiled when he handed it to her and raised it to her lips. A crimson drop of blood rolled from the tip of Lawrence's finger into the grass at his feet.

They seemed to have forgotten me, having slipped into a world all their own. Lawrence sucked the wound on his finger for an instant and then offered his other arm to Daphne. She took hold of it and they strolled to the house.

I was left alone in the rose garden, pondering Daphne's gratitude. Had she thanked Lawrence for reminding her of their newfound freedom—or for creating it?

Could I be mistaken and Virgil the intended victim all along? It nearly made me dizzy, contemplating yet again how many people benefited from his demise, how many could now breathe more easily. There could be no denying Derrick was one of them, according to what Grace had told me about the Monroe and Andrews families' entwined fortunes.

I had just added Lawrence to the list, and even Daphne. She might not have been on the *Vigilant* that day, but that didn't mean she and Lawrence hadn't conspired. Would they have had a reason to kill Wyatt as well? Virgil's will hadn't yet been read, as it was still in transit with the family lawyer from New York. Perhaps, Lawrence being out of favor because of Daphne, Virgil had left the bulk of his estate to his brother instead of his elder son. If so, the fortune would probably revert back to Lawrence in the event of Wyatt's death.

Round and round I went, as if on a carousel but never grasping the brass ring. Perhaps it would always elude me. I wanted answers, but I also wanted to be entirely wrong about suspecting Lawrence and Daphne. The sun grew hot on my back, sending a trickle of perspiration between my shoulder blades. I followed their path back to the house. Just before I reached the covered loggia, movement in an upper window caught my attention. I glanced up to find Nate holding a curtain aside and staring out at me. Solemn-faced, he didn't wave. Well, he would be pleased with the results I'd achieved, once he learned of them.

Inside, a telephone rang from some distant room—an office, perhaps, or a service room. The bell set my teeth on edge, but this wasn't my house, or my call. Otherwise the house remained quiet, the open windows admitting a fresh, salty breeze to the airy rooms. My footsteps echoed in the stillness. I had served my purpose here, and I needed to find a servant who could arrange my ride home to Gull Manor.

In the entrance hall, a footman approached me. "Miss Cross?"

"Yes, that's me. I was looking for someone who might have a carriage sent round . . ."

"There is someone calling on the telephone for you. If you'll please come this way."

"Oh. Yes, thank you." Puzzled, I let him lead me past the dining room and into the butler's pantry, where a call box hung from the rear wall. The ear trumpet lay on the writing table beside the telephone. I picked it up, and the footman bowed and left the room.

"Hello? This is Emma Cross."

"Good afternoon, Emma, it's Gayla," said Newport's main daytime operator. "Hold on, I have Miss Wilson on the other end."

The line clicked a few times and then Grace's voice sounded in my ear. "Emma, I'm calling on behalf of Marianne. She came home from town a little while ago, and it's taken this long to track you down."

My heart sped up, then skipped a beat. "What is this about, Grace? Is it Neily? Or Uncle Cornelius? He isn't—"

"No, Emma, they're fine as far as I know, and Neily would have telephoned immediately had there been any developments concerning his father. Hold the line and I'll have Marianne explain."

I heard another click and a burst of static.

"Miss Cross?" Though the line continued to crackle and buzz, Marianne's English accent identified her to me.

"Yes, Marianne. Do you have information for me?"

"I do, indeed. I was in town today doing some shopping for Miss Wilson, when I was approached by a young lady—a girl, really, perhaps in her late teens. She would not tell me her name, nor anything about herself. By her clothing I judged she was not a person of quality, yet there was something in her manner, a deference, that led me to believe she might be a maid-servant."

This lengthy description mystified me. "What did she want?"

"To talk to you, Miss Cross."

"Why doesn't she contact me directly, then?"

"When I suggested the very same, she became downright agitated. She said she daren't approach you or go to your home, or contact you in any other way that might link her to you. But she said she had vital information, and gave me a time and a place where you and she might meet. This evening."

Vital information. Could she know something about Virgil Monroe's death, or . . .

"Oh, Marianne . . . do you think she has information about Robbie?"

"That was exactly my thought, Miss Cross, for what else could it be? She was no one I recognized from among the servants at the Beechwood gala, so I don't believe she could know anything about the boating accident other than what is public knowledge. No, I believe you are right. This person might be able to enlighten us about the child."

"Where am I supposed to meet her?"

Marianne hesitated. "I cannot say. Not over the phone, for she made me promise I would only tell you face-to-face. If you could come to Shady Lawn, or I'll meet you at your home—"

"No, I'll come directly there." I glanced down at the brass clock ticking away on the desk. Five o'clock. My pulse clamored in fits and starts. "Can you at least indicate *when* she wants to meet me? I don't want to miss her."

"Eight o'clock."

As the sun would be setting, I thought, and the shadows lengthening. Several more clicks in my ear reminded me that Marianne awaited my response. Into the mouthpiece I said, "I'll be there as soon as I can," and hung up.

"Excuse me," I called out, hoping to attract the footman's, or anyone's, attention. When no one came, I returned to the call box, lifted the ear trumpet once more, and tugged at the crank.

"Operator, how may I direct your call?"

"Gayla, it's Emma again. Will you connect me to Gull Manor, please?"

"Of course, dearie. One moment."

I spoke to Katie, and then to Brady. "I need you," I told him without explanation. "I'm at Beechwood and I need to get to Shady Lawn immediately."

"The Wilsons' place?"

"Yes, please harness Barney and hurry over to Beechwood."

"I'll do better than that. I'll call over for one of Cornelius's curricles and a sure-footed Cleveland Bay."

"I don't care if you come in a chariot drawn by unicorns, Brady. Just be here soon!"

Chapter 15

✦

"Alone? I don't think so, Em."

Brady and I stood on Shady Lawn's front veranda with Grace and Marianne. Marianne had explained the instructions the mystery girl had given her.

"I don't like it either," I said. "Along the railroad tracks north of the Point? There's nothing there." A chill skipped across my shoulders. "Nothing and no one except a few stray dogs looking for garbage tossed out of the train windows, poor things."

"At that time of night there won't even be any trains passing through." Grace was right. The tracks ran from Long Wharf to the northern tip of the island, where they crossed the narrowest point of the Sakonnet River and continued on to Tiverton, Providence, and ultimately, Boston. But service became sparse after five in the evening, and only ran on certain nights. "You mustn't go, Emma. It's too dangerous."

"I don't know what other choice I have." I glanced at the golden sunlight slanting through the trees. I would have to leave soon if I was going to arrive at the assigned meeting place at the correct time. "Her need for secrecy could simply be for

Robbie's protection. If she is the individual who left him on my doorstep, she went to a lot of trouble to ensure no one else knew about it. Perhaps she's ready now to tell me where he came from, but doing so openly might endanger her life . . . and possibly Robbie's."

"And what about yours?" Grace reached for my hand. "Do not go, Emma."

"I have to." I gave her hand a squeeze, trying to impart a measure of reassurance. "For Robbie's sake."

"I'm going with you, and no argument." Brady widened his stance like a boxer.

"I think that's a good idea." Marianne adjusted the brim of her squat straw hat and raised her chin. "And I'm going, too. The girl already knows my face, and if anything happens I can help Miss Cross get away while Mr. Gale fights them off."

Brady swung round to face her. "Fights off whom?"

"I don't know." Marianne shrugged and tossed up her hands. "Brigands. Whomever this girl is hiding from."

"Come to think of it," Brady said, "how did she know you?"

Marianne shook her head. "She would only say she had her ways."

"Servants have means of finding these things out," I said. "Enough debate. It's time to go."

"Emma, you can't!"

"It's all right, Grace. Brady, are you ready? Marianne, are you certain you want to be involved any further?"

Marianne nodded and opened her mouth to reply, but Grace spoke first. "Then I'm going, too."

"Oh, no, you are not." Brady, Marianne, and I spoke at once, an army of three against one. I smiled to soften the blow. "I've already put you in danger once, Grace, and that is more than enough. Neily would never forgive me if anything happened to you."

That seemed to mollify her. At any rate she reached her arms around me in a tight hug. "Be careful."

However nimbly Brady handled the reins, it took a good while to negotiate Uncle Cornelius's curricle through town. With evening came concerts, plays, dinner parties, and balls, and the fine carriages of the summer set clogged the roads. Nervously I watched the sun dip behind rooftops and bit my tongue to keep from crying out that we must go faster. We went as fast as we were able, but our trek seemed to take an eternity.

Eventually we left the bustle behind us. The Point lay quiet but for the occasional carriage or horseback rider, and the voices of people through windows or from back gardens. We continued traveling north, away from the Point, past the U.S. Naval War College on Coasters Harbor Island, along a bumpy, pitted road that ran parallel to the train tracks. We were far from any depot, and at this time of night the rails and their flanking embankments felt empty and abandoned.

"There!" Marianne pointed several dozen yards ahead, to a scrap of fabric tied to a scrub pine beside the tracks. It danced and fluttered with the breeze, a forlorn little flag of welcome. "She said that would be her marker, and that you should wait for her there."

I unclenched my hands in my lap. Was this some kind of trap? "Brady, stop the carriage here. I'll go the rest of the way on foot. Alone."

"Em . . ."

"No, it's all right. You'll be able to see me, but perhaps this way we won't frighten her off." I climbed down from the gig, weeds and twigs crunching beneath my feet, and looked up at them one more time in warning. "Stay here."

Why did it seem the farther I walked from the curricle, the darker the evening grew? Though the tracks were clear, the vegetation around me consisted of clumps of pine, waist-high tangles of weeds and thickets, and tall, overgrown shrubs whose faded blossoms drooped from the weight of the summer heat. I searched the shadows for any sign of movement while that scrap of fabric, a strip of calico from an old dress perhaps, beckoned me on.

"I said to come alone," a voice hissed across the tracks from me.

I stopped short and turned my head to find the source of the whisper, but there was only the gently swishing foliage. "Where are you? Please show yourself. I—I only brought my brother and Miss Reid. You've already spoken to her, so you must have found reason to trust her."

There was silence and then a rustling. Had she run away?

"Please, if you have information for me, I very much wish to hear it." Desperation reduced my voice to a feeble murmur. "Is it . . . is it about Robbie?"

"Robbie?" So she hadn't gone away after all.

"The child," I clarified, but went no further.

There was more rustling and then a figure in an ill-fitting, faded pink frock stepped out from behind some trees. I remained perfectly still while she slowly picked her way through the brush and then over the tracks. I watched her, afraid to even peek over my shoulder at Brady and Marianne. Afraid to breathe too loud for fear of frightening this wraith off.

She was indeed young, perhaps no more than sixteen, with straight dark hair pulled tightly back beneath an old-fashioned cloth bonnet. A wan face peeked out from beneath the brim, her eyes large. She reminded me of Clara Parker, a young chambermaid who until last summer worked for my aunt Alva at Marble House. But unlike with Clara Parker, this girl's face struck no spark of recognition. She was a stranger to me, which meant she could not hail from Newport.

"Who are you?" I asked, still whispering, and afraid any sudden noise or movement would send her scampering. Looking at her thin shoulders and narrow build, I almost felt silly for having brought Brady and Marianne along for protection.

"My name is Naomi." She pushed her bonnet back off her

face. "That's all you need to know. It's who I worked for that's important."

"And who is that?"

She touched a trembling hand to her lips, as if she didn't quite trust the power of her own voice. "Is it true what they say, that Virgil Monroe is dead? That he went into the water and never came out?"

"Yes, it's true." But was it? I continued to wonder, and even feared he might be hiding somewhere close by at that very moment. I guessed, however, that any doubt on my part would silence this girl, this child, forever. So I said nothing more and waited.

"Are you certain they can be trusted?" She poked her chin toward the curricle.

"With my life, and yours. I swear it."

Before she spoke another word, she held out her hand and uncurled her fingers. Across her palm stretched a piece of delicate lace, shot through with golden thread.

I drew a shaky breath.

"I brought him to you, Miss Cross. I'm not from here, but I'd heard of you. What you do at your home . . . at your Gull Manor . . . is known throughout Rhode Island. Farther, perhaps."

"And so you brought him to us because you knew he'd be safe," I said to encourage her. "But from what?"

"From his father. And from growing up in the orphanage I was instructed to bring him to."

"Naomi, was Virgil Monroe your employer?"

"He was."

"And was he Robbie's . . . that is . . . the child's father?"

"That I don't know for certain. Virgil Monroe hired me to care for a woman living across the island, in a house in Portsmouth. It was an isolated place, no neighbors in sight. The woman was in the family way, Miss Cross, nearly eight months gone when I met her, yet she did a good job of hiding it. Until the very last weeks she might have gone anywhere wrapped in a light cloak and no one would have guessed. Some women carry that way. My older sister did."

Eight months gone and hardly showing. That last time Judith had turned up at home—how long had she stayed? Derrick hadn't said. Had it been a brief stay before she left again?

"Can you tell me who the woman is?" Once again, I held my breath.

"I never knew her name, but was instructed by Mr. Monroe to address her always as madam. I never knew his name either, until I saw his photograph in a newspaper the day after he drowned." She shuddered. "He was not a good man, Miss Cross."

I let that go without debate. "So he hired you to be this woman's maid. What then?"

"I helped her deliver her child, and when Mr. Monroe deemed enough time had passed, he charged me with taking the infant to an orphanage in Tiverton. He gave me money for my troubles, but he also threatened me, told me to go directly there and then to go home and never tell anyone what I'd seen or done . . . or he would find me and make me sorry."

"How cruel. For you, the child, the mother . . ." My heart ached for that new mother whose child had been stolen from her. "How did she react?"

"Dreadfully. Her screams followed us as we drove away, until I put my hands over my ears because I couldn't bear it. I thought she'd die from grief."

"Good heavens." Tears pushed at my eyes.

Naomi's remained dry, and as hard as ice. "That devil Monroe, he said no one could ever know about the child, it would ruin them and their families."

What it would have ruined, I thought, was his being able to divorce his wife and leave her with nothing. "You said, '*We* drove away,'" I prompted, remembering the poor man shot along Ocean Avenue the morning Robbie came to Gull Manor. This could no longer be a coincidence, not that it ever was in my mind.

"I convinced Charlie to help me," she said. "He was supposed to take us off the island, but he had a heart, he wasn't like Mr. Monroe. We realized we were being followed to your house and Charlie decided to cut off Ocean Avenue. He did it where the road curves sharply and the other carriage wouldn't see us. We'd barely come to a stop when Charlie pushed me out with the baby. I fell onto my knees, and I could hear Charlie whispering at me to run, to hide somewhere off the road. Then I heard the other carriage pass by on Ocean Avenue. After that it's all a blur. I kept well to the side of the road while I made my way to your house. It was full dark by then, but I still feared being seen, that the other carriage would turn around and I'd be caught. No one passed me, though. Whoever followed us must have kept going. . . ."

"He did," I said bleakly. "He went on ahead, and when he realized your carriage was no longer in front of him, he must have stopped and waited for Charlie to turn back onto Ocean Avenue. He must have believed you and the baby were still in the carriage."

"Charlie's dead, isn't he, Miss Cross?" She hung her head and a quiet sob dissipated into the deepening twilight.

"I'm very sorry, Naomi."

"Oh, Charlie," she whispered, a tight, forlorn sound. She raised her chin, her cheeks shiny with tears. "Now that I've told you everything, I want to leave this place and never come back. I want to go home."

"Where have you been staying until now?"

"A boardinghouse in town. I spent all but the train fare I'll need to get home, but I stayed because I wanted to find a way to meet with you without anyone discovering us."

"And you have family to go to?" If not, I'd bring her to Gull Manor.

She nodded. "I just want to go home, Miss Cross. I wish I'd never left."

"I'll help you get home, Naomi. But first, can you describe the child's mother to me?"

The girl shrugged. "She was like any other society woman. Beautiful and stylish, even while carrying the child. She—"

An explosive *pop* and a burst of flame mere yards from the tracks sent me stumbling backward. A wave of hot sulfur shoved me to my knees. Brady's and Marianne's shouts fought with the ringing in my ears. My eyes stung and I blinked rapidly. A smoky haze lingered in the air, and through it I saw Naomi still standing, hovering, her face frozen in bewilderment.

Then her knees buckled. She collapsed to the ground and rolled onto her back.

I struggled to my feet. "Naomi?" I coughed, my throat stinging from the sulfur.

From behind me someone gripped my shoulders and pushed me face-first to the ground. "Stay down," Marianne shouted.

"Naomi's hurt," I shouted back, but Marianne used all of her weight to pin me in place. Leaves and pebbles dug into my cheek. I tasted soil on my lips.

From the corner of my eye I glimpsed Brady's dark form dashing across the tracks, heard the thrash of his footfalls through the foliage. He was shouting, cursing. The din he made receded farther and farther.

And then silence fell.

But only for the span of several breaths. Then Brady was shouting and running again, only this time it was toward me, not away.

"Em? My God, are you hurt? Were you shot? Em?"

I shoved my palms against the ground in an effort to rise. "I'm fine. I'm all right. Marianne, please."

She rolled off me, sat up, and helped me do the same. The moment I was upright I scrambled on all fours across the ground . . . to Naomi, immobile on her back, staring wide-eyed up at the sky. Even in the dark I saw the insidious dark stain spreading across her chest.

"Miss Cross?" Her voice rattled in her throat, emerging as a weak croak.

"It's all right, Naomi. Don't speak. We'll take care of you." I lifted her hand in mine and felt the tide of warmth recede from her fingers. She remained focused on the sky. I leaned over her. "Naomi, listen to me. Keep listening. I'll send my brother for help, but I'll stay here with you, I won't leave you. . . ."

A pair of hands gently grasped my shoulders. "Em. It's too late. She's gone."

"No! She's not . . . she's . . ." But Brady was right. Though Naomi's eyes remained open, they no longer saw the sky or anything else. Her lips were parted but would never make another sound.

Bile rose up inside me and I scrambled again, this time dragging myself through the dirt as far as I could before my stomach emptied itself into the weeds.

Marianne followed, reaching to grasp the hair that had come loose from my coif and hold it away from my face. In a minute it was over. I was drained, empty but for the grief stabbing into my heart.

I sat up again and when I would have wiped a sleeve across my mouth, Marianne handed me a handkerchief. "It's clean," she whispered, and again stroked stray hairs back from my face. In her other hand she grasped my hat, which had fallen off at some point.

Brady stood a few feet away, looking ghostly pale in the rising glow of the moon. "Em?" He seemed to grope for words and found none, merely fisted a hand and bowed his head.

With Marianne's help I rose on shaky legs. We stood side by side, our arms around each other, my weight supported by her. I'm certain I would have fallen otherwise. Brady crouched beside Naomi and gently straightened her arms and legs, smoothed her skirts, and folded her hands together on her belly. Then he removed his coat and laid it over her.

"And the person who did this?" I asked in a small voice.

"Gone. I didn't get a good look at him." He gazed into the darkness across the tracks.

"He somehow followed us here," I said dully, numbly.

Brady shook his head. "I don't see how anyone could have without us noticing."

"Then he must have been following me from earlier . . . maybe for days." The attack on Neily and me on the *Vigilant*— had someone known we would be there? And Wyatt's murder at the hospital. Again, it was as if someone had known he would be there at that exact time. But who? Who had been clever enough to see all while not being detected? How had I been so blind, so oblivious? Even when I thought someone had been watching me, I all but dismissed it. And now this. . . .

"If only she hadn't worn that light color." Marianne pointed down at Naomi's pale pink hem trailing from under Brady's coat. "It made her too visible against the darkness. He might have missed her if she had worn brown or black or . . ."

"It's my fault." My voice shook, verging on hysteria. "I caused this."

"How is it your fault?" Brady thrust his fingers through his hair.

"I never should have agreed to meet her here. I shouldn't have come. If I had stayed away, she wouldn't have told her secrets and she would still be alive." Tears fell, brisk and hot against my cheeks. "Why was I so stupid, so selfish? I should have left well enough alone, or sent the police here to meet her. I—"

Two strides brought Brady to me. He gripped my shoulders and shook me none-too-gently. "Stop it, Emmaline!"

Brady rarely called me anything but Em. Occasionally Emma, but never Emmaline. I fell silent, my tears still flowing, Brady's face a streaky blur filling my vision. He was speaking, but it took a moment for the words to register.

"Whoever did this was waiting for his chance. Don't you see, Em? First the driver, then Wyatt Monroe, and now this girl. Everyone who knew about Robbie. Someone is silencing them one by one."

I rubbed the tears from my cheeks. "You think Wyatt knew about Robbie?"

"We all know about Robbie," Marianne whispered. She darted a gaze over the surrounding trees, along the tracks. "Are we next?"

Brady raised his chin, his ears pricked. "We're alone here now, I'm sure of it, and I don't think whoever it was will be back. We need to take care of . . ."

"Naomi," I supplied. "Her name was Naomi. She has a family somewhere. All she wanted was to go home." My throat closed painfully.

"Em, you and Marianne take the curricle into town and alert the police. I'll stay here with Naomi."

I thought to protest; I didn't want Brady out here alone. When I hesitated he again gripped my shoulders and brought his face close to mine. "I'll be fine, Em. We can't leave her here alone, lying on the ground. Don't argue, just go."

He was right. Leaving the poor girl here alone would have been callous and disrespectful. But we wouldn't need to be gone long. "We don't have to go as far as town," I said. "Derrick installed a telephone, and there's an officer guarding his house besides."

Marianne and I hurriedly retraced our steps. Marianne took the reins; I doubt I could have managed it. Yet, as we reentered the familiar surroundings of the Point, my brain began to work again.

"Judith Kingsley may be in danger."

"Mr. Andrews's sister?" Marianne asked. "How is she in danger?"

"Because she's Robbie's mother. I'm almost certain of it."

Marianne gasped.

"All this time I believed it must be Daphne Gordon. But Naomi said Robbie's mother barely showed her pregnancy until the very last weeks. And Derrick told me his sister acted erratically all winter and spring, and that she continually disappeared without a word of explanation. The last time he saw her was about two months ago. She would have been barely seven months along and able to hide her belly beneath her clothing." I turned on the seat to face Marianne. "And most telling of all, Judith Kingsley was furious with Virgil Monroe. I witnessed it at the ball, and I've also witnessed her bizarre behavior. Before she died, Naomi confirmed it was Virgil who hired her to take care of Robbie's mother and bring her child to an orphanage. She said the mother was distraught. Her screams followed them as they drove away with the baby."

"God forgive me," Marianne murmured, "but I'm glad the man is dead."

"Is he?" Our gazes met, hers shocked, mine steady. We were coming up on Walnut Street. "Turn here."

She returned her attention to the road and stopped where I indicated in front of the house. The street was quiet but for the melodic strains from a gramophone drifting from a neighbor's house. Nothing appeared unusual, yet a sense of foreboding gripped me. And then I realized.

The sidewalk in front of my childhood home lay vacant. "Where is the policeman? There's supposed to be one here at all times."

"Inside perhaps?"

I glanced up at the windows of the second-floor apartment. The electric wall sconces Derrick had installed appeared to be on. Bright light filled the room, yet I detected no shadows or movement of any sort within.

"It's too still," I said. We climbed down from the rig.

"Miss Cross—over there."

My gaze followed the line of Marianne's outstretched finger. A mound of . . . something . . . lay beside the box hedge that ran between this house and the one next door.

The mound took shape as we hurried over—arm and legs, a torso lying facedown. The blue uniform confirmed that we had found the missing policeman. We sank to our knees beside him. I reached out, then yanked my hands back.

"Oh, Marianne, I don't think I can bear another . . ."

"I'll do it."

She leaned to take hold of the officer's shoulders, and suddenly I was thrust back to the previous summer when I had performed a similar task beneath Uncle Cornelius's bedroom balcony at The Breakers. The result had not been a happy one then. . . .

The policeman's arm moved, and he moaned as Marianne rolled him onto his back. I released a great breath of relief and fell back on my heels. Marianne helped the man sit up.

"Are you all right, sir?"

"I think so—ow!" He touched the back of his neck. "Someone hit me from behind . . . Miss Cross, is that you?"

"Officer Dunlap?" I recognized him now, one of the newer men on the force. "Did you see anything?"

"No, help me up, please."

Marianne and I each took an arm and steadied Tom Dunlap until he achieved his feet and caught his balance. He rubbed his neck again. Then he broke away from us and hurried over to the front of the house.

"If you're worried about Mr. Andrews," I began, intending to reassure him that his charge would not have slipped away. Before I could speak another word footsteps echoed against the clapboards. I turned to find the source and bit back a gasp. "Derrick," I whispered instead.

Officer Dunlap heard his approach and whirled about. My heart hit my throat as he reached for his sidearm, but his hand came up empty.

"Where is it, Andrews?" Officer Dunlap assumed a half crouch, his fists readied for a fight. "Ladies, get back in your carriage and go. I'll handle him."

"I'm sure you're quite wrong about this," I blurted.

"Listen here, Officer." Derrick held up his hands, as empty as the policeman's. "I heard something, and when I looked out the window I saw you on the ground and the figure of a man dragging you to those bushes. I ran down to help, but by the time I reached the street whoever attacked you was gone. I thought I heard him running, so I took after him."

"I'll bet you didn't find him, did you?" Officer Dunlap said, more an accusation than a question.

"No, I didn't."

"Didn't think so. Miss Cross, go inside and call the station, please."

"Officer Dunlap," I said, "if Mr. Andrews attacked you, does it make any sense that he would have returned?"

The man thought for several tense seconds. "It does, if he thought he might make it back before I regained consciousness." He narrowed his gaze on Derrick. "Where's my weapon?"

"I don't know."

"You're lying."

"Officer Dunlap, please . . ."

"Emma, go in and call the station," Derrick said evenly. "Please."

"I . . ." I couldn't move, couldn't think what to do next,

what to say to convince Officer Dunlap that Derrick hadn't done anything wrong. That he was telling the truth.

Marianne placed an arm around my shoulders. "We came here to call the police, Miss Cross. We had better do it."

"Wait!" The policeman's order stopped us halfway up the steps to the door. "What does she mean, you came here to call the police? Why?"

I stared at the ground. "Something happened," I started, but stopped. How to explain that a young woman lay dead only minutes away?

I didn't have to. Marianne's protective arm tightened around me. "There was an incident. I'm surprised you didn't hear—it wasn't all that far away. A woman is dead. Shot."

The policeman's expression turned hard as stone. Derrick's chest rose and fell, and he quietly repeated, "Call the station, Emma."

Chapter 16

I made the telephone call that set the police in motion. Jesse told me under no uncertain terms that Marianne and I must not venture back to that lonely spot along the railroad tracks, but assured me a team of policemen would arrive there in a matter of minutes. I asked him to send an officer out to Gull Manor, then telephoned Nanny at home.

"Lock all the doors and windows," I told her. "And don't open to anyone unless you know who it is, and that you can fully trust them."

No doubt remained that Robbie was connected to the recent slew of deaths, and while part of me could not envision anyone hurting an innocent babe, Naomi's cold-blooded murder had taught me different. I longed to go home and protect Robbie myself, but there were matters here I needed to attend to. Besides, Nanny would safeguard that child to her dying breath, if it came to that. So would Katie, and I believed Stella would prove equally valiant. No, I could trust my formidable female army while I set my efforts toward helping to eliminate the threat once and for all.

Jesse arrived on Walnut Street with a handful of uniformed officers in tow. I wasted no time in confronting him with what in my mind were straightforward facts.

"Derrick could not have shot that poor girl. The timing is all off. Only a magician could have incapacitated Officer Dunlap, stolen his weapon, murdered Naomi, and made it back here at the same time Marianne and I arrived. Officer Dunlap would have been unconscious for more than half an hour."

Jesse's eyes softened in sympathy, but his jaw remained resolute. "It's possible, Emma. A forceful enough blow can render a man out cold for an indeterminate length of time."

"Can't you see this was an obvious attempt to make Derrick *appear* guilty of shooting that poor girl?" Jesse still didn't look convinced, but I hadn't finished. "There's another reason Derrick could not have shot Naomi. I stood close by, and he would not have risked hitting me." I raised my chin. My disclosure, with its reminder of Derrick's past affections for me, undoubtedly hurt Jesse. I was sorry for that, but necessity outweighed diplomacy.

He didn't react except to say, "Come with me." He drew me into Derrick's small kitchen and gestured for Marianne to follow. Once there it became clear to me he had nothing more to add to the debate, but merely wished to remove me from the procedure I had failed to prevent.

"Derrick Andrews, you are under arrest for the murder of an unidentified female. . . ."

"Her name is Naomi," I called into the main room. Tears of frustration squeezed past my efforts to contain them. "He's innocent. Jesse, you know he's innocent."

"I'm sorry, Emma, but I don't know anything at the moment."

The heavy clank of iron handcuffs reverberated like gunshot in my ears.

"Is that necessary?" I snapped. "He didn't attempt to escape even though Officer Dunlap didn't have a weapon to keep him from running away."

"It's procedure, I'm afraid." Jesse removed his bowler and whisked a sleeve across his brow.

"I need to speak to him before you take him away."

"I can't allow that."

I crossed my arms in front of me, my features so tight with anger they ached. Jesse made a noise in his throat and tossed up a hand. "Five minutes."

"Alone, please." I pushed my luck, but the worst he could do was deny my request.

He didn't answer, but a moment later he and Marianne vacated the kitchen. Derrick and I occupied the two chairs facing each other across the small table.

I was not about to waste those few minutes Jesse had granted me. "Was Judith having an affair?"

In the ensuing silence I feared he would refuse to answer. He drummed his fingers on the tabletop and met my gaze. "Yes, I believe so. It would explain her disappearances."

"Could that affair have been with Virgil Monroe?"

His cheeks immediately blazed as if I'd struck him. "What? No!" He frowned and glanced down. "I don't think so. . . . Good God."

"Derrick, that's not all. The day before Mrs. Astor's ball, someone left a baby, an infant, on my doorstep." He jolted back in his chair. I hurried on. "Again and again, all evidence led me to the Monroes. The girl who died tonight, Naomi, told me Virgil Monroe had hired her to wait on a pregnant woman— one who barely showed her condition until the very last weeks. Is it possible . . . ?" I couldn't complete the question, but Derrick's dawning look of horror told me he had followed the train of my thoughts.

"Judith . . . and Virgil?" He shook his head, but not in de-

nial. "It would explain her behavior these past months, her elu-
siveness, her defensiveness."

"And her recent hostilities," I added, remembering the many
times she had deliberately attempted to offend me, as well her implied accusations against Derrick. "Naomi told me when Virgil
ordered her to take the baby away, the woman's grief was ex-
treme. Your sister, if she is indeed the mother, has been living
under a terrible, desperate burden."

"My God, I have a nephew . . . *might* have . . ." Gripping the
table's edges, he came to his feet. "I have to go to her." He
darted a gaze about the room, as if searching for an escape
route.

"You can't."

"I must. She's my sister."

"You can't, Derrick, but I can."

"There's a murderer on the loose, Emma."

"All the more reason for me to warn your sister. I'll convince
Jesse to go with me," I added when he seemed about to oppose
the idea again. "According to Naomi, the mother has no idea
where the baby was taken, and Naomi was afraid to approach
her directly for fear of endangering everyone involved. If I tell
Judith what I know, and that her child has been sheltering in
my home, she might be willing to speak with me."

"And then what?"

"And then she can speak to the police. She can at least provide you with an alibi the day you left the island." Once again a
protest rose up in him, his complexion turning fiery. "Derrick,
stop being a martyr. Your sister is an adult, albeit a troubled
one. I understand she is bound to be fragile right now, but
don't you think reuniting her with her child will allow her to
heal? To become something of her old self again? And do you
honestly believe seeing you go to prison for crimes you didn't
commit will help her?"

He looked at me sadly. "There is no resolution to this where no one will be hurt."

"I'm afraid that is something we have to accept." I stood and circled the table to stand close to him. "And there is the child. By accepting what happened to Judith and not judging her harshly, your family will be saving that little boy. At Gull Manor, we've been calling him Robbie." I smiled.

He smiled back, his eyes filling with moisture. Blinking, he tapped a forefinger against my chin, just a slight touch that traveled through me. "Quite right."

Jesse poked his head into the room, making me wonder if he had been listening in and waiting for us to reach a conclusion before interrupting. "It's time."

Derrick calmly walked out of the kitchen before I could say good-bye to him; before I could convey any message, even the silent one pressing against my heart. But when Jesse also turned to leave, I stopped him.

"Let your men take Derrick in. We have important business elsewhere."

"You realize this only makes him look guiltier." Jesse held my hand and helped me down into the U.S. Life-Saving Service boat, a small, two-sailed steamer.

I nodded. "I believe that's why he didn't say good-bye when your men took him away. If his sister gave birth to Virgil Monroe's child, Derrick would certainly have a motive to commit murder."

"Not once, but all three times, Emma. The first out of revenge, the other two to silence the people who knew his sister's secret."

"You don't need to elaborate. I'm well aware of the implications. He's innocent." I turned my head to look out over the water as we pushed away from Long Wharf.

"I'm sorry."

"I know."

"If it were me, would you have this kind of faith in my inno-cence?"

My answer came without hesitation. "Of course I would. Some things you can know without a shred of evidence."

We cleared the other boats moored along the wharf. "The more truth that comes to light," I said, "the closer we come to finding the real killer. Or killers."

Jesse frowned. "Plural?"

"I don't know . . . I'm still not convinced Virgil is dead. With everything that's happened, he has the most motive to have killed Naomi." I shivered. "He probably would have killed me, too, if Brady and Marianne hadn't come running. It's possible he didn't realize they were with me."

"You're talking as if it's a foregone conclusion that Virgil Monroe is responsible for all of this."

I let out a humorless laugh. "In a way, alive or dead, he *is* re-sponsible."

Suddenly I no longer had Jesse's attention. He had shifted on his seat across from me. Face raised, he inhaled. "Do you smell smoke?"

I sniffed the air. "No."

Jesse glanced at the pilot, who shook his head.

"It's probably coming from one of the dockside taverns," I suggested. "Someone is always burning something in those kitchens."

Jesse only narrowed his eyes and continued to scent the air. "You must be right. I don't smell it now."

We were well out into the harbor by now, away from the many vessels crowded together along the wharves. *Lavinia's Sun* rose up in front of us, three decks tall above the waterline and crowned by three masts and a rotund stack that released the steam when they relied on coal to power the ship. Except for lights shining behind the lower portholes, a dark stillness claimed the vessel.

"I think you should wait here." Jesse carefully came to his feet as the pilot pulled alongside the hull.

"And how do you think Mrs. Andrews and her daughter will react to a man boarding their ship unannounced, and in the dark no less? From the looks of things, they've already retired for the night."

He paused, making a wry face. "All right. But at the first sign of danger I want you to make your way back here."

"What danger? Judith Kingsley's temper is volatile, true, but even at her worst she didn't threaten me with bodily harm. And when I explain to her why we've come, she'll very likely—" I broke off, inhaling. I couldn't be certain, but a sharpness in the air stung my nose. "Jesse, about that smoke you thought you smelled . . . I'm not sure, but . . ."

He handed me to my feet, and the two of us stood side by side, our heads raised. "Could also be a burnt pot roast down in the galley, or a loaf of bread."

I nodded. The pilot lifted a reflective lantern from the deck of the boat. "We can't take any chances. I'm going to signal the station to be at the ready."

Jesse and I climbed the starboard steps to the mezzanine deck. Polished, flawless teak gleamed in the moonlight. At first all seemed secure, but then the thinnest of wisps curled about our noses. I muffled a sneeze in my hand.

"Emma, go back down to the boat."

"It could still be something burning in the galley. But to be safe we need to warn everyone on board."

Jesse nodded and leaned down over the side to attract the pilot's attention. "Sound the alarm. Better safe than sorry."

A second later a sharp clanging rose from the water.

"If there *is* a fire it's most likely below," Jesse said to me, raising his voice above the clamor. Already we heard shouts from the lower decks. "I'll go down and help people out. You look for Mrs. Andrews and Mrs. Kingsley, and any servants who might be on the upper decks."

I started to move away, but he caught my wrist. "Please be careful. I couldn't bear it if anything happened to you." With that he pulled me into a hug. It lasted only an instant before he released me and started down the nearest set of steps.

I stood for a moment longer, dazed by the lingering phantasm of Jesse's regard. Then another acrid wisp jarred me from my thoughts and set me in motion. I tried to remember what little layout of the ship I'd observed on my first visit here. Were the staterooms on this level, as they were on Uncle William's yacht? With no hints in the form of lighted windows to guide me, I chose the closest door, opened it, and discovered a library within. Empty, but for the books lining the shelves.

I moved on, finally reaching the aft saloon, where I had met Judith when I came to deliver Derrick's message to her. The room lay dark and still, despite the disquieting memory of Judith's violent tirade.

Judith's violent tirade.

As I made my way around the stern, a new thought took hold. If Derrick had motive to commit murder, didn't Judith as well? Perhaps even more so. Virgil had taken her child away from her. I wondered, could she have persuaded Wyatt to carry out her revenge on Robbie's father—there was little love lost between the brothers—and then killed him, and Naomi, to protect her secret?

If she witnessed Naomi talking to me, then she would know where to find Robbie.

Icy fingers clutched my heart. Thank goodness I'd called Nanny to warn her of possible danger, and that Jesse had sent an officer out to protect the house.

I continued past the aft saloon, which stretched around to the port side, and shook my head at the jumble of theories I'd concocted. Daphne and Lawrence as Robbie's parents. Virgil, still alive. Now Judith, a murderess. In truth I knew only two facts. That Virgil had hired Naomi and paid her to take Robbie away from his mother. All else was conjecture.

Finally, I came to another door. I tried turning the knob, but it moved only slightly before clicking to a stop. Locked, which meant someone must be inside. From around the ship the bell continued clanging. Below me, on the lower decks, came the sounds of voices, tramping feet, and fists knocking on doors. I heard no indication of rising panic, merely an ordered procession as the staff and crew prepared to disembark if the need arose. Perhaps they were assisting Jesse in the search for fire. From this side of the ship I could no longer see the shore, but search beams skimmed the waves out beyond both stem and stern. Other U.S. Life-Saving Service vessels must be arriving. And a good thing, too. The smell of smoke was stronger here, and I thought I detected sooty tendrils rising out over the water from somewhere below me.

I pounded on the door. "Open up! There's an emergency! You must leave the ship!"

The door opened immediately, and Mrs. Andrews stood in a dressing gown buttoned to her chin. "What on earth is all that clanking about? Is there a fire?" Her beautiful features were taut with alarm, but then alarm melted into anger. "Miss Cross, is it? Is this your idea of a joke?"

"Mrs. Andrews, you must come at once. There may indeed be a fire on board."

"Where is my ship's captain? My lady's maid? Why haven't they come to assist me?" She pressed her hands over her ears. "Make them silence that infernal bell. Oh, if you don't go away at once I'll scream for help."

"Scream all you want, but you must come with me now." With the greatest difficulty I tamped down my growing impatience. "Mrs. Andrews, can you conceive of a single reason why

I would have rowed out to this yacht at what by now must be near the middle of the night merely to vex you?"

After a hesitation she stepped out onto the deck and sniffed the air. "Good heavens, you aren't lying! Where is it coming from?"

"I don't know. Please, Mrs. Andrews, you must come with me. There are boats waiting to take you away from here."

"I need to dress first. I'll ring for my maid. . . ."

I bit back a roar of frustration. "Mrs. Andrews, with any luck your maid has already left the ship."

"Without me?"

"Detective Whyte of the Newport Police would have insisted she, and all the other staff, leave at once. As you must do."

To forestall any further argument, I put aside all pretense of deference and seized her wrist. "We are going. Now."

Her cries filled my ears, but I didn't listen as I half dragged, half pulled her back around the aft saloon to the starboard side of the vessel. The bell clanged louder here, but once again I noted the air on this side seemed fresher, lighter. I no longer doubted the presence of fire, or that it originated on the port side. But how much longer would it be contained there?

Below us, staff members were swinging themselves from the lower decks onto the outer steps that led down to the water, where three Life-Saving Service cutters were slowly filling with individuals, some in their various uniforms, others in wrappers and nightshirts. Mrs. Andrews and I had nearly reached the steps when she tugged for all she was worth, surprising me with her strength and yanking free of my hold.

She backed away, her beautiful features twisted and bordering on feral. "Have you not heard a word I've said?"

In truth, I hadn't.

"I'm not going anywhere without my daughter. She's on the deck below us." With that, she turned toward the inner staircase.

I bolted forward and headed her off. "Mrs. Andrews, please go down to the rescue boats. I'll find your daughter." She was shaking her head at me, so I added, "I can move faster than you."

The staircase vibrated with footsteps, and a moment later Jesse emerged from the darkness below. "Emma, Mrs. Andrews, come. I believe we've almost got everyone off."

"Did you find Mrs. Kingsley?" I asked at the same time Mrs. Andrews shouted her daughter's name. She reached out to press a hand to the wall behind her.

"She hasn't been found yet. I'll keep looking."

"Oh, my daughter . . ." Mrs. Andrews's knees gave way beneath her and she slid down the wall to the deck.

"Jesse, take her—get her off the boat. I'll find Judith."

"No, Emma—"

"Please, just do it," I shouted. "I can't help her down the steps, I'm not strong enough to support her and we could both end up falling." I crouched and brought my face close to the sobbing woman's. "Mrs. Andrews, which cabin is Judith's?"

"Judith . . ." She fell into a fit of coughing, brought on more by her agitation, I judged, than by the presence of smoke. Just as I was about to take my chances and blindly search for her daughter, she recovered. "Port side, just below mine. Hurry. Please."

I bounded down the staircase. At the next level down I made for the stern and hurried around. Unlike the entirely open walkway of the mezzanine deck, the stern here was an enclosed, curving corridor, only open at its two ends. Smoke drifted in gauzy clouds, barely visible, yet my eyes and throat began to sting. I slowed long enough to struggle out of my carriage jacket and use it to cover my nose and mouth. Moments later I passed through a doorway and emerged to the open walkway on the port side and the relief of the harbor breeze.

Flickering radiance poured from the windows of the first cabin I came to. Instinctively I swerved to the railing, as far away from the glass as possible. In intense heat the panes would shatter. Yet I tried to peer in through gaps in the smoldering curtains. Was Judith inside? Was this her cabin? The door stood slightly ajar, the frame splintered as if it had been kicked in. Whirling smoke streamed through, pooling at my feet. Fearfully, I move closer to the door.

"Mrs. Kingsley? Are you in there?"

A scream from another cabin farther on carried on the breeze to dissipate over the water. I broke into a run.

Chapter 17

✦

I came to the cabin directly below Mrs. Andrews's. Another scream echoed inside. Was Judith trapped by flames? Did her room connect to the one I had passed? Before moving to the door, I peered at the windows, covered by heavy curtains. Some kind of light emanated from within. Lamplight? Or flames?

I dropped my carriage jacket and gingerly reached for the door, tapping the knob with my fingertips first to test the metal. Still cool. Holding my breath, I gripped it thoroughly, and to my great relief the door offered no resistance. I shoved inward and crossed the threshold.

Two things registered in my mind immediately. Plumes of smoke spiraled toward the ceiling, and Judith stood pressed into the far corner of the cabin, wedged in by the wall on one side and her bed on the other. Small flames, newly set by the looks of them, leaped over the bedclothes, curling the edges and sizzling against the satin. In the few seconds I watched, licks of flame spiked up the walls above the draped headboard, quickly spreading to consume costly carved woodwork. I shouted to Judith, but her gaze didn't find me. Her sights remained riveted on a spot directly in front of her, off to my left.

A man stood within the foggy vapors that swirled like a silver cape around him. He stretched out an arm to aim an accusing finger at Judith while his lips hurled obscenities at her.

My heart pounded violently. *Virgil.*

In his other hand, a lighted torch emitted streams of curling black soot. The odor of kerosene warred with charring wood and fabrics. I searched for a weapon, anything to knock Virgil down and allow Judith a path to the door. He stood between me and the hearth, where I might have snatched up the long-handled shovel or tongs. Then I saw it—an old-fashioned bed warmer, ornate silver with a long ebony handle, hanging on the wall behind him. I inched toward it.

In that instant, my movement must have caught Judith's attention. Her eyes opened wider, but somehow she had the presence of mind not to give me away. Vigil was still shouting at her, still swearing and accusing. His exact words eluded me as the flames leaped to an area rug and then a tablecloth. It didn't matter. What mattered was Virgil's impassioned rage keeping him distracted one more moment.

My fingers closed around the ebony and silver inlaid handle, but the object didn't simply lift away from the wall. Whoever had hung it had seen fit to secure it snugly. I had to tug, tug again, while the growing heat and smoke began to threaten my consciousness. I heard Judith coughing, but a quick look revealed her holding a trailing sleeve over her nose and mouth. Virgil waved his torch in front of her, his laughter and curses coming in shrieks like nails on a chalkboard.

I gave another heave, putting all my strength into it. The bed warmer ripped away from the wall, taking bits of paneling with it. Splinters flew like spittle into the air. One bounced against Virgil's shoulder. He flinched and turned to find the source of the tiny assailant. I saw his face at the same time I swung the pan of the warmer into the side of his head. His knees buckled and he fell. It was then I had my first good look at him.

No lines marred the smoothness of youthful features. It wasn't Virgil. It was Nate.

I had not a second to ponder this revelation. Instinct guided me over the sprawled body, a wide stride that almost compromised my balance and sent me stumbling into the flaming bed. By some miracle I remained upright and kept going until I was able to grasp Judith's outstretched hand.

The contact seemed to spark her into action, for I didn't have to coax her to move as I'd done with her mother. Hand in hand we picked our way to the door, sidestepping a burning chair, smoldering pillows . . . and Nate Monroe's prone form. The flames crept perilously close to him, and I looked back to see the edge of his coat ignite, victim of the torch he had used to start the fire.

Judith remained my first priority. She was coughing uncontrollably, nearly doubling over, and I could discern from the way she tightened her grip that she could no longer see where we were going. I took over. As we reached the door I wrapped an arm across her shoulders and, bent at the waist, we lunged for the railing. Here, at least, there was air to breathe, though smoke poured through the doorway after us. With a shove I started us moving again, following the railing down the length of the ship. Along the way we passed another smoldering cabin. Nate must have taken no chances. He had wished to send *Lavinia's Sun* to a fiery hell, and Judith with it.

"Are there port-side steps leading down?" I shouted. Even if those steps led us to the water and nothing more, I deemed the harbor safer than the burning ship and I daren't take the time to circle back to the starboard side.

Judith nodded and pointed. "That way."

At the same time, a cry came from below. I peered down, searching the waves. "Oh, thank heavens."

A cutter sat far below us, directing its searchlight at the port-side steps and guiding our way. Not far from it, a small skiff bobbed, dark and lonely in the waves. Nate's transportation here? Farther out, a fireboat—a steam tug equipped with pumps and hoses—cut a wide berth as it turned to approach *Lavinia's Sun*.

A figure made his way up the steps toward us, crablike in the darkness.

"Come," I said. "Let's start down."

Judith didn't need further coaxing. We opened the gate at the railing and more nimbly than I would have expected, she swung herself onto the top step and grabbed hold of the hemp banisters on either side. She didn't hesitate in starting down, or in gathering her voice past her raw throat and calling hoarsely to the man climbing up to meet her. He shouted a reassurance in return. He carried a blanket, no doubt dampened with sea-water, over his shoulder. In the event sparks began spewing from the boat, this would prevent us from being singed.

I, however, did hesitate, and when Judith realized I wasn't behind her she stopped and looked up at me.

"Miss Cross, what are you doing? Why aren't you coming?" Half of her words were swept away by the wafting breaths of the fire, but I understood her well enough. Even so, I couldn't set my feet on the steps. Not yet.

"I have to try!" I shouted back, my only further explanation conveyed by my actions. I moved away from the railing and retreated toward her cabin. She screamed at me. I heard the sound of my name—my first name. But I couldn't turn back. I had to try. . . .

I had only been gone a couple of minutes, yet flames all but consumed the cabin now. The heat pushed at me like a furnace blast. The sensation terrified me and called upon all my in-stincts to run to safety. But a path still existed from the door-way to the young man lying on the floor. Gathering my skirts close around me, I drew a deep breath, held it, and pressed through the smoke. I sensed rather than saw when I'd reached Nate, and in that moment I realized he had awakened. He stared up at the ceiling, his eyes blazing as intensely as the flames nipping at his cloak and outer clothing. His trousers—his legs. The odor of burning flesh nearly sickened me, but I bit back my nausea and screamed out his name.

His face twitched, his eyelids fluttered, but otherwise he gave no sign of hearing or understanding. Certainly he made no move to escape the inferno. Desperately I looked about for something to smother the fire. Little remained of the bed. I remembered my carriage jacket, dropped in a heap outside the door, but it would be no match for the spreading flames. Turning to the window, I grabbed an edge of the damask curtain and tugged until the rod came tumbling down. I fell on my knees beside Nate and beat the balled-up fabric at his legs, his right arm.

This all passed within seconds. He made no move to help me or to save himself. If I remained in the cabin any longer, we'd both die. The heat of the flames assured me of that. With one last effort, I seized his arm—the one that had not been burned—and put my weight into dragging him across the floor. He half lay on an area rug and this made my task easier. But he was nearly full grown, and his weight far outdid my strength, or should have. How I managed I would never fully understand, but somehow I hauled him clear of the doorway and along the deck toward the outer steps.

Like a phantom rising from the grave, he suddenly came alive. The strength I had harnessed now failed me. His wrist pulled violently out of my hand and he rolled, coming up on all fours and struggling to his feet. His legs swayed and wobbled. Pain contorted his features. His watering, reddened eyes continued to burn as brightly as the fire.

"Nate, please, come with me. We've got to get off the ship."

His gaze searched the skies over the harbor. His cheeks were soot blackened, and what skin showed through was scarlet and blistered. "Father, I tried my best."

"Nate! Listen to me!" I bounded forward, but he was too quick and lurched out of reach, at the same time holding up his charred arm to shield himself as if from attack. From down the deck, at the stop of the steps, came a shout. My name. An entreaty to move.

Jesse.

I glanced over my shoulder for the briefest instant, and in that moment Nate darted back to Judith's cabin.

"Nate, no!" My shout tore painfully from my smoke-roughened throat. I felt shredded inside, burned and half-dead.

Nate paused in the doorway, the angry orange glow inside framing him as though he were a demon at the gates of hell. "I continued his work," he shouted in a voice that grated like steel claws. "He can see me. He approves of me now. They betrayed him, and I've made it right. All of them. They got what they deserved."

"No, Nate. Please." I started forward, but arms locked around me from behind, pulling me away.

"The fireboat can't start spraying until you're out of the way," Jesse pleaded in my ear. He forcefully turned me about. In my last glimpse of Nate, he turned as calmly as a man without a care in the world and walked into the flames.

Blind instinct must have taken over then, for I can conjure no memory of descending to the waiting cutter. I have only Jesse's assurance that I did so by the power of my own two legs, and that my resilience made him proud.

Once ensconced in the safety of the rescue boat, someone tucked a blanket around my shoulders. I'd lost my carriage jacket somewhere back on the ship, and I'd been shivering beneath my cotton blouse. I found myself pressed up against Judith's side. Her mother sat at Judith's other side along the built-in wooden bench, and she reached over to cover our clasped hands with her own. This newfound affection served to heighten my disorientation and my sense of bewilderment. Were they not the very same women who had scoffed at me these many days?

I didn't have the energy—or the heart—to be angry with them or even skeptical of their present motives. It was enough that we were alive. The rest could be sorted out later.

Jesse asked us a few questions about what we had witnessed on the yacht.

"It was Nate Monroe," I said numbly. "Nate all along."

Arrow-like, Jesse's brows drew inward. "He admitted this to you?"

"In so many words, yes. I don't understand it all yet. . . . I don't know why, but Nate said he did it for his father."

"For Virgil? Then who killed Virgil? Wyatt?" Jesse, crouched on the floor before me, sat back on his heels. "I thought we'd have our answer. Instead, we have more questions."

Again, I decided we would sort it out later. Judith had fallen silent during Jesse's questions, letting me do the talking for her. An odd tremor passed from her side into mine, one that suggested she perhaps knew something the rest of us didn't.

"Don't argue with me once we return to town," Jesse said when we put into Long Wharf. He leaped onto the pier before the crewmen had a chance to extend the gangway. Once they did, Jesse extended a hand to help me across, then did the same for Mrs. Andrews and Judith.

A well-meaning swarm immediately surrounded us—officials, Life-Saving Service personnel, residents of the nearby Point neighborhood, even tipsy sailors and fishermen from the harborside taverns. Though I welcomed their collective concern, the myriad faces and voices assailed my senses like the whirling chaos of a carnival. Even Judith shrank from the attention. Her mother scowled, though she voiced no complaints.

Jesse herded us through the crowd to waiting vehicles. It was there I finally replied to his earlier command that we not argue with him.

"Honestly, I don't have the wherewithal, but why would we disagree?"

"Because you are all three going to the hospital."

"I'm fine, Jesse—"

"There you go. Arguing. Well, be advised it won't do you a lick of good." He turned to mother and daughter. "Help me convince Miss Cross she has no choice but to accompany us to the hospital."

"Oh, Mother," Judith said in a weary voice, "is that necessary?"

"I believe so, dear." With a sob, Mrs. Andrews pulled her daughter into her embrace. "Besides," she said in a choked voice, "where else do we have to go?"

"We could go to Derrick's house, couldn't we?"

Mrs. Andrews pulled back to regard her daughter, her eyes magnified by tears. "Why, yes, darling. We could go to Derrick's." Her gaze darted to me, and I saw the deep significance of what had just passed between them. This morning, or even an hour ago, Judith would not have suggested any scenario that included her brother. Had her anger dissipated into smoke and flame?

Jesse stepped closer to them, and I have no doubt his drumlike, reverberating footfalls against the planks were no accident. He wanted our attention and our compliance. "No one is going anywhere until they've been seen by a doctor."

When we arrived I allowed myself to be prodded. The doctor held a stethoscope to my front and my back while I breathed in deep and coughed. He tried advising me, but I couldn't listen; too many other thoughts raced through my mind. Fortunately, my old friend Hannah Hanson saw me arrive with the Andrews women. She listened to the doctor for me and wrote down everything he said.

"Emma, you should let us admit you. You've breathed in quite a lot of smoke. I cannot impress upon you enough how dangerous that can be."

Hannah's warning broke through the miasma that had taken hold of me. "Dangerous? But I'm breathing. I'm fine."

"Didn't you hear what the doctor said? He heard a slight wheeze. Your condition could worsen. You need rest."

I knew she was right and I had no intention of exerting myself, but neither would I allow anyone to tuck me into bed, extinguish the lights, and shut the door. I had more to do. I was about to tell Hannah so, when Brady and Marianne burst into the examination room.

"Good God, Em, we could see the fire from Third Street. Are you all right?"

"I'm fine, Brady. You needn't worry."

Marianne said nothing, just took up position at my side like a bodyguard. I introduced her to Hannah, and Brady's eyebrows surged in surprise.

"Little Hannah Hanson?" He surveyed her from head to foot in a way that would have been far too familiar—and disrespectful—if we hadn't known each other all our lives and played together regularly as children.

"It's good to see you again, Brady." Hannah smiled and extended her hand.

I could see Brady bursting with questions and a desire to become reacquainted—Hannah had blossomed into an attractive young woman—but now was no time to become distracted.

"Hannah," I interrupted Brady's inquiries about her time in Providence, "was Judith Kingsley admitted?"

"Yes, she's upstairs."

I jolted. "Not in her brother's former room, I hope?"

"Of course not. She's in the women's ward. There aren't currently any other patients there with her, so it's like a private room."

"Thank goodness. May she have visitors?"

"I'll check with the doctor, but I believe it would be permitted."

I spoke next to Brady. "Did you see Jesse on your way in?"

"In the waiting room. He was taking a statement from Mrs. Andrews."

I hopped down from the examination table. "I need to speak with him immediately."

"Em . . ."

"It's late, Brady," I said on my way out of the room. "Please take Marianne home."

I found Jesse sitting with Mrs. Andrews. They spoke quietly, and Jesse took notes. They looked up when I entered the room.

"Emma. We're about finished here for now and I was just coming to see you. Are you up to answering a few questions?"

"I am, but not here."

Looking puzzled, he asked, "Where, then?"

"In Mrs. Kingsley's room. But first we need Derrick here. Jesse, you've got to give the order to have him brought over."

"He isn't completely exonerated yet, Emma. Nate might be responsible for Wyatt and that young girl—"

"Naomi," I firmly reminded him.

"Yes, Naomi." He sighed, a forlorn, gusty sound. "But it's almost certain Nate didn't kill his father. Not where he was positioned on the *Vigilant*."

"I agree," I said evenly. "Nate didn't murder his father. But I believe I know who did."

Chapter 18

⚜

I refused to say more until Derrick arrived and the doctor could be persuaded to allow several of us to enter Judith's room at once. While Jesse explained to the man the urgency of our request in terms of his ongoing murder investigation, I made a telephone call. Stella answered; she was already up, having just fed Robbie his nighttime bottle. I told her what I needed and hung up.

Then I ran upstairs to check on Uncle Cornelius. I ground to a sudden halt in the doorway. "Neily!" I whispered in surprise.

He sat in a chair just beyond the foot of the bed, away from the dim shafts of light from the street lanterns outside. "What are you doing here this time of night, Emmaline?"

I entered the room, walking on tiptoe to avoid waking Uncle Cornelius. "I could ask you the same thing."

"Reggie's been keeping me informed on the sly. He tracked me down tonight with a message that Mother had finally gone home for some sleep. I took the opportunity to come and sit with Father."

"Does he know?" I went to Neily and put a hand on his shoulder. "Has he awakened?"

"No, and if he did he would probably order me away."

"Oh, Neily." I wanted to reassure him that his father would do no such thing, but after what I'd witnessed at The Breakers, I couldn't with any honesty speak those words. "I'm so sorry."

"I know you are." He craned his neck to look up at me, his eyes shining in the darkness. "Thank you for being my friend, Emmaline."

I bent down and hugged him.

"You haven't said what brought you here. Is someone at Gull Manor ill?" His face filled with alarm. "Robbie?"

"No," I hastened to assure him. "You needn't worry about him. Oh, Neily . . ."

I sank to my knees beside his chair and he took my hands in his own. "You're frightening me, Emmaline. What is it?"

"Tonight has been awful. A young girl died and . . . Nate Monroe is dead, too."

"Nate? My God . . ."

"He's our murderer."

"He killed his own father?" Revulsion filled Neily's voice.

I shook my head. "No, not his father. But the others." The sounds of low murmurs and ascending footsteps echoed in the stairwell. I held the arm of Neily's chair and pressed to my feet. "Don't stay much longer." I glanced at his father's sleeping form, wondering when he might awaken. Praying he'd awaken with his old self still intact.

Neily understood my meaning and nodded. "I'll leave soon."

"Go to Gull Manor. You're welcome to stay as long as you like. Brady's home now, too."

"Yes, all right. Thank you, Emmaline."

I left and met the others on the landing. Together, Jesse, Scotty Binsford—there to take notes—Mrs. Andrews, Derrick, and I filed into Judith's room, with the doctor following in the rear, undoubtedly to make sure we didn't overtax the patient. Hannah had remained downstairs, as I had asked her to.

Although I knew full well what Judith had endured earlier, her appearance nonetheless shocked me. No longer wearing the finery in which I'd grown accustomed to seeing her, and surrounded instead by stark, white linens and the even starker gray-white of the walls, she seemed smaller and younger, uncharacteristically docile. All the enmity once directed at me, her brother, and seemingly the world at large had been leeched away. As she gazed up at us all with glistening, sunken eyes, I couldn't help but think of dear cousin Consuelo, shaken and pale after one of her mother's tirades. Yet Judith had suffered much worse than a browbeating, and seeing her now in this tenuous condition—both physically and mentally—made me ashamed for ever having judged her. I should have known better. Should have remembered an ill-tempered disposition almost always stemmed from profound unhappiness.

Would I remedy that tonight? Could I right the innumerous wrongs of the past many days and weeks?

Derrick and I hadn't spoken since his arrival. We traded only one glance—his bewildered and somewhat wary, as if he didn't trust what appeared to be my latest whim, and mine an attempt to silently persuade him to trust me. After that I looked away, for if my plan didn't work, if my guesses proved incorrect, he would be taken back into custody. And that was a possibility I could not bring myself to acknowledge openly between us.

As we all took up positions around Judith's room, Jesse broke the rigid silence. "All right, Emma. You called this meeting. Perhaps now you'll explain why."

I raised a quick, wordless request that my aunt Sadie lend me a bit of her pluck. I would need it to prevail in the next several moments. Can one feel fortified and apprehensive at the same time? I did as I walked to the foot of the bed, from where Judith could meet my gaze without having to twist her neck.

"Mrs. Kingsley, it is time for the entire truth to come out." Her expression immediately became shuttered and I held up a hand. "No, Mrs. Kingsley. Judith, if I may. The time for reticence is long past. People have died. A coach driver. Virgil Monroe. His brother, Wyatt. A maid—one I believe you knew. And now young Nate Monroe."

Her mouth gaped. A few of those tears swimming in her eyes spilled over.

Heat buffeted my back and a voice spoke in my ear. "Now, see here, Emma. If you're implying that any of this is my sister's fault—"

I spun around to behold Derrick's handsome and, yes, angry features, yet I directed my next comment to everyone in the room. "No, not her fault. But all roads do lead back to Judith." I faced the bed once more. "Don't they?"

Her answer came like a faint stirring of wind across a headland. "Yes."

"Then stop me when I am incorrect." She nodded, her gaze never leaving mine. I was about to continue, but found I couldn't, not where I stood, at the foot of the bed looking down at her. My stance suddenly felt accusatory, as if I intended casting judgment, which I did not. I came around the bed and sat beside her knees, facing her. She didn't resist when I took her hand.

"You and Virgil Monroe had . . . an intimate association, yes?"

Behind me, her mother gasped. Even from across the room, and without my having to see him, I felt Derrick tense. If Judith noticed, she ignored them. She ignored everyone else in the room, her attention riveted on me.

"It began last summer," she said in a small voice. "When I came out of mourning. I was so lonely and he—he was so kind. So comforting. For a time," she added with a bitter note.

"And you became with child." She didn't respond, but she didn't correct me either. Her mother, to her credit, remained silent. Derrick swore so softly I might have imagined it. I heard his step, and out of the corner of my eye I saw him take up my former place at the foot of the bed. With both hands he gripped the iron bedstead, his knuckles whitening.

I went on. "To cover the evidence of the child's existence—to protect your reputation and Virgil's plans to divorce his wife and leave her virtually destitute—he determined that the child must be hidden away. Brought to an orphanage."

Judith's breath trembled. Her hand tightened around mine. "He changed. Became controlling, cruel. I began to hate him long before he stole my child."

I noted how she said *my child,* rather than *our* child, but for now I let that pass. "What you didn't know, I believe, is that the young maid Naomi, who cared for you, secretly refused to cooperate. Instead of taking the child off island, she brought him to me."

Judith's lips parted on a cry so mournful it traveled to my very soul. Her mother whimpered, then fell silent. Judith's eyes filled anew, and her free hand rose to press her lips.

"She left him on my doorstep," I said, "with only one clue as to his identity. A handkerchief edged with the lace Virgil Monroe brought home from Belgium last spring."

Judith bowed her head, her tears falling onto the sheets. "I wondered where that went."

"That same morning, the coachman who brought Naomi and the baby to Ocean Avenue continued on alone as a diversion." I paused until Judith looked back up at me. "And was murdered for his pains. Shot, out by Brenton Point."

"Good Lord."

"I believe it was Virgil who shot him."

"It's quite possible," she murmured. "He was away for hours that day. While I grieved for my child, he was nowhere to be found. . . ."

"What about Virgil's death, then?" Jesse prompted.

"An accident," I replied without hesitation. "But another man should have died that day, and it would not have been an accident. I believe somehow Wyatt knew about the child—is that possible?"

The way Judith's eyes closed when she nodded told me it was more than possible. It was a fact. I continued with my theory.

"And so Virgil rigged the boom on the *Vigilant* so that at the right moment, he could cause it to go swinging to the port side and knock Wyatt unconscious and into the water. He hadn't counted on the squall, though. He believed he could control the sea the way he controlled everyone in his life. But in the end, the sea proved too stubborn for him."

"And Nate?" Jesse moved to stand beside me.

"Took up where his father left off. I believe he decided it was his duty to do away with anyone who could identify the child. He indicated as much tonight before . . ." I tried to shake away the awful memory of Nate walking back into that blazing cabin.

"But why attempt to kill Mrs. Kingsley?" Jesse asked, his perplexity plain to hear. "She didn't know where the baby was until this moment. And why would he find it necessary to murder his father's mistress? Her only crime was to bear an inconvenient child."

"To avenge his mother, perhaps?" I suggested, but even to me, that sounded hollow. Nate had made no mention of his mother aboard the *Lavinia's Sun*. By his own admission, his foul deeds had been committed in his father's name.

Judith's reedy voice surprised us. "Out of everyone, I betrayed Virgil most of all."

"A woman can't help becoming with child," I gently told her.

She laughed, a harsh sound entirely without mirth. "You don't understand. The child is not Virgil's. He is Wyatt's."

Chapter 19

꧁꧂

Stunned silence enveloped the room and held each of us immobile in its grip. Seconds, perhaps minutes, passed. I scarcely breathed, aware of little else but the pounding of my heart and the blood rushing like an ocean in my ears. It was as if Judith had cast a spell on us, and only Judith could break that spell.

While we stood rigid with shock, she seemed more relaxed than I had ever seen her, sinking back against her pillows with something approaching a serene smile tilting her lips. Her expression perplexed me, nearly angered me, until I realized how tremendous a burden she had just released.

"I told you I'd come to hate Virgil," she said. "Only weeks into our assignations last summer, he stopped bothering to be charming." Her gaze slipped past me, to her brother, still gripping the footboard. "The mask he had always shown us as children finally slipped, you see. I saw the true Virgil—cruel, self-satisfying, indifferent to anyone but himself. I told him I had tired of him and would no longer see him, but he laughed in my face and threatened to expose me as a whore."

Mrs. Andrews gasped. "That insidious snake!"

"I didn't know what to do." Judith's calm exterior shattered. She clutched the edge of the sheet, dragging it to her chin as she sank lower in the bed. "He could not only destroy me, but our family. I knew that. He had powerful connections—he could buy anyone or anything and he was the kind of man who, once he had made up his mind, could not be deterred." She raised a remorseful gaze to her mother. "I knew he was already trying to buy controlling shares of the *Sun*. I feared if I didn't cooperate with him, he would dismantle the paper and everything Father has worked for over the years. He would put hundreds of people out of work. How could I allow that to happen?"

The footboard rattled slightly as Derrick finally released it. He moved to the other side of the bed, across from me, and held Judith's hand. "You should have come to me."

"And admit to the sort of situation I'd gotten myself into?"

I saw Derrick struggling to find the right words. He would know, as perhaps everyone in that room did, that no platitudes could undo the past. In the end, he coaxed her gently. "What happened next?"

"Virgil brought me to his New York townhouse. So brazen of him to have me there. It was late last summer, and Eudora and the children were at their Long Island estate. One day, while Virgil was at his offices in the garment district, Wyatt came by, quite unexpectedly. I'll never know why the maid who opened the door allowed him into the house, much less escorted him to the upstairs sitting room, where I was having my breakfast." She raised the sheet higher to dab at her eyes.

"I didn't know how to react to him being there, until he assured me Vigil wouldn't object. It seems Virgil had bragged to Wyatt about me, his conquest. The very thought sickened me—and Wyatt saw that. He saw my unhappiness. Little by little, on subsequent visits, we became closer. Sometimes under Virgil's very nose, for Wyatt hadn't lied. Virgil *had* told Wyatt all about us and took no pains to conceal anything from him. I believe Virgil enjoyed showing me off in front of his brother."

"God help me, if he weren't already dead . . ." Derrick let the thought go unfinished, but no one in that room could have wondered at his sentiments. His color high, he made a visible effort to bring his anger under control. "How did Virgil discover the child wasn't his?"

"Timing," she said succinctly. "He was away for much of that September, back on Long Island playing the loyal, if not quite devoted, husband."

"You could have come home then," Derrick interrupted.

"And face everyone's questions? 'Where have you been? With whom? Doing what?' No, it was easier to stay in New York. I took a small apartment of my own across from the park and hoped inspiration might strike and I'd find a way to free myself."

Here, Mrs. Andrews seemed to rouse herself from her shock and moved to the bedside. Silently I stood and backed away, allowing her to take my place.

"Oh, Mother," Judith said. "I never meant to make such a mess of things. I certainly didn't set out intending to be intimate with Virgil, a married man. But I was still hurting from Jonathan's death, and Virgil—"

"Took advantage of that fact, damn him." A vain thrashed in Derrick's temple.

His mother reached across the bed to touch his sleeve. "Let Judith speak. Go on, darling."

"Wyatt proved so different from his brother," Judith went on. "People thought they knew him. The sportsman, the dandy. The irresponsible one. He was much more."

"Was he?" Derrick's question came through clenched teeth.

"Do not judge him harshly, brother." A bit of Judith's former spark flared. "What happened between us was mutual, not forced. We found comfort in each other and became friends. And in truth there was only the one time." She relaxed back into the pillows again. "One time that made our child."

I took that as my cue. Slipping out of the room, I hurried

down the hall to the top of the stairs. There I caught Hannah's eye below and signaled to her. I returned to Judith's room to wait.

The doctor apparently had stepped out, too, possibly minutes ago when the conversation had turned so intensely personal. Jesse and Scotty Binsford had moved into the doorway, listening as unobtrusively as possible to the evidence they would need to finalize their case. As I passed them to reenter the room, they backed farther into the hall. Only the Andrewses were left, and me.

Though only for the next minute or so. Then Hannah entered the room with both Stella and Katie behind her. The two of them looked disheveled, with their hair—Stella's sleek black and Katie's wild bright red—hastily gathered and pinned, their dresses rumpled, their eyes puffy from lack of sleep. Yet both were smiling. Both blinked back the tears in their eyes. A bundle in Katie's arms wriggled.

Judith saw them and cried out, and stretched out her arms. "Is that him? Oh! I never thought . . . Please, please may I have him?"

Katie came forward, carefully unwrapping the knitted blanket from Robbie's pink face. She approached the bed and leaned, but when Judith eagerly pulled forward to reach for the child, Katie held on.

I came up behind her. "It's all right, you can let go of him now. Let his mother hold him."

Her arms reluctantly stretched forward to relinquish Robbie into Judith's trembling arms. Even then, Katie didn't completely let go, but held his head in her palm. "Like this, ma'am. Support his head, though he's doing quite a fine job of holding it up himself when he isn't sleepy."

"Katie, I believe Mrs. Kingsley knows how to hold her baby," I whispered.

My maid-of-all-work nodded with a sniffle and retreated from the bedside. My own throat tightened around a sob—of joy, of triumph, of immeasurable sadness. I had done what I had set out to do. I had found Robbie's mother and by all appearances, I had been correct in one essential assumption: that his family would ultimately want him. It had been that belief that kept me so single-minded in my quest. In all my life, being correct had never felt so gratifying.

Or so devastating. As I gazed from Katie to Stella, I saw my own sentiments mirrored in their forlorn expressions. We would be saying farewell to our visitor. No longer would anyone's sleep be interrupted at night. There would be no more bottles to warm, diapers to change, or extra linens to wash. Our daily burdens lightened, our lives would become our own again.

And at that moment, the future presented a dismal prospect.

But then, I could not come close to imagining what it had been like for Judith to have her child ripped from her arms, and to wonder if she would ever see him again, to agonize over his fate and attempt to find the will and the strength to salvage some kind of life for herself.

And to think I had judged her.

I dismissed the thought as something to be reconciled at a later time. I forced myself to rejoice for Judith, and for Robbie. For no matter how good we might have been to him, however much we might have loved him and formed a surrogate family, none of us could ever have been his mother. Only Judith could fill that role.

"He's gotten so big! So chubby compared to when I saw him last." Gingerly she unwrapped more of him, stroking his arms and dimpled knees, sprinkling both kisses and tears across his forehead. "Oh, look at his darling cheeks." She surprised me by addressing me next. "He's so rosy and healthy looking. Your sea air seems to have done him a world of good, Miss Cross. Or Emma, if I may. You took good care of him, and for that I'll always be in your debt."

"Oh, no, Judith. It's these two"—I gestured at Katie and

Stella—"and Mrs. O'Neal, my housekeeper, who deserve the credit. Most of Robbie's care fell to them."

"While you were out hunting down a killer." Derrick spoke in a low rumble that brimmed with emotion.

My throat went tight again, and I only nodded.

All the attention and fawning brought Robbie more fully awake, for he began to fuss and squirm. Judith touched her forefinger to his lips, and he latched on as if sucking on his bottle. Her peal of laughter echoed through the room and more tears spilled over, several splashing into Robbie's wispy, dark hair. As if reaching out to stroke a precious, priceless object, Derrick used his fingertips to wipe the moisture away. He said nothing, simply looked on with his slightly lopsided smile as if he couldn't quite believe what he was seeing.

Their mother moved back to the side of the bed vacated by Katie. She sat, leaned, and kissed her grandson's brow. Stella stepped forward then, holding up a cloth bag. "If you would like to feed him, ma'am, there's a bottle in here."

"Oh, yes, please!" With her gleaming eyes and heightened color, Judith had taken on the radiance of a new mother.

Mrs. Andrews reached for the offered bag. Her gaze bored into Stella then, and her brow furrowed. She went very still, and I remembered that she knew about Stella—knew of Stella's dark past. Would she cast judgment? Balk at having Stella in the room? I held my breath, ready to step between them, to deflect any derogatory comments Mrs. Andrews might make.

But then the woman's features smoothed. She nodded at Stella, even tilted her lips slightly upward. She turned back to her daughter and handed her the bottle. The family closed in around Robbie then, forming a protective circle. The earnestness and sheer power of that sight, of their joy, made me look away, and then move away. I didn't have to signal to Katie or Stella. Almost as one we quietly retreated to the hallway and closed the door behind us.

* * *

My exhaustion could have kept me in bed all the next day, but my hectic thoughts would not allow it. I dragged myself out from beneath the covers just after sunup, and after a quick breakfast I returned to town, to the offices of the *Observer.* There I sat down at the typewriter in the cramped office I shared with Ed Billings. He hadn't arrived yet, so in those rare few moments of privacy punctuated by the rumble of the presses at the far back of the building, I wrote out the basic facts of the murder at Beechwood that turned out to be no murder at all, but an attempted one gone awry. Virgil Monroe, out of jealousy and revenge, had schemed to stage an accident that would have killed his brother. From that point on, his deranged son sought to avenge his father's death.

As I had in the past, I left out much of the story, only outlining each murder as it happened, and perhaps dropping a hint or several about sibling rivalry, hostile buyouts, and financial fraud—all viable motives for murder, and all rampant among the members of the Four Hundred. As to the many truths I left out. . . .

For the first time in nearly a year, I thought about the unfinished manuscript moldering away in a desk drawer at home. Had I truly fancied myself a novelist, someone who endeavored to capture imaginations and emotions with the written word? Life, I had discovered, held thrills and dangers aplenty. I needn't make them up, nor could I have devised anything so fantastical as the events of these past two summers. Someday, perhaps, but not now.

Ed entered the office mere minutes after I proofed my account and declared myself satisfied.

"You're here awfully early," he said, his surprise evident. His expression became wary. "To what do we owe the pleasure?"

I tugged the page from the cylindrical platen and thrust it toward him. "Here. I listed the facts, Ed, but I must admit I have no stomach to write this story. I'm giving it to you."

He made no move to take the sheet of paper. "You're joking."

"No, Ed. Some events are too overwhelming even for me." The words nearly stuck in my throat, but I kept talking. "I think it best if you write the article." I stood and placed the page in his hand, forcing him to accept it or let it drop to the floor. Somehow I knew Ed would not let this unexpected boon slip from his fingers.

I plucked my hat from the coat rack and set it on my head. Ed made little noises in his throat as he skimmed my account. Then he glanced up.

"This is everything?"

I met his gaze without blinking. "Everything as I experienced it. If I missed anything, you'll have to hunt it down for yourself. But that shouldn't pose any problem for a reporter like yourself." With that I smiled and bid him good morning.

That very evening the *Observer* ran Ed's article nearly word for word as I had written it. Did it scald my professional pride to see Ed's byline beneath the commentary I had written? Of course it did. Just as having omitted key details mortified my reporter's ethics. But this wasn't the first time I had sacrificed journalistic integrity to protect people I cared about. No reporters would come swarming around Judith Kingsley hoping for a glimpse of her bastard child. Nor would anyone ever know Nate Monroe targeted her and her family for any reason other than greed and a misguided desire for revenge. That knowledge allowed me to hold my head up higher.

Chapter 20

❧

Two days later, I returned to Beechwood to visit what remained of the Monroe family.

"We're leaving for New York tomorrow," Eudora told me.

We sat on the loggia overlooking the sea and, closer, Mrs. Astor's rose garden. Mrs. Astor herself had returned inside, leaving us in privacy. A dry, sunny day, the air smelled crisp and sweet and stirred our skirts and hair gently. Butterflies hovered over the blossoms vying with the occasional bumblebee for nectar. In such idyllic surroundings, I found it hard to imagine the horrible scene we had witnessed on the awful day of the lawn party.

Likewise, in studying my companion closely, I detected no trace of the Eudora I'd encountered on my last visit here, a woman lost in guilt and excessive brandy. Or had it been something other than guilt driving her to drink? Perhaps she had feared, as I had, that her husband still lived and would return to retake control over her life.

"We set sail for France next week," she said after a sip of tea. "It's all arranged. I'm closing the Fifth Avenue house. Eventually, I intend putting it up for sale."

Her gaze drifted past me and beyond the roses to the two figures near the hedges that marked the Cliff Walk. They walked hand in hand toward us, waving as they came closer. I waved back.

Eudora watched them. "Daphne and Lawrence will marry in France, as soon as my husband's will has been executed. A small wedding. They don't desire anything fancy." She raised her cup to her lips as if to drink again, but set it back in its saucer. "People will talk, of course, without a proper period of mourning. But they don't wish to wait any longer than they must, and I haven't the heart to insist otherwise. It's time those children started living. Time we all did."

She lifted her teacup, yet hesitated again. "Nate *will* be mourned, Miss Cross. Wedding or no, he will always be in our thoughts. And in our hearts."

In the silence that descended, culpability bore heavily on me. "I'm very sorry, ma'am, that I wasn't able to save him. . . ."

"No, Miss Cross." The cup went back to its saucer with a clatter. Reaching across the table, she raised my chin on the tips of her fingers, forcing me to meet her gaze as Nanny used to do when she wanted my full attention. "Nate's death was not your fault. Just as the terrible crimes he committed were not his fault. Not really."

At my puzzled look, she scowled, though I had the distinct impression she was not scowling at me. Her next words proved me correct. "Nate was a boy who longed for his father's approval and never quite got it. Virgil knew that of all the ways to control a person, withholding one's regard from those who greatly desire it is the most effective method. My husband was a bad man. A murderer, even from the grave. He killed Nate and those other people, just as if he had performed the deeds with his own hands."

I wondered at the wisdom of voicing my curiosity, but went ahead and spoke my thoughts. "How do you suppose Nate came to know about . . . well . . . everything?"

"Judith Kingsley? The child?" Eudora stared out at the lawn again. "I don't blame her, by the way. You can relay that message to her, if you like."

"I will. She and her mother are staying with me at Gull Manor. I think she'll be very glad to hear it."

"As to your question." She sighed. "I suspect Virgil told him, perhaps to persuade Nate to help ensure that Wyatt went overboard during the race. And then when it was Virgil instead who went over . . ."

"It pushed Nate over the brink."

"Yes, I believe my son was quite insane in the end."

"I'm so sorry." How inadequate. I wished I had more comforting words for her. Lawrence and Daphne reached the loggia, coming up the steps and passing through its central arch.

"Emma!" Daphne held her skirts and ran up the last couple. She seized my hands, raised me from my chair, and danced me around in a circle. "I'm so happy to see you before we leave."

Suddenly her mirth ceased and she looked sheepishly at her guardian, soon to be her mother-in-law. "I'm sorry, Eudora. But we owe Miss Cross so very much." She turned a brilliant smile on me. "You will always be a favorite of mine. Shall we write? Often?"

I promised her we would. A more subdued Lawrence kissed my cheek and thanked me quietly. We sat around the garden table and talked for a little while longer. Then I wished them well and took my leave.

I had another call to make before returning home.

An eerie quiet blanketed The Breakers. I felt it the moment I drove Barney through the gates. The place felt forlorn and deserted, as if its very heartbeat had ceased. Even the sea sounded muffled and far away. Inside the house, my somber welcome continued as a subdued Mr. Mason escorted me into the Great Hall.

Aunt Alice called to me from the gallery above. "Emmaline, please come up."

She moved to wait for me at the top of the staircase, donned in perhaps the most casual attire I'd ever seen her wearing: a lawn shirtwaist tucked into a voluminous, navy blue skirt. Her graying hair had been simply dressed in an upsweep pinned at the crown. The only jewelry shimmering at me were a pair of gold earbobs and a brooch at the juncture of her collar.

When I reached her she took my hand and hurried me into her own bedroom, done up in soft creams and golds with a ro-tunda of windows like the music room below it.

"Is it true you're harboring Neily?" she demanded in a whisper.

"Harboring?" The accusation stung. "I would hardly call it that. He is staying with me, yes, but only because he's feeling very much alone right now."

"As well he should. When I think of what he has done to his father . . ."

My temper surged, yet I dredged up the patience due the wife of a critically ill man. "I won't take sides, Aunt Alice. Whatever I can do for you, I will do. Just as I'll do what I can for Neily. I love you all equally."

Alice Vanderbilt was one of the strongest people I had ever met, stronger perhaps than even her husband. So when her face crumpled and she reached for me, a significant piece of my heart shattered for her.

"Oh, Emmaline. You're a good girl, aren't you?" She pressed a damp cheek to mine, then pulled away, already reassembling her mask of composure. "All right. I shall make no further de-mands of you. Would you care to see Cornelius now?"

"Yes, if that's all right."

She started to lead the way, then stopped. "Brace yourself, dear. I know you saw him at the hospital, but it still may come as something of a shock."

That proved a greater understatement than I could have imagined. I entered Uncle Cornelius's bedroom to find him propped up in bed, one side of his face drooping lower than the other. But that wasn't what stole the breath from my lungs and made me sag despairingly against the door frame. No, it was the sight of the nurse, perched beside him at the edge of the mattress, a bowl in one hand while, with the other, she spoon-fed the man I had known all my life as one of America's, perhaps the world's, most powerful individuals.

I visited with Uncle Cornelius for about ten minutes before fatigue began to drag at his eyelids and his nurse shooed me from the room. In that time I held his hand and chatted quietly about nothing of great consequence. One might say I put my skills as a Fancies and Fashions reporter to good use, avoiding topics that might agitate him in the slightest. Needless to say Neily's name went unspoken, yet I felt it hovering between us, a splintered bridge that could not be crossed.

I returned home after that. After settling Barney in with a brisk rubdown, water, and fresh hay, I entered through the kitchen. A happy din at the front of the house met my ears. I immediately felt my spirit surge, renewed and revitalized, and I quickened my pace to the parlor.

The room was in shambles, with pillows tossed willy-nilly to the floor, some of the furniture moved, and a space cleared in between. In that space Brady sat with Robbie on his knees, bouncing him gently. Robbie had grown capable of holding up his head, and even sat upright with support. Neily and Grace, Mrs. Andrews, Judith, and Nanny surrounded the pair, and by their expressions I could see they had been enjoying themselves immensely. Nanny peered up at me through her half-moon spectacles and grinned, then nodded. All had been well in my absence, her gesture said. Mrs. Andrews greeted me with a fond expression, one usually reserved only for her grandson. Then she slid to the floor like a doting grandma to tickle Robbie beneath his chin.

I had opened my home to Lavinia and Judith. Although *Lavinia's Sun* had been saved, the fire, as well as the water that had doused it, had caused enough damage to render the yacht uninhabitable until the repairs were complete. Another development precluded their returning to Providence by other means—Mr. Andrews, upon learning of his daughter's circumstances, declared the disgrace intolerable and refused to speak to her or see her.

"He'll come around," his wife insisted. "His pride has been hurt and one can hardly blame him. He needs time. Once he understands he may not only lose his daughter but his firstborn grandson, he'll have a change of heart."

In the middle of August I received word that Neily and Grace had eloped. I rejoiced in their happiness, especially when Grace promised in her letter that they would visit Newport again in the fall. Even so, the news of their marriage drove home to me how quickly circumstances, and the world I had grown accustomed to, could change.

It was soon after one of Nanny's hearty breakfasts that Derrick arrived in a coach large enough to accommodate the family and the luggage they had brought to Gull Manor. My muffin and porridge curdled in my stomach, and judging by the sour expressions worn by Katie, Stella, and Nanny, they felt the same. Brady had said his good-byes to the Andrews family the night before and hadn't been seen since. It had warmed my heart in these past weeks to see my half brother so taken with a baby. He was so much a bachelor, I wouldn't have thought it of him.

While Judith and her mother readied themselves upstairs in the guest room they had shared, Derrick asked me to stroll with him out behind the house. Something in his voice made me wish to remain inside among the others where unwelcome words could not be spoken. But I steeled myself and followed him outside.

He wasted no time in getting to the point. "I'm leaving Newport with my mother and Judith today, Emma. I might not be back for quite some time." He angled his gaze toward the sea. "I wanted you to know."

"I think I already did. They need you." My throat tightened and I swallowed. "Your nephew needs you. It's only right that you be with them." After a hesitation marked by the ruckus of seagulls picking along the hollows of the rocky shoreline, I asked, "Where will you go?"

"Italy."

"Oh!" A shock went through me. I hadn't expected him to be so far away.

"My mother's sister, my aunt Elizabeth, lives in Tuscany. It's a beautiful estate, very private. There, Judith can be free from prying eyes and wagging tongues. She'll merely be a widowed relation visiting with her son."

"That sounds best." What had I just said? My reply had been automatic, for in that moment I had no inkling what words left my lips. *Italy* swarmed round and round my brain, drowning out all else.

"When I return, Emma, I'd like us to start over. Truly come to know one another." What was he saying? I only half heard, half understood. "You have been right. We have never had time—simple time that wasn't defined by danger and urgency—to learn about each other. Our likes and dislikes, our hopes for the future. It was folly, my asking you to marry me when I did. I can only hope we can forget our hasty past and start again. Slowly. Is that possible, Emma?"

"I . . . yes . . . When you return." *If you return,* I added silently.

Another silence stretched as my heart slowly descended to my feet. I would have given anything in that moment to keep him from leaving, from walking out of my life. But there was nothing I could say, or *would* say, to prevent him from letting his honor guide him.

I tried to be brave and smiled even as I blinked away a threat of tears. "Well, then." I extended my hand. "Have a safe trip and . . . and take good care of Robbie. Or whatever Judith will choose to name him."

He took my hand and tugged me to him, seizing me in a kiss that pledged he would return. Or, I amended silently as I kissed him back, pledged the *intent* to return. I believed with every fiber of my being that he meant it. His kiss carried that much power. Whether in reality he would return, or *when* he would, only time would tell.

We returned to the house to find everyone in the entry hall, Judith and her mother in their traveling clothes, Robbie wrapped snug and in his mother's arms. Tears streamed down Katie's cheeks. Stella looked devastated and practically stared a hole through the floor. Nanny folded her hands primly at her waist and gave last-minute advice to mother and grandmother. They nodded tolerantly.

Then Mrs. Andrews turned to me and opened her purse. "Miss Cross, I hope you didn't think we'd leave without paying you for your services. You've been most kind and accommodating, and my daughter and I wish to show our appreciation."

"My services . . . ?" Astonishment and yes, indignation made me rigid. A surge of heat engulfed my face. There it was, then. After everything we had been through and what had seemed to be a pleasant coming to terms, Mrs. Andrews still saw me as little more than a servant. Helpful, accommodating—to use her word—but certainly not her equal.

A strained and wounded silence settled over those of us who would be remaining at Gull Manor. Even Derrick shuffled his feet and Judith paid particular attention to an invisible speck of lint on Robbie's blanket.

"No payment is necessary, Mrs. Andrews," I said, once I'd reined in my pique enough to trust my voice. "Not to me. However, Katie and Stella—"

"Not me," Katie interrupted. She sniffled and wiped her sleeve across her wet cheeks. "I won't be paid for doin' what I loved doin'."

"Nor me, neither." Stella even took a step backward, as if to put herself out of reach of Mrs. Andrews's charitable hand.

"You could always make a donation to St. Nicholas Orphanage," Nanny calmly suggested. "It's in Providence."

"Yes, I know of it." Mrs. Andrews closed her purse and squared her shoulders. Had we offended her by refusing her offer? Then she knew how we felt. "Well . . . good-bye and thank you. All of you. We do sincerely appreciate everything you've done for us." She turned to her daughter. "Are you ready?"

"One moment, Mother." Judith beamed at us. She had become a happy and contented woman during her time at Gull Manor. "I was going to name him Bernard, after my grandfather. But I want you all to know I've decided to continue calling him Robert. Robbie. A part of you will always be with him."

Katie burst out crying and raised her apron to hide her face. Stella put an arm around her and I believe a tear or two fell from her eyes, and Nanny's, too. The Andrews women stepped outside then, but Derrick lingered.

"I promise I'll be back."

"You'll know where to find me." I smiled through a few tears of my own.

The door closed, and the four of us were left alone with our grief in a house that felt silent and empty.

Of course, that lasted only until Brady turned up later that afternoon. The front door banged open and his enthusiastic greeting filled the hall, traveled down the corridor, and out to the kitchen garden where Katie and I were picking herbs and vegetables for the pheasant Nanny planned to roast for supper. A crash from inside brought us to our feet.

"Oh, no." I pushed stray tendrils from my face. "What is he up to now?"

Katie and I traded a look, and I knew she guessed my thoughts: that Brady had been drinking. Another crash sent us running into the house.

We met Nanny in the kitchen, scowling as she wiped her hands on a towel. She followed us into the hall, where Stella had just reached the bottom step. From the parlor, Brady let out a yell.

"No, stay away from there! Get back here, you imp!"

"Land sakes," Nanny murmured.

I led the way into the parlor, hands on my hips. The first sight to greet me was a vase of wildflowers that had been knocked off the sofa table. Rivulets streamed and damp blossoms littered the area rug. Nanny's sewing basket lay on its side in front of the window seat with its contents spilling out. The small table in the corner sprawled on its side as well, the tray and brass goblets it had held strewn about—probably the first crash we had heard.

Lastly . . .

Lastly I found myself assailed by a knee-high bundle of brown and white fur—in big patches like a jersey cow. The creature barked and jumped at my legs, its lolling tongue finding my hand and leaving a slobbery trail across my palm and fingers.

"Surprise!" Brady stood grinning as if the animal hadn't been in the process of destroying the room.

At another jump, lick, and an eager bark, my annoyance dissipated. A blunt muzzle, big earnest eyes, softly rounded forehead, and ears that flopped with every excited movement worked their magic on me. I dropped to my knees and accepted more wet kisses on my chin and cheeks. When I combed my fingers through all that fur, my new friend rolled onto his or her back and offered me a tan and white belly. Katie and Stella sank at the pooch's other side and joined in lavishing our guest with a sound petting. Those dark eyes rolled blissfully.

"Oh, Brady, where did you find . . . him?" For I clearly saw now that our guest was male.

"Out on Long Wharf. Angus told me he's been hanging about for a couple of weeks now, begging for scraps. Probably came in on one of the boats, possibly a stowaway since no one has claimed him."

"And you brought him here thinking we need another mouth to feed?" Even as the chastising words left my lips, I knew it was too late. My heart had been captured even before Brady continued his explanation.

"He's an orphan, Em. He needs a home." He perched on the sofa beside Nanny. "Surely you wouldn't turn away a stray. Besides, I thought with Robbie leaving and all . . ."

I shook my head at him. "You're incorrigible." But I noticed Katie beseeching me with her eyes, and Nanny watching us fondly. "Well, what is he, then? Any idea?"

Brady shrugged. "Part spaniel as far as I can tell. As for the rest . . . I'm afraid that will remain a mystery. Does it matter?"

"He's a love," Katie said. "I'll give him that."

"One thing is for certain." I grasped one of his gangly paws. "He hasn't finished growing."

Suddenly the dog rolled and sprang to his feet, nosed my shoulder, licked Katie's ear, and bounded over to Nanny, presenting his head to be scratched.

"Well, Nanny, what do you think?" I gained my feet and crossed my arms. "Is there room at Gull Manor for another resident?"

She stroked behind his ears. "I think he needs us." She turned to gaze out the front window, her expression sad as she no doubt thought about Robbie. She said more quietly, "And I think we need him."

One thing I had learned about Nanny over the years, she

was almost always right. Patch, as we came to call him, might knock over a few more tables and vases before we trained him properly, but starting from that very afternoon, the ache in our hearts, so sharp that morning, began to subside, and somehow the future no longer seemed so bleak. In fact, I looked forward to Grace and Neily's visit in the fall, to receiving the promised letters from Daphne, to hearing news about Robbie's progress, and to seeing Derrick again.

But when a knock sounded at the door that very next morning and a Western Union delivery boy handed me a telegram, I knew it was far too soon for good news. With trembling hands and a fluttering pulse, I tipped the boy, closed the door, and leaned with my back against it.

I stared down at the unopened envelope so hard I might have burned a hole through it. Telegrams didn't always bring bad news, I tried telling myself. Sometimes they brought unexpectedly good news. Sometimes they merely contained a greeting, a reminder that loved ones far away held you in their thoughts.

Brady came toward me down the corridor from the morning room. "What do you have there, Em?"

The question jolted me out of my stupor. There was nothing for it. I slipped my finger beneath the seal and tore the thing open.

"It's from Mother and Dad."

"About time we heard from them. What's it been? Months?"

I acknowledged his observation with a *hmm* and kept reading as I strolled into the parlor. My perplexity grew with each word stamped across the page, until anger rose up and I all but crumpled the paper between my fingers.

"They need money," I said, shaking my head and wondering, yet again, how I had fallen into the role of matriarch of our little family. "They say it's an emergency, and they want me to go to Uncle Cornelius for it."

"In their defense, Em, they probably haven't received the letter you sent explaining what happened."

"And wouldn't I like to pretend I never received this telegram. Send money, indeed."

At the back of the house a door slammed, and soon thudding footfalls came barreling down the hallway. Moments later Patch skidded through the parlor doorway and launched himself at my ankles. I crouched to accept his enthusiastic greetings against my face and ran my hands from head to tail in return. Then I looked up to see Brady grinning down at me.

"What?" I demanded.

"You. You won't turn your back on Mother and Dad any more than you would with me or anyone else who stumbles into your life. I don't know what we'd all do without you, Em."

What, indeed? I sighed and pushed to my feet.

Afterword

✤

While the events that occur at Beechwood in the story are completely fictional, it is true that Mrs. Astor, as the reigning queen of society, typically kicked off the social activities of each summer Season. Caroline Schermerhorn Astor both led and defined Gilded Age society, and being a member of the Four Hundred (based on the number of guests who fit comfortably in her New York ballroom), was certainly seen as a mark of distinction. Being worthy of her notice meant a family had "arrived."

Mrs. Astor, considered "old money" (as opposed to the Vanderbilts, who had earned their fortune in trade), was nothing if not stubborn, determined, judgmental, and about as ruthless a society matron as could be imagined. When her daughter, Carrie, wished to attend a ball thrown by Alva Vanderbilt in 1883, she could not be invited because her mother had yet to recognize the "upstart" Vanderbilts as her social equals. Carrie's deep disappointment, however, persuaded Mrs. Astor to give in and call on Mrs. Vanderbilt, thereby paving the way for the two families to mix socially. Later, when Carrie wished to marry, it was to

Orme Wilson of the same Wilson family the Vanderbilts found so objectionable. Mrs. Astor disapproved of the match every bit as much as the Vanderbilts disapproved of Neily marrying Grace, but when Carrie proved determined (a family trait), Mrs. Astor gave in rather than lose her daughter. This, in my mind, suggests a mother who very dearly loved her daughter, who was capable of swallowing her own pride in favor of her daughter's happiness, and who was intelligent enough to realize what was at stake.

Sadly, such was not the case for Neily Vanderbilt. Although I have fictionalized the circumstances, *Murder at Beechwood* does trace the actual events leading up to Neily and Grace's elopement in August of 1896. One wonders, if Cornelius and Alice hadn't dug in their heels and voiced their disapproval so vehemently, would the young couple simply have danced a few dances in the summer of 1895 and ultimately gone their separate ways? To their credit, they did remain married until their deaths, but their years together served to emphasize the great differences in their personalities: Grace's love of parties and excitement versus Neily's quiet, studious nature. These differences would eventually create distance between them, until they basically led separate lives in their latter years.

As described in the story, the tension and estrangement between Neily and his parents reached a heartbreaking and dangerous climax in July of 1896. Some accounts claim father and son came to blows, while others discount that theory, but historians agree that the strife between them precipitated the first of Cornelius's strokes that would incapacitate him and from which he would never fully recover. Neily would be disinherited in favor of his younger brother, Alfred, and rather than being a partner in the family business he would merely hold a position at the New York Central Railroad for a modest salary. His ingenuity in modifying and modernizing train travel was extraordinary, however, and he came to be hailed a genius in his field. In time, his brother would restore a good deal of his inheritance as well.

In 2010, Beechwood was privately purchased and closed to the public, in order that extensive restorations could return the house to its original, Gilded Age state. The original arched loggia, which is also being restored, was destroyed by Hurricane Carol in 1954 and replaced with a relatively simple veranda, which will account for the fact that my description of the back of the house might seem unfamiliar to past visitors. It's my understanding that once the construction is complete, the house will reopen featuring a fine arts museum on the first floor, with select rooms on the second story open at certain times of year.

Please turn the page for an exciting sneak peek of
Alyssa Maxwell's

MURDER MOST MALICIOUS

the first book in her new Lady and Lady's Maid
mystery series coming in January 2016!

Chapter 1

December 25, 1918

"Henry, don't you dare ignore me!" came a shout from behind the drawing room doors, a command nearly drowned out by staccato notes pounded on the grand piano.

"Henry!"

Stravinsky's discordant *Firebird* broke off with a resounding crescendo. Voices replaced them, one male, one female, both distinctly taut and decidedly angry. Phoebe Renshaw came to an uneasy halt. She had thought the rest of the family and the guests had all gone up to bed. Across the Grand Hall, light spilled from the dining room as footmen continued clearing away the remnants of Christmas dinner.

With an indrawn breath she moved closer to the double-pocket doors.

"I'm very sorry, Henry, but it isn't going to happen," came calmer, muffled words from inside, spoken by the feminine voice. A voice that sounded anything *but* sorry. Dismissive, disdainful, yes, but certainly not contrite. Phoebe sighed and rolled her eyes. As much as she had expected this, she shook her head at the fact that Julia had chosen Christmas night to break this news to her latest suitor. And this particular Christmas, too—the first peacetime holiday in nearly five years.

A paragon of tact and goodwill, that sister of hers.

"We are practically engaged, Julia. Why do you think your grandparents asked my family to spend Christmas here at Foxwood? Everyone is expecting us to wed. Our estates practically border each other." Incredulity lent an almost shrill quality to Henry's voice. "How could our union be any more perfect?"

"It isn't perfect to me," came the cool reply.

"No? How on earth do you think you'll avoid a scandal if you break it off now?"

Phoebe could almost see her sister's cavalier shrug. "A broken not-quite-engagement is hardly fodder for scandal. I'm sorry—how many times must I say it? This is my decision and you've no choice but to accept it."

Would they exit the drawing room now? Phoebe stepped backward, intending to flee, perhaps dart behind the Christmas tree that dominated the center of the hall. Henry's voice, raised and freshly charged with ire, held her in place. "Do I? Do I *really?* You listen here, Julia Renshaw. Surely you don't believe you're the only one who knows a secret about someone."

Phoebe glanced over her shoulder, and sure enough, two footmen met her gaze through the dining room doorway before hurrying on with their chores. Inside the drawing room, a burst of snide laughter from Henry raised the hair at her nape.

"What secret?" her sister asked after a moment's hesitation.

"*Your* secret," Henry Leighton, Marquess of Allerton, the man Phoebe's grandparents had indeed invited to Foxwood in hopes of a subsequent engagement, said with a mean hiss that carried through the door.

"What . . . do you believe you know?"

"Must I outline the sordid details of your little adventure last summer?"

"How on earth did you discover . . . ?" Julia's voice faded.

It registered in Phoebe's mind that her sister hadn't bothered to deny whatever it was.

"Let's just say I kept an eye on you while I was on furlough," Henry said, "and you aren't as clever as you think you are, not by half."

"That was most ungentlemanly of you, Henry."

"You had your chance to spend more time with me then, Julia, and you chose not to. I, therefore, chose to discover where you *were* spending your time."

"Oh! How unworthy, even of you, Henry. Still, it would be your word against mine, and whom do you think Grampapa will believe? Now, if you'll excuse me, I'm going to bed."

"You are not walking away from this, Julia!" Henry's voice next plunged to a murmur Phoebe could no longer make out, but like a mongrel's growl, it showered her arms with goose bumps.

The sounds of shuffling feet were followed by a sharp "Oh!" from Julia. Phoebe's hand shot instinctively toward the recessed finger pull on one of the doors, but she froze at the marquess's next words. "This is how it is going to be, my dear. You and I are going to announce our engagement to our families tomorrow morning, and shortly after to the world. There will be parties and planning, and yes, there *will* be a wedding. You will marry *me*, or you'll marry no one. Ever. I'll see to that."

"You don't even know whether or not anything untoward happened last summer," Julia said with all the condescension Phoebe knew she was capable of, yet with a brittle quality that threatened her tenuous composure. "You're bluffing, Henry."

"Am I? Are you willing to risk it?"

Phoebe's breath caught in her throat at the sounds of shuffling footsteps. She gripped the bronze finger pulls just as Julia cried out.

"Let go of me!"

Phoebe thrust both doors wide, perfectly framing the scene inside. Julia, in her pale rose gown with its silver-beaded trim, stood with her back bowed in an obvious attempt to pull free of Henry's hold. A spiraling lock of blond hair had slipped from its pins to stream past her shoulder. Henry's dark hair stood on end, no doubt from raking his fingers through it. His brown eyes smoldering and his cheeks ruddy with drink, he had his hands on her—*on her!* His fingers were wrapped so tightly around Julia's upper arms, they were sure to leave bruises.

For a moment, no one moved. Phoebe stared. They stared back. Henry's tailcoat and waistcoat were unbuttoned with all the familiarity of a husband in his own home, his garnet shirt studs gleaming like drops of blood upon snow. Anger twisted his features. But then recognition dawned—of Phoebe, of the impropriety of the scene she had walked in on—and a measure of the ire smoothed from his features. He released Julia as though she were made of hot coals, turned away, and put several feet between them.

Phoebe steeled herself with a breath and forced a smile. "Oh, hullo there, you two. Sorry to barge in like this. I thought everyone had gone to bed. Don't mind me. I only came for a book, one I couldn't find in the library. Julia, do you remember where Grampapa stashed that American novel he didn't want Grams to know he was reading? You know, the one about the boy floating up that large river to help his African friend."

"I don't know . . ." Julia looked from Phoebe to Henry and back again. She brushed that errant lock behind her ear and then hugged her arms around her middle. "I'll help you look. G-good night, Henry."

"Oh, were you just going up?" Without letting her smile slip, Phoebe shot a glare at Henry and put emphasis on *going up*.

A muscle bounced in the hard line of his jaw. His eyes narrowed, but he bobbed his head. "Good night, ladies. Julia, we'll talk more in the morning."

He strode past Phoebe without a glance. Several long seconds later his footfalls thudded on the carpeted stairs. Phoebe let go a breath of relief. She turned to slide the pocket doors closed, and as she did so, several figures lingering in the dining room doorway scurried out of sight.

There would be gossip below stairs come morning. Phoebe would worry about that later. She went to her sister and clasped her hands. "Are you all right?"

Julia whisked free and backed up a stride. "Of course I'm all right."

"You didn't look all right when I came in. You still don't. What was that about?"

Julia twitched her eyebrows and turned slightly away, showing Phoebe her shoulder. Yes, the light pink weal visible against her pale upper arm confirmed tomorrow's bruises. "What was *what* about?"

"Don't play coy with me. What was Henry talking about? What secret—"

"Were you listening at the door?"

"I could hear you from the middle of the hall, and I think the servants in the dining room heard you as well. Lucky for you Grams and Grampapa retired half an hour ago. Or perhaps it isn't lucky. Perhaps this is something they should know about."

"They don't need to know anything."

"Why are you always so stubborn?"

"I'm done in, Phoebe. I'm going to bed." Her perfectly sloping nose in the air, she started to move past Phoebe, but Phoebe reached out and caught her wrist. Julia stopped, still facing the paneled walnut doors, her gaze boring into them. "Release me at once."

"Not until you tell me what you and Henry were arguing about. I mean besides your breaking off your would-be engagement. That comes as no great surprise. But the rest . . . Are you in some sort of trouble?"

Julia snapped her head around to pin Phoebe with eyes so deeply blue as to appear black. Her forearm tightened beneath Phoebe's fingers. "It is none of your business and I'll thank you to mind your own. Now let me go. I'm going to bed, and if you know what's good for you, you'll do the same."

Stunned, her throat stinging from the rebuke, Phoebe let her hand fall away. She watched Julia go, the beaded train of her gown whooshing over the floor like the water over rocks.

"I care about you," Phoebe said in a barely audible whisper, something neither Julia, nor the footmen, nor anyone else in the house could possibly hear. She wished she could say it louder, say it directly to her prideful sister's beautiful face. And then what—be met with the same disdain Julia had just shown her? No. Phoebe had her pride, too.

Eva Huntford made her way past the main kitchen and into the servants' dining hall with a gown slung over each arm. Lady Amelia had spilled a spoonful of trifle down the front of her green velvet at dinner last night, while Lady Julia's pink-and-silver-beaded gown sported an odd rent near the left shoulder strap. Eva briefly wondered what holiday activities could possibly result in such a tear, then dismissed the thought. Today was Boxing Day, but she had work to do before enjoying her own brief holiday later that afternoon.

"Mrs. Ellison, have you any bicarbonate of soda on hand? Lady Amelia spilled trifle—oh!" A man sat at the far end of the rectangular oak table, reading a newspaper and enjoying a cup of coffee. She draped the gowns over the back of a chair. "Good morning, Mr. Hensley. You're up early."

"Evie, won't you call me Nick? How long have we known each other, after all?"

It was true, she and Nicolas Hensley had known each other as children, but they were adults now, she lady's maid to the Earl of Wroxly's three granddaughters, and he valet to their houseguest, the Marquess of Allerton. Propriety was, after all, of the utmost importance in a manor such as Foxwood Hall. Familiarity between herself and a manservant wouldn't be at all proper. "A long time, yes, but it's also been a long time since we've seen each other."

He smiled faintly. "I saw you yesterday. And the day before that."

"True, but only surrounded by others, or when passing each other in the corridors." She turned to go. "In fact, I should—"

"Oh, Evie, do stay. I've craved a moment alone with you. Don't look like that. I only wish to . . . to express my deepest condolences about Danny. My very deepest, Evie. A bad business, that."

Her throat squeezed, and the backs of her eyes stung. Danny, her brother . . . She swallowed. "Yes, thank you. A good many men did not come home from the war."

"Indeed."

Hang it all, this would never do, not on Boxing Day. In a couple of hours she would be free to trudge home through the snow to spend the afternoon with her parents, and they must not glimpse her sadness. She gave a little sniff, a slight toss of her head. There. She smiled at Mr. Hensley. "Tell me, what are you doing down here at this time of the morning? Won't his lordship be abed for hours yet?"

"Already up and out, actually."

"On such a cold morning?" Shivering, she glanced up at the high windows, frosted over and sprinkled with last night's light snowfall.

Mrs. Ellison turned the corner into the room, her plump hand extending Eva's requested soda, fizzing away in a measuring cup. She handed Eva a clean rag as well. "Who's up and out on this frigid morning?"

Eva moved a place setting aside and spread the velvet gown's bodice open on the table. She dipped the rag in the soda. "Lord

Allerton, apparently." She looked quizzically over at Mr. Hensley.

He set down his newspaper. "At any rate, his lordship isn't in his room. I inquired with the staff setting up in the morning room and no one's yet seen him today."

"One supposes he's gone out for a walk despite the weather, then." Eva dabbed the dampened cloth lightly at the stain on Lady Amelia's bodice, careful of the embroidery and the tiny seed pearl buttons.

"Or perhaps a ride in that lovely motorcar of his?" Mrs. Ellison suggested with a sigh.

"No, I called down to the motor shed and his Silver Ghost is still there." Mr. Hensley frowned in thought, a gesture that did not diminish his distinguished good looks. He was several years older than Eva and had briefly courted her sister before entering into service as an under footman right here at Foxwood. The years had been more than kind to him, she couldn't help admitting. The slightest touch of silver at his temples might be premature for a man of thirty, but on Nick Hensley the effect was both elegant and charming. Perhaps more so than a valet needed, she added with a silent chuckle.

"Oh, wouldn't I relish a ride in that heavenly motorcar!" Mrs. Ellison took on a dreamy expression. "Ah well, back to work."

"I'm sure he'll turn up. Good morning, Vernon, Douglas." Eva greeted the two footmen, along with other staff members arriving for breakfast after finishing their morning chores of laying fires, sweeping floors, and setting up the breakfast buffet. An instant later Connie, the new house maid, skidded to a halt in the corridor and, with a visible effort to catch her breath, came into the room. "Good morning, Connie. Everything all right?"

The girl scanned the room with large, worried eyes. "Did Mrs. Sanders notice my late start this morning?"

"Were you late? Well, no matter," Eva assured her. She hoped she was correct, and that Connie wouldn't be facing a scolding later from Mrs. Sanders. "It's Boxing Day, and I suppose we're allowed a bit of leeway. Is everyone ready for their holiday later?"

Boxing Day, the day after Christmas, was a rare treat for the manor staff. Eva planned to spend the afternoon at her parents' farm outside the village, but first she needed to set her lady-ships' gowns to rights. After a final inspection of the now nearly invisible stain, she moved Amelia's velvet off the table to make way as more staff gathered round.

She was just on her way to deliver the gown to Mable, the laundress, before settling in with needle and thread to mend the beaded strap on Lady Julia's frock, when Lady Amelia came bounding down the back staircase and launched herself from the bottom step. She landed with an unladylike thwack mere inches away from Eva.

"Good heavens, my lady!" Eva sidestepped in time to avoid being knocked off her feet and spilling her burdens to the floor. She hugged the gowns to her. "Is there a fire?"

"Oh, I'm terribly sorry, Eva. I didn't mean to give you a fright." Lady Amelia's long curls danced loose down her back, and in her haste to dress herself she'd left the sleeves on her crepe de chine shirtwaist undone. "I was looking for you."

"You know I would have been upstairs to help you and your sisters dress in . . . what?" She glanced at the wall clock. "Twenty minutes."

Amelia Renshaw's sweet face banished any annoyance Eva might have felt. At fifteen she was a budding beauty. Not Lady Julia's glamorous, moving-picture-star beauty, but a quieter, deeper sort that one often finds in country villages like Little Barlow. Her hair was darker than Julia's, but still golden, a color reflected in her eyes, which sometimes shone hazel and other times brown, but always with those bright gold rims. If

Phoebe took after their dear but somewhat plain mother and Julia took after their dashing father, Amelia had inherited a pleasing combination of both that would surely endure throughout her lifetime.

"If you're worried about your frock, my lady, look." Eva held out the gowns, using one hand to unfold the bodice of Amelia's green velvet. "I've almost got the stain out, and Mable will vanquish what's left."

"Oh, I don't care about that," Amelia said with a dismissive wave. "You keep the gown. I wanted a private moment to wish you happy Christmas."

"Lady Amelia, where would I ever wear such a garment? And as for Christmas, you wished me happy yesterday." Slinging both gowns over her shoulder, she reached to button up the girl's wide cuffs. "Had you forgotten?"

"Yes, but yesterday was a work day for you, and this afternoon you'll be free to enjoy as you like." She switched arms so Eva could button the other sleeve. "I may wish you happy from one carefree person to another. That's quite different, don't you think?"

Puzzled, Eva frowned at her young charge, but only for an instant. "I think it's a lovely gesture and I thank you very much, my lady."

"There's more. I wanted you to know there's a special surprise in your box from Phoebe and me. Oh, there's something from Julia, too, something she purchased, very lovely and thoughtful, but Phoebe and I made our gift ourselves. But you're not to open your box until you're at home with your parents." Amelia bounced on the balls of her feet with excitement. "We made one for your mother as well."

"How sweet of you. But you're very mysterious, aren't you?" Eva reached out and affectionately tucked a few stray hairs behind Amelia's ear. In some ways she was blossoming into a gracious young lady, while in others she was still very much a little girl.

One with sadly too few memories of her mother. Poor child, one parent lost to childbirth—along with the babe—and the other to war. Eva hoped she helped fill the gaps, on occasion at least, even if only in the smallest ways. "Whatever it is, Mum and I are sure to love and treasure it always. Happy Christmas to you, my lady."

To her mingled chagrin and delight, Lady Amelia reached her arms around her and squeezed.

"With this deplorable weather keeping us inside, we'll have to use our imaginations to keep ourselves occupied this afternoon."

Maude Renshaw, Countess of Wroxly—Grams, as Phoebe and her siblings called her—stood as tall as she had as a young woman, if the photographs were any indication. If anything, she seemed even taller now, although Phoebe knew that to be an illusion created by her predilection to always wear uninterrupted black, from the high-necked collars of her dresses to the narrow sweep of her skirts. With smooth hair the color of newly polished silver worn in a padded upsweep culminating in a topknot at her crown, Grams was a study in dignified elegance that caught the eye and held it whenever she entered a room.

Strengthening the illusion of Grams's Amazonian height, Phoebe's youngest sibling, Viscount Foxwood—Fox—walked at Grams's side, her hand in the crook of his elbow. Fox had yet to enjoy a major growth spurt, much to his chagrin as this set him a good head shorter than many of his classmates at Eaton. Together they led the small procession of family and guests into the Petite Salon, tucked into the turret of what had been the original house.

This room was one of Phoebe's favorites. Its creamy paneled walls offset by bright white wainscoting and an airy cove ceiling made a welcome contrast to the dark oaks and mahoganies in other parts of the house, while rich colors of scarlet, blue, and gold, and the rotunda of windows overlooking the south corner of the gardens, lent warmth and a cozy touch.

An enthusiastic blaze danced behind the fireplace screen, and Mr. Giles and the footmen, Vernon and Douglas, stood at attention, waiting to serve. The table had been laid with leftovers from last night's dinner—roast goose and venison and beef, with Mrs. Ellison's savory apple-chestnut stuffing, among other delicacies, and for dessert, the leftover Yorkshire pudding and cranberry trifle. Phoebe hoped Amelia could manage to reserve all remnants of trifle for her mouth today and not her attire. At any rate, it was all easy fare designed to allow the kitchen staff, along with the rest of the servants, to finish up early and set out on their afternoon holiday. The day promised adventures for everyone—for the servants as they pursued their personal interests, and, Phoebe thought wryly, for the family and guests as they endeavored to look after themselves for these next several hours.

"Where is my son? It's not like Henry to be late to a meal." Lucille, Marchioness of Allerton, regarded her son's vacant seat at the table. It was no secret that Lady Allerton doted to extremes on her elder son—and always had. Phoebe regarded the marchioness. Where Grams's stoic self-discipline had sculpted her figure into lines of angular elegance, a less diligent outlook, and perhaps a habit of overindulgence, had softened the marchioness's figure, rounded her hips and shoulders and upper arms, and produced rather more chins than a body needed.

"He and Lord Owen must have gone out," Grampapa remarked. He turned his broad face toward Mr. Giles, who perceived the question without needing to hear the words.

"I believe Lord Owen is still in his room, my lord. If Lord Allerton has gone out, he left no message that I know of."

Lady Allerton's frown deepened. "Hmm . . . That, too, is most unlike Henry. Did he take his Silver Ghost?"

"No, my lady. His motor is still in the shed."

"Hmm . . . how very odd."

"Really, Mama, why all the fuss?" Lord Theodore Leighton—Teddy—reached for a roll and his butter knife with a bored expression. "Henry's a grown man."

He fell silent without any further reassurance and buttered his bread with meticulous strokes as if creating a work of art. This proved no simple task, not for Teddy, and Phoebe quelled the urge to reach over and offer her assistance. The knife quivered in his grasp, bringing attention to the scarred flesh of his fingers and the backs of both hands. The rippled skin ended at his sleeves and reappeared in angry blotches above his collar to pull the left side of his face into a perpetual sneer. Phoebe wondered that he hadn't grown whiskers to hide the scars. Like Henry, this second son of the Leighton family was handsome, or had been, before the war had left its mark on him.

Mustard gas, in the trenches of the Battle of Somme. Phoebe remembered the day a distraught Lady Allerton had telephoned to deliver the awful news. Teddy's injuries had taken him out of action for nearly six months, but when everyone had expected him to return home, he returned to the trenches instead. He made it abundantly clear at every opportunity he wanted no one's pity, no one's help. He'd butter his own roll, thank you, if it took all morning.

Phoebe tried never to feel sorry for him, even tried to like him, but he made it a ticklish task, especially in moments like this. This might be Henry they were talking about, but he and Teddy were, after all, brothers, and Teddy exhibited not the slightest concern.

Still, while the elder generation discussed where Henry might be, Phoebe couldn't help hoping he might never return. She glanced across the table at Julia. Had her argument with Henry driven him away? She noted that Julia's arms were well-covered in deep blue chiffon, with a velvet shawl draped over that, to hide any evidence of last night.

Well, as Teddy had said, Henry was a grown man who might

do as he pleased. Phoebe, on the other hand, saw little in her future now that the war had ended, other than an endless procession of luncheons, dinner parties, and a parade of potential beaux. She sighed.

A mistake.

"What's wrong, Phoebe?" Beside her, Amelia looked both pretty and smart in a new shirtwaist with blouson sleeves and ribbon piping that matched her eyes.

"Wrong? Nothing." She hoped Amelia never learned of Henry's boorish behavior of the night before.

"Then why are you moaning?"

"I am not moaning. I sighed. There is a difference." Phoebe leaned back in her chair and cupped her mouth to prevent Fox overhearing. Fox always seemed to be listening in on other people's conversations, storing away bits of information to be used at his convenience at a later time. "The truth is, I'm horribly bored, Amelia. I miss . . ." She paused. How to phrase this without sounding unfeeling and self-absorbed? "I miss the activity of the war. Not the war itself, mind you. I'm happy and relieved it's finally over. But we made a true difference to a good many people. And now . . . I fear life has lost its color."

Her sister nodded, her eyes keen with understanding. "That all we'll have to look forward to from now on are parties and such, like in the old days?"

"You read my mind exactly. And all that seems so purposeless now. I've been thinking—"

"You should be thinking of finding a husband before the dust gathers on that shelf you're sitting on," Fox whispered out of the side of his mouth, his gaze still fixed across the table at the elders as if he hadn't been listening in on Phoebe and Amelia.

"I'm *nineteen*, Fox. That hardly qualifies me for any shelf, and besides, what difference should it make?" Phoebe shook her head at him. "It's a new world, and women will no longer be relegated exclusively to the home. We have choices now."

"That's right," Amelia put in eagerly. "Many choices."

Fox finally deigned to turn his face to Phoebe, his lips tilting in a mean little smile. "You think so? As you said, the war is over. The men have come home. Time for you ladies to return to the roles God designed you for."

She nearly choked on her own breath. Only a throat-clearing and a glare from Grams prevented her from retorting—and perhaps wringing her brother's neck.

"I propose that directly following luncheon, Julia play the piano for us." Grams pinned her hazel eyes on Julia, turning her *proposal* into an adamant command that brooked no demurring.

"And following Julia, I wouldn't mind regaling everyone with a song or two." This came from Lady Cecily Leighton, Henry's maiden great-aunt. Phoebe glanced up at her, alarmed by the suggestion. Lady Cecily had proved herself thoroughly tone deaf on more than one occasion, and once Phoebe had had to endure an entire hour of jumbled and stumbling notes. If that weren't enough, the woman's outfit today reflected sure signs of a growing disorientation, with her striped frock overlaid by a knee-length tunic of floral chiffon. A wide silk headband sporting a bright Christmas plaid held most of her spiraling white curls off her shoulders and neck, giving her the appearance of some kind of holiday gypsy. The poor woman's maid must have been aghast when her mistress left her room.

"Of course, Cecily, dear." Grampapa spoke softly and gently, as he did when Phoebe was small. His perfectly trimmed mustache twitched as he smiled. "We shall look forward to it."

Phoebe managed to suppress a groan, but Fox could not. Grams shot another glance across the table, while Grampapa's eyebrows twitched out a warning.

"After Julia serenades us"—Fourteen-year-old Fox pulled a face—"and Lady Cecily, too, may we find something exciting to do? Grampapa, couldn't we take the rifles out for some skeet shooting? It's not so very cold. Is it?" He directed that last question to Henry's younger brother, Teddy, who thus far had been silently filling his plate.

"Fox," Grams said with a lift of one crescent-thin eyebrow, "I believe indoor activities are more appropriate for days such as this."

"Oh, Grams . . ."

"Fox." Grampapa's stern tone forestalled the complaint Fox had been gathering breath to utter.

Fox made a grinding sound in his throat and Phoebe whispered to him, "When are you going to grow up?"

"When are you going to stop being so boring?"

"Terribly sorry to be late for luncheon, everyone. I had some letters to write. Do forgive me." Clad in country tweeds, Lord Owen Seabright strode into the room. He bowed ruefully and took the vacant seat beside Julia. His gaze met Phoebe's, and she raised her water goblet to her lips to hide the inevitable and appalling heat that always crept into her cheeks whenever the man so much as glanced her way.

Lord Owen Seabright was an earl's younger son who had taken a small, maternal inheritance and turned it into a respectable fortune. His woolen mills had supplied English soldiers with uniforms and blankets during the war. He himself had served as well, a major commanding a battalion. Unlike Teddy Leighton, Lord Owen had returned home mercifully whole.

If only Papa had been so fortunate. . . .

She dismissed the thought before melancholy had a chance to set in. Of course, that left her once more contemplating Owen Seabright, a wealthy, fit man in the prime of his life and as yet unattached. After years of war, such men were a rarity. He'd been invited to spend Christmas because his grandfather and Phoebe's had been great friends, because Lord Owen had had a falling-out with his own family, and because Fox had insisted he come, with Grams's blessing.

If an engagement between Julia and Henry didn't work out, Owen Seabright was to be next in line to seek Julia's hand. Phoebe wondered if Owen—or Julia, for that matter—had been privy to that information. She herself only knew because Fox had told her, his way of informing her he'd soon have Julia married off and Phoebe's turn would be next.

Or so he believed. What Phoebe believed was that Fox needed to be taken down a peg or two.

"Henry isn't with you?" Lady Allerton asked.

Lord Owen looked surprised. "With me? No. Haven't seen him today."

"No one has, apparently." With a perplexed look, Lady Lucille helped herself to another medallion of beef Bordelaise. "I do hope Henry hasn't gotten lost somewhere."

"Odd, him going out on foot alone like that." Grampapa's great chest rose and fell, giving Phoebe the impression of a bear just waking up from a long winter's rest. "Ah, but he can hardly lose his way. He knows our roads and trails as well as any of us. Spent enough time at Foxwood as a boy, didn't he?"

"Yes, but Archibald," Grams said sharply, "things look different in the snow. He easily could have taken a wrong fork and ended up who knows where. Or he might have slipped and twisted his ankle."

"Good heavens," Lady Allerton exclaimed. "Is that supposed to reassure me?"

"Should we form a search party?" Amelia appeared genuinely worried. Phoebe sent her a reassuring smile and shook her head.

"Oh, Grams, don't be silly." Fox flourished his fork, earning him a sharp throat-clearing and a stern look from Grampapa. The youngest Renshaw put his fork down with a terse "Sorry, sir" and shoved a lock of sandy hair off his forehead. "But even if he *was* lost, he'd either end up in the village, the school, or the river. He's not about to jump in the river in this weather, is he?" The boy shrugged. "He'll be back."

He sent Julia a meaningful look. She ignored him, turning her head to gaze out the bay window at the wide expanse of snowy lawn rolling away to a skeletal copse of birch trees and the pine forest beyond that. Far in the distance, the rolling Cotswold Hills embraced the horizon, with patches of white interspersed with bare ground where the wind had whipped the snow away.

Phoebe brought her gaze closer and noticed a trail of footprints leading through the garden and back again. Henry? But if he'd gone out that way, he had apparently returned to the house.

Grams narrowed her eyes shrewdly on Julia. "I do hope there is no particular reason for Henry to have made a sudden departure."

This, too, Julia ignored.

"As Lawrence Winslow did last summer," Grams muttered under her breath. Although everyone must have heard the comment—Phoebe certainly had—all went on eating as if they hadn't. Grams seethed in Julia's direction another moment, then returned her attention to her meal.

Apparently, not everyone was willing to pretend Grams hadn't spoken. "Julia, you and Henry get on splendidly, don't you?" Fox snapped his fingers when she didn't reply. "Julia?"

She turned back around. "What?"

Phoebe was gripped by a sudden urge to pinch her. Though last night had obviously left her shaken, this sort of indifference was nothing new. It began three years ago, the day the news about Papa reached them from France, and rather than fading over time, her disinterest had become more pronounced throughout the war years. By turns her sister's apathy angered or saddened Phoebe, depending on the circumstances, but always left her frustrated.

"Stop it," Amelia hissed in her brother's ear, another comment heard and ignored around the table. "Leave it alone."

Phoebe observed her little sister. Had Amelia been privy to last night's argument, or had she merely grown accustomed to Julia's fickleness when it came to men?

"My, my, yes, he'll be back." Lady Cecily spoke to no one in particular. She had been intent on cutting the contents of her plate into tiny pieces, even her deviled crab sandwich. She didn't look up as she spoke, but next attacked an olive. Her blade hit the pit and sent the green sphere spinning off the plate and onto the tablecloth with a plop. She giggled as she tried without success to retrieve it with her fork, saying, "He must return soon, for isn't there an announcement Henry and Julia wish to make today?"

Lady Allerton leaned in close and plucked up the olive. With an efficiency born of habit, she deposited it back onto the elder woman's plate. "You asked that this morning, Aunt Cecily. And, no, there is no announcement just yet. Why don't you eat something now?"

"No engagement yet?" Lady Cecily looked crestfallen. She held her knife in midair. "Why is that? Julia, dear, didn't Henry ask you a very pertinent question last night?"

Julia finally looked away from the window as if startled from sleep. She blinked. "I'm sorry. Did you say something?"

"We were all very tired last night, what with all the Christmas revelry." Grams's attempt to sound cheerful fell flat. The Leightons might be second cousins, but they would not have been invited to spend the holiday at Foxwood Hall if Grams hadn't held out hope that Father Christmas would deliver a husband for Julia. The war had left so few men from whom to choose. "Henry and Julia shall have plenty of time to talk now that things have calmed down. Won't you, Julia?"

"Yes, Grams. Of course."

Phoebe doubted her sister knew what she had just agreed to. Fox sniggered.

"If you don't stop being so snide," she whispered to him behind her hand, "I'll suggest Grampapa send you up to the schoolroom, where you belong."

Fox cupped a hand over his mouth and stuck out his tongue. "Then you should stop impersonating a beet every time Lord Owen enters a room," he whispered back.

"I do no such thing." But good gracious, if Fox had noticed, was she so obvious? She sucked air between her teeth. But no, Lord Owen was paying her no mind now, instead helping himself to thick slices of cold roast venison and responding to some question Grams had just asked him. She relaxed against her chair. Lord Owen was a passing fancy, nothing more. He was . . . too tall for her. Too muscular. Approaching thirty, he was too old as well. And much too . . .

Handsome, with his strong features and steely eyes and inky black hair that made such a striking contrast next to Julia's blond.

Yes, just a silly, passing fancy . . .

"Well now, my girls." Grampapa grinned broadly and lightly clapped his hands. "I believe it's time to hand out the Christmas boxes, is it not? The staff will want to be on their way."

"Yes, you're quite right, Grampapa." With a sense of relief at this excuse to escape the table, Phoebe dabbed at her lips and placed her napkin beside her plate. "Girls, shall we?"

Amelia was on her feet in an instant. "I've so been looking forward to this. It's my favorite part of Christmas."

Julia stood with a good deal less enthusiasm. "Not mine, but come. Let's get it over with."

Eva could finally feel her fingers and toes again after slogging through snow and slush across the village to her parents' farm. Mum had put the kettle on before she arrived, and she was just now enjoying her second cup of strong tea and biting into another heavenly, still-warm apricot scone.

Holly and evergreen boughs draped the mantel above a

cheerful fire, and beside the hearth a small stack of gifts waited to be opened. Eva eyed the beribboned box from the Renshaws. She wondered what little treasure Phoebe and Amelia had tucked inside.

Mum huffed her way into the room with yet another pot of tea, which she set on a trivet on the sofa table. "Can't have enough on a day like today," she said, as if there had been a need to explain. "As soon as your father comes in from checking the animals, we'll open the presents."

"I think they're lovely right where they are," Eva said. "It's just good to be home."

"It's a shame your sister couldn't be here this year."

"Alice would, if she could have, Mum, but Suffolk is far, especially in this weather."

"Yes, I suppose . . ." With another huff, Mum sat down beside her, weighting the down cushion so that the springs beneath creaked and Eva felt herself slide a little toward the center of the old sofa.

A name hovered in the air between them, loud and clear, though neither of them spoke it. Danny, the youngest of the family. Eva's chest tightened, and Mum pretended to sweep back a strand of hair, when in actuality she brushed at a tear.

Danny had gone to France in the second year of the war, just after his eighteenth birthday. Not quite a year later, the telegram came.

"Ah, yes, well." Mum patted Eva's hand and pulled in a fortifying breath. "It's good to have you home for an entire day, or almost so. I'd have thought we'd see more of you, working so close by."

"Tending to three young ladies keeps me busy, Mum."

"Yes, and bless them for it, I suppose. It's a good position you've got, so we shan't be complaining, shall we?"

"Indeed not. Especially not today. But . . . I hear you huffing a bit, Mum. Are your lungs still achy?"

"No, no. Better now."

The door of the cottage opened on a burst of wind, and a booted foot crossed the threshold. Eva sprang up to catch the door and keep it from swinging back in on her father, who stamped snow off his boots onto the braided rug and unwrapped the wool muffler from around his neck.

"Everyone all right out there, Vincent?" Mum asked. She leaned forward to pour tea into her father's mug.

"Right as rain." He shrugged off his coat and ran a hand over a graying beard that reached his chest. "Or as snow, I should say."

"Come sit and have a cuppa, dear. Eva wants to open her gifts."

"Oh, Mum."

They spent the next minutes opening and admiring. Eva was pleased to see the delighted blush in her mother's cheeks when she unwrapped the shawl Eva had purchased in Bristol when she'd accompanied Lady Julia there in October. There was also a pie crimper and a wax sealer with her mother's initial, B for Betty. For her father, Eva had found a tooled leather bookmark and had knitted him a new muffler to replace his old ragged one.

From them Eva received a velvet-covered notebook for keeping track of her duties and appointments, a linen blouse Mum had made and embroidered herself, and a hat with little silk flowers for which they must have sacrificed far too much of their meager income. But how could she scold them for their extravagance when their eyes shone so brightly as she opened the box?

Mum gripped the arm of the sofa and pulled to her feet with another of those huffs that so concerned Eva. "I'll just check on the roast. Should be ready soon. Oh, Eva, you've forgotten your box from the Renshaws."

So she had. "There's something inside for you, too, Mum."

"You have a look-see, dear. I mustn't burn the roast."

"All right, I'll peek inside and then I'll come and help you put dinner on, Mum."

She picked up the box and returned to the sofa. Her father grinned. "So what do you suppose is in there this year?"

"We'll just have to see, won't we?" She tugged at the ribbons, then pulled off the cover and set it aside. The topmost gift was wrapped in gold foil tissue paper. The card on top read *To Eva with fondness and appreciation, from Phoebe and Amelia.* She carefully unrolled the little package, and out tumbled a set of airy linen handkerchiefs edged in doily lace, each adorned with its own color of petit-point roses. A pink, a yellow, a violet, and a blue. Eva didn't think there were such things as blue or violet roses, but her heart swelled and her eyes misted as she pictured the two girls bent over their efforts, quickly whisking away their gifts-in-the-making whenever Eva entered their rooms.

"Oh, look, Dad. See what the girls have for me. Aren't they perfection? And here's a fifth, with a tag that says it's for Mum."

He craned his neck to see. "Look a mite too fine for the use they're meant for."

"Oh, Dad." Eva chuckled and glanced again into her box. "And here's a card . . ." She took out a simple piece of white paper, folded in half. She unfolded it. "It reads, 'For the Hunt-fords, for their pains.' Odd, there's no signature."

"Isn't that jolly of the Renshaws to remember your mum and me."

"I'll bet it's a bit of cash, like last year. Let's see . . ." Eva bent over the box to peer inside. The breath left her in a single whoosh.

"Well? What's next in that box of surprises?" Dad leaned expectantly forward in his chair. "Evie? Evie, why do you look like that? Surely they haven't gone and given us one of the family heirlooms, have they? Evie?"

"I . . . Oh, Dad . . . Oh, *God.*"

"Evie, we do not blaspheme in this house," her mother called from the kitchen. She appeared in the doorway, drying her hands on a dish rag. "Eva, what on earth is wrong? You're as white as the snow."

"It's . . . it's a ring," she managed, gasping. Her hands trembled where they clutched the edges of the box. Her heart thumped as though to escape her chest. "A s-signet ring."

"Oh, that's lovely, dear. So why do you look as if you've just seen a ghost?" Her mother started toward her. Her father's rumbling laugh somehow penetrated the ringing in Eva's ears.

She held up both hands to stop her mother in her tracks. "Mum, stay where you are. Don't come any closer."

"Why, Eva Mary Huntford, what *has* gotten into you?" The sullenness in her mother's voice mingled with that incessant ringing. A wave of dizziness swooped up to envelop Eva. "What sort of signet ring could make my daughter impertinent?"

Eva looked up, the room wavering in her vision. "One that's still attached to the finger."